Mario Reading has led a maverick life with a [illegible] rom selling rare books to teaching riding in Africa and [illegible] nna, and from playing polo in India, Spain and [illegible] ch in Mexico. He has written for a num [illegible] *Sunday Times* magazine and the *Shootin* [illegible] e is also the author of the fascinating and hig [illegible] *Cinema*. He lives near Salisbury with his wife and so [illegible]

The Music-Makers

MARIO READING

This edition published in 2001 by House of Stratus, an imprint of
Stratus Holdings plc, 24c Old Burlington Street, London, W1X 1RL, UK.

www.houseofstratus.com

Typeset, printed and bound by House of Stratus.

A catalogue record for this book is available from the British Library.

ISBN 0-7551-0383-1

for Tim Manderson

Family Tree

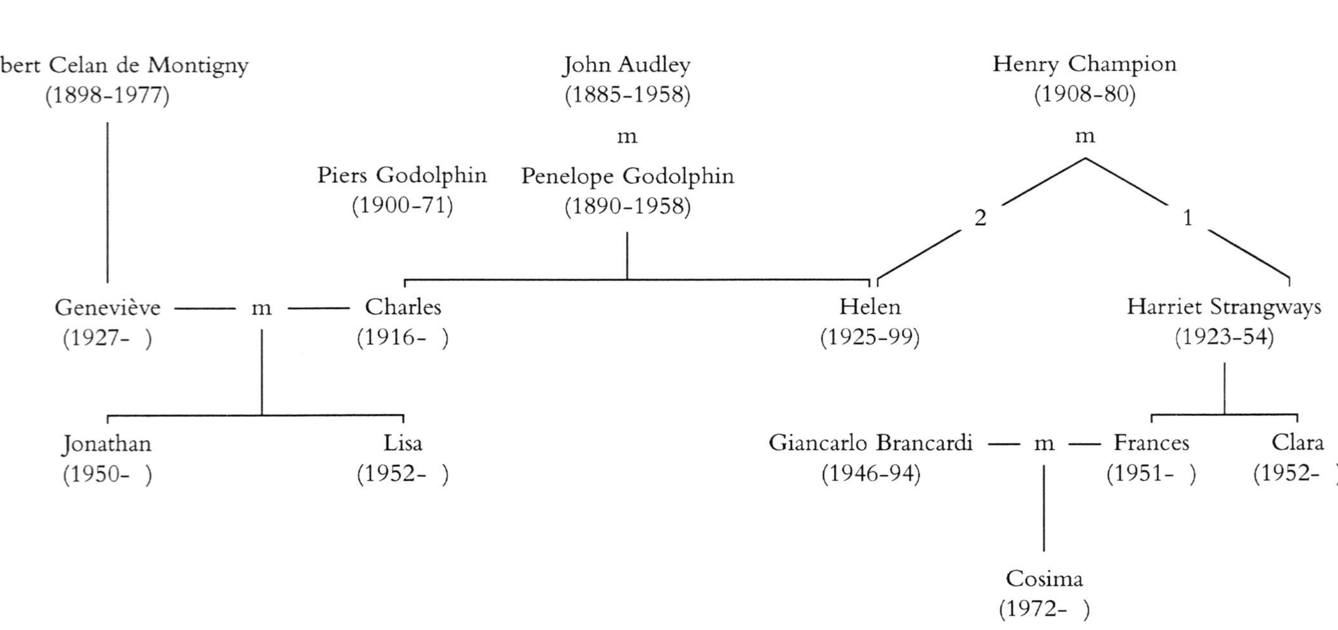

Hubert Celan de Montigny
(1898-1977)
John Audley
(1885-1958)
m
Penelope Godolphin
(1890-1958)
Piers Godolphin
(1900-71)
Henry Champion
(1908-80)
m
2
1
Geneviève
(1927-)
m
Charles
(1916-)
Helen
(1925-99)
Harriet Strangways
(1923-54)
Jonathan
(1950-)
Lisa
(1952-)
Giancarlo Brancardi
(1946-94)
m
Frances
(1951-)
Clara
(1952-)
Cosima
(1972-)

We are the music-makers,
And we are the dreamers of dreams,
Wandering by lone sea-breakers,
And sitting by desolate streams;
World-losers and world-forsakers,
On whom the pale moon gleams:
Yet we are the movers and shakers
Of the world for ever, it seems.

With wonderful deathless ditties
We build up the world's great cities,
And out of a fabulous story
We fashion an empire's glory:
One man with a dream, at pleasure,
Shall go forth and conquer a crown;
And three with a new song's measure
Can trample an empire down.

We, in the ages lying
In the buried past of the earth,
Built Nineveh with our sighing,
And Babel itself with our mirth;
And o'erthrew them with prophesying
To the old of the new world's worth;
For each age is a dream that is dying,
Or one that is coming to birth.

'Ode' by Arthur O'Shaughnessy

One

The smell of roasting coffee brought on the usual reflexive desire to vomit. Jonathan Audley took a deep breath and plunged through the swing-doors of Claudius Regaud Hospital. The stench was worse in here. His saliva tasted ominously of bile. He swallowed it quickly back, gagging, and hurried past the cafeteria, pinching his nostrils tightly shut with his fingers. A nurse he recognised exited the lift in front of him. He hunched his shoulders and tried to smile. She smiled back, canting her head prettily to one side, then crinkled her nose in sympathy.

'*Chimio*,' he mumbled, as the lift doors closed.

It was now three months since he'd had his final dose of chemotherapy, but the visceral memory still remained – the smell of espresso was the worst offender, followed by fried food and wine. Tobacco smoke came in a distant fourth.

Instinctively Jonathan reached up and touched the bulge of the portacath that was lodged under the skin of his chest, three inches above his heart. For the six months of his chemotherapy cure, that was where they'd plugged in the drip. He shuddered as he remembered the initial sharp prick of the needle, then the ice-cold sting of the poison through his veins. When his treatment ended Doctor Mézières had insisted that they leave the portacath in place, just in case the cancer came back. A typically sinister Mézières touch!

The lift doors wheezed open. Jonathan stepped into the familiar corridor with its intolerably cheerful Dufy prints of the Côte d'Azur. A man wearing a nylon dressing-gown, his jaw eaten away by cancer, approached him along the passageway.

'*Salut*, Jean-Paul.' Jonathan was relieved that he'd been able to summon up the name so rapidly. The nausea, thank God, was receding.

'Jonathan. How are you doing?' A line of drool fell from the man's distorted lips onto the flannel bib he wore around his neck.

'Where are you off to in such a hurry, J-P? The police still after you?'

The man attempted a smile. He pulled a pack of unfiltered Gitanes from his pocket, sniffed the wrapper luxuriously, then made an exaggerated smoking motion with his hand. '*Tu m'accompagnes*?' he said, hopefully.

'I can't. I'm sorry. Mézières wants to see me. It's crunch time.'

Jean-Paul rocked back on his heels. 'Good luck, then.' He used the forward momentum to re-launch himself up the corridor.

Jonathan watched the shuffling figure as it made its way to the smoking section above the balcony. Cracked voices were raised in welcome, then as suddenly hushed. A thick plume of blue smoke rose languidly into the air and was snatched away by the air-conditioning.

Dr Mézières poked his head out of the office. 'Monsieur Audley? I can see you now. My last patient has not arrived.'

'Perhaps he's died?'

Mézières pretended not to hear him. His sense of humour encompassed only those jokes told by himself.

Jonathan entered the office and took his usual chair. Mézières walked around behind the desk, poked idly through some papers, then sat down. His blue-black hair was freshly combed and his cheeks gleamed with health.

He looks as if he's just stepped off a pelota court, Jonathan thought to himself – all the passionless bastard needs to complete the picture is a black felt beret and a red spotted neckerchief.

'Can't you wean Jean-Paul off those bloody cigarettes?' The words came out more aggressively than he intended.

'What would be the point?' Mézières held Jonathan's gaze, his eyes wide open.

Jonathan looked down. He took a deep breath of hospital air. 'Perhaps I should take up smoking, too?'

'In your case I would advise against it.'

'Why?'

'Because, to all intents and purposes, you are now clear.'

Jonathan glanced at his fingers, still swollen from the Bleomycin. 'A year ago you gave me three months to live.'

'I was wrong.'

'Perhaps you're wrong on this?'

'I don't think so.' Mézières reached across his desk for a thick cardboard file. He sorted a CAT scan X-ray from the top of the heap and held it up to the light. He grunted in satisfaction. 'Your ganglions have shrunk. And you have no more pain in your leg thanks to the radiotherapy. Isn't that so?'

'Yes.'

'And you no longer require morphine?'

'No.'

'Well then?' He tossed the X-ray back on top of the file.

'They tell me I can no longer have children. That I'm azospermic.'

'You're forty-nine years old. You waited too long. Most men your age have grown-up families. Be thankful you're still alive.' Mézières's mouth had sculpted itself into a thin, disapproving line.

'I don't get erections any more.'

'It's early days yet. Your hair has grown back, why not your virility?'

'Because I've only got one ball left. And it's no good.'

'*N'exagérons rien.*' Mézières was becoming annoyed – self-pity repelled him.

Jonathan forced a smile onto his face. He minded what Mézières thought of him. 'You're right. I shall buy some pornography and start practising.'

Mézières waved a hand in irritation. 'Pornography? Bah. One testicle is better than none. And your last biopsy showed that it is healthy. If you continue to have problems there are treatments. Hormonal implants. Patches. Pills. Viagra. But it would be better if you addressed the problem yourself.'

'Viagra works on symptoms, not on causes.'

'The cause is in your head. You have been ill. You came close to dying. Your body is still in shock.' Mézières cleared his throat. He hated giving non-medical advice. 'Don't you know someone? A woman who loves you well enough to be patient with you?'

An ironical snort escaped before Jonathan could stop it. He disguised it with a cough. 'I knew one once. But I lost her.' The thought of Frances rocked him with bitterness. Twenty-eight wasted years. Twenty-eight years without her. And each year it got worse. Each year he realised, with increasing desperation, just what he'd forfeited and how it had poisoned his life. It was worse even than the chemo. At least that had served some purpose.

Mézières stood up. 'Well? Why don't you find her again?'

Jonathan glanced up at him in surprise. Watching Mézières's smooth, almost reptilian features, he felt a sudden, passionate connection to this man who had, by virtue of an inspired, if rather late diagnosis, saved his life. 'Find her again?' His heart beat dully below the portacath. His hand searched automatically for the now almost comforting bulge on his breastbone.

Mézières noticed the movement. 'You must have that out. I will write to you. A local anaesthetic, I think. You're not squeamish, if I remember correctly. When that is done, I shall expect to see you every six months. For perhaps five years. Then once a year after that. Your chances are good. You have been lucky.'

Jonathan shook the dry hand that Mézières held out to him. 'Thank you.'

'Thank Pasteur, not me.' Mézières was already thinking about his next patient.

On his way out Jonathan passed Jean-Paul shuffling back up the corridor, a miasma of used tobacco smoke trailing behind him.

'Well? Did he give you the okay?' Jean-Paul cocked his head quizzically, revealing the livid underside of his chin.

'Yes.' Jonathan felt himself reddening. 'Yes. He said I was lucky.'

'Lucky?'

'That's what he said. Yes.'

Jean-Paul used his bib to dab at some spittle that was escaping from the hole underneath his palate. 'Luck.' His head rocked backwards on the stem of his neck. 'Sounds funny, doesn't it? It's not a word I use anymore.' He raised a hand. 'I won't shake with you. Never know where it's been.'

Jonathan followed the dishevelled figure with his eyes as it shambled up the corridor towards its room. There goes a dead man, he thought to himself. A dead man walking. And I'm alive. I've won the fucking lottery of life.

The feeling was so singular that he paused for a moment before entering the lift. Forcing back the doors at the last possible instant, he inadvertently caught sight of himself in the mirror – a thin, pale man, no longer young, his eyes two empty vessels waiting to be pumped full of the next banal set of experiences.

He punched the ground-floor button. But a morbid fascination was drawing him back to the mirror once again. He attempted, for one unavailing moment, to sidetrack himself – to see himself as others would see him – but at each doomed attempt, the fearful image of Jean-Paul's grotesquely ruined face would superimpose itself over his own.

He barely noticed the road back from Toulouse to the Chateau de Montigny. Only when he came to the gates, with their conspicuous and rather kitsch armorial shields, did it occur to him that he had been the recipient of good news and that his mother would expect his demeanour to reflect that fact.

He followed the drive around into the courtyard, working vainly on his facial expression. He was surprised to see his sister's car pulled up alongside the mulberry tree. No wonder her paintwork always looked as if it had been scored with sulphuric acid. He speculated idly as to why Lisa should have been summoned, yet again, all the way from her London retreat. Moral support for his mother in the event of his imminent death? He shook his head in irritated disbelief.

Parking his car in the coach-house, he made his way past the serried ranks of walnut and greengage trees towards the front of the chateau. Hard as he tried, he couldn't get Mézières's parting words out of his mind. How long since he had heard any news of Frances? Five years? Ten? He'd written her an awkwardly phrased letter when he'd learned about the death of her husband, but he hadn't received a reply. Not surprising, really. Frances had married the ubiquitous Giancarlo on the rebound from him, and had probably considered the letter to be in particularly poor taste. Well at least she had a daughter for her pains. All he had was one kidney, a dubious ball, and semen – if he could ever procure some from himself again – the consistency of industrial waste. He bitterly regretted having spread it around (if that was the appropriate word) so cavalierly in his years of plenty.

'Jonathan?'

The two women were in the morning room. He could hear the familiar sound of his mother's heels tapping nervously across the marble tiles. He craned his head surreptitiously around the door. Lisa was perched on the edge of the sofa, pretending to read a paperback. Jonathan found himself smiling. The perfect end-of-the-millennium nuclear family: neurotic mother, lesbian daughter, sterile son. He had a sudden picture of his father, roosting luxuriously aged eighty-three, at his domain near St Tropez. He was the exception to the rule – the only one of them who'd lived his life the way he'd wanted to; not caring what anybody thought; not giving a fig for anyone. The old devil had hardly even noticed he'd been ill. So why, then, did he love him? And why did he feel so disconnected from his mother, who had stood by him this past year, and prayed for him, and tormented herself with innumerable morbid pictures of his death?

'It seems I'm to live.' He strode across the room, kissed his mother's hand, and, in a now habitual movement, inclined his head to let her brush his brow with her lips.

'J. I'm so pleased.' Lisa came up to him, stood on tiptoe, and rubbed her knuckles through his newly grown hair. 'You look like a Nazi.'

'The Nazis would have euthanised me. Actually I'm part-way there already. The *tebibs* assure me I'm sterile.' Putting the facts into words seemed, paradoxically, to reinforce, rather than to diminish them. 'You see before you the last of the Audleys. Unless you believe in the Immaculate Conception, that is.'

'Jonathan!' His mother had on her Catholic face.

'Didn't they freeze some of your…' Lisa hesitated, glancing at her mother, '…whats-it, before they started the treatments?'

'They caught it too late. I'm a hundred per cent azospermic, whatever that may mean. In fact they're not even sure if I'll be able to get it up anymore. The local virgins are safe at last, it seems.'

Lisa retrieved her discarded book. 'Well you've had more than your fair share of that sort of thing already. It'll do you good to leave the girls in peace for a few years.'

'All the more for you?'

'Your sister is not Sapphic,' said his mother, dabbing angrily at her eyes with a lace handkerchief. 'It is merely that she has not found the right man.'

Jonathan looked at her in mock horror. 'She's forty-eight years old, *maman*. When are you going to accept that she's a dyke?'

'Jonathan! What would your grandfather have said?'

'Now that's a question. What would he have said? *De la tenue*. You must not be *débridé*. You must have decorum. Didn't stop him from maintaining that ageing piece of fluff of his in Paris for nearly thirty years. I hear you even pay her a pension.'

'She's a lady.'

'Isn't Lisa?'

Geneviève Celan de Montigny Audley made a despairing gesture with her hand. 'I will never understand my children. I suppose you will be leaving us now? To go back to your father?'

'I can't stay here, *maman*. I have my work. I have my house.'

'You hate your house,' said Lisa.

'Well then I have papa's house.'

'Would he have helped you through your illness? Would he have stood by you as I have done?' said his mother.

'No.'

'Then I don't understand. I will never understand your relationship with him and that *gouvernante*. That...woman.'

'No, *maman*. You won't. And it's not your fault. Here. Let me kiss you.'

Jonathan took her face in his hands and kissed her on either cheek, then once, lightly, on the mouth.

'*Mon fils*...' She raised a fluttering hand to his face as if she were about to bless him.

Lisa raised her eyes to heaven, then began to fan herself dramatically with her book.

With an affectionate, mock-ingratiating smile, Jonathan gave her the finger behind his mother's back.

Two

Charles Audley buttoned his waistcoat, adjusted his eye-patch, then screwed a monocle, with a fluid movement, into his remaining eye. He wore the eyeglass to irritate the tourists, but on this occasion it served a secondary purpose as well. It allowed his gaze to linger, in astonishing detail, over the lace-clad *derrière* of Madame Josseline's newest eighteen-year-old recruit. Aware of his appreciation, the girl turned around and posed for him, coquettishly.

'You ever been with an antediluvian before?' he asked her.

'What is that?'

'A clapped-out eighty-three year old.'

'Perhaps.'

'Fibber.'

She giggled, and went back to smoothing her stockings.

'Come up to scratch, did I? Or was I a bit of a let-down after all those young men you have sniffing around? No. On second thoughts, don't answer that one.'

She turned and moved, wide-hipped, towards him. Standing as close to him as she could, she inserted a small hand into his unbuttoned trousers and felt around, pouting. 'Scratch? What is that?'

'Did I please you?'

'Mmm. Yes and no. Not bad for an old man.'

She withdrew her hand and turned her back on him. He gave her bottom the expected slap. God, he loved women. He walked over to his jacket and took out his wallet. Selecting two five-hundred-franc notes, he laid them carefully onto the dressing table. 'For you. Not Madame.'

She kissed him on the cheek, '*Vous êtes mon vieux protecteur*,' and crumpled the notes inside her bag. 'When do you want to see me again?'

'I'll need at least a week to get my energy back.'

'In a week I have the curse. How about two weeks today? At the same time?'

'Perfect. If I'm still alive.'

'You'll be alive, Cha-cha. Men like you never die.'

Charles paused tellingly at the door. 'So my late father told me.'

Even though he'd spent the last six hours driving and his leg ached, Jonathan decided to take the long route from the RN 98 up through Gassin. The sudden panorama from below the Barri always pleased him. It smelled of his childhood up here – the glorious, vacant summers of his youth.

He parked the car under his favourite Aleppo pine tree and stepped outside. Stooping down, he picked up some of the fallen needles and rubbed them between his fingers. Closing his eyes, he inhaled deeply. Yes. It still worked. Smiling, he took a few paces forwards, enjoying the feel of the sunshine on his shoulders. The Baie de Cavalaire stretched majestically in front of him, the Mediterranean brash blue, the triple islands of the Porquerolles like truffle-flakes on her surface.

He picked out Le Levant, the island where he and Lisa had spent their August holidays as children. After her first day there his mother had refused to set foot on the island ever again because people insisted on walking around naked, or wearing those 'absurd pieces of string'. When Charles had rejected her entreaties that he take his family to a more civilised environment, she had sent her housekeeper, Antonia Gauberti, to look after the children for her. A mistake, thought Jonathan, because Antonia was only twenty-four at the time, and his father a lusty thirty-six. Jonathan couldn't be sure if anything had gone on between them, but Antonia, now seventy-one, still ran Charles's household, and his mother, terminally Catholic, had recently celebrated her twenty-second year of living alone at her late father's chateau in the Lot.

He glanced at his watch. Six o'clock. With luck Charles might be home and not playing bridge for a change. Bridge, or chemin de fer at the Sainte Maxime Casino. Jonathan knew that he had, at the most, a five-hour window of opportunity. He snatched a last glance at Le Levant and climbed back into his car. Half a lifetime ago Frances and Clara had joined them there for a week, without their father's knowledge – a week that had changed his life. Perhaps he should go back? See what had become of the place? The swimming, if not the memories, might prove good physic, as long as he remembered to keep out of the sun. His radiotherapist had warned him about that.

Without thinking he pulled up his shirt and scrutinised the tattoos delineating the radiotherapist's hit-zone. He ran his finger down the livid eight-inch biopsy scar that stretched from below his sternum down to his navel. The six-inch incision through which they'd extracted his ball was now almost hidden by the re-growth of pubic hair. Six months ago there hadn't been a single hair on him – not even an eyelash. And now look! His body had become a foreign country to him, an object he could only coincidentally count on.

Cursing himself for a fool, he slowly unzipped his trousers and gazed down at himself in morbid fascination. 'Stand up, you bloody thing.'

After a moment's bemused silence he refastened his trousers and started the engine.

Charles Audley parted the beaded fly curtain and stepped into the hall. Antonia straightened up from her dusting.

'Where have you been?'

'Cannes. The *Croisette*.' The curtains made a swishing sound behind him, scattering the afternoon light.

'You've been with that girl again, haven't you? Aren't you scared of getting ill?' She put down her duster and moved towards him.

'I'm already ill. I'm eighty-three years old, Antonia. I'll be dead of natural causes before Aids, or syphilis, or prostate cancer, or any of the other piddling little diseases lying in wait for me have the chance to carry me off.' He let her help him out of his coat. 'Anyway, Josseline's girls are clean. They have a health check twice a month.'

'And you believe that?'

'I choose to believe it, yes. Just as I choose to believe that I'll beat the house from time to time at the casino. It makes getting old more bearable. When I lose faith, I'll shoot myself.'

She snatched an anxious hand to her mouth. 'You wouldn't do that.'

'Try me.' There was the distant crunch of gravel as a car pulled up in the yard. Charles jerked his head to one side. 'Now who the bloody hell is that?'

Antonia moved to the window. 'It's Jonathan.' She turned back towards him, smiling.

Charles drew himself up with a sigh. 'So. She's let him out of her clutches at last. The poor devil's probably crawled down here to die. Back to the elephant's graveyard. We must endeavour to make his last days as comfortable as possible. I shall take him to the casino with me tonight.'

'But Jonathan hates gambling.'

'Nonsense. Every Audley for the past ten generations has enjoyed a flutter. That's why we're down to our last five million.'

Antonia gave him a stern look, then hurried to the front door. 'Jonathan!'

'Anto.' Jonathan kissed her twice on each cheek. 'Is papa here? Don't tell me he's bolted again?'

'He's gone ahead to the library. He's waiting for you.'

Jonathan snorted. 'That would be a first.' He started up the stairs, then abruptly caught himself. 'Anto?'

'Yes?'

'You can stop worrying.' He made a circle with his thumb and forefinger. 'They gave me the all-clear. I'm as fit as a fiddle. Everything patched up and back in working order.' He could feel the bitter taste of the half lie jetting across his tongue.

Antonia crossed herself, then snatched up the crucifix that she wore around her neck and held it to her lips. '*Dieu soit loué.*'

Jonathan grinned at her. He continued up the stairs and through the mezzanine. It was comforting to know that someone in the household gave a damn, anyway. 'Papa?'

'Come over here and take a look at this.' Charles was seated in his favourite wing armchair, leafing through a leather-bound book. 'Maggs have just sent it to me. Sublime. D'Alessandri at his best. Hand-coloured, of course. I've only got it on approval, but I intend keeping it. Stiff price they're asking, but they may come down.'

Jonathan peered over his father's shoulder, trying to conceal his smile.

'He's enjoying three at once. There's a fourth, see? Reflected in this mirror. She's working on herself and watching the others. Brilliant design, if a little lacking in essential detail.' Charles cleared his throat self-consciously. 'Your pre-Revolutionary Frenchman certainly understood the arts of love. So did the Ching-dynasty Chinese, of course, before the Taiping rebellion. People always seem to make the most of things when they sense the end of an era. It's a bit like ageing, really. You know you've only got so much credit left in the bank. Piers called it the triumph of decadence over civilisation. I call it plain common sense.'

'Are you trying to tell me something, by any chance?'

'Whatever can you mean? I thought you appreciated this sort of thing.'

'*Lauso la mare e tente'n terro.*'

'I don't understand. Is that Italian?'

'It's an old Provençal proverb. It means, "praise the sea and stay on land". Apposite, don't you think?' Jonathan moved across to the window. He stood there for a moment, looking out. The skin on his face felt ice-cold. 'The stupidest part of it all is that I don't even know if I can manage it with one woman any more, let alone four.'

'They didn't cut it off, did they? Seems an extreme measure. I thought they were treating you for cancer, not priapism?'

Jonathan turned back towards the room. 'I lost a ball, Dad.'

'So did Johnny Carteret, at Montecassino. To an anti-personnel mine. Didn't stop him bedding half the tarts in the West End when he got back.'

'It's not just the ball.'

'Then what is it? Did they lobotomise you as well?'

Jonathan let out a snort. He took the chair opposite his father.

'Scared to try it out, is that it?' asked Charles.

'Something like that.'

'Well, Josseline's got a new recruit. Gorgeous little thing. Mouth like a guppy. I'll treat you. She'll get you going again. You'll never look back.'

'I don't think that would be a good idea.'

'Can't for the life of me think why not.'

'Because I've lost my libido.'

'Then you'd better find it again. Loss of libido is the worm at the core of the Protestant work ethic. *Pace* your mother, who was something of an exception to the rule, I always thought Catholic countries managed these things so much better than we did. It was one of the reasons I took off for

Paris after the war. That, and your uncle Piers, who was an expert at avoiding the currency restrictions.'

'Speaking of Piers, have you been over to check on his house? I suspect that André may have been holding wild parties there while I've been away.'

'Wouldn't put it past him. Can't understand why you don't get rid of the place and come and live here. It'll be yours soon enough, anyway. And Antonia hasn't got enough to do, just looking after me. I'm sure Piers never expected you to keep on *La Giraudère* after his death. He was many things, but he wasn't a sentimentalist. The Cap is finished, of course. Full of bloody Arabs and their harems.'

'It's a good place to paint.'

'So's a field. And there's less to maintain.'

Jonathan stood up. He unconsciously massaged his leg. 'Do you mind if I stay for dinner? I wouldn't want to catch André unawares. Might be forced to sack him, and that would never do.'

'Stay the night. Antonia's making bouillabaisse. We can play some chemmy afterwards. I ordered a dozen bottles of the '82 Lafite from Berry's. Want to try one tonight? See how they're coming on. That's something I don't mean to leave you when I croak.'

Jonathan couldn't help laughing.

'See,' his father said, 'I've cheered you up already.'

Three

It took six loud honks of the horn to persuade André to emerge from the lodge. Stretching sleepily, he wheeled open the heavy wrought-iron gates to the house. Jonathan eased his battered Aston Martin Volante up the gravel track.

His great-uncle, Piers Godolphin, had bequeathed him *La Giraudère* in 1971 as the result of a deathbed fit of pique against Charles. Jonathan had been grateful at the time. He'd needed somewhere to hide after the devastating loss of Frances. Now the place was a brick and plaster albatross around his neck.

Jonathan garaged the car and started up the tiled path. *La Giraudère* was one of the last great villas left on the Cap d'Antibes. It was surrounded by four acres of garden that André tended whenever the fancy took him. Absorbing the desolation around him, Jonathan decided that the fancy had rarely taken André in the past few months. He couldn't blame him of course – he didn't care for the house himself. In recent years he'd used it as a glorified studio and as a place to store his clobber. In fact, he decided, *La Giraudère*'s gentle decline eerily mirrored his own ever since he'd given up trying to paint great works of art in favour of commissioned portraits. His clients, when they saw where he lived, not unnaturally assumed that it belonged to a wealthy and eccentric patron, and Jonathan did nothing to disabuse them.

He allowed André to muddle through his usual excuses for not doing this or maintaining that, then sent him back to his lodge. Relieved to be alone at last, he mounted the stairs to the first floor and threw open the shutters. The furniture was still covered in dust sheets, which suited his mood perfectly.

He'd call for the cleaning woman in the morning. It would probably take her the best part of a week to get the place up and running again. Meanwhile he had other things on his mind.

He crossed the hallway to his studio. The one change he'd made to Piers's layout was the insertion of a north light into the roof, above what had been the old *buanderie*. He strode around ripping dust sheets off the stacks of canvasses piled against every wall. He was looking for something. Dust motes twinkled hysterically in the shafts of sunlight. Here it was. He eased a canvas from behind the stack and carried it over to one of the easels. He set it up carefully, then stepped back. It was an unfinished nude of Frances.

The photograph from which he'd been working was still attached to the lower stretcher. He unpinned it and carried it over to the light. Frances was taking off her blouse and was naked from the waist down. She'd been in the act of turning towards him when he'd snatched the shot. She'd rushed at him, calling him all sorts of names, and had tried to grab the camera. They'd tussled, and ended up making love on the floor. She'd forgotten all about its existence, afterwards.

Jonathan held the photograph closer to his face. He was briefly tempted to sniff it, but that would have been obscene and rather pointless. Had he really made love to this girl only scant moments after her image had been distilled into the bowels of his camera? You could just make out the tip of one of her breasts. He ran his finger over it. The memory, surprisingly, aroused him. Of the dozens of women he had known in his life, not a single one had made him feel what Frances had made him feel.

He closed his eyes. The after impression from the photograph reverberated behind his eyelids. A staccato succession of images superimposed themselves across the one in the photo – he was holding Frances for the first time, touching her hair, watching her perform in the Zennor show, lowering his mouth to her nipple. He remembered her as he had first seen her, on the cliffs above Penhallow, nine years old, her mouse-coloured hair whipping across her cheeks, her rounded chin almost too strong to carry the delicate lines of her upper face. She had brown eyes, a straight, slightly uplifted nose, a hesitant and subtle mouth that matched the generosity of her gaze, which was wide – wider than normal – but was given point by her eyes, which, from the very first moment he had seen them, had held him in thrall.

The painting was a failure of course. He hadn't caught her expression, or the natural design her body made against the Persian sofa and the window behind her. He hadn't caught anything.

He pinned the photo to the upper stretcher and began to set up his palette. Now was the moment. Now he would catch her, moulding her to the background until she became a part of it, and it, her. It would be his first painting in nearly a year. Since his illness. And it would mark the start of his maturity.

Charles reached across and replaced the telephone in its cradle. He stood for a moment as if listening for an echo of his recent conversation, then walked slowly back to his armchair and sat down. He stretched out his hands, massaged the fingers absent-mindedly, then rested them heavily on his knees.

It was bad news. Worse than bad. His sister Helen had died. Helen, who had stood up for him, all those years ago, when their father had threatened to disown him. Helen, who had supported his quixotic abandonment of his studies at the Slade in favour of his brief, if disastrous, campaign of support for the Republican cause in the Spanish Civil War. A crypto-fascist of the old school, John Audley had never been able to forgive his son, despite his loss of an eye, for siding, as he saw it, with the communists. Later, Charles hadn't been remotely surprised to hear that the old man had signed Penhallow over to Helen, with the proviso that it should entail back to Jonathan when she died.

He had, however, been more than a little astonished to receive notice, after his parent's fatal air crash in Kenya in 1958, that his father had left him the bulk of the Audley family holdings, valued at a conservative six million pounds. He put that down, not to blood ties and to family honour, but to John Audley's profound hatred of Henry Champion. It was a feeling with which he wholeheartedly concurred. That had wiped the smile off old Henry's face, he thought to himself. The greedy bastard reckoned he'd had the lot in the bag: Helen, Penhallow, and the Audley millions. Well he hadn't. Charles was delighted when Henry had a stroke, in 1980, followed closely by another, which finished him off. It had served the bugger right.

But Helen? Charles wasn't a sentimental man, but he'd always had a soft spot for his sister. Nine years younger than him, she'd been all set to remain a spinster, living quietly with her parents at Penhallow, when Henry Champion had chanced along in 1955. He'd recently been widowed, and had been left with two infant daughters, Frances and Clara, and a house at Breage, which he couldn't afford to keep up. He'd managed, somehow, to winkle from Helen that she was to inherit Penhallow, and not unnaturally assumed that she was to inherit the Audley millions as well. Ha!

There was a tentative knock at the door. 'Charles?'

'Come in.'

Antonia manoeuvred the tea tray around the library door. It was only when she'd safely beached it on the map table that she noticed Charles's face. She'd looked after him, body and soul, for forty-five years. His expression and his mannerisms were an open book to her. 'Charles? What is it? Are you feeling unwell?'

'Fine. Fine. It's not me. I'm fine. I only wish it were.' He raised a quick hand then let it drop, flutteringly, to his lap. 'Helen's dead.'

Antonia made a fist and held it to her mouth.

'She didn't come down to breakfast. So Clara went up to see what was the matter. She was still in bed. Clara thought she was asleep. She'd already turned to leave when for some reason she had second thoughts. She went over to the bed. Helen had passed away sometime during the night. Quite peacefully, it appears. The sheets were still smooth.' Charles snorted. 'Can't complain, I suppose. The powers that be give me my son back with one hand, then snatch my sister away with the other.' He felt in his pocket and retrieved a handkerchief. He blew his nose, then noisily cleared his throat. 'The funeral's on Saturday. At Zennor. I shall go, of course.'

Antonia took an anxious step forward. Her first instinct was to dissuade him, but she knew it would do no good. It wasn't her place, and never had been, to interfere in whatever family arrangements he might care to make. 'Of course.'

'I shall go by airplane. Jonathan can take the car and meet me at Exeter airport.' He blew his nose again and replaced the handkerchief. 'I haven't forgotten anything, have I?'

'Geneviève.'

'Good God! You're right. I must call her. Didn't Jonathan say that Lisa was visiting Montigny? That'll make things easier. They were very close, you know. Geneviève loved Helen very much.'

'So did you.' Antonia walked over to the chair. Charles glanced up at her and held out his hand. She took it in both of hers and kissed it, then gently rested her cheek on top of his head.

The phone was ringing downstairs. Now who the hell was that? No one knew he was back at *La Giraudère*. Probably someone trying to sell him life insurance or a bloody mobile phone. Jonathan turned back to his painting. The ringing continued.

'Damn. Bloody damn. Damn the bloody machine.' He put down his palette, gazed lingeringly at the canvas, then spun around and started for the stairs. The ringing echoed through the empty house like a call to matins. He strode down the final three steps and snatched up the receiver. 'Who is it?'

'Me.'

'Who's "me"?' He wished people wouldn't do that. 'Oh. Clara. Is that you?' Incredible how one could identify a person by one word. In Clara's case the word 'me' had always fitted the bill perfectly.

'Jonathan.' Then silence.

Jonathan held the phone away from his face and squinted at it. Was the woman drunk again? He put the receiver back to his ear. 'Clara. It's so good to hear from you. How's the antiques trade? Passed off any good forgeries recently?' He loathed gossiping over the telephone. He cradled the mouthpiece against his clavicle and stared around the hall. It was worse than he'd thought – the place was seriously in need of a make-over. Piers would be turning in his crypt. He'd always liked everything just so. Jonathan sucked in his breath with an impatient sigh. 'And how's my aunt doing? Is she there? If so you can put her on when we're through. I've been meaning to call her for some time. Bring her up to date. Clara, you must be psychic.' He could feel himself rapidly running out of polite conversation.

There was a distant crash, then Clara's voice appeared right next to his ear, as if she'd been talking for some time and had only now decided to place the receiver near enough her mouth to be heard. '…so that's why I'm calling.' She began to sob.

'Clara? Whatever's the matter?' He could scarcely believe his ears. Clara, sobbing? Water might as well flow uphill.

'It happened last night.'

'What happened? Clara, I didn't catch a word of what you said.'

'Helen. She died.'

A rush of emotion almost left him speechless. 'Oh God, Clara, I'm so sorry.' His eyes flailed wildly around the room, searching for some metaphorical hook to hang himself on. 'So very sorry.' An uncalled-for thought occurred to him. 'Frances. Does she know yet?'

'Jesus. Trust you.' Clara managed a damp sniff. 'No. I haven't been able to contact her. She's in Italy. Cosima's doing her farewell show for Donatella Versace. They're somewhere in Milan.' She found herself listening, against her will, for the sound of his breathing.

'And my father?'

'He already knows. I phoned him first.' Clara caught sight of herself in the hall mirror and self-consciously touched the incipient alcohol flush at her throat.

'That was decent of you.' And also completely out of character, thought Jonathan. What the hell was going on? 'How did it happen?'

'How do you *think* it happened?' Jonathan heard something else fall, followed by Clara's mumbled curse. Then the sound of a deep breath. Clara's voice sounded wet when she next spoke. 'I thought she was asleep. Out like a light. But she'd been lying there half the night.'

'Clara. Listen to me. She was seventy-four years old. It had to happen sometime.'

'She wasn't old. And there was nothing whatever the matter with her. In fact I was just thinking the other day how well she looked. And she loved restoring the antiques.' This with a slightly guilty edge.

Jonathan could make out the distant tinkle of glass against the neck of a bottle. Then the explosive sound of Clara blowing her nose near the earpiece.

'You'll probably laugh when I tell you this, but we were finally on our way to becoming friends – not stepmother and stepdaughter any more. Oh, we argued, and we bickered, and we pissed each other off...'

'I'm not laughing, Clara. And I'm really glad you came to feel that way about Helen. She was special.' He shook his head in wonderment at his capacity for platitudes. He found himself remembering Helen's many small kindnesses: the unassuming way she'd coped with his passion for Frances; the masterful way she'd fielded the awful Henry until matters had been taken out of her hands, in 1968, in Paris. He cleared his throat self-consciously. 'Do you want me to contact Frances? It'll be easier from down here. Milan's only a few hours away.'

Clara groaned. She felt like a child again, talking to Jonathan – a deprived child, second-best loved, second-best admired, second-best everything.

'Well?'

'I don't know. She might not like it.'

'Clara. It's been twenty-eight years. She's buried a husband. Borne a daughter. I'm not exactly a threat to her anymore. She must have forgiven me by now.'

'I wouldn't be so sure, if I were you.' One part of Clara hated herself for saying it, the other part gloried in the vestige of power it still gave her over him.

'You weren't exactly an innocent party yourself.'

'I wasn't in love with her.'

That stopped him in his tracks. 'All right. Point taken. So?' More silence. Jonathan held his breath. He was briefly tempted to yank the phone from the wall and toss it across the room.

Clara sighed long-sufferingly. 'They'll be staying at one of the big hotels. Somewhere in the centre of Milan. Or else she'll be someone's house guest. In that case you'll never find her. We'll just have to hope she gets in touch before Saturday, won't we? I don't see that there's anything more we can do.'

'Is that when you're holding the funeral?'

'Yes. At Zennor. At the church. Eleven o'clock. I was going to say that you're welcome to stay at Penhallow, but then the house is entailed to you, isn't it?' There was a thinly disguised edge of bitterness to Clara's voice. 'You don't mind if I stay on for the time being, do you? Until I can find somewhere to store my things?'

'Oh for God's sake, Clara. Of course you can stay on. I'm not going to evict you from your own home.'

She took a long, shuddering breath. 'Do you still love Frances? No. Stupid question. Forget I ever asked it.' She snorted sarcastically. 'Helen always said that age would mellow me. That I'd start accepting things for what they were. Stop kicking against the pricks. She was wrong, wasn't she?'

Jonathan tried to think of a tactful reply, but failed.

'I suppose you think I'm a cow for not asking about your illness? Well I got all the guff from Helen, who got it from your mother. And Lisa still calls, when she can find the time between book-signing tours. I know you nearly died. I wasn't sorry.' Clara could feel the tears pricking at her eyes again.

'Thanks a million.'

'Do you want to know the real truth? If you'd died before Helen, I'd have inherited Penhallow. I sound like a bitch, don't I? But there's virtue in honesty. And I'm a middle-aged woman now, and don't have many other pleasures left in life.' Her laughter had an edgy quality to it. She cast another bleak glance at herself in the hall mirror. 'You'll be delighted to know that, in addition to everything else, I've lost my looks. I always was the brassy one, wasn't I? Just that little bit too obvious. While Frances was born elegant. And she's as beautiful as ever. Fucking Frances.' Her hand reached automatically for her glass.

Jonathan waited until he was sure she had nothing more to say, then gently replaced the receiver. He paused for a few moments to give his heart time to resume its normal pace then lifted the phone again.

He dialled quickly this time, holding the phone tightly to his ear. 'International Directory. Milan. Thank you. I'll wait.'

Four

He ran Frances to ground on his eighth try, at the Antica Locanda Solferino.

'Yes. *La Signora* and *la Signorina* Brancardi are registered with us. Shall I put you through to their room?'

'Please.' Pray God I don't get the daughter. 'Thank you.' Jonathan waited. He could hear the phone ring a scant two hundred miles away from where he was standing. Why am I doing this, he thought to himself. What's possessed me, after twenty-eight years of silence, to telephone Frances out of the blue simply to tell her that her stepmother has just died? It's surreal.

'Their room doesn't answer. Shall I give them a message?'

'No. I'll phone back later. Thank you. Thank you very much.' He was relieved. Now he'd have time to think. To marshal his resources.

Would Frances agree to him picking her up in Milan? No. Of course not. What a stupid idea. She'd want to travel by plane, not car. He'd have to wait until the funeral to see her. Would she stay at Penhallow, then? Of course she would. So he couldn't very well stay there as well. All right. He'd spend the night at the pub. Go to the house for dinner. Meet her there. That would be safer.

And then there was his father. He'd want to go to the funeral. Except that he hadn't been outside France for years. Probably hadn't even kept his passport up. It was out of the question, of course, that Antonia should travel with him. His mother would leave at once were she to appear. But Antonia had tact, thank God, whether she'd been his father's mistress or not. One day, before it was too late, he would have to ask Charles, point-blank, what the situation really was. Strange how they could talk about anything but that.

As for his mother, Lisa would travel up with her. That was easy enough. He wondered what his parents would find to say to each other after so many years? He'd love to eavesdrop on that conversation.

So when it finally came down to it, he wasn't really needed at all. The notion rather surprised him. He quickly shunted it to his mental out-tray for incineration. One thing was certain: the rest of the family would count on him staying at Penhallow, so Frances couldn't expect him to skulk off somewhere else, then, could she? Clara would certainly have her work cut out. Serve her bloody well right. That crack of hers about inheriting Penhallow if only he'd had the courtesy to die was below the belt. And it was his bloody house now, wasn't it? He'd enjoy rubbing Clara's nose in the fact. If he stayed away he might as well daub some red paint on a placard and walk around with it stretched above his head as they all drove up. 'Jonathan hasn't seen Frances for twenty-eight years, but he's still in love with her. Sadly, she hates him.'

He felt flustered and irritable. Why did this have to happen to him? And at this particular time? He'd been building up to something, he knew it. Some action that would have sorted things out once and for all. The painting was part of it – even his impotence had a part to play (if he could allow himself the pun). Why did Aunt Helen have to choose this particular moment to die? To precipitate things before he was ready?

His thoughts were taking him in the same direction they always did – to the fact that before he'd fallen ill he'd been able to live with the loss of Frances. It had seemed rough justice. He hadn't been worthy of her. But the illness had changed all that. It had marked a belated rite of passage. Now he wanted to reclaim what had been lost. Make up for the past. Could it be done? Only one way to find out. He picked up the phone again.

Frances Brancardi watched her daughter prance down the catwalk, swirl left and right, then pleat her flimsy dress in her fingers and show the world her underwear. Or what little there was of it. She glanced over at the photographers. They were behaving, as usual, like slavering beasts, snapping their photos, flashing their bulbs and shouting to Cosima to reveal even more of herself. As if that were possible. I'm glad she's retiring, Frances thought to herself. Glad that age has finally caught up with her. These fashion shows aren't about real life, they're make-believe. All very well for a girl of eighteen, but Cosima was twenty-seven. She should be thinking of settling down. Raising a family. What would Giancarlo have said? She smiled as she thought of his face when Cosima had announced her intention to take up modelling.

'What do you mean modelling? Modelling like Twiggy? Like Verouschka? Modelling like...who is that black girl with the beautiful figure? Like that? Do you want men to look at you like that? To undress you with their eyes? You don't know how they can be.'

'Yes I do, papa.'

'What? Which question are you answering?'

'Both. And you're a man, papa. And you aren't like that.'

'I am. I'm no different.'

'Well, I'm not scared of you looking at me, so why should I be scared of them?'

'Aiee. Francesca. Speak to your daughter. Tell her what I say is true.'

'You speak to her. You're her father. She'll listen to you.'

'Of course I'll listen to you, papa. Now what did you want to say?'

'Bah. *Raggazzi*. Mad. You will do what you want. I'll be a laughing stick. My friends will cut pictures of you out of the magazines.'

'A laughing stock.'

'A what?'

'You'll be a laughing *stock*, papa. Not a stick.'

'Why don't you speak Italian any more? I knew your mother was wrong to send you to that English school. In Italy you would not have become a model. Would not have made me a stock. What decent man will have you when he knows you have stripteased in front of half of Europe.'

'Giancarlo!'

'All right. I know. I know. She is not stripteasing. But it comes to the same thing. And nothing you tell me will make me think different.'

He'd gone along, of course, in the end. And been proud of her. And boasted to his friends how Cosima now modelled for Dior, and Yves St Laurent, and Versace, and Gianfranco Ferre, and that, unlike all the other models, she had brains and spirit. Poor Giancarlo. He'd had a bad death. They'd been separated when the accident occurred, but she'd gone to him nevertheless; looked after him, those last few days in the hospital.

Should his infidelities have mattered to her so very much? He'd sworn, after all, on his mother's soul, that he loved only her. That he couldn't help himself. Frances snatched a hand to her breast. A memory was forcing its way into her consciousness. A memory from long ago. But she wouldn't let it come. She'd fight it, as she'd always fought it. She wouldn't be held back.

When she looked up again, Cosima was gone. The show was over. She'd missed most of it, with all her useless thinking. She stood up and looked around herself. No point in going backstage. She knew all too well the sort of bedlam that would be occurring in the fitting-rooms. Better to go back to the hotel and wait for Cosima there. She threw her coat around her shoulders, oblivious, as ever, to the admiring glances she received.

Standing in the via Gesú, she hesitated before hailing a taxi. What was she doing? Why was she here, standing in this Milan street, so far from anything that mattered? Cosima didn't really need her. Giancarlo was dead. She had no lovers, no husband, few friends. God, the self-pity's starting to well again, she thought. What was that silly rhyme, the one Jonathan and Lisa used to trill when we were children? About Lord Dudley? 'He promised much, did little, and died mad.' She held her hand up for a taxi. She'd promised much, and done little. Married at twenty. A first in history of art from Cambridge in the same year. Joint-owner, with Giancarlo, of her own gallery in Paris at twenty-five. Deceived wife at thirty. And then what? The last eighteen years had passed like stolen kisses.

The taxi pulled up. The driver wound down his window. '*Dove, bella*?'

'Antica Locanda Solferino.'

She curled up on the back seat and watched the shops flash past. She was forty-eight years old. She was three years into her menopause. She had a liver spot on the back of one hand. And the taxi driver had called her '*bella*'. She put the liver-spotted hand up to her face. Perhaps it was just a sun freckle, after all. But how much longer could she get away with it? How many more good years could she count on? And what was good about them anyway?

'The beautiful lady is sad?'

'No, no. The not-so-beautiful lady is not sad.'

'*Donna, se' tanto grande e tanto vali, che qual vuol grazia ed a te non ricorre, sua disïanza vuol volar sanz'alli.*' (You, Lady, are so great and so precious that whoever craves grace and does not turn to you, his desire would fly without wings.)

'Dante! I recognise it. It's magnificent.' A taxi driver who quoted Dante? Strange days. '*Nel mezzo del cammin di nostra vita mi ritrovai per una selva oscura che la diritta via era smarrita.*'(In the midst of life's journey I found myself in a dark wood where the straight way was lost.)

'You know Dante, Signora?'

'I've read him. But my Italian is poor. I understand so little.'

'No one understands Dante. You feel him. It is an instinct.'

'An instinct. Yes. That's it.' The taxi was pulling up at her hotel. 'We lose our instincts, don't we? All too often. In places like this?'

He turned to answer her, but the doorman already had his attention, forcing new clients on him. Frances paid the driver and stepped onto the pavement. '*Grázie*,' she said.

'*Prego*.'

The moment was gone. She'd felt herself grasping at something, something she'd been searching for for a long time. But it was like the lost memory of a dream.

Jonathan waited impatiently while the phone rang in Frances's room. It was his third try. Give it ten more rings, he thought to himself, then hang up for good.

'*Sì*?'

'Frances?'

'Yes? Who is that?'

'It's Jonathan. Jonathan Audley.'

Frances felt an almost fatalistic lethargy creep over her. She must do something. She scrabbled in her handbag for a cigarette. She was in the process of giving up. Down to five a day. Cosima smoked like a chimney. Made the excuse that it kept her weight in check. Frances placed the cigarette in her mouth and lit it with her father's battered Dunhill lighter.

'Frances? Are you there?'

She drew in a deep cloud of smoke. She could feel the nicotine eating into her bones. I suppose it'll be osteoporosis next, she thought to herself.

'Frances?'

'Jonathan? Is that really you?'

'It's really me.' Why had he said that? It made him sound like a complete ass. Why the hell shouldn't it be him? 'It's good to talk to you again. I've been thinking of you recently. Been meaning to call you. Find out what's been going on in your life. I was sorry to hear about your husband.' Oh God, he was blathering. Then it suddenly struck him. Helen! He'd almost forgotten. 'Clara asked me to run you down...' Run her down? That's what had happened to Giancarlo. Talk about Freudian slips! '...to find you. Which hotel you were in.'

'Clara? She asked you to find me?'

'Yes. I know it seems crazy after all these years. But...well, you see...'

'Jonathan. For God's sake. What is it?'

'It's Helen.'

'Helen? What about Helen? Has she had an accident?'

'It's worse than that, I'm afraid.'

'Worse than that?' Frances let her cigarette flutter, unnoticed, into the ashtray.

Jonathan cleared his throat. This was terrible. He must have been mad. Clara must have known what it was going to be like. She'd been a step ahead of him, as usual. She'd simply opened up the lift-shaft door and let him step through it. Just as she'd done in 1971, on the island. 'Helen died in her sleep. Last night. Clara didn't know where you were staying. I'm only a few hours away, so we thought it would be easier if I called around the hotels. I hope you don't mind?'

'Mind?'

Jonathan put a hand over the mouthpiece and made a face. This wasn't turning out quite as he'd expected. But then, what had he expected? A tearful reunion? A nostalgia trip back to the good old days? He'd ballsed it up, good and proper. 'The funeral's on Saturday. At Zennor. She's to be buried in the churchyard. I'm driving up. Charles will probably fly. *Maman* is to go up with Lisa, on the Eurostar. They'll spend the night at Lisa's house, then take the train to Penzance. I was wondering if you wanted me to come to Milan?'

'You? Come to Milan? What on earth for?'

'To pick you up.' This was a disaster. Jonathan's toes curled in on themselves inside his shoes. 'I suppose you'll want to fly too? No one in their right mind would choose to drive for fifteen hours in a clapped-out open-top sports car if they could possibly avoid it.'

'A sports car?' What *was* he on about? 'I'm sorry, Jonathan. I'm a little distracted. I'm probably not making much sense.' It's not me who isn't making sense, thought Frances; he's the one who's maundering on. She'd heard he'd been ill. Perhaps it had affected his brain in some way? All those anaesthetics and scans.

She could feel her guilt over Helen begin to gnaw at her extremities. She'd seen her, what, five times in the last fifteen years? Now Helen was dead, and it left her cold. It was as if she'd heard the news of her nanny's death.

'Yes. I will take the plane,' she heard herself saying. 'Clara will need me. There'll be a lot to organise. I'll fly today. Cosima can follow later.' A thought occurred to her. 'If you want to be of help, perhaps you could pick Cosima up in London? Drive her down?'

'Who?'

'Cosima. My daughter. You'll be coming via Calais, won't you? London isn't that far.'

Jonathan made a face. He'd actually intended to travel via Roscoff to Plymouth. Save hours on the journey. 'I'd be delighted to. Shall I call you at Penhallow? Nearer the time? We can make the arrangements then.'

'Call me on my mobile. Have you got a pen?' She reeled off the number.

'Got it. I'll call you on my way up. Work out times, etc.'

'Thanks, J.' What on earth could she think of to say to him? His voice sounded strange after all these years. Unfamiliar. As if someone had made a recording of her youth and was insisting on playing it back to her. 'It'll be odd meeting at Penhallow again. Do you remember?' Remember what? Their childhood? Their love affair? His betrayal of her with that foxy little bitch Clara? Frances tasted the anger again. For a moment it overwhelmed her – she felt almost faint with the sudden rush of feeling. Why had the men in her life always betrayed her? Was it something in her nature? The in-built status of a murderee, perhaps? Wasn't that what D H Lawrence had been going on about in *Women in Love*? 'I'd better go now. Cosima will be arriving any minute and I need time to think. I don't want to spoil her farewell party because of this.'

'Her farewell party?'

'I'll speak to you soon. Thanks for calling. Goodbye, Jonathan.'

She put down the phone and reached for another cigarette. Her mind was seething. Her hands shook as she raised the lighter to her mouth.

Five

Penhallow, Cornwall. 1960

Frances Champion. Frances Champion. Frances Champion. She looked up from her diary. Through the window she could see the mossy green grass leading down to the sea, broken, here and there, by angry rocks. Frances Champion, she wrote again, Penhallow, Cornwall, England, Europe, The World, The Universe, Infinity, God. Could a person live in God? She supposed so, as the Reverend Darby had explained that one could, during his Sunday-school lesson. God was certainly a good deal bigger than infinity, anyway.

There was a sudden scraping in the hall. 'Is anybody there? Clara?' She said the name apprehensively, rather hoping that there wouldn't be an answer. A squeaking canine yawn reassured her that it was only Mr C.

She'd been avoiding her younger sister recently, ever since Daddy had lost his temper with her on Clara's fibbing say-so about the broken Dunhill pipes. She'd known how Daddy loved his pipes. She'd never have broken even one of them, let alone three. But there they were, in smithereens, looking like somebody had stamped on them – like *she'd* stamped on them.

'Clara says she saw you.'

'But Daddy, she's lying.'

'I think I can tell who's lying in this household and who isn't. Clara can hardly *reach* the mantelshelf yet. You can.'

Frances had glared at her sister in what amounted to a final supplication. She'd *try* to love her, *try* to forgive her for all the ghastly things she'd done, the lies, the tricks, the endless attempts to ingratiate herself with Daddy and please

Helen – even her campaign against Mr C staying in the house instead of in the kennels with the *real* gun dogs – if *only* she'd own up about the pipes.

Clara's voice had been flat and emotionless. 'She reached up and took the pipes and then she stamped on them. I saw her do it.'

'Clara, you didn't!' Frances burst into uncontrollable tears.

Henry Champion lowered his head as if he had just received a severe, but well-deserved, prison sentence. 'It pains me to say it, Frances, but you're beginning to take after your mother. If you think that all you have to do to get me to believe you is to cry and to flutter your eyelashes, you're making a very big mistake.'

Frances had raged at him through her tears. 'Don't talk about Mummy like that. She's dead!'

'How dare you raise your voice to me, young lady!' He had looked around the room for support. Helen had dropped her gaze. Nanny Cruikshank had hovered in the corner, biting her lower lip, waiting, in despair, to pick up the pieces. When he'd turned back to Frances, his eyes were big, like a wolf's. 'And whose fault is it if she's dead? Nobody asked her to abandon her family. Nobody asked her to behave like a strumpet and humiliate me in front of the entire community.'

'Henry! Please. *Pas devant...*'

'Helen, I'll trouble you, please, to mind your own business. You may be the children's stepmother, but I'm their father. Clara's too young to remember her mother, but Frances isn't. And I'm absolutely determined to stop her following...'

Frances sprang up from the table and squeezed her eyes tight shut against the memory. Think of something else – something nice – she intoned to herself. Then it'll go away. Then Mummy will come back from heaven and take me off with her and we'll live like gypsies, in a gypsy caravan, and we'll eat our dinners over an open fire, out of a pot.

The well-rehearsed litany worked. She carefully closed her diary, hid it behind a row of books, then walked composedly into the hall. Her new cousins, Jonathan and Lisa, were due to arrive with their mother and father in good time for tea. She felt a first, tentative surge of excitement. They weren't really 'new' of course; it was only that she hadn't met them yet. They'd been around for quite some time, actually. They lived in France.

'Come on, Mr C.' Her elderly black Labrador eased himself up from his bed by the hall fireplace and clicked across the floor towards her. 'We'll go and wait for them.' She opened the glazed half-door to the porch and squeezed through. 'Shush, Mr C, or they'll hear us.'

Once out of the house, she began to run. Mr C lumbered behind, dewlaps flapping. 'Come on, Mr C, come on!' The warm summer breeze lifted her hair. She could feel the heat of the sun on her knees. The sea twinkled invitingly. Seagulls swung and ducked over the cliffs. Frances followed the driveway, then struck out towards Boskedder Rocks. Ten minutes later she was out of breath. Mr C had fallen so far behind that he was now only a small black dot in the field below. Frances stood on the top-most rock and looked out to sea. A Dory, with tight red sails, was beating around Portwidden Point. Frances waved. One of the fishermen waved back. 'Good luck!' she shouted, but her words were eaten by the distance between them.

Mr C reached the summit, panting, his tongue lolling from his mouth. 'Come here,' she called. He came and stood close to her leg while she kneaded the deep flesh of his neck with her hands. 'Is that better?' It was what her stepmother did for Daddy sometimes, when he was tired from shooting.

In the distance, on the road from St Ives, she could make out the metallic glint of a car. If it turns right at the crossroads it will be coming to us, she thought to herself. And they'll be inside it. My new cousins. Lisa and Jonathan. She watched the car approach. It seemed to hesitate for a second, then it turned right and headed towards the sea and the coast track. Frances darted down the hill. Mr C watched her for a moment with a sad expression, then picked himself up and started after her. 'Come on, Mr C. We'll be late!'

Frances ran faster and faster, the slope so steep that she felt headily out of control. 'Help!' she shouted ecstatically. She raised her arms and for a brief moment imagined that she could actually take off, that she could feel herself rising, out over the stone walls, over the stunted trees, high over the cliffs and curling around the headland and back towards Penhallow. 'I'm flying, Mr C!' Her foot caught a half-buried stone, breaking her stride. She felt herself start to go, tried vainly to steady herself with windmilling arms, then crashed to the ground. 'Owww!'

She lay there for a few moments, winded. Slowly she eased herself into a sitting position. She could hear Mr C panting his approach somewhere behind her. She looked down at her foot. There was something wrong with it. Her ankle was swelling and turning blue. She tried to get up, but fell down again. Mr C reached where she was and flopped down beside her. 'Oh, Mr C,' she said, 'can you help me?' He gave her cheek a cursory lick then groaned comfortably and laid himself flat in the sun. Frances began to cry.

Jonathan watched the stone walls flashing past him from the back of his father's 1955 Facel-Véga Cabriolet. He loved the car, with its brown leather upholstery and lean black lines. At a hundred miles an hour it would boom and rock alarmingly. One time, on their way up through France, he had stood up and held out his arms, allowing the heated wind of its passage to caress his body through the thin fabric of his shirt and shorts.

'Jonathan. Get back in your bloody seat this minute.'

'Charles, you are driving too fast,' said his mother.

'No point in having a car like this if you don't intend to drive it. Jonathan! Back in your seat.'

That morning they had landed at Hurn airport, and a man had driven the Facel-Véga out of the nose of the aeroplane. 'That's a very fine car if you don't mind me saying so, sir.'

'I don't mind at all.'

Hearing his father's response, Jonathan had edged forward and put his hand possessively on the warm bonnet. He had felt, for one sensuous, utterly complete moment, as if the car were his.

Now they were approaching Penhallow, the place where his father had grown up as a child. He was looking forward to meeting his cousins – except that they were girls. He supposed that Lisa would find more to say to them. He was nine years old, after all. Ten next month. The oldest, by a long shot. He could always go off alone if the girls annoyed him.

Charles Audley turned right at the crossroads. 'Not far now.' They were his first words for nearly an hour.

Jonathan put his hand in Lisa's pocket and tried to prise out the remaining half Mars bar he knew she still had in there.

'That's mine! You ate yours hours ago.'

'Then why don't you eat yours? It's not fair keeping it back like that. And why do you take so long to eat them, anyway? You do it just to annoy me.'

'*Mes enfants*.' Their mother turned around in her seat. 'Look at you.' She started brushing hair and smoothing eyebrows and plumping collars. 'What will your cousins think?'

Charles pulled up at the gates. He opened the car door, stepped out and took a few paces forward. He stood there, staring down the driveway, his hands held tightly to his sides. Half a mile distant a dozen tall chimneys, like disarranged but unbowed skittles, poked above the canopy of copper beeches. The magic of Penhallow seemed to radiate towards him through the trees. He closed his eyes and allowed the past to wash over him. In a quarter of a mile the drive would curl around to the right, below a great bank, with the sixteenth-century house spread out below. He could almost feel the soft sheen of the winding carved-wood staircases and the oak-panelled corridors beneath his hand. He could smell the musty attics and the junk-rooms in which he and Helen had played as children, creating enchanted caves and castles from the jetsam of five centuries. The house was built in the form of an E – in honour of Elizabeth I, he supposed – and had been little changed by succeeding Audleys in the years since its construction. The stone had weathered to a lichen-tainted yellow and grey, and more lichen, dark green this time, dotted the roof-tiles, as if some giant had taken ink and blotting paper to it, randomly damping the spilt tincture. But the place, despite itself, seemed to work; to belong there, nestled away from the Atlantic storms in a glade, which, on summer days, reflected its heat high into the sky, then reflected it back again so that the fields and woods, coverts and coppices, appeared almost Mediterranean in its amber glare.

'Charles? What is it?'

'I'm going to leave you here.'

'Charles?'

'I'm sorry. But I can't face two weeks as the guest of that stupid bugger Champion, playing host to me in my father's house.'

'But Helen? What about Helen?'

'Helen will understand. Jonathan, help me with the luggage.'

Excited, despite himself, Jonathan ran to his father's side and began unpacking their bags from the boot. 'Come on, Lisa.'

'I'm staying with *maman*.' Lisa was standing beside Geneviève, clutching her hand.

'Charles, how are we going to get to the house?'

'Send the boy. There's a short cut over the hill. Stacey can bring one of the cars and ferry you down.'

'Where are you going?'

'London. I shall be at my club.'

'Charles. You won't go to the Clermont. You won't gamble. You promise me?'

'Can't promise anything of the sort, old girl.'

'And you won't...' He turned quickly towards the children.

'Goodbye you two. Enjoy yourselves. Try and annoy Henry as much as possible. There'll be two bob in it for you every time he loses his temper. I shall have to trust you, Jonathan, to keep an honest record.'

'I will, papa.'

'Good. Look after your mother and sister. Goodbye, darling.' He gave Geneviève a cursory kiss. His thoughts were already on the fleshpots of London. 'Go on, Jonathan. Go and find old Stacey. The round trip shouldn't take you more than twenty minutes. Up over that hill, then down around the back of the house. You'll find him in the stables, tinkering. Give him this.' He handed Jonathan a ten-shilling note.

He fired up the car, made a smart three-point turn, then disappeared up the road, spraying gravel. Jonathan stood looking after him. He worshipped his father.

'Jonathan. You heard what your father said. I shall stay here with Lisa. Go and bring the man. Hurry now.'

Some instinct caused Jonathan to turn back when he was halfway up the slope. His mother and Lisa were still standing, hand in hand, with their backs to the house, watching the empty road down which his father had gone.

Frances had got as far as her knees. She eased her good leg forward, but when she put her weight on her other foot, the pain lanced up it like a lightning bolt. 'Please, Mr C. Go and get help. Go on,' she wailed.

Mr C stood irresolutely by. He knew that something was wrong, but not what, exactly. He raised his snout and sniffed around, then moved back towards Frances. 'All right. We'll have a rest. But then I'm going to start crawling.' She pulled Mr C down and snuggled up to him. From her prone position she had a strange, abbreviated view of the surrounding country.

A cow, or an animal of some sort could walk right up to her and she would only see it at the very last moment. She craned her neck backwards. Her tummy grumbled. She was starting to feel hungry. She wondered if her cousins were already tucking into their tea, back at the house. Perhaps when Mr C felt hungry he might go home and raise the alarm? She didn't want to spend the night here. Maybe they'd send a search party, like in *Lorna Doone*?

A shadow fell across her and she screamed. Not out of fear, exactly, but more by way of having been taken by surprise.

'Why did you scream?'

It was a tall boy, his blonde hair in a crew cut, his face very brown for this early in the summer. She craned her head to look up at him, but the sun was blinding her. Noticing this, Jonathan moved forward and crouched beside her. He had very green eyes.

'Are you all right?'

'I've hurt myself.'

'Show me.'

Frances pointed to her foot. Jonathan moved down and took a closer look. 'Do you think it's broken?' she said, apprehensively.

'Can I touch it?'

'Be careful. It hurts a lot.'

He lifted the foot in his hand and carefully stroked the swollen skin. 'Does that hurt?'

'Not really.'

'Then it's probably not broken. I'll tell you what. I'm going to bind it up with my handkerchief, then you can lean on me and I'll walk you home.'

'Is it clean?'

'What?'

'Your handkerchief.'

He held it up for her appraisal. 'The maid gives me a fresh one every day.'

'You have a maid?'

'Not just for myself. She's for my sister Lisa, too.'

'So you're my cousin?'

'Yes.' He was binding her foot. It felt nice. 'I'm Jonathan. Are you Frances, or Clara?'

'Guess.' He considered her for a moment. Frances liked the feeling of being looked at so closely. 'Well?' she asked, coquettishly.

'You're Frances.'

'How did you know?'

'I just did, that's all. You don't look like a Clara.'

'What does a Clara look like?'

He seemed almost abashed. 'Not like you.'

'And how do I look?'

He swallowed, his Adam's apple bobbing in his throat. 'You're pretty. I like the way you look.'

'Very pretty? Or just quite pretty?'

'Very pretty.'

'All right then. You can help me up.'

She was a head smaller than him and as light as a feather. He ducked, so that she could place an arm around his neck.

'Do you want to kiss me?'

'All right.'

She closed her eyes and poked her chin towards him. He watched her for a moment, a moment he would remember all his life. Her pale skin. The light down on her cheeks. Her almost translucent eyelids. So different from him, and yet the same. He closed his eyes and gave her a brief, tight-lipped kiss.

'Was that nice?' She'd opened her eyes at the very last moment and was looking at him intently.

'Yes. I liked it. Did you?'

'Girls don't like those sorts of things. They just let boys do it to them.'

'Oh.' Jonathan didn't quite know what to say. This was a revelation to him. 'Are you sure you didn't like it?'

She seemed uncertain. 'My stepmother said that to Daddy. She said there were things men liked that ladies didn't. I heard them. In their bedroom.'

'Are you sure they were talking about kissing?'

'That's what people do in bedrooms, isn't it?'

'You're probably right.' He was beginning to feel weary. 'Can I do it again, some time?'

She looked up at him. She liked leaning against him. Liked having him all to herself. 'Only when we're alone. And you must never, ever, tell Clara. You promise?'

'I promise.'

Mr C let out a bark, and started an awkward gallop towards the house.

'Oh no,' said Jonathan. 'Just my luck.'

'What?'

'I've forgotten *maman* and Lisa.'

Six

'I can't understand it. Can't understand it at all.' Henry struck a third match, held it to the bowl of his pipe and began to suck. 'The man drives up to the front gates, stops his car, unloads his wife, then buggers off. Would you call that sane, Helen? Would you call that normal, civilised behaviour? Perhaps when Franco blew out his eye, a stray piece of shrapnel got in there? Been playing havoc with his brain ever since.'

'You know very well why he wouldn't come in.'

'Oh? And why is that?'

'I'm not going to say.'

Henry finally got the pipe going to his satisfaction. 'I've carried my point then, it seems.'

'It seems.'

'Are you being sarcastic, Helen?'

There was a knock at the door. 'Geneviève. Come in.' The two women kissed. Henry raised a hand, then pretended to be busy with that morning's *Times*, which he'd already read, cover to cover. Helen shot him a look, then turned back to Geneviève. 'Have you settled in already? That was quick. Where are the children?'

'Frances is holding a salon in her bedroom. She looks like Madame de Staël. The other three are in attendance. I hope the injury to her leg isn't serious?'

'Dr Mabley says it's just a sprain. Cruikshank will look after her. If I know Frances, she'll be on her feet and hobbling in a day or two. As soon as the children lose interest in paying her court.'

Henry cleared his throat. 'I'm going over to talk to Baldwin. He's having sparrowhawk trouble. Want to make sure he's setting his gins and not using those bloody useless cage traps.'

'Henry! Gins are illegal. You told me so yourself.'

'I will not have the bloody government telling me what I can and can't do on my own estate. Do you know how many chicks those buggers kill? Have you any idea? And then they tell me I can't gin 'em.'

'But what if Baldwin gets caught? Sent up in front of the bench?'

'I'm the magistrate. I'll let him off with a warning.'

'Oh Henry.'

Henry thrust the newspaper under his arm, restored his pipe to the rack and prepared to leave. 'Glad to have you here, Geneviève. Make yourself at home. Helen will see to everything. I'll catch up with you girls at dinner.'

The two women watched him silently as he walked out of the door. When he was gone, Helen took a deep breath and glanced across at Geneviève. 'Henry loves his shooting. July is always an upsetting time for him. Nothing much to do except annoy the gamekeeper.'

Geneviève smoothed the pleats at the front of her tweed skirt. She gave herself one final pat, then looked up. 'Helen. Please don't be upset at what I'm about to say, but are you sure it's convenient for us to stay for two whole weeks? Wouldn't it suit you better if we stayed for just a few days, then vaporised away?'

'Geneviève!' Helen almost ran across the room, then stopped, as if afraid of the impression her haste would make. 'It's Henry, isn't it? What am I saying? It's always Henry. Please, please, please, don't let him put you off.'

'Of course it's not Henry.'

'Don't be so tactful. It's not necessary. Look. I'm going to be honest with you. Honest and un-English. Do you mind?'

'Mind? I am un-English. I'm French.'

Helen darted an anxious look at the door as if she feared that it might suddenly burst open again, revealing her husband. She reached impulsively for Geneviève's hand. 'Oh dear. This is going to sound so disloyal. And I don't want to be disloyal to Henry.'

'Helen. *S'il vous plaît*. Please. Just this once. Be un-English. Like you said.'

Helen managed a weak smile. 'All right then.' She let go of Geneviève's hand and walked over to the fireplace. She picked up Henry's warm pipe, fiddled with it, then replaced it in its holder. 'I don't want you to go because I shall be lonely.' She turned quickly around, the sharp movement unsettling her hair. It transformed her, for a moment, into the young girl she must once have been. She took a hesitant pace forward, bringing the palm of her hand unconsciously to her chest. 'The truth of the matter is that Henry has managed to alienate the entire county. It was more or less confined to the east at first, but since he's had the running of Penhallow he's seen off the south and the west, too. There may be a few people up in the north, around Bude perhaps, who haven't heard about us yet, but that can't last long.'

'I don't understand.'

Helen's voice took on a higher timbre, as if she had sucked in a lungful of pure nitrogen. 'When my father disinherited Charles, it didn't go down at all well with the people who count around here. The big estates. The old families. Those sorts of people. It's the same in France, isn't it?'

'I suppose so.'

'Well Charles, as you know, had what they call a 'good war'. So it was considered that Daddy had acted too harshly towards him, and that he should make amends. But it was too late by then. He'd got into one of his tempers and done the irrevocable. And Charles was proud. He'd be damned if he was going to climb down.'

'But Helen, I don't see what this has to do with Henry. And Charles loves you. I know he does. He doesn't hold what his father did against you.'

Helen was wringing her hands. 'Everything would have been all right if I hadn't married. But I did. Henry was the first man who ever asked me. I was thirty. On my way to becoming an old maid. I was flattered, of course, even though he *was* seventeen years older than me. And the children were adorable. So I went ahead and married Henry, thinking it would be years and years before I inherited the estate, before Mummy and Daddy would die. And that something would happen in between to make everything all right.' She groped in her sleeve for a handkerchief. 'And then came the accident in Kenya. On the day of their fortieth wedding anniversary. Daddy had hired a plane as a surprise for Mummy.' She clutched the handkerchief to her mouth. 'I'm sorry. I never cry.'

Geneviève rushed across and steered Helen to a sofa. They sat down. She put an arm around Helen. Helen lowered her face until her forehead was touching Geneviève's shoulder.

'The trouble is that Henry won't ever take a back seat on anything. It was fine when we were at Breage. Nobody cared. But controlling the estate seems to have gone to his head. He's been marching around putting everybody's backs up.' She straightened herself and looked directly at Geneviève. 'Now people I've known all my life cut me dead in the street. Henry doesn't notice, because the men all take him up on his shooting invitations and only laugh at him behind his back. But the wives won't come. They make silly excuses. And they don't invite Frances and Clara to their children's parties. I try to tell Henry but he won't listen. "Stuff and nonsense, old girl," he says. "Give the old hags time. They'll come around." But they won't. I know this county. I know them. And they won't. Ever.'

Geneviève felt as if she'd just picked up a rosy-looking apple, bitten into it, and discovered half a maggot wriggling in the remains. 'But, Helen. Surely. It can't be as bad as you say?'

'No, Geneviève. It isn't. It's worse.'

Clara watched Frances as she lay, propped up in the bed, with Mr C sprawled on the counterpane beside her. Then she looked across at Jonathan. He was pretending to read a 'Babar the Elephant' book, but every now and then he'd steal a glance at Frances when he thought she wasn't looking. Clara felt a hot pang of jealousy. Why wasn't it me who sprained my ankle on the hill? Why wasn't it me he helped back to the house? Why did things always come easily to Frances and hard to her? She pursed her lips. Well at least Daddy loved her the best – that was obvious. The fuss about his pipes proved that. She'd felt guilty at first, lying to everyone like that. But later, when she'd thought about it, she'd realised that she'd really been telling the truth. Frances had probably *wanted* to smash the pipes and just not let herself. In future, she vowed to herself, she'd try to reveal the real Frances for everyone to see, whenever and wherever she could.

The door opened and Cruikshank came in. She took one look at Mr C and pointed silently towards the stairs. Mr C jackknifed up and landed with a thud on the floor. He tapped across the floorboards and disappeared into the corridor.

Frances raised herself up on her elbows. 'But Crookers, he's making me better. In the old days they used to put dogs across sick people's legs to cure them of the gout.'

'That was children. And you don't have the gout. And Mr C has fleas. He also drools and smells. The sooner you're up and walking again, the sooner you can entertain Mr C. Now I'm going to take your temperature. You other children go and play. But remember, supper's at seven. I'll expect to see you, hands washed and hair combed, at the kitchen table before the last chime of the hall clock. Understood?'

'Yes, Nanny.'

Clara ushered Lisa and Jonathan out ahead of her. Her heart was thumping in her chest. At last! 'Come on, you two. I've got something to show you.'

The three children clattered down the stairs. Once in the garden, Clara struck off down the path to the plantation.

'What is it?' said Lisa, hurrying to catch up. 'What are you going to show us?'

Jonathan cut away from the path and ran parallel to the girls through the trees. 'It doesn't matter. I'll probably not want to see it anyway.'

'But we're nearly there,' shouted Clara. She desperately hoped Jonathan wouldn't go all boyish on her and disappear, lumbering her with Lisa. She broke into a nervous trot. 'Come on. It's this way.'

Jonathan swung down through the trees, picked up a stick, and sent it swinging overhead.

'Look.' Clara stopped and pointed to the tree house. 'It's mine. Stacey built it for me.'

'Isn't Frances allowed to use it?'

'Yes. But only when I let her. Do you want to see inside?'

'Okay.'

Jonathan cut smartly in in front of the girls and pulled himself hand over hand up the rope ladder. 'It's a bit sticky. What have you put on it?'

'Stacey painted it with something. He said it would stop it rotting.'

'Come on then, scaredy-cats. What are you waiting for?' Jonathan slithered inside the tree house.

He looked around, absent-mindedly sniffing the creosote on his fingers. I'll come here with Frances when her leg gets better, he thought to himself.

We'll scrounge some biscuits from Cook and have a feast. And if I'm really lucky she'll let me kiss her again.

He spat some saliva onto his hand, reached down and carefully rubbed it into a graze on his knee.

Lisa poked her head cautiously over the rim. 'Oh Clara, it's really nice. We could even sleep up here.' She climbed inside.

Clara followed her through. 'It gets a bit scary at night, though. All the trees creak, and the owls hoot, and the pheasants cluck. And then you think someone's going to come up the rope ladder and climb in.' The two girls sat side by side and looked at Jonathan expectantly.

'Aaaarghhh!!' Jonathan leaped to his feet and pointed through the window, his mouth wide open in horror. The girls shrieked and ran for the trapdoor. Jonathan let them go. As they slithered down the rope ladder, he manoeuvred his head across the opening and grabbed his throat with one hand, pretending to fight off his invisible assailant with the other. 'He's got me! He's strangling me! Go for help!' He let out one final gurgle and lay still, with his head hanging down below the platform.

'Jonathan?' Lisa stood beneath him, her face white with shock. 'Are you pretending? You *are* pretending. I'll tell *maman*!' She turned to Clara. 'He's always doing things like this.' She looked up again, uncertainly.

'Perhaps we'd better climb up and see?' said Clara.

'There might be something up there with him.'

Jonathan let out a groan, then began jerking himself inside, with his knees bent.

'It's pulling him in!'

'I'm going to get Mummy.' Clara turned around and ran back along the path.

'Wait for me!'

The two girls pelted up the track.

'I was only joking.' Jonathan poked his head out of the window. 'It was a joke!' He allowed his voice to tail off. They were already out of earshot. He could just imagine what Aunt Helen would say.

He scrambled down the rope ladder and walked disconsolately up the track. He stopped at the top and looked down towards the house. Which window was Frances's? He started counting them off from the left. One. Two. Three. Four. It must be that one. He wondered whether it would be possible to steal a ladder, climb up and surprise her? Perhaps not. With his luck he'd choose the wrong window. Catch Cruikshank sitting on the bog! That would really tear it.

'Jonathan!' It was his mother, calling to him from the house. 'Jonathan, come here this minute.'

He took a shaky breath and started back. He'd get even with those two girls. Really frighten them. Serve them right for sneaking on him. He cast around for a dead mouse or a piece of hedgehog. A slow-worm would be good.

'Jonathan! Hurry up.'

A face appeared in an upstairs window. It was Frances. Jonathan could just make out the ruffles at the neck of her nightdress. As he watched, she raised a hand and waved at him.

He stood stock still, staring up at her, his face hot, his heart thumping, his hands glued to his sides.

Before he had time to respond she heard something behind her and darted away. But not before blowing him a kiss.

Seven

Forty years later, Jonathan would recall that summer of 1960 as if it had been all the summers of his childhood, magically distilled into one ageless, timeless moment. The sun was hotter, the sea was bluer, the sky wider and the grass greener than they would ever be again. Each stone-walled field was a maze, each sarsen a soldier guarding hidden treasure, each quoit an ogre threatening to devour him or to sacrifice him on some pagan altar in a mysterious glade. Just now he was Heros the Spartan, leader of a cohort of Roman soldiers, and he was returning to Rome through the strange land of the Vorgaths.

'Are you paying attention?' Stacey was adjusting tappets in one of the old stables Jonathan's grandfather had converted into a garage after the First World War.

'Sorry?'

'Tappets. Tappets. These little levers here. How the blooming heck are you going to learn about the internal combustion engine if you stand there dreaming all the time? What will Mr Charles say?' Stacey walked across and unhooked a spanner from its place on the wall. He disappeared behind the car.

'Have you always known my father, Stacey?'

'Ever since he were a little boy.'

'You must be awfully old.'

'Oy!' Stacey reared up over the motor. He cleaned his hands briskly on a piece of rag, his eyes sparkling humorously. 'I'll have none of that. I'm only a youngster. My hair's still black.'

'Clara says you use boot polish on it.'

'Does she now? Well what Miss Clara says, and what Miss Clara knows, are two different things entirely.'

'Look, Stacey. I didn't mean to sneak. You won't tell her I told you, will you?'

'Tell her? 'course I won't tell her. Little girls is little girls, and little boys is worse. That's what my mam said. And she were right.'

Frances poked her head around the garage door. She beckoned urgently to Jonathan. She caught Stacey's eye and smiled.

'You'll be off then,' said Stacey. 'At the siren's behest! Don't want to get your hands dirty, I shouldn't wonder. Not like Mr Charles. He was always into an engine. Hard as you tried, you couldn't keep him away.'

'I'm sorry, Stacey.'

'That's all right, Master Jonathan. You're not your father and he's not you. And you're both the better for it. You can thank Mr Charles for the tip. And you can tell him from me that we'll be raising a glass in his honour at the Tinner's Arms, come Saturday night. To the King across the water.'

Jonathan hesitated, instinctively aware that he was missing something, some mysterious adult thing to which he ought to be attending. He opened his mouth to speak, but Stacey had resumed his banging beneath the cowling of the Daimler.

'J, come on!' Frances picked up Jonathan's duffel bag, her face flushed with excitement. 'Hurry up, or Clara and Lisa will see us. Then everything will be spoiled.'

She hobbled off in the direction of the woods, a panting Mr C behind her. Jonathan, with a final glance at the Daimler's upraised bonnet, trotted to catch up. 'It's really nice, your Daimler. I like the way the wheel rims come all the way down the sides.'

Frances looked back over her shoulder. 'I don't like cars. And I don't like the Daimler. It smells of old leather. And it makes me feel sick when it goes round corners.'

'Gosh. What *do* you like then?'

'Horses. Horses and dogs. And cats. And I quite like sheep. But I don't like cows at all. They smell. And their bottoms are always dirty.'

'How about people?'

'Some people. Others aren't nice. Horses and dogs are always nice. Aren't they, Mr C?'

Jonathan paused and scanned the park. His cohort of Roman soldiers fell neatly into line behind him. He tapped at an invisible sword hanging from his waist. 'Where do you think they are?'

'Who?'

'The others.'

'I don't know, and I don't want to know.'

Jonathan lowered his voice to a false bass. '*I don't know. And I don't want to know!*' He turned around and jogged backwards for a few paces. 'You know who you remind me of when you say that? The Man In Black.'

Frances stopped, her eyes wide. 'Do your parents let you listen? I so want to, but Crookers says I'll get nightmares. But I wouldn't. I really like ghost stories.'

'I'll tell you some later, then. I've got some good ones from school. Have you heard The Monkey's Paw? That one's really frightening. And The Brown Hand? Sinclair Minor had to sleep in *Matrona*'s room for three nights after Fenwick-Jones told it to him.'

'Who's *Matrona*?'

'Miss Marks. Our matron. Mr Crow insists we call her *Matrona*. That's Latin. *Latine legendum est.* You'll probably learn Latin too, when you're a bit older.'

'I'm nearly as old as you.'

'I shall be ten in August.'

'Well I shall be ten in March.'

'March next year!'

Their walk had brought them as far as the tree house. A soft south-westerly breeze was drifting through the woods, causing the rope ladder to twist and turn. Afternoon sunlight filtered through the leaves, throwing the children's shadows far out in front of them. Jonathan pointed excitedly. 'Look. Our heads are joined together. If I raise my arms like this...' he threw both hands into the air, '...we become a palm tree. And if I do this...' he corkscrewed on the spot with his hands held high above his head, '...we become...'

'...an oasis?' Frances darted a look at him.

The expression in her eyes flustered Jonathan. He blushed. Annoyed at himself, he glanced upwards to deflect attention from his burning cheeks. 'Is it really Clara's tree house?'

Frances sucked her breath in through her teeth. She grudgingly followed the direction of Jonathan's gaze. 'Of course not. It's both of ours. Is that what she told you?'

'Yes. That it was hers. That you could only use it with her permission.'

Frances's expression changed. She hobbled over to the rope ladder and squinted upwards. 'I don't think I'll be able to climb up. I'm not even supposed to be here. Crookers said I wasn't to leave the park. I think I'll go home now.'

Jonathan hurried to her side. He took her arm, imploringly. 'Please, Frances. Don't go. If I climb in first, I can pull you up. You'll only have to manage the first two or three rungs. Please. Give it a try.'

She weighed his offer in her mind, then looked at him, her eyes clouded with thought. 'All right then.'

'Give me the duffel bag.' Jonathan looped the bag over his shoulder. He grabbed hold of the rope ladder and swung himself up, enjoying showing off. He disappeared inside the tree house then reappeared, minus the bag, with his arms held out. 'Come on.'

Frances put her good foot onto the bottom rung. 'You stay there, Mr C. And you're not to bark.' She stepped up carefully. 'It still hurts. A lot.'

'Only one more rung and I can reach you. Come on, Frances. Please.'

Frances, brow furrowed, put her weight onto her weak ankle, then took the strain with her other foot. 'Quickly. Quickly. It hurts.'

Jonathan stretched down as far as he could and grabbed her hand. 'I've got you. It's all right.' He pulled her towards him. She seemed heavier, somehow, than the other day. 'Put your good foot onto the top rung. That's it.'

Frances slithered through the gap. She came to rest on the edge, with her legs dangling. She glanced down over her knees. 'I don't know how I'm ever going to get down again.'

'I could tie a rope around you. Like they do in the Fleet Air Arm.'

'We don't have a rope.'

Jonathan flung his arms wide, like a magician, then clapped his hands together dramatically. 'But we *do* have tea.' He bowed low and held out his hand, palm upwards, towards the duffel bag. 'Abracadabra Zoobitty-Doo. What have we here?' Frances crawled towards him, smiling. Jonathan threw open the bag. 'There's barley water, and apples, and squashed-fly biscuits and a Milky Way each. What are these?'

'Lardy-cakes. They're Cook's speciality.'

'Scrumptious.' He snagged a piece of sugar with his finger, then licked it off. 'Oh. I forgot to tell you. Cook said we're not to leave a mess, or we'll get her into trouble. Encouraging ants, and such-like.'

Frances made herself comfortable on the bench. 'Daddy wouldn't dare get angry with Cook. I heard my stepmother telling him off one day. "If Cook goes, I go." He didn't say anything after that. And Cook's still here.'

'We'd be awfully hungry if she wasn't.' Jonathan sat below Frances on the floor of the den. He looked furtively up at her. She was wearing a red, green and yellow beaded bracelet, and gold clip-on earrings. Her arms had a faint down on them. She had very neat fingernails, too. Not bitten to the quick, like his.

'Did Clara really tell you that I could only use the tree house if she let me? You're not fibbing?'

'I never fib. She really did say it. Ask Lisa.'

Frances spread the contents of the duffel bag in front of her. Her expression was thoughtful. 'What would you like first?'

'I'm not really hungry yet. Do you mind if we wait a bit?'

'What shall we do then?'

Jonathan hunched forward and stared down through the trapdoor. 'Do you think Clara and Lisa suspect where we are?'

'Not if we don't make any noise.'

'Shall I pull up the rope ladder? That way, if they come, they won't be able to climb up.'

'All right.'

His heart was beating uncomfortably fast. He reeled in the rope ladder, then rolled it carefully up. When he was finished he squatted down opposite Frances, watching her again. A half-painful, half-pleasurable sense of expectation was worrying at the pit of his stomach. 'I think you're much prettier than Clara.'

'I think you're handsome, too.'

'Me?' Jonathan shifted his weight in astonishment.

Frances nodded. 'I like the colour of your eyes. They're green. Like jade. Like one of Mummy's necklaces.'

He'd never really thought about the colour of his eyes before. Perhaps it was a thing girls did? Like lacrosse. 'Your eyes are brown. Like conkers.' That didn't sound quite right. 'Like a polished-up horse before a show.' That was better. Frances liked horses. He racked his brains for something else to say. Some way of continuing their conversation. It was such a nice feeling, talking like this, that he didn't want it to end.

'What do you like best about me?'

Jonathan rocked back and forth, thinking. He was aware of himself in a way he'd never been before. His skin was almost throbbing with the energy of his thoughts. 'I like the way you're littler than me. And soft.' He closed his eyes. 'And you smell different.' He opened his eyes again. 'I liked it when you let me help you, the other day, when you hurt your leg. A boy would never do that.'

Frances watched him as he rocked backwards and forwards in front of her. His knees were turning unnaturally white with the strain of his crouching. His blonde hair gleamed in the late afternoon sunlight that filtered in behind him through the window. He looked like one of those Greek heroes in the *Oxford Myths and Legends* book which Daddy had bought for her last Christmas, she decided. If she'd been born a boy, she'd have wanted to be just like Jonathan. 'I'm jolly glad I'm not a boy, then,' she declared, in unconscious paradox.

'So am I. Really.'

'Really?' They smiled at each other. They could have been touching, so strong was the connection between them. Frances plucked idly at her dress. 'Do you think we could be friends? For all our lives?'

Jonathan pretended to think. Then he nodded. He tried hard to swallow, but the saliva wouldn't go down. 'We could be married, even. When we're bigger.'

Frances bit her lip. A shadow suddenly crossed her face. 'I don't know. I wouldn't ever want you to be angry with me.'

'I wouldn't. Not ever.' Panic-stricken, Jonathan could sense her slipping away from him.

'Daddy always is. To my stepmother. And then she cries.'

'I won't ever make you cry.' He put his heart and soul into the words, grasping at concepts he barely understood.

'Do you promise?' Her eyes were wide and dark in the steadily muting light of the den.

'Scout's honour.' He spat on the palm of his hand and held it up. 'I, Jonathan Hubert Audley, promise never to make Frances...do you have a middle name?'

'Mary.'

'...promise never to make Frances Mary Champion cry. Ever.'

'What will happen if you do?'

Jonathan thought for a moment. 'I'll get ill. Just like King Arthur did when he got angry with Guinevere. And I'll only get better when you forgive me.'

'All right.' The shadow left her face. She took a deep breath, her chest rising and falling in measure.

Jonathan lurched up from his squatting position. 'Ouch. My leg's gone to sleep.'

She held out her hands. 'Come on over here and I'll rub it for you. Crookers rubs my leg for me whenever I have pins and needles.'

Jonathan hopped across to the bench and sat down beside her. 'I'm going to have a squashed-fly biscuit.' He chewed on the biscuit while she pulled down his woollen sock and started to rub. The skin beneath her parting was very white. Her hair flopped either side of her face in rat's tails. The bridge of her nose broadened a little in one spot, then narrowed again. She was like a strange country to him.

'All finished. Does it feel better?' She tore open a Milky Way and began to eat.

'Lots, thanks.' His leg tingled where her fingers had been touching it. He watched her finish the chocolate. 'Lisa takes hours over her Milky Ways. A Mars bar's even worse. I've seen her keep one for two days, just nibbling on it. You finished that one in three bites.'

'The rubbing made me hungry. Do you want some barley water?'

A flake of chocolate had lodged itself at the corner of Frances's mouth. Jonathan couldn't take his eyes off it. 'Wait.' Abandoning all conscious thought, he leaned forward and teased it off with the tip of his tongue.

Frances looked at him strangely. 'That felt funny.' She was breathing very rapidly again.

'I don't know why I did it. I'm sorry.'

She shook her head gently. She was acutely conscious of the damp mark at the side of her mouth that he had left with his tongue. 'Do you want to kiss me properly?'

'How do you mean?'

'With your eyes shut.' Taking his willingness for granted, she snuggled back into the corner and raised her chin. After a moment's hesitation he eased himself across her until he was poised above her face. 'You mustn't look,' she said, 'the *whole* point is not to look. Do you promise?'

'I promise.'

She closed her eyes. He leaned forward, inches from her face. A soft heat seemed to emanate from her skin. He hesitated, watching her, some instinct impelling him to seize the moment.

'Are they really closed?'

He swallowed; her fluttering breath fanned softly against his cheeks. 'Now they are. Yes.'

'Then you can kiss me.'

As their lips met, Jonathan could feel himself sinking, becoming one with Frances. It was as if he were seeing with her eyes, feeling with her skin. He was flying and sinking and breathing, all at the same time. Her mouth opened very slightly under his pressure until he could feel the shape of her teeth against his lips.

When he pulled back from her he was breathless, like a diver emerging from the sea, the wonders he has just seen vanishing like the forgotten remnants of a dream. 'Will you marry me? Please, Frances. When we're grown up. I won't shout at you. I won't make you cry.'

Her eyes were unnaturally black, their pupils swollen in the semi-darkness of the den. 'Yes, J. I'll marry you.'

He grasped her hand and covered it in kisses.

A small stone struck the open lintel of the window and bounced onto the floor. 'We know you're up there! We know you're up there! We'll throw some more if you don't come out.'

Frances sat up, white-faced. 'It's Clara,' she whispered.

Clara's voice boomed up from below. 'Mr C's here. That's how we know. And the rope ladder's gone. So it's no good whispering. We're not as stupid as all that.'

Jonathan moved to the trapdoor. 'Clara. You fibbed. You said the tree house belongs to you. Well it doesn't. It belongs to both of you.'

'We know you're having a feast up there! Cook told us. If you don't share, we'll tell Cruikshank.'

Jonathan glanced across at Frances. Her face echoed his anxiety. 'Shall we let them up?'

'We'd better. Clara sneaks on me all the time. If she tells Crookers I climbed up into the tree house, I'll be made to go to bed again. Then we won't be able to see each other so much.'

Jonathan poked his head through the trapdoor. 'All right. Frances says you can come up.' He let down the rope ladder. 'But there's only one Milky Way left, and it's mine. We can all share the biscuits and the lardy-cakes. Agreed?'

'Agreed.'

He turned to Frances. The rope ladder was already creaking with Clara's weight. 'I love you.' His words came out in a whisper.

'I love you too.' Her words were mouthed near-silently, but he heard them, nonetheless.

Eight

That night Lisa lay beside Jonathan in the bed they shared. 'Why don't you like Clara, J?'

'I do.'

'She says you don't. She says you've liked Frances right from the beginning better than her. But Clara's really clever too, you know. She's a year ahead at school, same as Frances.'

'It isn't because Frances is a year ahead of school that I like her. In fact, normally speaking that would be a pretty good reason *not* to like her. I like Frances because…' He began chewing on the inside of his cheek. '…well, just because.'

'You still haven't told me why you don't like Clara?'

'Well you like her, don't you?'

'She's my best friend.'

'What about Danielle?'

'She's my best friend in France.'

'You can't have a best friend in France and a best friend in England. If you have a best friend, she should be a best friend everywhere.'

'Then Clara's my best friend everywhere.'

'I'm glad that's settled. Now go to sleep.'

He lay back and closed his eyes. Was Frances his best friend? Did he love her more than *maman* and Daddy? Or didn't that matter? His feelings pressed like an anvil on his chest. He turned over and lay on his stomach.

'Stop wriggling, J.'

'I can't help it.'

'Perhaps you've got fleas. Cruikshank says Mr C gives them to everyone.'

'Then you've got them too.'

'No, I haven't.'

'Yes, you have.' He sprang up and began to tickle her.

'J. No!' She shrieked and tried to wriggle out of his grasp.

He grabbed a foot, tucked it under his arm, and went to work on it. Lisa kicked out with her other foot. Jonathan ducked his head. 'If I stop, will you persuade Clara not to spy on us anymore?'

'Spy on who?' Lisa was still struggling.

'On Frances and me. She follows us everywhere. With you trailing along behind her like a pet monkey.'

'I don't!'

'Monkey! Monkey!' He turned her over and started tickling her flanks.

The bedroom lights burst on. 'What's going on in here?' Cruikshank was standing at the door in her dressing-gown. 'You were meant to be asleep hours ago, both of you. Do you want to disturb your mother? Lisa, your shrieking could be heard all over the house. I shall put you in separate rooms if you're not careful.' The two children flattened themselves obediently on the bed. 'Now, no more talking. I want to hear complete silence from both of you.'

'But you can't *hear* complete silence.' Jonathan had no idea why he said it. Perhaps his father would have found it amusing – anyone other than Nanny Cruikshank.

'You come with me, young man. Your mother's going to hear about this.'

'Please, Crookers. I didn't mean anything. It just came out.'

'Just came out?'

'He says things like that sometimes,' piped in Lisa. 'It's always getting him into trouble at school. But he doesn't mean it.'

'Your sister's very loyal. Is it going to happen again?'

'No, Nanny.'

'Very well then. Let that be a lesson to you. I'll see you both in the morning. Good night.'

She closed the door. Jonathan let his breath out in a rattling sigh. He looked across at his sister. 'Thanks, monkey. If you weren't so hairy and smelly I'd give you a kiss.'

'Then I'm glad I'm hairy and smelly. Ye-uch.'

'Let that be a lesson to you.'

'Let that be a lesson to *you*.'

'Shhh!'

'*Shhh!*'

Clara was chasing a pea around the plate with her fork. She glanced across at Jonathan to see if he was watching her. He was staring at Frances. As usual. Clara looked at Lisa. Lisa blushed. Cripes Almighty!

'Clara, either eat that pea or leave it alone. Are those the sort of manners they teach you at school?'

'No, Mummy.'

'Well then.'

Clara speared the pea and ate it. At least Jonathan was noticing her now. She gave him an exaggerated smile. Why didn't he like her? Why didn't he pay her as much attention as he paid Frances?

'Heard from that errant husband of yours yet?' Henry was dabbing at his mouth with a napkin. They were the first words he had uttered all lunch-time. Staring fixedly at Geneviève, he shovelled a forkful of roast beef into his mouth. He tapped his wineglass with his knife. 'Cantenac-Brown '29. Over thirty years old and still got legs. Charles doesn't know what he's been missing.' He took a long pull from his glass. 'Let me tell you something. The French know next to nothing about wine. It took the English to teach them the importance of ageing in the bottle. Yet they still persist in drinking the stuff too young.'

'Henry. Geneviève's French. You're being unforgivably rude.'

Henry stifled a belch behind his napkin. 'I'll give that much to your father, Helen. He kept a damned fine cellar.'

Helen made a nervous movement with her hand. 'It's not all ours, dear. Half of it belongs to Charles.'

'Well he should come over here and bloody well drink it then. If he thinks I'm going to ship it back to France he's got another think coming. This sort of wine doesn't travel. Best leave it where it is. Another thing we taught the French.'

Geneviève caught Helen's eye and smiled. Helen managed an embarrassed grimace in return.

'Can *we* have some wine?'

Henry scanned the room like a weasel scenting prey. 'Which child said that? Clara?'

Geneviève cleared her throat. 'In France we give the children red wine mixed with a little water. We think it's good for them.'

Henry wheeled on her. 'Well we don't do that sort of thing over here. We don't believe in turning our young into alcoholics. Clara. Off you go.'

'But Daddy. Please.'

'If you can't behave yourself at the grown-ups' table, you can go back to the nursery and eat junket.'

'But I can't stand junket.'

'Please, sir. She didn't mean any harm. It was my fault she said it.' Jonathan could feel the eyes of the table swivel onto him.

Henry reddened. The two whiskies he'd had before lunch and the wine he'd had with it were beginning to take effect. 'You can go too, young man. I'll not have any cheek at this table. Both of you. Up you get. You can leave your food. Helen, call Cruikshank and tell her she's got customers.'

'But Henry. It's Sunday. Cruikshank has the afternoon off.'

'Damned bloody woman! I thought you gave her Thursdays off, like those precious Hyde Park nannies. Don't tell me you give her Sunday afternoons as well?' He hesitated, marginally aware of the spectacle he was making of himself. 'All right, then. Just this once. But I don't want to hear another squeak out of either of you. Do you understand me?'

The children nodded. Clara glanced over at Jonathan. He gave her a faint smile. When he looked across at Frances, she was staring down at her plate. He felt a sudden immense guilt. By taking Clara's side, he had betrayed her. He yearned to be able to speak. To tell her that it didn't matter. That he'd only been responding in the way they'd taught him at school.

Clara watched their interaction triumphantly. At last! Jonathan had finally stood up for her. In front of everybody. Now he'd *have* to pay attention to her. Now, perhaps, she'd no longer have to be saddled with that little drip Lisa all the time.

Jonathan stretched his leg under the table in an effort to touch Frances, but it wouldn't reach. He considered dropping a roll, then hunting for it, but instinct told him that Frances's father was just longing for an excuse to punish him. He waited, in excruciating impatience, as the summer pudding was passed around. No, he wouldn't have any cream. No, he wouldn't have a second helping. At last. Coffee for the adults.

'All right. You children may leave the table. Frances, you must take especially good care of your foot. It's not properly healed yet. I don't want you to go more than three hundred yards from the house. Is that understood?'

'Yes, Mummy.'

'Jonathan. You make sure she does as she's told. As the oldest, I'm holding you responsible.'

'Yes, Aunt Helen.'

'All right then. You can go.' The four children clattered out.

'Slowly! Slowly!' Henry's voice boomed down the corridor behind them.

Once outside, Frances made straight for her room. Jonathan started up the stairs behind her.

'Jonathan.' Clara was standing by the entrance to the library. 'I've got something to show you.' Lisa was standing behind Clara, looking imploringly at her brother. With a groan, Jonathan moved away from the stairs and towards the library door. Lisa brightened visibly.

Clara stepped up to one of the book shelves. She felt around behind it and pulled out a book. 'Look at this. It belongs to Frances. She's been keeping it a secret. It says Frances Champion, Her Diary, on the front. She's been writing about all of us.'

Jonathan took a step towards her. 'Then you shouldn't be looking at it. You'd better give it here.'

'Don't you want to hear what it says?'

'No. Come on, Clara. Hand it over.'

Clara darted behind the sofa. She opened the book and licked her finger in anticipation.

'Clara!' Lisa was wringing her hands together. 'You shouldn't read it. Frances will be terribly upset.'

'Too late. I've already read it. Listen to this.' Clara cleared her throat and held up the book. '*I let Jonathan kiss me. Then Mr C started barking. Clara told him I wasn't allowed in the tree house. Later we hid up there. Jonathan said he'd marry me. Then I let him kiss me again.*' She looked up. 'When I tell Daddy, he'll shoot you with one of his shotguns.'

Jonathan vaulted the sofa and snatched the book away.

'J, I think I've wet myself again.' Lisa lifted up her dress and peered underneath.

'Mummy!' shouted Clara. 'Quickly!'

Jonathan gave Clara a withering look. He moved towards his sister. 'Is it a big wet, or a little wet?'

'A big wet.'

'Come on. Let's find *maman*.'

He hid Frances's diary under his shirt and took Lisa's arm. Clara stood behind the sofa watching them. She didn't shout again. She knew she'd lost something, but she couldn't think what.

'Frances?' Jonathan knocked a second time. 'Can I come in?' He pushed the door open and peered around it. 'I'm coming in anyway. Okay?' He stepped through the crack and closed the door behind him. He looked around. There were two lumps under the bed covers. 'I've brought you your diary.'

The bedclothes flew back. Frances sat up. Mr C was beside her. He immediately began to scratch himself behind one ear, grunting. 'What do you mean, my diary?' she demanded.

'Clara found it. Behind some books in the library. She wanted to read it out. I stopped her and took it away.'

'You stopped her?'

'Yes. I told her she shouldn't read someone else's secret book. We had a fight.'

'You had a fight?'

'Well, I tried to put my hand over her mouth. Then she screamed. Then Lisa wet herself.'

'Did Daddy hear?'

'Yes. But *maman* and Aunt Helen thought Clara had screamed because of Lisa. So I got away with it.'

'Can I have my book?'

'Here.' He walked over to the bed and sat down. 'I stopped her before she'd read much, but she did read a bit.'

'What bit?'

'The bit about us kissing. And deciding to get married.'

'Oh.'

'She said she'd tell Uncle Henry. And then he'd shoot me.' He glanced at the door apprehensively. 'You know why I stuck up for Clara, don't you? At table.'

Frances looked away. She clutched the notebook to her chest. 'No I don't.'

'Because that's what they tell us to do at school. Stick up for the younger boys.'

'But Clara isn't a boy.'

'You know what I mean. If we see a younger boy getting into trouble, we've got to stick up for him.'

'Is that the only reason?'

'Yes. I promise. I told Clara that I'd never stick up for her again. After she read your book like that.'

'Did you?'

'Yes. You can ask Lisa. She didn't want Clara to read your diary either. That's why she wet herself. She always does it when she's upset.'

'You mean she *actually* wet herself?'

'Yes. She used to wet her bed until they put her in with me. Now she's better. But she still does it during the day sometimes. It's usually only a little. But this time it was a lot. It was all over the carpet.'

'Gosh.' Frances made a face, but her mind was elsewhere. 'Did Clara tell Daddy what I wrote?'

'No. I think she was scared to. He was so angry about the carpet.'

Frances opened the book. 'Did you read it?'

'No.'

'Do you want to?'

'It's your private book.'

'It's about you. A lot of it. And Mr C.'

'You could read it to me.' He climbed up onto the bed and snuggled down beside her. Mr C groaned and collapsed between them.

'All right then.' She looked down. 'Do you still want to marry me?'

'More than ever.'

'Good.'

Nine

Cruikshank was shooing them towards the cars. 'Hurry up, children. We're going to be late. The Merry Maidens will have turned to stone waiting for us.'

'But they're already made of stone!'

Henry had allocated himself the Daimler. Stacey was to drive the shooting brake. Both cars were emitting pungent plumes of smoke from their exhausts.

'Gosh. Are we travelling in the Daimler?' said Jonathan.

'No. The grown-ups are in the Daimler. We're to go with Stacey. You can get in now, all of you. Jonathan, as a special treat, you can go in the front. The girls and I shall travel in the back.'

'The front? Thanks, Crookers.'

'What have we got for our picnic?' said Lisa, clinging to the inside leather strap.

'You'll soon find out. There'll be more than enough for everybody.'

Henry emerged from the house. He was wearing a check driving coat, cavalry twill trousers and a pair of tan pigskin gloves, turned over at the wrist. He stood and surveyed his estate. A woodpigeon clattered off from a belt of oak trees forty yards from the house. Henry raised his arms and pretended to shoot it.

'Won't you be too warm, dear?' Helen said, glancing up at the sun. 'The forecast is rather good you know.'

'Stacey!' Henry beckoned with a glove. 'Mrs Audley is still powdering her nose. Or whatever else women find to do on occasions like these. I suggest you take the advance party and get going. We'll catch up with you later.' He turned to Helen, his feet moving geometrically, as if he wished to negotiate a perfect right angle. 'No, I shall not be too warm, Helen. And if I find that I am too warm, I shall simply take the jacket off.'

After waving goodbye, Helen walked over and made a great show of inspecting the dog roses that were trained up either side of the front entrance to the house.

Henry glared at her, then shot another woodpigeon. 'I can tell you one thing, though. I'll be glad when this damned trip's over. Can't stand picnics. Messy affairs. Can't taste your wine. Can't sit properly. Food stale. Wasps in your jam.' He slapped his thigh impatiently. 'How much longer is that bloody woman going to be?'

'I can hear her coming down the stairs now. You said eleven o'clock, Henry, and it's still only five to.'

'I'll be pleased when they're gone and we can get back to our normal routine. It is tomorrow, isn't it?'

'You know very well that it is. You made the travel arrangements yourself.'

'Did I? How chivalrous of me. I hope you're not thinking of making this an annual event?'

'Oh Henry, the children all loved it so.' Helen raised her chin and looked at him with as pugnacious an expression as her normally passive demeanour would allow. 'And I've already promised Geneviève that we'll take Jonathan and Lisa for the occasional half-term *exeat*. In fact whenever it's inconvenient for her to come to England.'

'Then it'll always be inconvenient for her to come to England.'

Geneviève emerged from the hall, patting her sleeves into place. She smiled seductively at Henry. 'You'll be glad to know that I'm ready at last. You did say eleven o'clock, didn't you? Didn't he, Helen?'

'Yes, he did.' Flashing Henry a dark look, Helen hurried over and took Geneviève's arm. 'I can't bear the thought of you going tomorrow,' she whispered. 'I simply can't bear it.'

Geneviève gave her a squeeze. 'Helen. Please. I want you to promise to bring the girls over to St Tropez. Charles would love to see you. Perhaps for Christmas?'

Henry snapped a look over his shoulder. 'Can't miss the Bank Holiday shoot. Out of the question.' He was already striding towards the Daimler.

'Winter, the whole winter, is out of the question. I need Helen for my shooting lunches.'

'Easter, then? Or in July, perhaps? We could make it a yearly thing. One time here, the next at St Tropez?'

'Come on, you two. Get in. We're already running five minutes late.'

'Thanks for trying,' whispered Helen. Then, a little louder, 'Henry has never really liked travelling.' She settled herself in the back seat next to Geneviève and waited.

Henry's eyes glared back at her from the dashboard driving-mirror. 'What do you mean "Henry has never really liked travelling"?' There was the crash of gears. 'Bloody pre-selector boxes. Why didn't your father buy a Rolls Royce or a Bentley instead of a bloody dinosaur like this? God knows he could have afforded it.' He pumped the clutch three times. The Daimler jerked forward, protesting. Henry twisted around in the seat. 'Went to Truro just the other day. And what's this, if it isn't travelling?'

'Henry, please watch the road. Geneviève meant to the South of France.'

'The South of France? Couldn't possibly. Baldwin needs me. Refuse to pay a dozen people's wages while I'm boiling on the bloody beach.'

'Perhaps I could take Nanny and the children then, dear? On the Mistral. Or else we could fly from Hurn.'

'Alone?'

'Not really alone. There would be four of us.' She patted her headscarf. 'While you stay here and run the estate.' She glanced at Geneviève, who gave her hand a conspiratorial squeeze below Henry's sight-line. 'You know how you like being by yourself. You could even make a start on your memoirs. You've been promising to for ever such a long time. And people so enjoy reading about the war.'

'Were you awfully brave?' Geneviève nonchalantly checked one of her gloves.

'Well...' Henry glanced swiftly into the rear-view mirror. 'Don't like speaking about it, actually. You can understand that, can't you?'

'Henry was in the Royal Engineers.' Helen was starting to enjoy herself.

'He must have looked very dashing. All that red.'

'He built bridges. Didn't you, dear?'

Henry cleared his throat. 'Well, somebody had to. We couldn't all go gadding off like bashi-bazouks behind enemy lines.'

'Like Charles, you mean?'

Henry grunted. 'Always surprised me how they let him in with that one eye of his. It was his master eye, too. Shouldn't have thought he'd have been able to shoot a sitting partridge with it, let alone an angry Fritz. But I'm probably wrong. Don't suppose he got his MC for nothing. Although you never can tell with those things. Family connections and all that.'

The two women sat placidly in the back of the car.

Thirty minutes later, as they were passing St Buryan, Henry finally cracked. 'I think I will make a start on my memoirs. Put the record straight. Describe the war from the journeyman officer's point of view. Before I forget.'

'Such a good title,' said Geneviève. ' "Before I forget." I can see it now: *Before I Forget – A Memoir of the War*, by Henry Champion.'

Henry's face cleared magically as he contemplated his apologia.

'Does that mean I can take Nanny and the girls to France?' said Helen.

'Don't see why not. Give me time to clear the decks. Engage myself a secretary. Keep things in order for once. House is a total shambles as things stand.'

'Lisa. Do you want to come with us to see the Pipers?' Frances was already beckoning to Mr C.

'I'd rather stay here with Clara.'

'All right then. But don't complain later that we're ignoring you.'

'I won't.' Lisa looked wildly around. 'Clara! Clara! Wait for me.'

Frances clipped the lead to Mr C's collar. 'Crookers, can we go over the road, please? I want to show Jonathan the Pipers.'

'If you remember to put Mr C on the lead.'

'We already have. Look.'

'All right. But I want you back here in twenty minutes. Mummy and Daddy and Mrs Audley are sure to have arrived by then.' She returned to laying out the picnic.

The two children passed Stacey, struggling manfully under the burden of a hamper.

'Stacey. Catch!' Jonathan made a pretend overarm throw.

Stacey faltered, then caught himself. 'That's not funny, Master Jonathan. If Mr Charles knew you was up to them sorts of tricks, he'd give you a good hiding.'

'I'm sorry, Stacey. I wasn't thinking.'

'Does your daddy really beat you?' said Frances later, as they crossed the road.

'Never. But don't tell Stacey that. He's given me smacks, of course. And they really hurt. Does your father smack you?'

'No. He just gets angry. Sometimes I think I'd rather be smacked.'

'They beat us at school, though.'

'What do you mean?'

'With a slipper. On the bottom. Mr Crow gets us up to his study. Then we have to stand outside in a line until he's ready. Then we go in and choose the slipper. Or the cane, if we've been really naughty. Then he gives us six.'

'Is his name really Mr Crow?'

'Yes. Corvo Crow. And Corvo means crow, too, in Latin. I think his parents were pulling his leg. He doesn't know we know, though. One day, if he whacks me too hard, I'm going to tell him.'

'He'll probably whack you even harder then.'

'Then I'll put something in his sherry. He keeps it behind a screen in his study. The older boys say he always takes a few swigs before he whacks us.' His face darkened. 'To get his courage up, I suppose.'

Frances caught the look. She knelt down and untied Mr C. 'All right. You can go and run now. Go on Mr C.' Mr C waddled a few paces, then turned around expectantly. Frances stepped forward and shooed him on. 'He used to run all over the place. Now he's so old, he doesn't want to go anywhere without me. Do you Mr C?'

'Is he going to die soon?'

Frances looked up, her eyes brimming. 'I don't think so. He could go on for years and years. That's what Mummy says. He's my only friend. I'd miss him terribly.'

Jonathan swallowed. 'Will you miss me, too?'

Frances turned her back on him and stood looking out across the fields.

Jonathan took a tentative step towards her. 'Frances?'

She turned around so quickly he was taken by surprise. 'I don't want you to leave! I want you to stay forever. I don't see why grown-ups should boss us around all the time. Or why Mr Crow should beat you. Or why Clara should hate me so much when I've never done anything to hurt her.' She was crying properly now, her cheeks glistening with tears.

Jonathan stared at her. He felt panic-stricken, frozen to the spot by the force of his emotions. He wanted to comfort her more than anything in the world, but he was uncertain of the line he ought to take. 'We could run away,' he said tentatively. 'I could work somewhere. Look after you. Or I could steal!' That was more like it. 'We could become bandits. Or even pirates. Escape on a boat. To France. To Paris, even. Like The Scarlet Pimpernel.'

'They'd catch us. And then we'd never be able to see each other again.'

Jonathan remembered his handkerchief. He scrabbled in his pockets and brought it out. 'It's clean. Remember? Our maid packed enough for two weeks. This is my last one.'

Frances took the handkerchief. For a moment their hands touched. She stepped up to him and carried his cupped palm to her cheek. Her ear felt warm. Her hair tumbled lightly across his knuckles. He took a step towards her and gathered her in his arms. She snuggled against him, the top of her head just reaching his chin. He squeezed her tightly and kissed her forehead repeatedly, his mouth tightly closed, just as his father did when wishing him good night.

Mr C inserted himself between them and glared challengingly across the fields.

By the time they got back to the Merry Maidens, the picnic was already underway.

'Where have you two been?'

'Jonathan wanted to see the Pipers.'

'Well you certainly took your time about it. You could have been to Penzance and back by now.' Helen's expression softened. 'You must be starving. Come over here and sit down. Cook made potato salad especially for you, Frances.'

'Thank you, Mummy.'

'Thank Cook. She spoils you rotten. Clara? Why aren't you eating?'

'Because I feel sick.'

'What sort of sick? Icky sick, or the other kind?'

Cruikshank sprang up from her place on the rug and hurried across.

'Icky sick. *And* the other kind.'

'You can't be both.'

'I can, so!'

'Clara! Whatever's the matter with you?'

Clara glared across the blanket at Jonathan and Frances. Cruikshank put the palm of her hand on Clara's forehead. Clara shrugged her roughly away. The blood was already beginning to drain from her cheeks and forehead.

'Clara! Whatever do you think you are doing?'

'I saw Jonathan and Frances hugging. Lisa did too. They were hugging!'

Helen glanced meaningfully across at Geneviève. Cruikshank straightened up, a hurt expression on her face. Henry emitted a plume of smoke from over by the cars, comfortably out of earshot. He waved his pipe at Stacey and started to cough.

Helen returned her attention to the children, instinctively lowering her voice. 'Frances? Is this true?'

'Jonathan was hugging me because he's going away tomorrow. We like each other. We're cousins. We didn't do anything wrong.'

Helen looked relieved. 'Well then.' She looked across at Clara. 'You mustn't tell tales out of school, Clara. And you mustn't pretend to feel sick when you're not. And you mustn't push Cruikshank away like that.'

Clara jumped up, her arms flailing, and sprinted beyond the periphery of the stone circle. She slumped melodramatically to her knees and started to retch.

'Oh dear.'

'What the devil's the matter now?' Henry had already started towards them. 'Has everybody gone mad? Clara!'

Helen ran to Clara's side. 'Clara,' she hissed, 'stand up this minute. Your father's coming over.'

Behind her, Geneviève reached across and grabbed Jonathan by the shoulders. 'What has been going on? *Ne me mentez pas.*'

'I don't know. I promise, *maman*. I was giving Frances a hug and Clara got jealous. She and Frances hate each other, everybody knows that. And Frances and me are friends. Clara's got Lisa all to herself, so I don't know what she's complaining about. She's only making trouble. She's not really sick.'

Helen straightened up. Clara was hunched on the ground like a caterpillar. 'Cruikshank?'

'Yes, Mrs Champion?'

'We'd better call off this afternoon's trip to Porth Curno.'

Henry was out of breath. He tapped his pipe violently on a sarsen, as if he meant to shatter the stone into a thousand pieces. 'We most certainly shall not call off this afternoon's trip to Porth Curno. I haven't come all the way here to pack up sticks and head straight back home again. If Porth Curno is on the agenda, it will bloody well stay on the agenda. If Clara feels sick she can remain in the car. Cruikshank can find her a bowl. In my time, one tiny person didn't spoil everyone else's fun because of a spot of over-indulgence.'

'I didn't over-indulge. And I'm not sick.' Clara was shouting by now. 'And Frances and Jonathan have been kissing. Up in the tree house. I read it in Frances's book.'

'Frances's book? What book is this? I don't know of any book.'

'Clara!' said Helen. 'That's enough. We'll have no more of this. You are becoming hysterical.'

'But I saw them.'

'What do you mean you saw them? You just told us you read it in Frances's book.'

'Saw them hugging.'

Henry clapped his hands. 'That's it. You've finally convinced me. We're all going home again. I've got better things to do with my time than listen to this bedlam. Clara, nine-year-old children don't know how to kiss. Your imagination has run away with you. Frances, we'll have no more of this hugging nonsense, thank you very much. And you too young man. If you want to hug something, hug a scrum machine. Stacey! We're packing up.'

'Darling, don't you think we might go to Porth Curno after all, now that we've come this far? The children are dying to see the open-air theatre.'

Henry spun around, an unbelieving expression on his face. 'Helen, only two minutes ago you were insisting that we all go home. I don't understand.'

'I've changed my mind.'

'Changed your mind?' Henry looked vainly around for support. 'Changed your mind!' He was suddenly aware that all eyes were on him. 'I told you I hate picnics. Didn't I? In the car. On the way out here. Something always goes wrong. Well, worse than picnics, I hate women who persistently change their minds. And children who pretend to be sick when they're not. And sneaks. And I hate little boys who go around hugging people. And dogs that won't pick up birds and are gun-shy...'

'Henry, Henry.' Helen stepped up and took his arm. 'Let's just go, shall we. No need to say any more. Is there, dear?'

Henry looked around uncertainly. After a moment's hesitation he replaced the pipe in his mouth with a clack, shrugged Helen roughly away, and started back towards the car.

The summer holiday, it seemed, was finally over.

Ten

Penhallow, Cornwall. 1999

Clara slammed down the receiver. So slippery old Jonathan had pulled it off yet again. Saint God Almighty Frances was coming to the funeral after all – in fact she was sitting on the Penzance train this very minute, blabbing down her mobile phone and probably irritating the hell out of the other first-class passengers. Her and her flashy Parisian ways. Well serve them bloody well right!

She lit a cigarette and walked through into the drawing-room. It was only three days since Helen's death, but things were already starting to fall apart. Today should have been cleaning day, but she'd had to cancel Mrs Gibbs through lack of funds. She hadn't admitted as much, of course. 'Grief prostration.' Those were the words that she'd used. The old bat had oozed false sympathy down the telephone.

Clara collapsed languidly onto the sofa and draped her feet over the arm. Worse, much worse, was the fact that Frances now intended to help – read interfere – with the funeral arrangements. What evil moon had made her tell Jonathan that Frances was in Milan? She ought to have guessed that he'd phone every hotel in town in some desperate attempt to find her. Failing that, he'd have put the Carabinieri, and probably even Interpol, on her trail.

No. The one fact that really stuck in her craw was that Frances had never cared for Helen the way she had. She'd pretended to, of course. Done all the right things. But ever since Daddy's death, her detachment had become increasingly obvious. And now she'd come gliding in, with all her glamour and her money and that stick-thin daughter of hers, to gloat. Clara could feel the resentment eating away at her. She stood up and petulantly flicked her half-smoked cigarette into the fireplace.

She'd been prettier than Frances. Everyone had said so. Even Jonathan had succumbed to her in the end. And pathetic little Lisa, too. Who wasn't so pathetic now, by the way. Writing breathless books for dykes. She'd let Lisa do it to her once, on the island, and the silly brat had been vomit-inducingly grateful. As if she'd given her a benediction or something.

Lisa would be travelling over with Geneviève, of course. Now there was a woman you could admire. But Geneviève hadn't played her husband well. If Clara had hooked a man with five million in the bank, she'd have made damned sure she held on to him – not given him over to the nearest available housekeeper on permanent loan.

Mind you, Geneviève wasn't short of a bob or two herself, with that ritzy chateau of hers, and her grand name – Chanel suit, court shoes and a triple string of pearls, that had been Geneviève. Charles hadn't even come near, until he'd lucked back into the Audley millions. Old lecher. Mind you, she'd liked how he used to look at her on Pampelonne beach, during the school holidays. He hadn't been so old then. Late forties maybe. God! Same age she was now. But not bad looking. In fact *particularly* well preserved. No morals, though. He'd put his fingers inside her bikini top once. Said he'd seen an ant climb in there. Made out it was a joke. Had he given her a diddle? Told her not to tell anyone? Or was she just imagining it? She couldn't remember now. Well, she hadn't been born yesterday. And she hadn't been underage, exactly. Or had she? She ticked off the years on her fingers. 1967. Mmm. Fifteen and a half. Dirty old man! Perhaps she'd remind him of it, now that she was going to see him again. Give him a heart attack. Then Jonathan and Lisa would get all the dosh. If she re-seduced Lisa she'd be rich. Ha!

She stepped in front of the mirror. Christ. She prodded at the puffy flesh beneath her eyes. The years hadn't been kind. She needed a face-lift *and* a body-lift. In fact she needed a total bloody overhaul – reconditioned engine, new gearbox and a better set of brakes. Too many men and too many drinks, that was the trouble. But no children. Well thank God for small mercies, anyway. And while she was on the subject of drinks, she didn't see why she shouldn't have one now. Helen wasn't around to disapprove. No one was around to disapprove. Nobody gave a damn anymore what she did. She approached the cabinet.

Strange how things had turned out. As a child, she'd always been the one who was going to go away. Become an actress. Have the world at her feet. And what had she done? Nothing. Sold a few antiques. Slept with half the county. Livened up a few dull parties. And there was dowdy, boring, flat-chested little Lisa, selling five hundred copies a week of her up-market porn to closet lesbians. Ten-to-one she'd turn up at the funeral with one of her lissom literary groupies in tow. A twenty-two-year-old comparative literature graduate, probably. Even now the thought made Clara a little jealous.

She poured the drink, then slurped soda into it. Men. They'd loved her and left her, most of them. If you could call it love. Maybe she'd have been better off riding tandem at that? What did the Spanish call it? *A bicicleta.* One leg either side of the saddle. Trouble was, she'd never really fancied women. Tits always got in the way. She liked her men lean and hard, like Jonathan, all those years ago on Levant. He'd been drop-dead bloody gorgeous. She could hot up just thinking about him – knowing all the time what was going on between him and Frances. The jammy little bitch used to mince around the harbour at St Tropez like the cat that got the cream.

Clara made a petulant moue at herself in the glass of the drinks-cabinet door. Grumpy, grumpy. Shouldn't think Jonathan was any great shakes in bed anymore, though. What was that joke, the one about the bloke's girlfriend when they finally got it together after his fourth consecutive nuclear scan? She lit up like a pinball machine! Ha ha ha! She downed her drink and poured another. A small one. Best watch it. She'd promised to pick Frances up from the station. Wouldn't do for PC Plod to come along and nick her license again. Probably never get it back this time. Shame Daddy wasn't still on the bench. He'd have let her off.

She topped the glass up a third time, promising herself that it would be the last. Oh God. Where was she going to live when Jonathan turfed her out? The business wasn't going well. There was hardly enough money left to keep her in booze, let alone buy a shop. Maybe Helen had left her a legacy? Failing that, she could always sting Jonathan for a few thousand.

No. On second thoughts, better not. Jonathan might look soft on the outside, but he was hard as granite in the middle. He'd never forgiven her for screwing up his grand passion with Frances. Well it had been his own fault, hadn't it? Should have kept his trousers buttoned. Mind you, she'd worked on him long enough. It had been the hash cake that finally did it. That and the Slivovitz. But the hash cake had *really* tipped him over the edge. Bloody fool.

Why were men such innocents? Because they never admitted to themselves what they really wanted, that was why. Find one who could do that, and he'd be formidable. Most of the bastards were perfectly happy to be led around by their you-know-whats.

'Another wee dram and we'll set off for the station.'

Clara made a face at herself and tipped the rest of the whisky into her glass. She wouldn't bother with the soda this time. The stuff was flat anyway.

Frances replaced the mobile in her handbag and glanced at her watch. Only three-quarters of an hour to go. How distant Clara had seemed on the telephone. Abrupt, even. Nothing new in that, of course. If you graded people as sandpaper, Clara would be the extra rough variety.

Outside her window the train clattered comfortingly across a set of points. She adored trains. She remembered the time Jonathan had made love to her in a railway carriage, somewhere between Ventimiglia and Nice. She'd got the giggles. The fake leather of the seat had stuck to her bottom, and she'd ended up making ridiculous squeaking noises with each thrust of his hips. He'd taken the precaution of pulling the corridor blinds down, but he hadn't bothered with the main window. The look on his face as they'd drawn into the station! His furiously pumping buttocks must have sailed past a hundred gaping commuters before he'd realised what was happening.

That had been the summer of 1971. Their last summer. The summer of Fauré's Quintet in D. They'd discovered the music together in Paris, during the May '68 riots; then they'd heard the piece again in Venice, three years later, at a concert given in the old casino. It had become their music. Their theme. Others of their generation had the Beatles, or the Bee Gees, or the Mamas and the Papas – she and Jonathan had the first movement of the Fauré quintet. It had made them different, somehow; had seemed, dare she say it, to reflect the special quality of their love.

Smiling secretly to herself, Frances squinted through the darkness outside the carriage window. Had they crossed the Tamar yet? She checked her watch a second time. Only forty minutes to go until Penzance, so they probably had.

She brought her heels up and snuggled further into her seat. She remembered the particular look Jonathan used to get on his face when he was feeling randy. He'd press his lips together and narrow his eyes. Then his mouth would start working in a scissors action, as if he were chewing on something, or as if he were about to burst into an uncontrollable fit of the giggles. He'd been completely unaware of what he was doing, of course, and she'd never once brought it to his attention. It had been her secret. Just like his smell. Sometimes she'd be walking behind him and he'd smell so good she just had to run up and bury her nose in his shirt. Oh God.

The young man across the way was pretending not to look at her. She turned back to the window. Yes. He was at it again. She could see him reflected in the glass. Why were the English so diffident? At least Italian and French men looked you straight in the eye when they lusted after you. She smoothed the skirt over her knees. The young man glanced quickly down. Not much to look at. Marginally overweight. White collar on a striped shirt – always a bad sign. And his shoes were cheap.

She wondered what Jonathan looked like now. Strange, but she was suddenly looking forward to seeing him again. Curiosity, she supposed, more than anything else. She didn't have that many ex-lovers to look back on. Would he be grey-haired? Or bald? He'd been, what, seven months older than her? That made him forty-nine. Not a bad age for a man. Murder for a woman, though, as she knew only too well. What had his star sign been? His birthday was in August. During the holidays. A Leo. Yes. Of course. He had to be a Leo.

He'd sounded odd on the phone. Like a boy working up his courage to ask for a date. Had he been married? No. She didn't think so. Clara would have enjoyed telling her that. And he'd nearly died. Some sort of cancer, apparently. Poor Jonathan. He wasn't the sort to take illness lightly. All that Leonine energy. She remembered him dancing like Zorba the Greek, stark naked, on the beach at Le Levant. And he really could dance. Not like most Englishmen. But then he wasn't completely English, was he? That aristocratic dash of French blood set him off from the others. Gave him a veneer. He'd probably lost all of it by now. Beaten down by life, and age and illness.

'I was just wondering...would you like me to bring you something from the buffet car?'

Frances looked up. The white-collared man was looming over her, swaying gently to the rhythm of the train. He wasn't as young as she'd first thought, she realised. And where had all this 'young man' business come from anyway? She wasn't as old as all that. She must stop talking herself down. 'That's sweet of you. But I don't think so. Thank you.'

He hesitated, then gave up gracefully. Frances smiled to herself as he zigzagged down the corridor. He'd try once more, of course. When he came back. She'd give him the same answer, and he'd retire content. 'Met this gorgeous woman on the train. She tried to pick me up, but I wasn't having any of it. Bit too old. Now if she'd been ten years younger, who knows?' There you are. She was doing it again!

She looked at her watch – it was fast becoming a nervous tic. Twenty minutes to go. She prayed Clara wasn't on the bottle again. In which case she'd have to drive them both back to Penhallow. She'd always had trouble switching from right to left. That's when she most missed having a man. Stupid, wasn't it? And such a cliché. But there it was. She liked having a man to open doors for her, drive the car, pick up the bill in restaurants. Giancarlo had been perfect for that. There were times when she really missed him, despite the horror of their final years. Perhaps his behaviour had been far more her fault than she'd ever really acknowledged? She'd never, God knows, been a hundred per cent committed to their marriage. And he'd been such a child. He simply couldn't say no to a pretty face. His mistresses (not to mention the occasional boyfriend) had been like an endless succession of eager young mothers, offering their tender and milky breasts to their hungry and oh-so-very-appreciative grown-up baby.

She shook her head sadly. She'd always known, of course, when he'd been having an affair. Well not at the beginning, perhaps. But later. Back he'd come, like a beaten dog, begging her forgiveness and fearful that she'd leave him – take a lover herself. But she never had. Why? There'd been opportunities galore. Once she'd even gone as far as making an assignation – what a stupid word that was. She'd chickened out at the last minute, of course. The whole thing had suddenly seemed so dirty and underhand. And anyway, she hadn't even loved the man.

Perhaps she wasn't highly sexed enough? Heaven knows she hadn't felt like it these past two or three years. Only now did she understand why middle-aged women wore cardigans and why middle-aged men took young mistresses. The menopause was for suckers. At night you broke into hot sweats, and sex, when it was offered, hurt. Giancarlo had tried to be good about it, but she'd seen it had bothered him. She'd be pleased when it was all over and she could relax into a comfortable middle age. Recently she'd gone eleven months without her period, and then, just when she'd thought she'd weathered the worst of it, it had all started up again. God! She could almost scream.

The man was back. He hesitated, thinking of something to say. Would she let him off the hook? No. Not this time. He could do his own dirty work.

'Are you sure you wouldn't like some tea? I've got a spare cup here.'

'No. You drink it. I don't like tea.'

'Oh.'

She speared the phone out of her handbag. Cosima would be through customs by now. She'd try her once more, just in case. Warn her that she'd arranged for Jonathan to pick her up from the flat first thing in the morning.

She stopped short in the act of tapping out the number. Why had she done that? Why had she put Cosima and Jonathan together, in a car, for five hours? She exhaled angrily. She was no closer to understanding her own motivations now than she had been – how many years ago was it? Twenty-eight? More than half a lifetime, anyway.

And the strangest thing of all was that it felt like yesterday. As if the years between had simply melted away.

Eleven

Clara left the house lights blazing and the front doors wide open. Let the burglars come. They could clean the place out as far as she was concerned – threadbare carpets, dubious antiques and all. Bugger Jonathan and his bloody estate!

She reeled drunkenly towards the stables. She was running late. If the car started, all very well – if it didn't, then Frances could sit on Penzance station until her quim froze off. Serve her right. Perhaps some maniac would come along and rape her, then chop her to pieces with his electronic buzz-saw and store her bits and pieces in his freezer. She always had been a frigid bitch.

Chortling quietly to herself, Clara tugged at the door of her eleven-year-old Volvo estate. It burst open, causing her to stagger. Whoops! Keys on the dashboard. That was lucky. She'd thought she'd forgotten them. She squeezed in behind the wheel. After three near misses she succeeded in spearing the ignition. Funny thing, thinking of the keys, but it had always baffled her how men ever managed to find the spot, with their John Thomases dangling three-and-a-half feet below their heads. Just look at horses. And chickens. You'd think they'd never hit the mark. And what about giraffes? Yet another bloody miracle of nature!

She turned the key. The engine caught first time. Good cars, these. Never let you down. Not like you-know-what and -who.

She was halfway up the drive before she remembered the headlights. She switched them on with a flourish. *Voilà!* Now at last she could see. Should she go up the Try Valley, or use the main road? Better the short cut. Less chance of PC Plod and his little plastic bag – the thing would probably turn puce, with insanely ringing bells, if it caught even a whiff of her breath.

Ten minutes later, passing the ghostly silhouette of Treen Downs in the dusk, she gave a superstitious shudder. The place had always given her the creeps – ever since her childhood when she'd dreamed that the bogeyman was really the bog-man, and that one night he'd climb out of Treen swamp, dripping with slime, and come to get her. Mind you, there wasn't any great Freudian mystery about that one. The US army had lost a Sherman Tank and its crew down there during the Second World War. She remembered Stacey telling them the story, one windy night, in the garage, with the storm lamps guttering. All four of them had sat in the back of the Daimler, while Stacey had busied himself polishing the headlights and trim.

'They made a bet with the locals, see. You young 'uns won't remember how them Yanks were at that time. Boastful-like. "Nothing can stop one of our tin cans," they'd say. "Those things'll go anywhere – through anything." "Well they won't go through Treen bog." That was Toby Penrice talking. Him that used to farm up near Gear. "I've lost three head of cattle to that place in the past thirty years," he says, "and what's more, my granddad told me that blasted bog swallowed a clergyman, whole, and spat out his horse like it were a fish bone, just about the time of the Battle of Waterloo." '

'The Battle of Waterloo!'

'That's what he said.' Stacey had shaken his head sadly, relishing their attention. 'And I believed him, as would you. But did those Yanks pay any attention? No. Because there'd been some drinking, see? And you know what drink does to people. You remember that, Master Jonathan. It's a good lesson to learn while you're still young.'

'Come on, Stacey, tell us.'

'Very well then.' He'd cleared his throat dramatically. 'So that there US crew simply climbed into their tank, drove it up to the downs, and set the thing full tilt at the bog. And a good thirty mile an hour they must have been doing when they hit the edge of it.'

'And then what happened?'

'That was the last anybody saw of them, is what happened. The next day the army dug down one-hundred-and-fifty foot, with their pipes and suchlike, and still they couldn't find hide nor hair of 'em. They give up in the end. Place become a war grave. But those four men are still down there, you mark my words, locked tighter than potted sardines inside that tank.' He'd made a particularly ghoulish face as the image occurred to him. 'Preserved for ever in the primordial ooze.'

Bloody Stacey! He'd scared the living daylights out of them all. Even Jonathan, who'd always relished telling ghost stories above all things. They'd refused point-blank to go back to the house, she remembered, until Stacey promised to walk with them, holding up his torch to light the way ahead. God, though – what a way to die. Clara gave a convulsive shudder. She'd feared tight, claustrophobic places ever since. She tightened her grip on the steering-wheel. Even as a child, she'd been able to imagine the slime leeching through every available crevice as the tank slid slowly, inch by deliberate inch, down through the swampy waters. Surely there must have been air trapped inside it for quite some time? Had the men clung to each other for comfort? Prayed? Screamed in horror?

Come on! Change the bloody subject, Champion.

She hooked a sharp left towards Carnaquidden Farm and put her foot down. The sooner she got away from there the better. Belting past Chysauster at sixty miles an hour, she pooped her horn at a Range Rover backing out of a farm track. The Volvo swerved briefly, then recovered. Clara switched on the radio. Yes! Yes! 'Sitting on the Dock of the Bay.' That was more like it. She began to sing, hammering the steering-wheel for effect. A car passed her, its horn wailing. 'What's wrong, you stinker!' Then, in a John Wayne drawl, 'There's not enough road for the both of us.' She erupted into giggles, then her voice trailed off. For a moment there, she'd forgotten what she'd come out to do.

Reaching Badger's Cross she didn't stop but simply swung across both lanes of the B3311 and down towards Penzance. No traffic. Too late at night. And you could see the other cars coming from miles away.

Half a mile further on she hit it. She didn't know what it was, just some white thing running out at her. It slammed into the side door and bounced backwards. She jammed on the brakes, leaving smoking tyre marks for fifty yards behind her. The Volvo conked out abruptly on the corner, its radio still blaring. Clara turned in her seat and looked back. The white thing, whatever it was, was lying in the road, half illuminated by some cottage lights. Now the door was opening. People were coming out.

Clara dry-retched. Headlights were approaching rapidly half a mile ahead of her. Her heart hammered impatiently at the inside of her ribs. It was now or never. She turned the key in the ignition. The engine coughed once, then died.

'Come on. Come on you bastard!'

She switched off the radio and headlights, and tried again. The starter motor whirred twice, then caught. Thank God! She waited until the approaching car was on the cusp of the corner, then put her foot to the floor. The Volvo surged forward, its tyres screaming. All the oncoming driver would see would be the flash of her face as she went past. Let him deal with the thing in the road. It was probably only a deer, anyway. Or somebody's bally pet dog.

Stone-cold sober now, Clara negotiated her way through the brightly lit outskirts of Penzance.

Delayed shock hit her a quarter of a mile before the railway station. She pulled onto a double yellow line and rested her head against the steering-wheel. What she needed was a drink. A brandy would do the trick. She'd heard that if you were seen drinking after an accident, the flatfoots couldn't breathalyse you.

She raised her head and looked around for a pub. The lights of an off-licence beckoned merrily from fifty yards down the street. Clara staggered out of the car. She was surprised to find that her hands were shaking. She rubbed them angrily down the side of her jeans. Oh God. No money.

'Clara?'

Clara twisted, squinting anxiously down the neon-lit street. Hell. It was only Frances. Approaching purposefully from across the road. She must have been nearer the station than she'd supposed.

'I thought you'd forgotten you were picking me up. I finally got tired of waiting and came out to find a taxi. Is anything wrong? Why didn't you park nearer the station?'

'Lend me twenty quid, will you? We're out of brandy.'

Frances recoiled. Clara smelt like a wine cellar. 'Don't get any brandy in on my account.'

'It's not on your account. It's coming straight out of your pocket. Ha ha ha.'

Frances grimaced and felt around in her handbag. So it was going to be one of *those* nights. 'I've no cash. Only credit cards. I had to hurry to catch the train.'

'Bring the credit cards then.' Clara strode ahead of her down the street.

Frances shrugged her shoulders and followed. Clara looked terrible. More raddled even than the last time they'd met – how long ago was it? Three years? Four? Yes. That was it. Four years ago. At Helen's seventieth-birthday party. She mustn't, really mustn't, get the guilts about that. 'I've left my luggage at the station. And I promised the man I wouldn't be long. He wants to go home.' Clara, it was obvious, was on a jag. Now she'd have to drive back to Penhallow after all.

'It doesn't take long to buy a bottle of brandy,' said Clara, disappearing into the off-licence ahead of her. 'Or don't you remember?'

Frances bit her lip in concentration. Drive on the left. Drive on the left. Drive on the left. She tried to conjure up a mental image of the last time she'd driven on English roads, but failed.

'Don't take the short cut!' Clara brandished the bottle wildly.

'For heaven's sake, Clara, there's no need to shout. I'm not deaf. And stop waving that bottle. Why shouldn't we take the short cut? We always take it.'

'Because the road's up. That's why I was late. Got stuck behind a red light for hours. They're laying sewage pipes or something.'

'At this time of night?'

'Well how am I to know what they're doing? I'm not an electrician.'

Frances sighed. 'All right. All right. I'll go up through Nancledra then.'

'No! They're working below Badger's Cross. You'll have to go all the way past the Leisure Park.'

'Oh for God's sake!'

Clara sat as far back in her seat as she could and cracked the seal on the brandy. She was hallucinating. Must be. One minute the white thing was coming at her, its eyes blazing, the next it was rearing up and scrabbling at the window. 'You want a swig?'

'Of course not. I'm driving.'

'Scared it'll bite?'

'Well it's obviously bitten you.'

Clara lit a cigarette. Her hands were shaking badly. Frances opened her window to let out the smoke.

'God, Frances, don't tell me you're off the fags as well? Don't you have any vices left? The occasional snort of cocaine? A predilection for orgies?'

Frances crashed the gears. 'Oh, I have vices. But they're my own affair. I just don't parade them in front of the first person who chances along.' She'd been tempted to drift into the right lane after that last turning. She must catch hold of herself – now was certainly not the moment to cause a pile-up. Why on earth did Clara insist on driving such a tank? 'Do you *have* to stare at me like that all the time? I feel like Jack the Ripper's next victim.'

Clara muttered, 'If only,' under her breath, then turned away and closed her eyes. But the white thing was still there. Lurking. Almost as if there'd been a Polaroid camera behind her pupils when she hit it. 'Do you have to dawdle quite so much? We should have been home ten minutes ago.'

Frances bit back her answer. Why start another row? She and Clara would be living together, willy-nilly, for the next few days, so an armed truce might be in order. She modulated her voice. 'Clara. Look. Let's not get off on the wrong foot. We've done too much of that already in our lives. I'm desperately sorry about Helen. It seems silly for me to say this, as she was stepmother to us both, but I know how particularly fond of her you were.'

Clara blew a thin stream of smoke through her nostrils. 'Well, jolly old Frances. Always the right word at the right time.' The white thing was gone, thank God. Whatever it was. Whatever it had been. She drew herself up in her seat. 'Helen and I both enjoyed the visits you never made.'

Frances tensed. She wanted to bite back her words, but she simply couldn't manage it. She could feel her stomach swooping, just as it had done so often when they were children. 'And how was I to make them? Whenever I came, you went out of your way to make me feel unwanted. To make me feel I didn't belong. Penhallow is my home too, you know. I have as much right to be there as you.' She stopped herself, then managed a broken smile. 'Go on. Pass me a cigarette, then.'

'Ha! Grace under pressure indeed.' Clara lit a second cigarette, then handed it to Frances. 'Well you can kiss goodbye to those rights of yours, ducky. Penhallow is winging its way back to its lawful owner. Jonathan, a.k.a. "quick-zip" Audley.'

'Clara!'

'Did he ever try that trick on you with the ice-cubes? He'd put one in his mouth...'

Frances jammed on the brakes. Tyres squealed behind them. A white van hooted, then overtook angrily, the driver's face a malevolent blur through the passenger window. The smell of burnt rubber began to permeate the interior of the car. Frances pulled unsteadily into the lay-by, the Volvo grumbling over the stones. She cut the engine and turned to Clara, her eyes flashing. 'Clara. Look at me.'

Clara responded with a sarcastic smile.

'I shall say this once, and once only. I do not want to hear all the gory details of what went on between you and Jonathan. Either twenty-eight years ago or last week, for that matter. I have my own life now. And you're not a part of it. Neither is Jonathan. I'm here for Helen's funeral. After that, we shall probably never meet again until either one or the other of us is on our deathbed. And that suits me just fine.' She flicked her un-smoked cigarette out of the window. 'It's pointless trying to pretend.' She restarted the Volvo. 'We never did get on. Even when we were girls. And nothing's changed. You still despise me for what I am, and I'm utterly indifferent to you. Let's just leave it at that, shall we?'

She checked over her shoulder and pulled back into the traffic. Her upper arms were shaking. She steeled herself for the tongue-lashing Clara was doubtless preparing for her. Silence. When she glanced over towards Clara's seat, Clara was crying. 'Clara! What on earth's the matter?'

Clara flapped her hand and turned towards the window. 'Nothing. What should be the matter?' The white thing was back again. Only worse, this time. She kept hearing the thud its body had made against her door. It must have been a dog. Or a fawn? Yes. That was it. A fawn. That would account for the white. But it had been bigger than a fawn, surely? What if it had been a child?

'Do you want me to stop? Look. There's a pub over there.'

Clara brandished her bottle. 'I'm carrying my pub with me. Or hadn't you noticed?' She must snap out of this or Frances would become suspicious. Start asking silly questions. Put two and two together. 'Look,' she said. 'I've lost Helen, my home, and my financial security, all in the space of a week. Then you show up, looking like a fucking film star. I'm drunk and I'm feeling sorry for myself. It's nothing new. Don't go worrying your little head about it.' Now here goes with the placebo, she thought to herself. 'And that crack about

Jonathan. The one about the ice-cubes. It wasn't true. It was some other bloke that did that. There have been so many, I've forgotten exactly which one it was now.' She blew out her cheeks sarcastically. 'Jonathan only had me the once, and that's stretching it. I tricked him into it. He was high as a kite. Bastard probably thought he was dreaming the whole thing. Does that make you feel any better?'

They passed Lelant and Carbis Bay and were travelling along the upper road through St Ives. Frances turned sharply away so that Clara wouldn't see her expression. Then, instinctively, as she'd always done at this point in the road, she glanced down at the town, so elegantly spread beneath her.

She was surprised to find that it gave her the same cosy feeling it had given her as a child; she knew each bay, each cliff, each tree and rock for twenty miles in every direction. This was her country. Her mother's country. Even her father's country, God help him.

Anchor lights were winking around the port. She could just make out the green and red signal lamps of a fishing boat, far out to sea. Five or six streets below them was the flat that Jonathan had taken during the summer of 1968, two months after he'd kidnapped her from school to join the student riots in Paris. She smiled to herself. God, but Daddy had been livid when he'd found out. He'd forbidden Jonathan, on pain of death, ever to see her again. So Jonathan had taken the flat in St Ives to get around the ban. They'd met in secret all that summer. Helen had known, of course. And Stacey. But Clara had never caught on. Too busy chasing boys of her own.

She wondered if the flat was still there – still as wonderfully shabby? If you craned your neck out of the studio window you could just make out the far corner of Porthmeor Beach. And if you looked the other way, you could see Godrevy Island like a pinprick in the distance. The lavatory only filled if you tugged on the stopcock with a piece of string. The shower came away from the wall when you turned the water up to more than a trickle. At night, you could hear the raucous cheers and the laughter swelling up from the pubs around the harbour. Catch the tang of freshly caught fish from the old salting works, drifting on the breeze.

Her heart clenched with the memory of it all. She cracked the window and breathed in the fresh salt of the sea. As the full force of the damp night air struck her, she realised for the first time that she was coming home.

Twelve

Jonathan sighed and pushed away the remnants of his breakfast. Reaching inside his jacket he took out an envelope. He shook it onto the table, revealing a dried poppy, which still retained a little of its colour, and a desiccated four-leaf clover. He withdrew a single, yellowing sheet of folded bond paper from the envelope and spread it out in front of him. It was tattered now, the paper soft with thirty years of age and handling. Slowly, rationing himself, he leaned forward and began to read.

Wednesday...after I recovered.

The power of words... Deliquescent with desire, I ran out into the fields. My friends were making hay and the unused adrenaline went into hoisting bales and jumping about in the sun. I apologize to your exciting personality, your challenging wit, your sensitive nature, your deep moss peat of culture, your artistic talent, your musical flair, your intrepid spirit of survival, your open-mindedness, your sporting glory and your touch of class...but you just turn ME ON!

Your voice, your sensuous lips (*lèvres gourmandes*?) your well-tuned brown body, your mapped out strategy... I can call it anything you want; it feels like, it looks like, it IS lust! I have endless fantasies of me lying there helplessly, only making the merest attempt at retaliation.

Why do I cry when you make love to me? I've thought: Go into heaven. Turn into a cloud. Float. Up. Up. Then change atmospheric conditions. Low pressure. I rain. That's why – I rain –

I feel sooooo good after our telephone conversation. The complete experience. You are very enjoyable. When we next meet, will it be fireworks or short circuit?

Leos, tigers, dragons whirling around an innocent (?) Pisces. She might, like St Blandine, keep the beasts in check. Hmm what do we do to her?

I love it so far. You will be my special pilgrimage.

I send you a mess of kisses and caresses. You are the expert. You sort them out. I am rapidly losing control.

But I'm not giving in.

– Frances

During that summer of 1968, Jonathan had taken a holiday let above the old harbour in St Ives – a shabby place, smelling of fags and fried breakfasts and Woolworths' perfume, just a few streets up from where, forty years earlier, Christopher Wood and Ben Nicholson had discovered Alfred Wallis painting his magical driftwood galleons. It had red flock wallpaper and a nylon carpet. On one wall was an overexposed photogravure of Constable's The Hay-Wain; on the other, a print, framed in rope, of Sir Francis Chichester's Gypsy Moth rounding the Horn. The sofa pulled out to make a bed – it had seen much use, that summer, he recalled. The shower had a mind of its own and the lavatory didn't work. Strange to think the room still existed, subtly changed, no doubt, with other people's odours and other people's memories etched upon its walls.

That year his father had given him a Citroen *Deux Chevaux* as an advance eighteenth-birthday present and to celebrate his expulsion from school. He'd driven it up through France (it had taken him twenty-four straight hours), the knowledge that he was to see Frances acting like a dull weight in his groin. How did one ever lose that first, strange madness? He remembered the curve of her breasts beneath her blouse. The smoothness of her legs. The toss of her hair. Sometimes he'd run his hand up the back of her thighs, then cup her buttocks inside the thin cotton fabric of her pants. At a bus-stop, in the cinema, in the car, he'd caress her – then catch her scent, later, on his fingers, when he was alone.

He folded the letter back inside its envelope. No woman would ever love him as Frances had done. It was impossible. She'd given herself completely, as no man ever could. As *he* couldn't. He sometimes wondered whether his cancer wasn't a belated form of punishment – he'd been given something of infinite value and he'd abused it. What was that vow he'd made to Frances, in the tree house, at Penhallow? 'I'll get ill. Like King Arthur. And I'll only get better when you forgive me.'

Each day, that perilous summer, she'd cycle out to Tremedda Common to meet him. They'd hide her bicycle behind a rock. Later, they'd drive somewhere for lunch – a cosy pub, the old Lamorna café, fish and chips on Mousehole harbour. Most times, consumed with lust, they'd stop somewhere on the way – he particularly remembered a wood, with a river and a medieval bridge, somewhere near Trewoofe. She'd leant over the bridge to look for trout and he'd come up behind her, raised her skirt (she'd been naked underneath), and they'd made love, looking down into the river, oblivious of anyone but themselves.

Once, after three days of continual heat, they'd taken sleeping-bags and hidden out on St Michael's Mount, long after the tourists had gone home. That night, the night of his eighteenth birthday, they'd sat on the rocks, surrounded by candles, with the lights of Penzance glittering across the bay. It was then that he'd asked her to marry him. To make good her promise of eight years before.

'Later,' she'd told him gently. 'When we're older. It's too complicated now. Too much bad karma in the family.'

Perhaps he'd accepted too easily? Been too eager to preserve the status quo? Youth, after all, in its spurious infinity, had stretched ahead of them.

'Some more toast?' The waiter hovered expectantly.

Jonathan looked up. How he hated English chain hotels, with their tea machines, and their trouser-presses, and their plastic bags of free biscuits – they were temples of loneliness, and their secrets weren't worth knowing. 'No. No, thank you. I must be going.'

'As you wish, sir.'

As you wish, sir? Jonathan glanced at his watch. Rush hour on the M25. Why had he ever agreed to drive Cosima down to Cornwall in the first place? Catching sight of himself in the hall mirror, he smiled at his own evasions. Because he couldn't say no to Frances, that was why – and besides, sitting next to her daughter for five hours hardly constituted a penance.

Midway through re-packing his overnight case, the happy thought occurred to him that Cosima might want to stop off for lunch on the way down. All those skinny models liked to eat, didn't they? Thanks to his illness, it had been more than a year since he'd dined alone with a woman. He would suggest some snug little pub. The Nobody Inn at Doddiscombsleigh, for instance. That wasn't too far off their road. They could talk about Frances, and gorge on scallops and *Coteaux de Layon* (if he didn't still feel sick at the smell of wine, that was) and he could look at Cosima, and flirt, and pretend he was young again.

Jonathan eased the Aston Martin into Prince of Wales Drive. He scrutinised the piece of paper with Cosima's address on it. Yes. It was here all right. He glanced up at the façade. Just the sort of place a model would live. Mansion block. King's Road a short walk away. Fulham just across the river. He shook his head. If anyone had suggested to him thirty years before that any daughter of Frances's would have ended up on the catwalk, he'd have laughed in their face. An art historian, maybe. Or even an actress. But a model? Mind you, with Giancarlo as a father… Jonathan found himself gripping the steering-wheel with vicious intensity.

They'd met Giancarlo in Paris, during the May '68 riots. It had been a crazy time for everyone, where youth was king and the old order was being put to the question. The customary barriers and deterrents to communication were being torn down forever – or so they'd fondly thought. There'd been graffiti everywhere – plastered over cars, on *pissoirs*, sprayed onto the glass fronts of shops: *Here, Imagination Rules*; *Society is a Carnivorous Flower*; and his favourite, *Time Reveals Nothing*. God, but they'd been callow.

Giancarlo had latched onto them at the height of the Denfert-Rochereau street disturbances; later, he'd invited them places, shared the contents of his capacious wallet with them at nightclubs, restaurants, cafés. Jonathan had been suspicious of him from the start, but Frances had been charmed by the sleek Italian, and had taken to treating him like the romantic older brother she'd never had.

Giancarlo had written to her when she'd returned to school, Jonathan knew that much, and she'd written back. Innocent letters, he supposed, even now. But they hadn't seen each other again for three years. Then, hearing that she was to spend a term in Venice as part of her art history course, he'd called and offered her the use of his late father's house in Sant'Alvise.

He'd become an odd sort of fish in the intervening years. Inheriting his father's estate, which included the Venice house, art galleries in Paris and

Milan, and a holiday cottage in Sicily, had made Giancarlo, paradoxically, insecure. It had brought out his peasant blood. He took to hanging around Frances during the months she spent in Venice like one of those scrawny young gorillas you saw on nature programmes – biding their time before cutting in on the dominant male.

Well the bastard had cut in all right. He'd been waiting for her the day she got back from the island, smarting from his infidelity with Clara. They'd been married in less than a week. Bloody young fool that he'd been – what unbelievable folly had possessed him to leave it so long before going after her?

When he had eventually arrived in Venice, Constance, Frances's friend, had been there to meet him at the station. It was she who had told him about the marriage. Frances and Giancarlo had already left on their honeymoon – to Sicily, of all ironical places. He and Frances had been planning a visit there the next summer. Blushing furiously, Connie had admitted that she'd only known he was coming because Frances – fearing something like this? – had asked her to pick up any telegrams and deal with them while she was away.

At first the devastating fact of Frances being married hadn't really hit him. He remembered laughing, grotesquely, when Connie first told him, as if he suspected that some obscene practical joke was being played on him. Frances couldn't cut off from him that fast, could she? It wasn't possible. Not after eleven years. And with Giancarlo? Surely he could rely on her to forgive him. He knew he could. She was the strong one, after all.

Afterwards, he'd paced the Venice streets, half-enjoying the *Sturm und Drang* of his belated grief. Finally, exhausted, he'd taken a shabby room in some God-forsaken *pensione*. He remembered drinking most of a bottle of grappa, secretly hoping that he'd come down with alcoholic poisoning, upon which Frances would rush back from Sicily to administer first aid to him in a hospital, which, in his half-waking dreams, suspiciously resembled the one in *A Farewell To Arms* where the injured young Hemingway had contrived his passion for Agnes von Kurowsky.

Two days later, the hangover long forgotten, he'd stood in a corner of that same hotel room and cried – long, gut-wrenching tears, worse even than the tears he'd shed when his parents had first abandoned him to the tender mercies of his public school. Frances had been his forever – they'd both known it – from that very first moment, in the field at Penhallow, when he'd bandaged her ankle with his handkerchief. How could they have got it so wrong? He had counted on their love. It had been such a fundamental part of each of them that nothing, ever, should have caused them to question it.

Cosima was watching him. He was aware of her out of the corner of his eye. She'd been at it, now, for a good ten minutes. He sighed dramatically. 'Go on, then. A penny for your thoughts.'

She cocked her head at him. 'All right. You asked for it.' She curled herself against the passenger door, folding her arms protectively across her belly. 'Did you and Mummy ever have an affair?'

They'd already passed Stonehenge. Great Ridge was on their right, with Grim's Ditch passing through it. He remembered shooting there, some years ago – the strange, almost primordial feeling of the woods. Over to his left, hidden somewhere beyond the furthest belt of trees, was the ruined shell of Fonthill Abbey. 'I'm sorry?'

'Did you and Mummy ever have an affair? Don't pretend you didn't hear me.'

He hadn't got over the frightening resemblance that Cosima bore to Frances. Hair a little lighter. Amber eyes, not brown. But that same, gloriously rounded chin. The same slight broadening of the ridge of her nose. She was taller than her mother (all the young were, weren't they?), but she had her mother's high breasts, and the shape of her legs, beneath the Russian-style miniskirt and matching jacket she was wearing, marked her, beyond a shadow of a doubt, as Frances's daughter. 'Have you asked her?'

'I'm asking you.'

Why was he havering? Hadn't he driven into London that very morning with the express intention of discussing Frances with her daughter? What harm would it do him to speak honestly for once? It might even afford him – the French had the best word for it, as usual – *soulagement*. The nearest English equivalent, 'relief', had a massage parlour ring to it.

'I don't think the word "affair" quite covers what your mother and I had together.'

'Why ever not? Were you unique? Different from the rest of us in some way?'

Jonathan moved awkwardly in his seat. The little minx had a sharp tongue on her, and an even sharper capacity for intuition. Come on, Audley. Spit it out. In three hours you'll be seeing Frances for the first time in twenty-eight years. The boil needs lancing. He cleared his throat. 'Not unique, no. I wouldn't dare to call it that, although it seemed so to us at the time. But I was truly in love with her. Passionately. And she with me.'

'How do you know she loved you?'

He looked at Cosima in astonishment. 'She couldn't hide it. No true woman ever can. And your mother was certainly that.' He pretended to concentrate on the road ahead. 'No. The only one who hid it was me. From myself.'

'I don't understand.'

'Neither do I. That's what's so bewildering about it.' He shook his head uncomprehendingly. 'My only excuse is that I was barely twenty-one when our relationship ended, and I might as well have been ten. I had more sense, though, when I was ten.' Cosima was still watching him, but he refused to meet her gaze.

'How long did it go on for? Your relationship, I mean.'

'Eleven years.'

'Eleven years!'

He swallowed. He had a sudden urge to close his eyes. To shut off what he was saying from himself – but the road – the road. 'I met your mother when I was nine. It was at Penhallow. My first time there. I was running across the fields to fetch Stacey – he was your grandfather's odd job man – when I came upon your mother. She'd sprained her ankle. She was sitting in the middle of a meadow, on a hillside, with a moth-eaten black Labrador beside her.' He glanced swiftly at Cosima to gauge her reaction. 'I was lost the first time she looked at me. There's no other way of putting it. Like twin souls. You've read Plato, haven't you?'

She nodded.

'We were like two halves of the same person, and we'd been looking for each other. All our lives. I know how it must sound. Like something out of Rider Haggard. But it wasn't simply a matter of recognition. It was more visceral than that. It was a sort of *knowing*. I can't put it any better than that. I'm a painter, not a poet.'

'It sounds frightening.'

'That was it. That was it exactly.' He slapped the steering-wheel lightly with the palm of his hand. 'It frightened me. I didn't know what to do. How to manage the thing. And I had this absurd and patronising idea that it was up to me to manage it. That I should take responsibility for both of us. For what both of us were feeling.'

'You weren't giving Mummy much credit, were you?'

'That was the way it was in those days. However ridiculous it might sound now.' He slowed down for the Chicklade speed cameras. 'Well, maybe it wasn't so ridiculous after all. Because your mother *did* need protecting. From herself. And I failed her.'

'How do you mean?'

'Oh, it's so long ago now.' He pushed himself awkwardly back in his seat. 'I don't know that it's worth going over again.'

'It obviously is, or you wouldn't have started telling me about it.'

Damn the girl! She'd certainly nailed *him* to the wall. He cleared his throat. He could feel the dark, clammy weight of the past, like a recently disinterred corpse, pressing familiarly against him. 'She was too trusting, perhaps. That's what I really meant. She thought I was just as I appeared to be. And I wasn't.'

'What did you do? To make her leave you. Because I suppose it *was* her that left you?'

He attempted a laugh. 'Oh God! What didn't I do? I couldn't have thought up a meaner or a more vicious betrayal if I'd spent those entire eleven years doing nothing else.' He stopped abruptly, feeling that he'd gone too far. 'But maybe I'm kidding myself. Maybe she didn't care that much? Perhaps I'm exaggerating something that happened a long, long time ago.'

'You know that's not true.'

He turned to her in astonishment. 'How come you're so acute? In my experience, daughters know very little about their mothers. And guess less.'

'I'm twenty-seven years old, Jonathan. Seven years older than Mummy was when you broke up with her. I lost my father twenty years too soon. I've enjoyed the sort of success most people would kill for. I've had more lovers than I care, in my darker moments, to remember.' She hesitated, then reached across and touched his arm. 'So you see, I'm not the bewildered and malleable little girl you think I am. I'm not Frances's cute little daughter, who looks so much like her, and who reminds you, when you're willing to entertain the idea, of what it was like in the good old days of your youth, and whom you'd secretly, if rather incestuously, quite like to bed. I'm through the hero-worshipping stage. You missed all that. Fortunately.'

'I see.'

'Do you?' Her eyes were challenging him. 'Do you really?'

Thirteen

St Tropez, France. 1967

Charles Audley bought the *Domaine de Canteloube* in 1949, using his new wife's money. St Tropez was a quiet little place then – a few writers and artists, a smattering of 'yachties', and a small, rather artistic homosexual community. There was only one decent road from the mainland and little prospect of further building. The harbour of *La Ponche* teemed with fisherman, not gin-palaces, and some of the houses around the old port, which had largely been destroyed by the Germans during the aerial bombing of 1944, were still under reconstruction.

Delighted with their new home, Charles and Geneviève set about planting vines – Charles had viticultural aspirations – and also olives, figs, almond, jujube and citrus trees. Along the periphery of the one-hundred acre property they sowed parasol, alep and maritime pines, eucalypti, and cedars of all sorts. Geneviève, who had a way with animals, kept three goats, a donkey, some ducks and a fluctuating army of chickens. Within three years the property was up and running, and within five years – following the birth of Jonathan and Lisa – and with the help of three permanent staff, it was supplying the local markets of Grimaud, Cogolin, and La Garde-Freinet. At a loss, of course.

In 1957 Brigitte Bardot and Roger Vadim arrived in St Tropez to film *Et Dieu Créa La Femme*, and all hell broke loose in paradise. During the next ten years the population grew from the 4,161 souls left *in situ* after the war, to more than 70,000 at the height of the frenetic August annual holidays. 'Bardolaters' abounded. Dress consisted of a pair of gaudy slacks, a bare midriff and a tight sailor top. The hippest bars were the Café des Arts and the Escale; the hottest restaurants were Les Mouscardins and the Auberge des Maures. For antiques, there was Barry, on the port. If you wanted drugs, you went to Jojo, at the Citadelle. Madame Palma, at her brothel on the rue de Marisson, had no trouble procuring a steady stream of Bardot look-alikes for the delectation of her discerning and well-heeled clientele.

In extreme contrast, and situated a bare two miles east of town on the road to Les Salins, was Monsieur Dutron's restaurant, A La Bonne Ensignure, where old-guard *Tropéziens* could still buy themselves an unhysterical three-course lunch, with wine and coffee, for between twelve and twenty francs.

On the first Saturday of August 1967, Charles Audley was seated on the terrace of the Ensignure playing host to his summer guests. The party consisted of his thirty-nine-year-old wife, Geneviève, his two children, Jonathan and Lisa, and their cousins, Frances and Clara Champion. Charles's uncle, Piers Godolphin, was also present, with his long-time lover Jean Toquet, who had recently completed his valedictory season as lead choreographer for the Ballet National de France. Jonathan's seventeenth birthday party was to take place in three days' time, and there was an air of excited anticipation amongst the teenagers.

Piers stopped stroking the cravat he was wearing under his pigeon-blue handmade Lanvin shirt, and cleared his throat dramatically. 'What would you say, Charles, to Jean and I giving the boy a *mobylette* for his birthday? He's a touch long in the tooth for another bicycle, don't you think?'

'I don't think. He has trouble staying put on a piddling three-speed Raleigh already. Give him something with a motor attached and he'll be a fully paid-up quadriplegic within the year.'

'But, Dad! All the other boys have one. And they all got theirs when they were fourteen.' Jonathan looked hopefully towards Piers and Jean. 'And I'm seventeen. Or as near as damn it.' He caught his mother's eye. 'Sorry, *maman*. I didn't mean to swear.' The fact that his father hadn't said no straightaway was a justifiable sign of hope. 'You don't have to pass a test, you know, papa. You just need insurance. And that only costs eighty francs a year.'

'Aren't you forgetting fuel, medical bills and a cast-iron crash helmet with India-rubber shock absorbers?'

'The boy has shock absorbers if nothing else,' said Jean. 'You saw those high dives he did at the Eden Roc? Sublime. What it is to be young.'

'You see?' Jonathan flashed an excited glance at Frances. He could as good as feel the solid weight of the machine between his legs; hear the racket it would make after he'd rammed a poker up its exhaust pipe. Frances smiled back. She crossed her fingers surreptitiously over her chest.

'Well I don't want Lisa travelling on it,' said Geneviève.

'She wouldn't be allowed to, *maman*. Only people over fifteen are allowed on the pillion, and Lisa isn't fifteen for another week. I could take Frances, though.'

'Your Aunt Helen would never forgive me. And I thought you said fourteen, a moment ago?'

'It'll be all right, *maman*. It really will. I'll be ever so careful. And I wouldn't put Frances up straightaway. I'd practise first.'

Piers sat as far back in his seat as he was able, all the more to enjoy the elusive pleasure of having stirred things up.

'Can we go to the beach now? We've finished our lunch.' Clara, aghast at the prospect of Frances and Jonathan disappearing into the countryside together on the back of a motorbike, was prepared to do anything, even miss Monsieur Dutron's famous tarte Tatin, in order to change the subject.

'You may,' said Geneviève. 'But you are not to go anywhere near the nudist beaches. You must promise me. All of you. You know the sort of people who lurk there.' She darted a meaningful look at her husband. 'Frances? Clara? Don't forget that I'm responsible for you to your mother and father.'

'We won't, *tante*. We'll only go as far as the café. We promise.'

'But *vitch* café?' said Jonathan, as soon as the restaurant doors had closed behind them. '*Zat iss zee operative qwestion. Iss it not so, Kameraden?*' He grinned at Frances and Clara. 'Come on. If we hurry, we can be at Pampelonne beach in twenty minutes. Absolutely everybody goes starkers there.'

The two girls had worn their bikinis to the Eden Roc swimming pool the day before, and Jonathan had spent a long and feverish night speculating on what further wonders the thin strips of red and blue gingham might conceal. As a direct result of his *nuit blanche*, the 'Great Pampelonne Plage Nudist Plan' had sprung, fully formed, from the fervid wells of his imagination at around five o'clock that morning. 'Go on. Don't be spoilsports. We might even see a police raid. I've heard that the *flics* come running down the beach with their batons hanging out.'

'Jonathan!' Lisa was going through one of her sporadic prurient phases.

'If the thought of yet another naked body makes you blasé, Lisa, you can stay here and go shrimping with the infants. Frances, you'll come, won't you?'

'If you'd like me too.'

'So will I,' said Clara. 'When you go shrimping, Lisa, do watch out for those beastly rogue oursins. I'm sure they'd love to sink their poisonous spines into those nice, pink, well-cared-for feet of yours.'

'Don't be nasty, Clara. You know I loathe oursins.'

'Come on, children. Don't bicker. We'd better hurry up before the grown-ups tumble out and think up something else for us to do. Lisa, last chance. Are you coming or not?'

'No, J. I told you. You'll just get us all into trouble.'

'All right then. See you later. But if you tell *maman*, I'll personally cover you in treacle and stake you out over that anthill by the *cabanon*. Understood?'

'You wouldn't dare.'

'It'll be weeks before you're found. And you'll be nothing but a skeleton by then. Picked clean of all your flesh. They say that carrion crows always go for the eyeballs first. Remember what happened in *The Four Feathers*?'

'You're disgusting.'

'Well come with us, then, and avoid your miserable fate for yet another year.'

Lisa sighed, allowing her shoulders to rise and fall dramatically. This was what she'd wanted all the time. To be needed. To be the centre of attention for a moment or two. Clara and Frances ignored her at school just because she happened to be younger than them, and in another house. Well here on holiday they were going to have to acknowledge her. She *was* J's sister, after all. And it was utterly obvious to everyone that they both had crushes on him. 'I will then. But I won't take my clothes off. I had enough of that on Levant, with you and Daddy. And I hated it.'

'Nobody's asking you to. We don't all want to be traumatised.'

'Ha, ha. Very funny.'

They climbed onto their bicycles.

'Come on then,' said Jonathan. 'Last one to arrive at the beach has to hide all the bikes.'

* * *

Clara, resplendent once again in her red gingham bikini, was pointing at a naked man. She let her mouth fall open in mock horror. 'Look at that one. He's got sunburn on his willy. It's horrible. Like a peeled aubergine.'

'Clara!' Lisa was genuinely shocked. 'He'll see us looking at him. You heard what *maman* said.'

'*Vous*! *Les enfants*! *Allez-vous en*.' A woman with pendulous breasts and three layers of stomach was levering herself up from her sun-lounger.

'Oh my God,' said Jonathan. 'It's a jellyfish.'

'*Méduse*! *Méduse*!' shouted Clara.

'Clara. Shh. Please.' Lisa was squirming with embarrassment.

The woman's husband hoisted himself up beside her. They stood side by side on the warm sand, rocking gently.

'Look. Another one's emerged.' Jonathan circled his fingers in front of his eyes like binoculars. 'God! He's so gross, you can't even see his winkle.' He put his hands to his mouth and imitated the sound of a megaphone. '*Nous allons appeller la police. Vous êtes tous des débauchés*.'

Frances took his arm. 'Please, J. Let's go. It's no longer funny.'

Her pleading had the usual calming effect on him. 'All right.' He touched her fingers lightly with his. His face abruptly changed expression. 'Everybody! I know of the perfect place. It's not far up the beach.' He broke away from them and sprinted to the water's edge. He turned and began jogging backwards along the line of the surf, his heels cutting wedges into the wet sand. Clara, without bothering to check whether the others were coming or not, followed immediately behind him.

Frances hesitated for a moment, frowning, then abruptly changed her mind about not joining them. 'Come on, Lisa. You can't stay here alone. We'd better go with them.'

'Where to?'

'It's somewhere Jonathan knows.'

Lisa shook her head doubtfully. 'I know all about Jonathan's places. I told you he's going to get us into trouble. Don't say I didn't warn you.'

'No he's not. He's very careful. Really.'

'You *would* say that.'

Clara caught up with Jonathan and began running beside him. She was very conscious of her breasts jigging up and down. She wondered what Jonathan thought of them. 'So where's this place you're taking us to?'

'Just around the corner. We can strip off there and no one will be able to see us.'

'Strip off?'

'Of course. This *is* a nudist beach. Don't tell me you're scared?'

'Scared? What do you think?'

'I think you're scared.'

'You'll see.'

Jonathan came to a bank of seagrass and vaulted over it. He rolled three or four times full-length, then came to rest in a dell, totally sheltered from prying eyes. He sat up, covered in sand. 'See. I found it years ago. Before the beach turned naturist. I used to imagine bombarding all the bathers from here. I bet it was where the Krauts placed their machine-guns during the war.'

Frances and Lisa had caught up with them. The three girls stood silently at the top of the dune, watching him. He craned his neck to get a better angle of vision against the sun. It was hard to tell which one of them had the bigger breasts. Except for Lisa, of course. She had fried eggs.

'Clara says she's going to strip.'

'I bet she won't,' said Lisa. 'She's just winding you up, J. Can't you see?'

Clara dug Lisa in the ribs and took a step forward. 'What about you, then? You're a boy. And you've been going to that horrible nudist island ever since you were little. You should do it first.'

Jonathan swallowed. He stood up and brushed himself off. 'All right then. I will. Frances?'

Frances shaded her eyes. She was feeling curiously light-headed. 'I'll undress if everybody else does.'

'Lisa?'

Lisa turned her face to the sea. 'I said I wouldn't outside the restaurant, and nothing's changed since then. I'm just not going to. That's all.'

'Then you don't count.' Jonathan looped both fingers in the waistband of his swimming trunks. 'Ready?'

'Are you sure no one can see us?' said Frances. She glanced uneasily down the beach.

'Don't worry. Nobody comes this far up. They all want to be near the bars. And if the police come, we'll see them from miles off.' Anticipation was burning a hole in the pit of his stomach. 'So. On the count of three. Okay? Ready... Steady... Go!' He slid his swimming trunks down his legs and stepped out of them. He looked up. Frances had begun to take off her bra. There was the sudden flash of a nipple beneath the wiring of her bikini top.

Clara burst out laughing. Jonathan looked across at her angrily. She was staring at him and pointing. He looked down. Oh hell! Clutching himself in both hands, he vaulted across the tussock of seagrass. He flattened himself, red-faced, on the far side of the dune.

'What are you doing over there, Jonathan?' It was Clara's voice. It *had* to be. 'We're all standing here nude. Except Lisa, of course.' Clara murmured something under her breath, but Jonathan couldn't catch it. There was the sound of concealed giggling. 'Why are you hiding, Jonathan? You're not scared, are you? We're only girls, after all. Naked, pubescent, glorious girls.'

Jonathan's cheeks were burning. He felt both aroused and ashamed at the same time. He tried to think of something neutral. Something matter-of-fact to quieten the throbbing between his legs. His bicycle for instance. Or the new *mobylette* Jean and Uncle Piers might buy him. He'd put Frances on the back and they'd go up into the hills. Around Grimaud. They could take a picnic with them. She might even let him kiss her breasts. Damn! There he went again. He twisted his head around. Frances, Clara and Lisa were standing above him, their bikinis firmly in place. He felt the sudden, swooping fall of a forever-lost opportunity.

'Do you think we're blocking his sun, girls? Perhaps he's trying to tan his bottom. It *is* rather white, compared to the rest of him.'

'Go to hell, Clara.'

Clara stuck out one hip, tantalisingly. 'Well, J, us girls are going back to the bikes now. We don't want to get into any more trouble with your parents. You just go ahead and tan yourself to your heart's content. But don't worry. We're taking these horrid old things with us. You won't be needing them now, will you?' She dangled his trunks in her hand.

'No you're not.'

'Yes we are. You just try and stop us.' She darted past him, heeling a spray of sand into his face, and sprinted up the beach.

Jonathan lurched to his feet. Clara had a ten-foot head start on him. God, but the little hell-cat could run fast. 'Give me back my trunks. Clara! Come on. Stop it. This is silly.'

'Save your breath, dopey. You'll be needing it if you want to catch me.'

'Damn!' Jonathan set off in pursuit. He hardly dared look down to see if his erection had subsided. This was rapidly turning into one of the worst days of his life. All he needed now was for *maman* to see him. Or for the *flics* to come. That would make it just perfect.

He increased his pace, his chest expanding with the strain of his breathing. He was starting to catch up. He could see Clara's furiously pumping buttocks beneath the thin cloth of her bikini. He'd get the little bitch. He really would. And when he did, he'd whack her a smart one across the rump. That'd serve her right.

Clara was starting to tire. Jonathan closed the last few yards between them, then made his tackle. He tapped her flying ankle with one hand and caught her around the thighs with the other, just as Mr Trevor had shown him time and again during scrum practice. Clara hit the ground, the breath exploding out of her. Jonathan landed with his full weight on top of her. 'Now, bloody well give me my trunks!'

Clara jerked her knee instinctively between his legs, then as suddenly stopped. Jonathan squatted on top of her, pinning her upper arms with his knees. She looked up at him, sand caking her face and hair, nostrils flaring with the effort of running so far. 'Kiss me,' she said. 'Kiss me hard. Before Frances comes. Go on. Do it.' She wet her lips with the tip of her tongue in anticipation.

Jonathan slowly became aware, through the hot, almost random desire of his breathing, of where he was and what he was doing. He was relishing the unfamiliar pleasure of physically dominating a female – even a female as terminally annoying as Clara. At the same time he felt frustration at his inability to control the undiscerning rush of his sexual urges. He wanted to rip off Clara's bikini top and sink his teeth into her nipples. He wanted to tear off her pants and take her right there on the beach. In front of everyone.

He stood up and slipped on his swimming trunks. 'Not tonight, Joséphine.' His attempt at a Peter Sellers voice was a failure. Clara kicked out at him, missing his ankle by an inch. 'Touchy. Touchy.' He glanced back over his shoulder. Frances and Lisa were approaching at a snail's pace across the dunes, gossiping. They hadn't seen him, then. He hadn't blown it after all. 'I'm going for a swim.'

With a brief backward glance at the girls he sprinted to the water's edge and executed a flat racing dive into the sea. He caught the wave perfectly and reappeared in a surge of spray, flashing his wet hair to right and left.

After a few more show-off rolls he emerged from the water, self-consciously tensing his stomach muscles. He fervently hoped that both Frances and Clara were watching him.

Fourteen

Piers Godolphin watched as Geneviève negotiated her way around the neighbouring tables, and, with a brief word to Monsieur Dutron, made her way out towards the *vestiare*. Only when she had passed completely through the swing-doors did he turn back towards his host. 'A refined and beautiful woman. You are luckier than you deserve to be, Charles.'

'Thank you for that.'

'And she's given you two magnificent children.'

Charles cocked an eyebrow at him, then readjusted his eye-patch. 'Piers. I know you too well. Get to the bloody point.'

Piers fixed a Sullivan Powell into its ivory holder, and Jean reached across and lit it for him. Piers briefly cupped his hand. '*Merci, mon chéri.*' He inhaled deeply and turned back, trickling smoke. 'Very well then.' He tapped his cigarette against the rim of the ashtray, as if calling for everyone's attention. 'You realise, of course, Charles, that Jonathan has a roaring crush on the eldest of the Champion girls? And that her younger sister is sick to her jealous little heart thinking about it?'

Charles snorted. He leaned forward and stubbed out the remnants of his cigar.

'There'll be blood on the sand before the holidays are over, you mark my words. Whether virgin or otherwise is a moot point.' Piers took a sip of his coffee, then patted his mouth dry with his napkin. 'It was this fact, and this fact alone, which prompted my generous and, I felt, under-appreciated offer of the *mobylette*. It had occurred to me that it might serve to split the opposing parties into two, shall we say, rather more compatible camps? We shall call them, for the sake of simplicity, the Lesbian and the Cretan.'

Charles signalled to the waiter. He felt around for his money-clip. 'Piers, it constantly astonishes me how you can deduce so much from so little. It's almost become an art form with you. What brought on this recent revelation?'

'It all depends on what you're looking for. Buggers like Jean and I are always on the lookout for other buggers. Like Gagool, we *patapoufs* can sniff each other out at fifty yards. If you'll allow me the pun.'

'The point, Piers, the point.'

'Ah, the point.' Piers glanced dramatically at Jean, then sighed. 'Well you'll be glad to know that your only son, Jonathan, is a dyed-in-the-wool heterosexual. As is his exquisite paramour.' He flicked the ash from the tip of his cigarette with an errant gesture. 'Her sister, on the other hand,' he glanced quickly at Jean for support, '*comme-çi, comme-ça*, wouldn't you say so, Jean?' Jean shrugged. Piers tapped the mouthpiece of his ivory holder delicately against his signet ring. His manner had become hesitant.

'Piers, say what you have to say and fucking well be done with it.'

Piers stopped tapping. 'Very well then. I will. But you must promise not to fly off the handle?'

'Piers…' Charles spoke warningly.

'All right, all right.' Piers cleared his throat self-consciously. 'Your daughter Lisa – and here is the climax I've been leading up to so laboriously, my dear Charles – is first-class dyke material. She just doesn't know it yet.'

Charles flopped heavily back in his chair. He steepled his fingers and placed his thumbs against his mouth, then clicked his teeth with his nails, considering. 'Stuff and bloody nonsense,' he said after a moment. 'She's not even fifteen yet, Piers. So I'm going to give you the benefit of the doubt and assume that you're seeing the world through your customary vermilion-tinted spectacles.'

'I can assure you I'm not. Jean and I have been watching her for days and there is not the slightest doubt about the matter at all. Jean told me you'd react this way, but I refused to believe him. I was, of course, labouring under the perilous delusion that you were an adult.'

Charles sat up abruptly. 'I am an adult. And if it's so, it's so. I've nothing in the least against lesbians. But I guarantee you're wrong.'

'Ignorance is its own privilege.' Piers allowed his gaze to wander languidly over the neighbouring tables.

Charles glared across at Piers as if about to spear him in the cheek with a fork. 'So why, may I ask, have you chosen this particular moment to make your dubious little revelation?'

Piers leaned towards him. 'We've known each other intimately for over thirty years, my darling boy, and I love you dearly, but tact and discretion are not your strongest points. Geneviève, as I'm sure you'll agree, is quite incapable of acknowledging, let alone understanding, a Sapphic daughter. You, on the other hand, are.' He reclined backwards in his chair. 'Lisa is my god-daughter, Charles, as well as being my great-niece. And I'm feeling particularly Delphic today. By telling you this now, I'm doing her a service for which she'll thank me her entire life through. I simply don't want either you or Geneviève to force her, through heterosexual ignorance, into a way of life for which she may be unsuited.'

'Bloody hell, Piers!' Charles fanned out some bills for the waiter, then doled out a handful of coins on the top. The waiter bowed, and moved away. Charles replaced the money-clip in his pocket. He looked curiously deflated. 'Are you sure?'

'Positive.' Piers stood up to his full height of six-foot four, and threw out his arms majestically. 'And here is Geneviève, back again from the Stygian depths. Darling, we were just talking about you.'

'Kindly, I trust.'

'Always.' He lingered an inch above her outstretched hand. 'Now Jean and I must leave. We have a *vernissage* to attend. And Barou so hates people turning up late to his little affairs. *Adieu, mes enfants.*' He kissed Charles on both cheeks. 'Be good, Charles. And remember what I told you. Uncle Piers is watching.'

'Why do you always tease Jonathan like that?' Lisa was seated on the edge of the Canteloube swimming pool, paddling her feet.

'Like what?' Clara checked around, then undid her bra at the back. She eased herself into a more comfortable position. 'Oil, maestro, please.'

Lisa sprang up and went to fetch the *Piz Buin*. 'All over, or just on the back?'

'All over.'

Lisa began rubbing in the oil. Clara had flawless skin, and breasts to kill for. She looked down at her own. What had Jonathan called them? *Oeufs au plat.* Fried eggs. It was too late, she supposed, to hope that they would grow any bigger. She was going to be fifteen, after all, in a few days. Three shadowy days after Jonathan's own birthday, to be exact. It would have happened by now, if it were going to happen.

'Is anyone watching? Your lecherous old father, for instance.'

Lisa checked around. 'No.'

'Then you can do me on the front.' Clara turned over. 'Deeply in, please. I want to get so brown this summer that the other girls at school just die from jealousy.' She closed her eyes.

Lisa swallowed. She started on Clara's shoulders. 'You *are* pretty, Clara.'

'I know I am.'

'Is that why you tease Jonathan? To get him to notice you?'

Clara opened her eyes. 'Oh, he notices me all right. It's just that he's got this bestial attitude that he has to be true to Frances. It makes me sick.' She closed her eyes again. 'You can do my tits, too. They're not going to bite you.'

'Are you sure?'

'Oh for goodness sake.'

Lisa started rubbing the oil very lightly over Clara's breasts.

'Mmm. That's nice. I'm going to keep my eyes closed and imagine you're Jonathan. Do you mind?'

Lisa could hardly speak. She continued massaging in the oil. Some of it trickled down Clara's tummy and lodged in her belly button.

'Do you masturbate?'

'What?'

'You heard me, Lisa.'

'No. Of course not. You know what Mrs Kapell said to us.'

'Do you at least know how to?' Clara opened her eyes. 'Is anybody around?'

'No. I've already said no.'

'Give me your hand then. Go on. Don't be shy. Here. That's it. Now rub my tits with oil at the same time. Yes. You've got it. Go on. Just like that.'

Lisa could feel her face burning with shame. At the same time she felt almost painfully aroused.

'Don't stop. Don't stop.' Clara abruptly groaned and turned over onto her stomach. She thrust a hand beneath her belly and made a few spasmodic movements with her hips. Lisa sat back on her haunches, her eyes wide with shock. Clara sighed contentedly, stretching herself like a leopard. She glanced back at Lisa over her shoulder. 'Not bad for a first time, I suppose. Now you'll know exactly what to do. With boys it's a bit different, of course. But you'll find that out for yourself soon enough. Now I'm going to sleep. Be sure to wake me up in twenty minutes, will you? I don't want to burn.'

Frances dropped the empty coke bottle into her bag and reached across for Jonathan's hand. They were returning from an unsatisfactory visit to the beach café. 'Jonathan, please don't snap at me when I tell you this. But Clara fancies you like mad. You do know that, don't you?'

'No. I don't.'

Frances dropped his hand. 'Come on, J. You must have noticed? She's always running after you and making eyes at you and flirting.'

'Is she?'

'She even boasts about it at school. How she's going to take you away from me.'

They paused outside the Canteloube gates. The faded blue of a *Byrrh* sign was still visible on the outside wall – Charles had refused to have it painted over, saying it reminded him of a Marcel Pagnol film. Frances leaned against the blue of the sign, her arms behind her back, resting on her shoulder-blades, watching him. Jonathan walked towards her, smiling. He leaned forward and kissed her lightly on the breastbone, then on each bare shoulder.

'Do you like her? I mean, do you find her attractive?'

Jonathan straightened up. Why was Frances asking him all these questions? Did she want him to fancy Clara or something? Or was she just trawling for compliments, like girls did? Either way, it was irritating. 'Of course she's attractive. But a bit obvious too.'

'Like me?'

'I don't know what you mean.' He suddenly clicked. 'Oh, for God's sake. Of course not like you.' Angry with himself, he pushed on through the gates. Why was he talking like this? He loved Frances. His heart stopped every time she came into the room. Why couldn't he simply tell her and have done with it? 'Of course you're not obvious. Not obvious at all.' His tone was all wrong. He was feeling bewildered. Things used to be easier, surely? He couldn't think what had changed – but everything, all of a sudden, seemed so bloody complicated. He made a conscious effort to soften his voice. 'Fran, you're nothing like Clara. I promise.'

She followed him through the gates. They took the path down towards the swimming pool. She felt a sudden, panicky urge to placate him. She hated it when he was cold towards her. It was like dying. 'J. If you get the *mobylette* tomorrow, for your birthday, will you drive me up into the hills? We could take a picnic with us. I really want to see the lavender fields before they tear them all out.'

'Why would they do that?'

She hurried to catch up. 'Because they're using chemicals to make the perfume now. Fragonard in Grasse don't need real lavender any more. Jean told me so. In a few years there won't be any lavender fields left at all.'

He stopped and turned towards her. 'If I take you to see the lavender fields, will you think about what I said? What I asked you?' Frances hesitated, then walked on ahead of him. 'I'd have to know, you see? I'd have to buy some of those things.'

She turned quickly towards him. 'Don't talk like that, J. I hate it when you talk like that. It's horrible. When we do make love, I want it to come naturally. Not be thought out beforehand.' She spun on her heel, took a few steps, then stopped and looked back. 'Sometimes you're not very romantic.'

Without realising it they had reached the pool. Clara turned over lazily at the sound of their voices. 'Who's not very romantic? Not Jonathan, surely?' She sat up and began to fasten her top. 'Lisa, did you hear that? Did you know your brother's not very romantic?'

Lisa slid into the pool. She began a slow breast-stroke.

Frances set down her bag and straightened one of the deck-chairs. 'Clara, it doesn't take all day to fasten your bikini.'

Clara grinned mockingly. 'I know, I know. It's just that I always have such trouble finding the catch at the back. Jonathan, perhaps you could help me?'

'Sorry, Clara.' Jonathan ducked into the changing room.

'Lisa, then.' Clara sat up and turned towards the pool. 'Lisa, do this up for me, will you? I can't reach.'

'Do it up yourself. You've always managed before.' Lisa ducked under the water and began swimming along the bottom.

'I'll do it.' Frances walked over to where Clara was sitting and knelt down behind her. She yanked the two halves of the material together, then let them slacken again.

'Ouch!'

'Sorry.' She leaned forward and whispered in Clara's ear. 'Clara, if you carry on the way you're going, I'll put acid in your shampoo.' Clara jerked around. Jonathan was still out of earshot, and Lisa had submerged herself once again in the pool. 'Believe me, Clara. I'm serious. There are dozens of boys in St Tropez for you to choose from. And Jonathan's mine. He doesn't want you. So don't tease him all the time, and flirt with him, and try to wind him up.'

Clara pulled herself free. She massaged her breasts, grimacing. 'Worried, are we?'

'Not worried. Just determined.'

Clara turned to her. 'So. You'd put acid in my shampoo? How dramatic. What sort of acid? Citric?' She laughed. 'God, Frances, I know you too well. You couldn't hurt a fly. You're a wet at school, and you're a wet here. And you've got about as much sex-appeal as a crested newt.' She stood up and ran her hands slowly down her flanks, spreading the excess oil over her belly. 'That's why you're scared about Jonathan, isn't it? He wants more than you're prepared to give him.'

Frances looked away, angrily.

Clara flicked the oil off her fingers. 'Well you're damned right to be scared. It's true. I do fancy him. And I'm going to offer myself to him.' She dried her hands on her towel, then threw it in Frances's lap. 'In fact, I'm fed up to the very back teeth with being a virgin. So put that in your pie dish and eat it.'

Fifteen

Lisa smoothed the thin cotton bedspread beneath her and lay down. It was three o'clock. The hottest part of the afternoon. Outside her window *grillons* were sawing. The scent of wild thyme wafted through her bedroom on billows of warm air.

Somewhere inside the house her father was playing Schubert's *Winterreise* on the gramophone – Hans Hotter and Gerald Moore were just starting on *Gute Nacht*. Funny music for papa to choose in the middle of a sweltering hot summer's day.

Lisa lay back, listening. Her German was rather good. She was specialising in it at school – though all her teachers insisted she was perverse not to have chosen French. She began to translate. It was hard at first, but she felt she'd got the hang of it by verse three. '*Why should I stay longer, until I am driven away? Only stray dogs howl in front of their master's house. Love loves to wander from one to another – God made us so. Love loves to wander. Dear love, good night!*'

She turned over, languidly. Was she really in love? At the thought of Clara her heart began to beat so intensely that she was forced to rest a hand against her ribs as if to suspend its motion. Why had Clara forced her to do that thing at the swimming pool? It was animal. Clara was an animal. Mrs Kapell had warned them often enough about the sins of the flesh.

Lisa closed her eyes and took a deep, languorous breath. She allowed her hand to brush lightly across her nipple. God, but she was a bad fibber. She'd lied to Clara, just as she was lying to herself now. Of course she touched herself. Been doing it for nearly a year. And to heck with Mrs Kapell. She'd been doing it ever since India Petersen had shown her how, in the showers, when she'd come in late from games one day. She enjoyed it, just as Clara obviously did. But it was cruel of Clara to pretend it was Jonathan doing it to her. The very thought made her feel sick. She'd seen Jonathan's willy lots of times, but never like that day on the beach. Standing up like a flag-pole. Ugh. The thought of wanting something like that stuck inside you, whatever the other girls said. She dreaded the thought of getting married and having babies.

She stiffened on the bed. In her heart of hearts, of course, she knew perfectly well that Clara was using her. Ever since their first meeting at Penhallow. But she didn't mind. Not really. Not if it meant that Clara paid attention to her.

Recently, Clara had taken to knocking on her door whenever Jonathan didn't notice her. 'Come on, Lisa. Let's go out. The love-birds are at it again. Little Miss Frances Frigid-Pants is busy spinning her web. I need some air.' And the sad thing was, she was always so pathetically ready to go. To be near Clara. Good old Lisa. Always second in line. Always playing second fiddle. The eternal bridesmaid, never the bride.

The record ended abruptly. Lisa sat up. She suddenly knew, with a horrifying certainty, that if she ever told Clara how she really felt about her, her life would end. She could just imagine all the nightmarish comments at school. 'Audley's got a pash on! Audley's got a pash on!' Her stomach lurched at the thought of it. Perhaps if a boy really kissed her, kissed her properly, something magical would happen and she'd forget all about Clara? But boys just didn't seem to notice her. And she certainly wasn't going to make a special effort to get their attention. That was *too* yucky a thought.

Now Daddy was playing Beethoven's *Pathétique* sonata. That was better. She began to calm down a little. Perhaps, with time, she could bring Clara around to her way of thinking? Make her see that she, too, was worthy of being liked – that she wasn't just the little swot everyone thought she was. Maybe if she allowed her devotion to show, did anything Clara asked of her, then, one day perhaps, Clara might even let her kiss her? If that happened, she couldn't very well close her eyes and pretend that it was Jonathan.

Lisa was ready now. She snuggled over onto her tummy, holding onto the image. Closing her eyes, she eased her hand under her belly and thrust her head deep into the pillows, just as Clara had done at the swimming pool.

She began the familiar mantra, the one that had accompanied her on so many lonely nights. *Clara. You bitch. I hate you. Clara. Clara. I love you. Clara.*

'Come on, Fran, let's go over to Da Lolo.' Jonathan was chaining their two bicycles to a plane tree outside the Hotel de Ville. On the terrace of the café, three waiters, in bright red trousers, were performing an impromptu cabaret, twirling laden trays around their heads to cheers from the onlookers.

'Can you afford it, J?'

'I've still got twenty francs left over from the fifty Piers gave me the other day. We could have a coke each. And maybe a *beignet aux pommes* between us.'

'We could buy the *beignets* later. At the booth.'

'Yes, Fran, and we could buy our cokes there too, and save lots and lots of money. But then we wouldn't have been to Da Lolo, would we?'

Frances turned quickly away.

Jonathan straightened up beside her, his hands at his sides, cursing himself. Why was he snapping at her all the time recently? It was his birthday tomorrow. He was out with Frances. Ten minutes ago they'd stopped at the edge of the woods, on the way into town, and she'd let him kiss her breasts and touch her a little through her pants. Things were going swimmingly. Yet here he was, feeling wretched. It was absurd. 'I'm sorry, Fran.' He put his hands on her shoulders. She shook her shoulders free and started across the square. 'Come on. *I'm sorry.*' The last thing in the world he wanted to do was to visit Da Lolo now. 'Fran. Look. Let's do what you suggested. We'll get cokes and *beignets* at the booth, then we can go and sit by the harbour and watch the world go by. Okay?'

Frances stopped. She turned towards him. There were unfamiliar anxiety lines between her eyes. 'I know I'm being boring, J. I know Clara would leap at going to Da Lolo – or anywhere for that matter, so long as it was with you. Don't you think I want to make you happy? Make you pleased with me?' She moved a few paces closer. 'I love you so badly sometimes, it hurts. It literally hurts me. Here.' She pressed the pads of her fingers violently against her breast.

'Frances. People are watching.'

'I don't care.' She refused to look around. 'I don't care what people think. And I don't care about Clara, either, and all her snide little suggestions, and her sex, and her…' She stopped abruptly, closing her eyes. 'Oh God, what am I saying. One day you're going to hate me, and I'll have brought it on myself.'

He took a hesitant step towards her. 'Fran, you know I'll never hate you. That's insane.' He was searching for the right words – words that would break through the wall that seemed to have sprung up so bewilderingly between them. 'I'm not very good at saying things. You know that.' His voice fell away.

She opened her eyes and looked at him, utterly vulnerable.

He had a sudden flashback to that day in the tree house, seven years before, when she'd faced him in much the same way. Waiting. Trusting him. For some reason beyond his capacity for understanding they now found themselves on the edge of the very same precipice – but this time Frances was asking *him* for help. He knew that he mustn't let her down. It was inconceivable. Before he had time to exert any control over his words, he heard himself saying, 'I love you, Fran. I really do. More than anything else on earth. I always mean to say it, and then I can't get it out. Or the moment goes. Or I feel silly.'

Frances thrust her fingers against his lips. 'Shhh.' Her eyes brimmed with tears. They began to flow, unchecked, down her cheeks.

Jonathan felt a passionate rush of emotion overwhelm him. 'You're more precious to me than life itself, Fran. If anything ever happened to you, I'd die. I'd kill myself. I really would. That's how much I love you.' The words sounded strange to his ears, as if someone outside himself were saying them. His feelings had internalised themselves to such an extent that his skin felt almost numb with their weight. When he attempted to move towards her, he stumbled, and she had to steady him.

'Are you sure, J? Really sure? I've wanted you to say it for so long I can't quite trust myself to believe it.'

'I couldn't before, Fran. I couldn't.' He felt himself choking. 'I don't know why.'

'It's all right.' She drew him inside her arms, sensing the strength return to him. 'Kiss me on my forehead. The way you used to. Lots of little closed-mouth kisses.'

He laughed, and kissed her. 'Do you know why I did it like that?'

'Why?'

'Because it's the way my father used to kiss me goodnight. It made me feel cosy. I wanted you to feel the same.'

She smiled up at him. 'I did. That's just the feeling I always had when you did it. Cosy. As if nothing could ever hurt me while you were there.'

'Did you really feel that?'

'As if you would protect me. Yes.'

He shook his head at her in wonder. 'That's funny. I never thought someone would ever feel that way about me.'

'That's because you're not a girl, and you don't feel as we do.' She hesitated, weighing him up. 'That's why you've always got to go with your instincts, J. All through your life. As you did just now. You'll never go wrong then, I promise you. I don't know how I know it, but I do.'

He looked at her strangely. 'I don't understand you sometimes, Fran. You're so soft. And yet there's something strong about you at the same time.' He shook his head. 'I feel strong – physically. But then, when it comes to saying things, I feel incredibly weak. As if I don't know what to do. As if I'm floating outside myself, in a sealed chamber, somewhere far up in space, and I can't get out.'

She reached out and caressed his cheek. 'When that happens you must think of me.'

'I don't understand.'

She held his face between her hands. 'Because I'm part of you, J. Part of you.' She squeezed him even tighter. 'I've known it ever since we first met.' She smoothed his hair and stepped backwards. 'Next time, when you think you're all alone in that chamber, sealed up, drifting in outer space, I'll be with you. Then we can break free, both of us, and float off like comets beyond the stars.'

'Beyond the stars?'

'Yes. You're not scared, are you?'

'Not any more.'

'And you'll protect me?'

'Always.'

She looped her arm through his, smiling. With a shy motion, she buried her face in his shoulder, breathing him in. Then she looked up at him again, consciously flirting. 'Da Lolo?'

He hesitated for a moment, not quite sure of how to respond. Then he burst out laughing, and kissed her once again. 'Da Lolo.'

Sixteen

Clara threw herself into the chair opposite Jonathan. She was wearing a white cotton tennis skirt with pink piping and matching panties, set off by a brand new emerald green Lacoste top. She thought she looked very tasty. If she were a man, she decided, she'd fancy herself something rotten.

She smoothed the skirt down self-consciously over her thighs. When she was certain of Jonathan's undivided attention, she flashed him a mischievous smile. 'Happy birthday, Jo-Jo. Many happy returns of the day. So what do you want for your present?'

'Come on, Clara. You don't have to give me anything.'

'Oh, but I do, J.' Clara's heart was beating uncomfortably fast. Behind her confident exterior, she wasn't a hundred per cent sure of the wisdom of what she intended to do, nor of how Jonathan would respond when she did it. The last thing she wanted was for him to end up hating her. 'I *am* your second favourite cousin after all.' She smoothed back her hair, unconsciously sniffing her fingers just as she'd done when she was a child. 'How about one of those great big blow-up dolls, for instance? The ones they advertise in the back of that girlie magazine you have hidden under your mattress?'

'Ha bloody ha.' Despite valiant efforts to the contrary, Jonathan could feel himself beginning to blush. 'And what were you doing looking under my mattress? Searching for fleas?'

Clara gave a fake grin. 'Actually, it was your mother who discovered it, not me.'

Jonathan froze. For a moment he found it hard to swallow. Then relief bloomed. 'Sorry, Clara. No dice. *Maman* never makes my bed. Only I do. Or Antonia. So it had to be you. What were you doing? Sniffing my sheets?'

What a bloody fool he'd been. He'd bought the *Mayfair* three days before, at the *Maison de la Presse* in the old port, out of misguided protest, sheer frustration, and just the slightest hint of righteous pique at Frances's sexual recalcitrance, with a vague view to letting her stumble across it – accidentally on purpose, of course – in the forlorn hope that she might take the hint and let him make love to her.

It had taken him more than an hour to build up the courage to even go inside and take it down from the top shelf. He'd sandwiched the magazine between copies of *Télé Sept Jours* and *Le Monde Merveilleux Des Animaux*. At the last moment, just before paying, he'd come near to losing his nerve. The middle-aged peroxide-blonde wife of the owner had unaccountably emerged from the back of the shop to take over from her husband at the counter. Jonathan had been third in line at the time, with another woman standing behind him. He'd looked wildly around for a possible escape route, but hadn't dared take it in case they thought he was shoplifting.

When it had finally come to his turn he'd flipped the magazines with false nonchalance onto the counter. In agonisingly slow motion, the woman had leafed through each magazine, noting the prices. He'd managed a sickly grin when she came to the *Mayfair*. She'd dropped it back on top of the pile, in full view of the other customers, as if the magazine had been coated in a thin film of glutinous grease.

'*Vingt-trois francs cinquante, Monsieur.*'

He'd scrabbled in his pockets for Piers's fifty-franc note. When she'd at last deigned to hand him the magazines, he'd hurried for the entrance like a thief escaping the scene of his crime.

'*Monsieur! Monsieur! Je vous dois encore vingt-six francs cinquante.*'

That had been the worst moment. He'd been forced to walk the gauntlet of the entire length of the shop and back to the counter to fetch his change. The woman who'd been in the line behind him had seemed to clutch her infant daughter even tighter to her side as he approached. He could just imagine what was going through her mind. Pervert, she'd be thinking to herself – young pervert.

He'd accepted his change with another sickly smile, then eased his way back past the outraged woman and her child. As he'd left, a flurry of passionate conversation had broken out behind him. It wasn't easy sometimes, being a man.

He gave Clara a caustic grin, belying his true confusion. 'We call them flog-mags at school. Everyone buys them. They're airbrushed, of course. But at least they're more realistic than *Health & Efficiency*. I hope you put it back when you were finished with it?'

Now Clara was blushing. Victory! Snatched from the very jaws of defeat. Jonathan decided that he'd twist the knife in a little further, while he had the chance. 'If I'd known you fancied women when I bought it, Clara, I'd have offered it to you myself. You must tell me when you want to borrow it again.'

All the colour drained from Clara's face. 'So you *did* see.'

'See what?' said Jonathan, with a mock innocent tone. He had no idea what she was talking about.

'Nothing.'

'Go on, Clara. What did I see?'

'Nothing, J. I was only joking.'

'Oh. Do you mean at the swimming pool?' It was a shot in the dark. But he'd picked up something there, the other day, when he and Frances had emerged from the woods, and it was the only thing he could think of to say on the spur of the moment. He'd never had Clara so much on the defensive before, and he wanted to enjoy the feeling. She was concealing something from him. He knew it. But what?

Clara blanched. 'Did Frances see?'

Jonathan pretended to hesitate. What was going on? What had Clara been doing? 'I don't think so. No.'

'Are you going to tell her?'

This was better than he'd hoped. This was the birthday present to end all birthday presents! He pretended to consider. He had a sudden, overwhelming urge to burst out laughing. 'That all depends.'

'Depends? Depends on what?' Clara was licking her dried-out lips.

'Make me an offer.'

Clara closed her eyes. She appeared to Jonathan to be deep in thought. Actually, she was jubilant. When she opened her eyes again, she knew exactly what to say. This was even better than she'd hoped. Jonathan was propositioning *her*, rather than the other way around. Now she had him. One slip, one obvious slip, and Frances would never speak to him again. Guaranteed. 'Do you want to do the same thing to me? The same thing Lisa did?'

Lisa? What on earth was she talking about? What had she let Lisa do? This was mystifying. But he didn't want to let it go yet. He'd have to play this very carefully indeed if he didn't want his canny little fish to wriggle off the hook. 'Maybe.'

'Maybe?'

'Perhaps I want more than that.'

Clara could feel her stomach tightening. 'How much more?'

Light was slowly beginning to penetrate Jonathan's darkness. Bloody hell! He could scarcely believe it. Lisa? Sexless old Lisa with *Clara*? God, this one was weird. What the hell had they been doing? What could they have been doing together? 'Everything. I want everything.'

Clara stood up abruptly. 'When?'

Jonathan looked at her legs. Her skirt had hitched up over one thigh. Her breasts jutted against the thin fabric of her tennis shirt. He could just make out the imprint of her nipples behind the material. This was crazy. Was Clara actually offering herself to him? Jesus Christ! He felt almost criminally aroused. What was he going to do now? He couldn't go through with it, however much he might be tempted. Clara would have him over a barrel.

'Do you want to see my panties?'

He swallowed. What should he do? Clara slowly raised her skirt and stood looking at him. His eyes were so wide open, they hurt. What if Frances walked in on them? She'd never speak to him again.

'Shall I turn around?'

Jonathan couldn't trust himself to speak. Clara pivoted slowly on her toes and lifted up her skirt at the back. Jonathan clamped a hand over his crotch. Clara let her skirt fall back and turned to face him, smirking. 'Was that nice? I suppose you want more?' She could feel the saliva building up at the back of her mouth.

Jonathan breathed out, shakily.

'The cat got your tongue?' She moved towards him, spread her legs either side of his, put her hands on the back of his chair and leaned towards him. 'Do you want to feel my tits?'

There was the sound of approaching footsteps on the tiles outside. Jonathan leaped to his feet, pushing Clara roughly out of the way. He sprinted for the French windows, manhandled them open, and plunged out into the garden.

He may have been imagining it, but he could have sworn he heard the echo of Clara's laconic laughter as he ran frantically down through the vines.

The truck arrived with his new *mobylette* just as lunch was ending. The entire company stood in an awkward line as it was wheeled down the ramp, some still holding their napkins.

'Gosh, Jonathan. It's bigger than I thought.' That was Clara.

Jonathan closed his eyes. He could feel the humiliation eating into him. Sooner or later Clara was bound to say something utterly disastrous. She wouldn't be Clara if she didn't. He felt powerless. A moral coward. One thing was certain – he could never give away the secret of what she'd done with Lisa. *Maman,* if she ever heard about it, would have a coronary. Then Clara and Frances would be banned from visiting them, Lisa would be an outcast, and that would be that.

No. He'd sold his soul to the devil, that's what it came down to. He ought to have stopped Clara early on, before things got out of hand. Now that she'd convinced herself he was after her, she'd never let go. He just knew it. He looked across at Frances. She met his eyes with a happy smile. Oh God.

'Well, Jonathan, what do you say?'

'I think it's great, Dad.'

'You'd better phone Piers and Jean this evening and thank them.'

'I will, Dad, I promise.'

After shaking hands with the van driver, Jonathan went over to stand by his new machine. It was pale blue, and had a silver badge on the petrol tank.

'J'ai fait le plein. Monsieur Godo...uh...le grand monsieur. Avec son ami. Il m'a demandé de le faire.'

Charles gave the man a tip. 'Jonathan, don't just stand there. You can take the thing for a spin if you wish. We'll consider your birthday lunch finished, as of this moment.'

'Thanks, Dad.'

He should have been happy, but he felt utterly wretched. He looked around. The eyes of the entire household were on him. Even Antonia had come out to watch. Sighing, he straddled the *mobylette,* easing it up on its plinth. He started to cycle, holding the throttle forward. The engine turned over, then sparked. He locked the brakes and kicked back the plinth. The engine chugged satisfactorily. 'Frances? Do you want to come with me?'

'You'd better try it alone first. You can come back and fetch me later. When you've got the hang of it.'

Relief washed over him. 'OK. I won't be long.' He raised one hand and accelerated up the drive, slipping and sliding on the gravel.

As he approached the corner, he glanced back over his shoulder. Everyone was going inside. The show was finally over.

He stopped on the far side of the front gates and got off the *mobylette*. He cut the fuel switch and waited as the engine stuttered out. Even the cicadas had ceased their strumming.

He stood forlornly in the utter silence, looking down the drive towards the house. The pregnant, oily smell of the two-stroke mixture wafted past him unnoticed.

Seventeen

The mountains of the Massif des Maures were so immeasurably ancient that they had shed much of their original glory and eroded back into hills. In the villages, on a hot summer's day, the shutters remained tightly sealed against the reflected sun, just as they had been for generations past. The blank houses, four storeys high, still echoed with the voices of schoolchildren and the distant rush of the village fountains.

Jonathan raced his *mobylette* through the empty streets of Grimaud, enjoying the clatter the machine made against the cold stone of the buildings. It was lunch-time. Everyone was indoors avoiding the heat – digesting, or having their siesta. The deep-shadowed streets belonged to the two of them.

Frances snuggled tightly against him, curving her form to the contours of his body. Jonathan reached back a hand and squeezed her bottom.

'J, stop it, or we'll fall.'

At the steepest part of the hill, the two-stroke engine began to lose some of its tempo. Jonathan was forced to stand up and begin pedalling.

'Shall I get off?'

'No. We'll make it. Hold on.' They approached the flattened summit and the engine began to pick up speed again. Jonathan sat back on the seat. 'Grab on like you were doing before. It's nice.'

They took the D558 out of Grimaud and headed up into the mountains. After the relative darkness of the village, the sunlight hit them with blinding force. The *mobylette* travelled so sedately up the inclined road that they picked up the scent of rosemary and hot pine needles on the swollen currents of air.

'We'll have to forget the lavender fields. With two of us up she'll never make it. Sorry, Fran.'

'I don't mind. This is fun anyway. Where shall we go instead?'

'To *Notre Dame de Miremer*. You can see the sea from there. We'll have our tea up there too.' He glanced backwards, the wind causing his eyes to water. 'What did you bring with you? I'm starving.'

'We've got a thermos of coffee, and some of that pear tart Antonia baked for your birthday lunch. And I nicked a *Salambo à l'Orange* from the bridge tray.'

'Bloody brilliant. Good choice, Fran. Thank goodness I've got a sweet tooth.'

'But you haven't, J.'

'Ah ha!'

Whenever he was alone with Frances, everything appeared so simple. All she had to do was look at him, with those wide-apart eyes of hers, and he felt transported. There was no question then of Clara, or of any other girl. It seemed he had only to summon up the courage to reach forward and he could touch her very essence with his hands.

They hiked up the last part of the track, with Jonathan pushing the *mobylette* and Frances walking beside him, carrying the picnic basket over one shoulder. At some point she'd tied the tails of her blouse together, exposing her bare midriff. Jonathan glanced furtively at her. Her stomach was as flat and smooth as Carrara marble.

Approaching the summit, the view gradually opened out across the tiled roof of the chapel until they could see far beyond the distant villages of Cogolin and La Croix Valmer to the crescent-shaped *Baie de Cavalaire* and to the turquoise-tinted sea beyond.

'Oh J, it's beautiful.'

'*Maman* brought us up here once. I think it was that very same summer we first met. Papa still had the Facel-Véga, anyway. We left it down at the *Oratoire* because it kept bottoming out on the rocks and he was scared of losing the exhaust.' His brow furrowed, then relaxed itself. 'It's a funny thing, but I seem to remember the walk up here as being utter murder – Lisa complaining all the time and me having to carry all the blankets and the cold water. Now it seems so easy.'

'*You* may find it easy. My legs are aching all the way up to the top of my thighs.'

'We may just be able to rectify that. I have healing hands, they tell me.'

'You should be so lucky!'

Jonathan gave her a broad smile. The thought of Fran's buttocks was tantalising. Still savouring the image, he began to cast around for a suitable place to set up the picnic. He could feel an underlying edge of excitement nudging at his subconscious.

'How about beneath that umbrella pine?'

'Okay.' Jonathan began spreading out the blanket.

'Where is everybody, anyway?'

'Frying themselves down on the beach, probably.'

Frances laid out the thermos and the plastic cake box. 'Doesn't this remind you of that picnic we had up in the tree house? When Cook made us the lardy-cakes and you first asked me to marry you?' She blushed. Then her expression abruptly changed. 'And then Clara had to come by and spoil it all.'

'Well she won't come by this time. Unless she can fly, that is.' He shielded his eyes and checked around. 'Nope. No sign of her yet.'

Frances kicked off her shoes and stretched out beside him. She closed her eyes and sighed luxuriously. A gentle, satisfied smile played around the corners of her mouth.

Jonathan squatted nearby. The sudden mention of Clara's name had reminded him of the resolution he'd made earlier that afternoon, standing in the silence left by the cicadas at the Canteloube gates. He swallowed. His throat felt unbearably dry. 'Fran. Promise me you'll keep your eyes closed. I've something important to tell you.'

She pursed her lips. 'All right. I promise. But why do I need to keep my eyes closed? Not that I mind. I'm feeling so good, just at this moment, that you'd better watch out or I'll doze off right in the middle of your speech.'

Jonathan sat back on his heels and gazed across at the chapel. Did he dare? Did he dare tell her about Clara, and his criminal stupidity at leading her on? Once he did, there would be no turning back, he knew that. It was now or never.

He took a ragged breath. 'Frances. I've got a confession to make.'

* * *

By the time he got through, his body was coated with a thin sheen of sweat. He held up his arms, like a cormorant, for the warm breeze to dry him off. It was done. He'd said what he had to say. Whatever happened now, he'd cleared his conscience and things felt straight again. Controllable.

'Can I open my eyes now?'

'Yes.'

Frances sat up. At first she wouldn't look at him. Icy fingers of panic needled his heart. He allowed his arms to drop fatalistically to his sides.

'Is that everything? You promise me there's nothing more, J?'

'I promise. I know I made a fool of myself…'

'Shhh.' She turned and laid her fingers against his lips, just as she'd done the day before, in the square at St Tropez. 'I haven't given you your birthday present yet.'

'But Frances…'

'Shush.' She made a disapproving face. 'I told you to shush.' She felt in the basket and brought out a small box wrapped in gold foil. It was tied with a red silk ribbon. She laid it in front of him, smiling. 'Happy seventeenth birthday, J.'

Hesitantly, he reached for the package. It was as light as a feather. With a quizzical look at Frances he untied the ribbon to reveal a small cedar-wood casket no bigger than a box of kitchen matches.

'Go on. Open it. But be careful. It's very fragile.'

He slipped the catch and opened the box. Glancing at her for confirmation, he peeked inside. 'You can't be serious. Frances?' He was grinning all over his face.

'I'm deadly serious. That's your birthday present, J. Take it or leave it.'

'Now?'

She glanced about. 'Now's as good a time as any. I don't see anyone around. Do you?'

He placed the box to one side and moved towards her. She lay back, smiling, her hand playing at the buttons of her blouse.

'Are you sure? Really sure?'

'What do *you* think?'

They returned to the house a little after dusk. The bridge party was well under way, and no one noticed their arrival. Frances leaned forward and kissed him sloppily on the side of the mouth. 'Happy birthday again. Did you like your present?'

'I liked it so much I want another one, exactly the same.'

'I think we can arrange that.'

'I don't have to wait until this time next year?'

She put both hands over her eyes. 'Not even until this time tomorrow.' She made a face at him through her fingers. 'But from now on, *you'll* have to visit the chemist. I've never felt so ashamed in all my life.'

'It was like me with the magazine.'

'Not quite, thank you very much!' She raised her chin pugnaciously. 'Are you going to be buying many more such magazines, do you think?'

'*Nay, my lady. A thousand times nay.*' He thought for a moment, searching for a rhyme. '*I'll have no further need of images now the real thing's come my way.*' He grimaced at her, more embarrassed than he cared to acknowledge. 'How was that? Apart from the fact that it didn't scan?'

'The real thing, huh?' She eased herself gingerly off the seat.

He parked the *mobylette* and slung the basket over his shoulder. He gave her a guilty sidelong glance. 'I didn't hurt you, did I?'

'Do you want an honest answer, or a fib?'

'A fib.'

'It didn't hurt in the least, I'm not sore, and I shan't have to rinse my panties in the bidet in case Antonia sees them and apprehends straightaway what you've done to me.'

Not for the first time in his life, Jonathan felt a furtive admiration for the complexities involved in being a woman. Frances seemed to grasp instinctively what it took him much laboured thought to comprehend. He swallowed. 'What do you want me to do about Clara?'

'Nothing. *I* shall do it. And enjoy it.' She looked up at him, intently. 'She'll hate you, J. You know that? Just like she hates me. It'll be war.'

'War?'

'Oh Jonathan, you've no idea, have you?'

'Of course I have.'

She let her gaze linger on his face. He looked so beautiful, standing there, in all the glory of his newly won virility. The virility that she'd accorded him.

'Come on then. Let's creep in. Then we can wander downstairs and make believe we've been back for hours. They'll be so deep in their bridge game by then that they wouldn't even notice if you started making passionate love to me across the dining-room table.'

'That's one hell of an idea.'

She smiled conspiratorially. 'It is at that.'

Eighteen

Penhallow, Cornwall. 1999

Frances allowed her slice of bread to drop with a dull thud onto the plate in front of her. Even toasting hadn't improved it. And what remained of the marmalade was growing a loathsome variety of white fungus. Did Clara ever bother to eat breakfast, she wondered, or did she simply drink it, as she was doing now? Something would have to be done – Cosima and Jonathan were due to arrive after lunch, and the rest of Helen's family were descending on them tomorrow. It was looking more and more like a disaster.

Silence wafted between the two women like a poisonous fog. They'd exchanged barely half a dozen words since crossing paths in the hall that morning, and Frances was finding it increasingly difficult to convince herself that the person sitting opposite her was really her sister at all. Nothing new in that, mind you – for the first twenty years of her life she'd fantasised that someone had switched Clara's cot at the hospital, and that her real sister was living with another family nearby; that someday, across a crowded room perhaps, or in some forgotten street, they'd recognise each other. Fat chance of that now.

She cleared her throat. She'd have sold her soul for a glass of fresh orange juice. 'Do you get the St Ives paper?'

'The what?'

'The local rag.' Frances took a sip of her tea, then spat it surreptitiously back into the cup. The milk was off too. She glanced up in resignation. 'Come on, Clara. You heard me. Your hangover can't be as bad as all that. I want to arrange for Helen's flowers. Florists advertise. Local florists advertise in local newspapers. Or have you sorted it out with the funeral people already?'

More silence.

Frances pushed her plate wearily to one side. 'Look, Clara. I'm sorry to insist on this. I know how wretched you must be feeling. But did Helen at least have a cleaning woman?'

Clara was still recovering from the thought of the local paper. It came out on Thursdays. Today was Thursday. How could she have forgotten? Perhaps there was a story about last night? Maybe she was already splashed across ten thousand front pages? 'Hit And Run Driver Leaves Scene Of Crime. Child Left To Die On Isolated Country Road.'

For she was convinced by now that it had been a child. It couldn't have been anything else. It had been too small for a deer. Too big for a dog or a fawn. Oh God.

Fearful notions began to force their way through her alcohol-befuddled brain. Was there blood on the Volvo? Dents? Broken lights? Thanks to the booze she hadn't even thought to look last night. She'd just stumbled up to bed and collapsed, fully clothed, onto the quilt. And what if someone had recognised her? The man in the Range Rover, for instance. Everyone in the neighbourhood knew who she was. She was renowned, for God's sake. A fucking bloody celebrity.

'Clara? Are you listening to me?'

'What?'

'Do you have a cleaner? The house is a sty. And not a single one of the spare rooms is made up. Perhaps she could sleep in over the funeral?'

'Who?'

'The cleaner!' Frances glared at her sister across the table. 'What's the matter with you? You've been acting strangely ever since I arrived. Anyone would think you'd committed a murder or something.'

'What do you mean?' Clara sat up straighter. 'What do you mean, "committed a murder"?'

'Oh come on, Clara. It was just a manner of speaking.'

'No. No. You meant something more than that.'

'Something more than what? What more could I have meant?' Frances slapped the table and widened her eyes dramatically. 'Who have you got rid of? An unwelcome ex-lover? The local vicar? The master of foxhounds? Don't tell me you've been sucking the blood from young virgins again?'

'Ha bloody ha!' Clara darted out her hand for the brandy bottle, then realised it was empty. Blast. What a skinflint Frances was. She might at least have stumped up for a twin. 'You never used to have such a witty sense of humour, Frances. Just the opposite, in fact. What was that name they gave you at school? After Daddy dragged you kicking and screaming back from Paris?' She pretended to think. 'Ah yes. The "grim weeper", wasn't it?' She glared triumphantly across the table. Boy! That one had *really* struck home. She could almost see Frances reel from the force of it.

'Clara, you can be unbelievably cruel sometimes. You know perfectly well why I couldn't stop crying. Yet you persisted in tormenting me. You and your little band of cronies.'

'Then you shouldn't have run off with Jonathan, should you? Playing at Girl Guide revolutionaries, or whatever the hell you were doing over there. And don't put on that long-suffering face. It was you who got him banned by Daddy and booted out of his school, not me. Not that the board of governors can have thought him any great loss – he always was as thick as two short planks. You were just too besotted to notice. He'd have been lucky to get a place at Bude polytechnic, let alone Oxford or Cambridge.'

'That's not true!'

'Perhaps you'll finally realise that I was doing you a favour when I told Mrs Kapell about your love-nest in the rue de Florence. Saving you from a fate worse than death. Jonathan always did suffer from a terminal case of testosterone overload – not to mention a seriously roving eye. You just refused to admit it to yourself, that's all.'

Now Frances was gazing open-mouthed at her across the table. What was the matter with the bloody woman? She looked as though she'd seen a ghost.

'So it was you! You were the one who told them where we were. God how stupid! I'd always thought it was all Daddy's doing.'

Clara snorted. 'Daddy didn't have enough imagination. He was convinced you'd eloped to Gretna Green. No, it was me who winkled the truth out of Lisa. After that, I thought it would save everybody a great deal of trouble if I went down and told Mrs Kapell straightaway.'

'Clara. You utter cow!' Frances leaped to her feet, knocking back her chair.

'Oh do shut up. Stop being so dramatic.'

Without stopping to think, Frances picked up her side plate and hurled it at Clara. She missed by at least a yard, and the plate bounced harmlessly off the wall.

Clara glanced over her shoulder in mock alarm. 'Marvellous! The first time in your life you actually do something original, and you can't even bust a bloody plate. Look. This is how to do it.'

Clara grabbed the nearest available dish and smashed it to smithereens on the edge of the table. Then the one beside it. The third plate she hurled through the plate-glass French windows behind Frances's head. 'See? *That's* how to bust the fucking crockery. And believe me, I've had some practice.'

Cosima was doing her make-up in the passenger-seat vanity mirror. She dabbed expertly at an eyelid with the tip of her index finger, then glanced coquettishly at Jonathan. 'You realise this is my first visit to Penhallow?' They'd just passed through St Ives and she was feeling strangely apprehensive.

Jonathan stared at her. Unself-consciously, she began to apply her lipstick. She opened her mouth wide, then pursed it shut again, chewing on her lips. He felt an unexpected surge of desire. God, but she's young, he thought to himself. He had a sudden vision of her smooth and unblemished skin stretched out beside his own beaten-up, battle-scarred body. 'You're kidding, surely?'

'No, I'm not. Mummy never brought me here. Granny would come up to visit us whenever we were in London, but I never came down.'

'Why ever not?'

'You can't have forgotten the way Mummy and Clara feel about each other? Mummy didn't want her tender spring lamb anywhere near her diabolical younger sister.' She dabbed at her mouth with a tissue. 'Now I'm wildly looking forward to meeting her. It's not often you have to wait nearly twenty-eight years before encountering the black sheep of the family. What's she like?'

'Oh Christ. Please don't ask me that.'

'That bad, huh?'

Jonathan grimaced. 'No. Not that bad. But I don't want to prejudice you.'

'Prejudice? *Moi*? Impossible. Mummy's already tried that. She hasn't been able to mention Clara's name without retching ever since I can remember.'

A sudden thought occurred to her. 'Clara didn't, by any remote chance, have anything to do with you and Mummy breaking up?'

Jonathan kept his eyes firmly fixed on the road ahead. 'Now what gave you that idea?'

'No reason. Only it does seem a little strange that Mummy's been holding a grudge against Clara for so long. They hardly ever see each other. And what you said earlier, about hurting Mummy so badly. Nothing would have hurt her so badly as you shagging Clara.'

'How delicately you put it.'

'Was she pretty?'

'Clara?' He bought himself a little time by pretending to ponder the question. 'Yes. I suppose you would have called her pretty. A little obvious, perhaps.'

'Like me?'

Jonathan laughed. 'Now you sound just like your mother. It's extraordinary how women are able to turn any conversation about sexual attraction back towards themselves. It must pass down through the generations in a sort of spontaneous morphology.'

'A what?'

'Forget it. I was just trying to impress you with my intellectual credentials.'

'Well you haven't succeeded. And don't think I haven't noticed how you've greased your way out of answering my question. If you don't own up, I shall take a spontaneous and morphological look at Aunt Clara and decide for myself whether you've had her.'

'You'd have done that anyway.'

'Bull's-eye. Strike one for the veterans!'

'The veterans?'

Cosima giggled. 'Don't look so surprised. You're not exactly in the first flush of youth, are you?' She cocked her head to one side. 'How old are you, anyway? Fifty? Fifty-one? Well preserved, though. At least you've kept your figure and most of your hair.'

'Thanks for nothing.' He was angry that Cosima should think him old, and flattered at the same time that she should feel interested enough in him to bring the subject up at all. 'I was forty-nine in August, if it's any of your business. But it's not the age. It's the mileage.' He smiled weakly. 'I didn't make that one up, by the way. I got it from a movie.'

'Yes, I know. It's Indiana Jones. *Raiders of the Lost Ark*. I'm a seventies baby remember. I was nine when it came out.'

'Uh-oh. I should have known. Thank God I confessed in time.'

She dabbed her wrists and behind her ears with the stopper of her perfume bottle. 'Do you mind about getting old?'

He considered for a moment. A sexy, musky smell began to suffuse the interior of the car. 'No. But I *do* mind about getting ill.' He breathed cautiously in, and then exhaled with more confidence. Three weeks ago the scent of the perfume would probably have made him vomit, thanks to the lingering effects of the chemotherapy.

'So what was wrong with you, then?'

'Oh. Didn't your mother tell you?' He choked off his words. Why the hell should she have? He was nothing to Frances any more. He swallowed awkwardly – his saliva tasted bitter again, just as it had at the hospital. Strange how the tastes and the smells of his treatment seemed to linger, in some odoriferous memory bank, ready to pounce when he least expected it. He cleared his throat angrily – now he could taste the wine and the scallops from lunch. Goddamn the whole bloody process of getting ill!

He took a shallow breath, letting the air hiss out through his nose. 'I had cancer. It may have started in one of my balls and moved up from there into my lymph system, but nobody really knows for sure. It's the sort of cancer that normally affects younger men, so by the time they picked it up, I'd sprouted enough ganglions to keep a medical convention in free samples for the better part of a month.'

'That's not funny. Cancer scares me.'

He allowed his false smile to fade. 'You're right. It should do.' He was tempted for a moment to let the subject drop, but he was already too far engaged. 'You see, they only told me, barely a week ago, that I was finally in the clear. Up to that point I'd been more or less accepting that I was done for. Dead meat.' He glanced across at her. 'Now, paradoxically, I seem to be having trouble getting used to the idea that I may be able to live a normal life again.' He smiled grimly. It was impossible to tell how she was responding to his story.

She began to brush her hair. 'Did you ever think about suicide?'

He nodded immediately, caught unawares. 'Yes. As a matter of fact I did.' He was disconcerted by her apparent nonchalance and by his own passive response to it. 'When the pain from my tumours got really bad.' He laid a hand on his leg in an unconscious echo of his former habit. 'There was no longer any real reason to carry on, you see. I had no wife. No kids. I'd saved up more than enough pills. It would have been pitifully easy to up my dose of morphine to the point where I simply slid into a coma and didn't re-emerge.'

She paused in her brushing. 'Then why didn't you do it?'

They were approaching the turning to Penhallow. He caught a brief glimpse of Tremedda Common, and below it the spot where he and Frances used to hide her bicycle during the long, furtive summer of 1968. 'I haven't the faintest idea. It wasn't fear, I can tell you that much. I was at that stage in my illness when it takes more guts to go on living than it does to snuff yourself out.' He laughed ironically. 'Unfinished business, I suppose.'

'You mean Mummy, don't you?'

He nodded, suddenly serious. 'Yes. Yes, I do.'

He took the right fork. Now he could see the hill where he'd first met Frances – how small it seemed. He could remember cresting the bluff, all those years ago, out of breath from his running, to find her curled up at his feet, wide-eyed and just a little frightened.

A light rain began to fall. He flicked the wipers to clear the screen. The Penhallow gates were leering at him like a gigantic mouth through the drizzle. 'Do you mind if we stop here for a moment?'

'Of course not.'

He switched off the engine and stepped out of the car. When he turned back, Cosima was already leaning across the soft top of the Aston Martin, staring out to sea.

'It's very beautiful. It really is. All those different colours. I suppose it's all yours now?'

Jonathan raised the collar of his jacket. He thrust his hands deep into his coat pockets, warming himself. He hesitated, searching for the right words, knowing he must say more; knowing, also, that she did not expect him to.

She came up beside him. She was so tall that her head was almost on a level with his. To his intense surprise, she took his arm. Feeling that she wanted him to, he rested the palm of his hand lightly across her fingers. It was, he realised, the first time they'd actually touched. She was watching him. Intently. Almost hungrily.

He dashed the rain out of his eyes with his free hand. '*I should have been a pair of ragged claws, scuttling across the floors of silent seas.*'

She frowned, trying to place the poem. 'I give up.'

'T S Eliot. *The Love Song of J Alfred Prufrock.*' He shook his head slowly, languidly. As if assessing the very parameters of his brain.

She waited. Silently. So like Frances. Watching him.

Without really knowing why, he leaned forward, very gently, and brushed her rain-dampened forehead with his lips.

Nineteen

Clara stood in the Zennor village phone box, scrunching herself as far as possible against the back of the booth. A copy of the local paper was folded open beside her on the metal shelf. There'd been nothing in it, of course. Nothing at all about the accident.

'Hello. Yes. Yes.' She gave the phone a dirty look and waited, tapping the back of the receiver with her nail. 'Hello? Yes? I have a question. A question! Yes.' She mouthed a silent curse down the speaker. 'Could you tell me when exactly the paper gets printed? No. Not the advertisements. The news pieces. The news. Yes.' Another pause. 'I mean, if, for instance, there was an important event – a car accident, say – on a Wednesday night, would it get printed in the Thursday issue?' She listened for a moment. 'The television? It would appear on the television? But I don't have a television. What if I want to read it in the newspaper?' She held the handset six inches away from her face and glared at it. 'I'd have to wait for next week? That's not much of a bloody service, is it? The Internet? Oh, for God's sake.'

She slammed down the receiver and manhandled her way through the phone box door. She'd parked on purpose near the museum so that no one would see the Volvo and have their memories jogged – unlikely, but you never knew. Perhaps she should get the car repainted? No. That wouldn't be a good idea. It would make it even more obvious that she had something to hide. And she couldn't afford it anyway. Thank God there hadn't been any blood on the car. And no dents. If only she hadn't been so drunk, she might remember better.

She toyed for a moment with the idea of cruising past the cottage where it had happened. Just to check. It would be madness, of course, and nothing to be gained. What on earth could she expect to see there? Blood in the road?

Her heart lurched unexpectedly. Flowers. Yes! People always put flowers near to where their relatives had been killed. And they'd be even surer to put flowers there if it had been a child. It couldn't possibly hurt if she were to drive swiftly past. And if there weren't any flowers, then it must have been an animal after all. Then, perhaps, she could sleep again, and get a little peace.

She giggled nervously. No Flowers For Rover. Sounded like the title of one of those James Hadley Chase thrillers Daddy used to read. *No flowers for Rover, who got runned over.* She felt a sudden, unexpected pang of loss, and glanced down at her convulsively shaking hands. If only Daddy were alive – he'd have told her what to do. How to get out of it. But at least by checking out the cottage she'd be doing *something*. She couldn't just sit around waiting for the plods to pounce on her.

Already, as she started the car, she was beginning to doubt the validity of her own logic.

·

'They're here!' Frances had no idea why she called out. The act seemed to come naturally, despite herself – a last, desperate attempt at normality perhaps?

She paused in front of the hall mirror and patted her hair. What would he see? She squinted at herself, trying to discern the truth behind her familiar image. One thing was for sure – it wouldn't be the nervous, irresolute twenty-year-old who'd bolted from him on the Levant ferry twenty-eight years before.

She closed her eyes, blotting out her reflection in the glass. Had she acted like a fool? Should she have confronted him and Clara? Forced him to make a choice? After all this time she still couldn't believe what he'd done. The irony, of course, was that she'd been perfectly willing to tolerate in Giancarlo what she couldn't stomach in Jonathan. If she was honest with herself, Giancarlo's infidelities had almost suited her. They'd kept him off her back, so to speak – both literally and metaphorically. But with Jonathan it had been different. She'd loved him. And he'd betrayed her with a woman she loathed.

What, then, had been the significance of all that drunken nonsense Clara had been spouting in the car the night before? That Jonathan had been as high as a kite? A likely story. What was Clara fabricating? What had she and

Jonathan been up to in that sordid little hut? And had it really been him with the ice-cubes? He'd certainly never done that to her, and they'd tried just about everything else. She felt almost cheated. But Clara was an adept little liar when it suited her. Always had been.

'Oh God!' Frances stamped her foot in irritation. She hadn't felt like this for years. She was behaving like some stupid little virgin on the eve of her deflowering. And speaking of Clara, where had she got to? She could certainly use her now – as a red herring, if nothing else. What was it those bombers had dropped in the war to confuse the enemy radar? Jonathan was always batting on about it when they were children. Confetti? Something like that. That's what she needed now. Confetti.

'Mummy!' Cosima ran past the front door and hugged her mother. Then she stepped back and looked at her appraisingly. 'You look absolutely gorgeous. Surely you haven't gone to all that trouble just for me?'

Frances blushed. 'I don't know what you mean.'

'Oh, it's all right, silly. Jonathan's told me everything. We had a long chat in the car.'

Frances took a step backwards. 'He's done what?'

'You mustn't be angry. But I grilled him. The opportunity was simply too good to miss.'

'Cosima!'

'So I know all about you and him and you don't have to hide anything.'

'Really!'

'And I know all about Clara, too.'

'What do you mean? What about Clara?'

'Oh, this and that. Where is she, by the way? I'm dying to meet her.'

Frances felt as if she'd been doused with a bucket of cold water, and then, before she could even begin to recover, doused with another one. 'And where, may I ask, is the source of all this exciting new knowledge of yours?'

'Himself, you mean? Out in the car getting our things. He'll be in in a minute. Panting to see you, I shouldn't wonder.'

'How nice.' Frances backed away. She could feel the familiar tingling in her nose that presaged tears. 'Well, I'm going to go upstairs and look for Clara. I've made all the beds, and I've done my best to tidy the place up a little. But it still leaves a lot to be desired.' She stopped abruptly. 'As does your discretion, Cosima. And Jonathan's too, for that matter. For future reference, please remember that I don't like being discussed behind my back. And certainly not by my own daughter and a man I haven't seen for nearly thirty years. *Capisco*?'

Cosima blanched. 'Oh come on, Mummy? You're not really angry are you?'

'No. I'm livid.' No question of tears now.

Cosima took a tentative step towards her. 'Then why did you arrange for me to travel down with him? I don't understand. You must have known we'd discuss you?'

Frances squeezed her eyes tightly shut. What a disaster. She must have been mad. Had she really wanted this to happen? If not, why else had she thrown them both together? She could hear Jonathan's feet scrunching imminently towards her on the gravel. 'I'll see you both later.' She turned on her heels and ran in the direction of the stairs. 'Don't try any of the milk, by the way. It's off. Clara promised to take me shopping over two hours ago, but she's disappeared – probably to Tibet. Frankly, I don't blame her.'

'Mummy! You can't just go like that.'

Frances was already halfway towards the hall landing.

'Mummy!'

Jonathan pushed his way through the front door and dropped the cases he was carrying loudly onto the floor. 'Phew! I'm certainly not as fit as I once was. What have you got in this thing? A travelling dressing-room?' He glanced around expectantly. 'Funny. I could have sworn I heard voices. Isn't Frances here?'

Cosima glanced up at the empty staircase. Then she looked back at Jonathan. 'I'm afraid she's bolted.'

'Bolted?'

Cosima took a deep breath. 'Perhaps I'd better explain.'

Clara was retracing her journey of the night before. She passed near the Treen Downs bog (it wasn't so scary in daylight), then Try Valley, then Chysauster and the farm where the Range Rover had been backing out. Not a soul about. Well thank heavens for that, at least. Her hands felt disgustingly clammy against the wheel, but the shaking had subsided a bit. She rubbed them impatiently against her jeans.

What if the police were waiting for her? Didn't they say that criminals nearly always go back to the scene of their crime eventually? Well she was doing it sooner, rather than later. But then she wasn't really a criminal, was she? She hadn't done it on purpose. In fact it wouldn't have happened at all if ruddy Frances hadn't decided to turn up for the funeral. Or if Jonathan hadn't found her. Or if she hadn't blurted out to Jonathan where Frances was.

I suppose this was what you'd call a chain reaction, Clara thought to herself. One thing leading to another, leading to another. If she hadn't tricked Jonathan all those years ago, he and Frances would probably have been married, divorced, and hating each other by now, and all the bombs defused. Oh well.

She reached Badger's Cross and turned right at the junction. She was very close now. In fact there was the cottage, half a mile down the road. She must have passed it a thousand times over the last forty years, and never noticed it. She slowed down. No sign at all of the plods. No flowers either. And no blood on the tarmac. Perhaps she'd been imagining it after all?

As she was cruising past the cottage, the front door opened. A tall, grey-haired man stepped out into the road. Without thinking, Clara rammed her foot onto the accelerator and sped away, tyres shrieking. She glanced wildly into her mirror. The man was standing in the middle of the road, staring after her with a quizzical expression on his face. God, she must have been mad. He probably wouldn't have noticed her at all if she'd only behaved normally.

Now he was patting his pockets. She could see him in the mirror. Looking for a pen, probably, and a piece of paper to write down her number with. Her entire body shuddered as if someone had just walked over her freshly dug grave.

Twenty

Benenden School, Kent. Sunday, 5 May 1968

Jonathan watched from his concealed vantage point as the girls emerged from matins at the Benenden village church. Almost immediately he caught sight of Lisa, gossiping with one of her friends. She took her companion's arm and they leaned towards each other, giggling. Jonathan inched backwards into the shadows. Lisa had grown up since last Easter holidays – she was actually becoming quite pretty, despite her tomboy figure and her flat chest. *Maman* had allowed her to cut her hair into a page-boy bob, and it suited her. He felt curiously disconnected as he watched her, so self-possessed in her straw hat, white collar and brightly coloured frock – almost as if he were an only child, and she his imagined sister.

Clara came next, surrounded by an older group of girls. They spent a long time chatting and fiddling with their hats, studiously avoiding the younger fry. Clara cracked a joke, and her little crowd of sycophants peeled back like lilies in the wind, then swayed forward again, the thin sound of their laughter travelling across the gravestones towards him.

Some instinct made him glance back at Lisa. Her eyes were now fixed on Clara's face. Her companion made a doomed attempt to drag her away, but Lisa refused to budge. The girl finally let go of her arm and stalked off. Lisa kept her gaze locked on Clara. When Clara did eventually turn her way, Lisa raised a hand and smiled at her. Jonathan's heart went out to his sister. He could sense what was coming.

True to form, Clara cocked one quizzical eyebrow at Lisa, then turned back to her older friends, cutting her dead. White-faced, Lisa continued watching, while the endless, unseen, chattering line of girls swept past her. Fifty yards separated them, but Jonathan could feel Lisa's pain as if it were his own – it was a strange feeling, and he was unused to it.

Frances was the last to come out. She straightened her hat and glanced up into the sunlight. She, too, caught Clara's eye, but she immediately looked away – even a stranger would have observed that there was little love lost between these sisters. Jonathan could make out the tap and crunch of her shoes on the gravel as she started down the path towards him.

He waited until Clara's back was turned, then stepped out from behind the yew tree he'd been using as camouflage. Frances was walking freely, her hips swaying in cross time to the hem of her frock – she already looked like a woman, not the young girl she still undoubtedly was. Jonathan took a subtle, almost solipsistic pleasure in watching her. She was his. He had possessed her. *Did* possess her. If he called to her now, she would run to him, giving herself.

With a wary eye on Clara, he raised one hand in the air. The movement caught Frances's eye. She stopped, snatching a knuckle to her mouth. Jonathan put a finger to his lips, then retreated behind the tree. Frances looked anxiously around, then changed direction and hurried towards him. In the distance Clara and her gaggle of friends were moving in the direction of the playing fields.

'Jonathan!' Frances ran the last few yards and fell into his arms.

He kissed her furiously, across her cheeks and mouth and hair. She responded, her eyes wide open in sensuous shock – for the space of a minute they were like two animals, nosing each other out. She finally broke away, burying her face inside his collar.

He drew her swiftly under cover of the branches. 'Shhh. We mustn't be seen.'

She pulled back, surprised by the urgency of his tone. 'Why not, J?' Her senses were rapidly returning to normal – all of a sudden she was taking in his jeans, the faded shirt, the hunted expression on his face. 'Are you having a Sunday out? And why aren't you in school uniform? Where are your parents, J?'

'I'm alone. And I'm not having a Sunday out.'

She shook her head. 'I don't understand.'

He took her hand, rolled back her school glove, and kissed the mound of her palm. 'I've decided to run away. I'm going to Paris. To join the students.'

She took a further step backwards, unconsciously reclaiming her hand. 'You've run away? But you can't have, J. You're joking with me. What about your A levels?'

He shook his head vehemently. 'There won't even be such things as A levels in a few months' time. Or universities even.' He was looking out over her shoulder, as if he were reading his text from a cue card held up against the sun. 'People will have the right to go where they want. Do what they want.'

'J. What on earth are you talking about?'

'Come on. Haven't you been reading the newspapers?'

'Yes, of course I have, but…'

'It's really getting serious, Fran. I've been following the build-up for the last few months. Our history teacher's a socialist, you see. He's been explaining everything to us. He'd go over there himself if it wasn't for his family.'

'Go? Go where? What do you mean, J?'

'To Paris. To join the uprising, of course. It's already been going on for two days. We've simply got to make it over there while we still can.'

Frances shook her head in simple amazement. 'We?'

'Yes. You and me. That's why I've come to get you. I've got money. Nearly a hundred pounds. We can buy you some clothes and then cross over tonight on the Dover/Calais boat.'

Frances gazed wildly around herself. She dropped her voice to an unbelieving whisper. 'But J. Even if I wanted to go with you, I couldn't. I don't have my passport. Daddy always keeps it.'

'Then I'll smuggle you onto the ferry.' He took her by the shoulders. 'Come on, Fran. Don't you see that we've got to go?'

'No, I…'

'For crying out loud! Do you want the whole world to change while we sit on our arses and do nothing? Do you want that, Fran? Do you want to have to explain why we didn't go to our children?'

'To our children?'

'Of course to our children. They're the ones who are going to inherit the world we leave behind. Mr Cameron says it's all been building for years. Since the war. And that they're not going to stop now. They've gone too far.' He was beseeching her with his eyes. 'France is my country too. I've got to go. Can't you see that?' His voice ended on a dying fall, as if his argument failed to convince even him.

She reached up and took hold of his collar. 'Yes, J. Of course I can see it. But what about your parents? You'll be throwing ten years of education away overnight. I thought your father desperately wanted you to go to Cambridge?'

He shook his head irritably. 'Papa never desperately wants anything. He's so laid back he's only ever done one completely selfless thing in his life, and that was to fight in the Spanish Civil War. And it cost him Penhallow and the use of an eye. I've always respected him for that.' He squeezed her hands against his cheeks. 'Paris could be our Spain, Fran. Our civil war. Please say you'll come with me?' His eyes were searching passionately across her face. He could sense that she was faltering. 'We can stay at my uncle Piers's flat. You'd be safe there. No one would ever find us.'

'J. This is crazy. It's still not too late for you to go back and explain things to your housemaster. Mr Cameron, or whatever his name is, will back you up. I'm sure he didn't mean you to take him literally.'

Jonathan stepped back from her, glowering. 'Well? Are you coming or not?'

'What? Now? This very minute?'

'Yes.'

She shook her head. 'I can't, J. You must see that? Daddy would never forgive me. You know I've been promised a place at Girton if I get two As and a B.' She could feel the tears building behind her eyes.

Why was Jonathan doing this to her? She'd always assumed they'd go to Cambridge together. Live a charmed life. Love each other like the characters out of books. She began to cry. 'If you do this, you'll spoil everything. They'll never take you back at school. You'll be wrecking your future for some bunch of left-wing loonies who don't even know you and who wouldn't care about you even if they did.'

He took a step towards her, his hands pressed uselessly to his sides. 'Please Fran. Don't cry.' He'd lost her. He knew it. He felt the despair of utter loneliness. 'I've made my mind up, you know. It's too late for me to turn back now.'

'What do you mean?'

'I did something stupid. Painted something on the walls of the Temple Speech Room. They'll know it was me by now. So even if I did go back, I'd be expelled. What would be the point?' The emptiness was building behind his heart. 'Do you know what I'm going to do? I'm going to walk straight out to the main road and start to hitchhike. Then I'm going to take the very first lift I'm offered.' Each word seemed to mark a separate part of his death sentence. 'It's not too late to change your mind, you know,' he added, lamely.

'Don't,' she said. It was more an animal sound than a recognisable utterance.

He reached forward and kissed her cheek. 'I love you, Fran. It's funny, but I have no problem saying it now.' He backed steadily away. 'I'll write you a postcard, bring you up to date on what's happening in the real world.'

'Jonathan!'

He could no longer think rationally. He broke away from her and began dodging through the gravestones. He'd known she wouldn't come. But still the bitterness stung at his eyes. It was as if he were ripping the still-forming scab off an unhealed wound.

'Jonathan. Don't leave me like this!'

He nearly hesitated then. Nearly turned around. But he was too unsure of himself. Of his commitment. Her voice grew steadily fainter the faster he ran.

Frances felt sick. She placed a hand against her diaphragm and leaned unsteadily against the trunk of the yew tree. Some girls walked by and looked at her strangely, but she ignored them. She couldn't let Jonathan go like that. He was stealing something from her. Something she had a right to. He was stealing himself from her.

Sobbing now, she began to run too. She simply had to catch Jonathan before he reached the main road. Talk to him. Persuade him from this madness. She hadn't liked that half-crazed look in his eyes. As if he were on drugs or something.

'Frances!'

She swerved around, her heart pounding. Lisa was squatting against the fence, her arms clutched around her knees. Frances hurried across to her. 'Come on, Lisa. Get up.'

'What for?'

'Come on. Quickly. We haven't much time. It's Jonathan.' She grabbed Lisa by the wrist and pulled her to her feet.

After a moment's instinctive resistance, Lisa fell in beside her. The two girls hurried along the path. 'What about Jonathan?'

'He's here. At the school. He wants to go to Paris. Join in the riots.'

'I knew he would.'

Frances stopped in her tracks. She turned to face Lisa. It was only then that she noticed the dried traces of tears down her cheeks. 'You knew he would?'

'Oh, come on. It's obvious. Jonathan's been looking for a cause for years. And this is perfect. He's always wanted to be a hero. Just like Daddy.' The countenance she presented to Frances was curiously blank, as if she saw no virtue any more in unnecessary displays of emotion. 'He'll probably get himself killed. Or, and this is more likely if good old Audley luck runs true to form, horribly maimed.'

Frances grabbed her by the shoulders. 'What do you mean, Lisa? Tell me!'

Lisa shrugged herself out of Frances's grasp. 'Only that if you love him, you'd better go with him. That's all I'm saying.' She took another pace backwards. She could feel her face twisting up. 'Come on, Frances. I'm not telling you anything you don't already know. Jonathan's always been a tragedy waiting to happen. Just like papa was. Just like I am. It's in our blood. If we're not loved, we destroy ourselves. Grandfather was the exception. Grandmother truly loved him. So he destroyed them both.'

'Don't be so stupid.'

'I'm serious. I've read all the family histories. There's a blight on every generation of Audleys. Men *and* women. Jonathan is just the most recent misfit in a long and not very salubrious line.'

Frances glanced nervously back over her shoulder. 'Come on. He'll be nearly at the road by now. We can talk about this later.'

'No. You go on. I'm staying here. He's *your* boyfriend.'

'He's *your* brother.'

'Don't you think I know that? Which is why I won't try to stop him. Won't try to talk him out of it. He wouldn't be Jonathan otherwise. I've learned that much.'

Frances hesitated. She was seeing a new side to Lisa, a side she'd never suspected before.

Lisa reached out and took her cousin's hand. 'Go on, Frances. Go and find him. He wants you to. And when you find him, go with him. You're the only one who can steady him. He's lost alone. We both are.'

Frances closed her eyes as tightly as she could. Her heart was struggling to pump sufficient oxygen into her bloodstream.

'Don't think about it.' Lisa stretched out a hand and touched Frances lightly on the cheek. 'It doesn't bear thinking about. Just go.'

Twenty-one

'Blast. We're running late.' A few of the foot passengers were already starting to board the Calais ferry. Jonathan grabbed Frances's hand. 'You see that party getting off the coach? We'll filter in amongst them and cross the barrier like that. You move on through when I tell you. But don't stop. Don't look back, okay? Act like you're deaf or something.'

Frances nodded uncertainly.

'We can't think about this, Fran. We just have to do it. Are you ready?'

She nodded again, more confidently this time.

'All right then.'

People were feeling around for their passports. The tour operator was flapping his wad of tickets and trying to get his flock into some sort of order. Jonathan elbowed his way through the crowd, waving his passport for everyone to see, his ferry ticket plainly visible behind it. He hesitated until he caught the purser's eye, then gave Frances an encouraging shove.

'Hey! Are you the purser? I think I'm with the wrong group. I don't recognise these people. Can you tell me if the rest of my team are already on the boat?'

'Your team? What team's that then?'

He had the purser's full attention now. From the corner of his eye he saw Frances slip past him and up the gangplank.

The purser put out his arm and stopped the man next to Jonathan. 'You wait there. One at a time. I'm dealing with this gentleman.' He glanced at Jonathan. 'Now, sonny. I haven't seen any team.'

'They'll all be carrying rucksacks. We're travelling to Calais to play the French National Schoolboy side. We're called the Waverley Terrace Wanderers. All the way from Waverley, Warwickshire.' Jonathan could scarcely keep a straight face. A heady sense of triumph was overwhelming him now that Frances was safely on board.

'You're having me on. I don't know of any team with a name like that. Show me your ticket again.'

Frances was leaning over the railings, watching him.

'Oh look. There's one. They're on board already.' He waved to a non-existent team-mate on the upper deck. Frances ducked.

The purser was still scrutinising his ticket and passport. 'All right then. This all seems to be in order. You give those Frogs a good bashing, do you hear?'

'Loud and clear, Captain!' Jonathan saluted and started up the gangplank. He put on an exaggerated Guy Gibson accent. 'Don't worry. I'm coming, chaps.'

'Boy's been drinking,' said the purser, to no one in particular. 'They start younger every year.'

Frances sat hunched against the companion-way, trying not to giggle. She placed both hands across her eyes in mock horror. 'Jonathan. Please! I can't bear it.'

'It's all right. I read it in John Buchan. One of Peter Pienaar's tricks. The best way to dupe an enemy is to do the obvious. Not try to conceal yourself. Just brazen it out. Fit in with the surrounding terrain.' He shook his head in stunned surprise. Untold new horizons of possible trickery loomed. 'We'll do the same thing in France. With the passports.' He sounded more confident than he felt.

'What do we do now, though?'

'What do you think?' He reached down and jerked her to her feet. 'Come on, girl, I'm starving. Let's hurry and get to the restaurant before the plebs beat us to it.'

Frances was unable to sleep on the Paris train. From the first moment she tried to close her eyes she began to fret. What were they saying about her back at school? And what would Daddy be saying? She'd really, really blown it this time. Clara must be ecstatic.

She sat up, brushing the hair out of her face. Jonathan wasn't sleeping either. She lowered her voice so as not to wake the man in the opposite seat. 'J. What if they call the police?'

Jonathan was staring at the blackness outside their carriage window. He turned to her in surprise. 'Come again?'

'What if they call the police? Or Interpol?'

'Interpol? For God's sake, Fran, why would they do a thing like that? They don't even know we're abroad.' He glanced outside again – it was as if the darkness was trying to withhold some secret from him. 'We are both seventeen, after all. I mean, it's not as if we've robbed a bank or something.' He didn't sound convinced by his own argument.

'I suppose so.'

Frances's gaze was still tormenting the back of his neck. He swivelled around to face her. 'Think about it this way. If we both came from poor families, we'd be out in the world earning a living already. You'd probably be behind a checkout counter in Woolworths and I'd be sweeping the streets. Or delivering milk. That's something else the revolution's going to change.'

Frances sat up straighter. 'Do you really believe that, J?'

He fiddled idly with his collar. 'Of course I do. Mr Cameron…'

'I don't want to know what Mr Cameron says. I want to hear it from you.'

Too late she saw the desperate uncertainty behind his eyes, the victimised look. She wished now she'd never asked the question in the first place.

He cleared his throat. 'I don't know all the ins and outs of it, of course, but it's sort of against the Americans.'

'Against the Americans?'

'Yes. It's about trying to stop the capitalists from taking over the world. Vietnam and all that.'

'But we're all capitalists, J. You. Your father. Daddy. All of us. Otherwise we couldn't live as we do.'

He hunched towards her. 'But that's just the point, don't you see?' His eyes were a deeper green than ever. 'Look, Fran, don't get me wrong. I'm not saying I'm some great revolutionary or anything, because I'm not. But there's something special happening here. Something that won't occur again in our lifetimes. And I want to be a part of it. I want *us* to be a part of it. Byron would have been here. And Shelley. Shakespeare and Wordsworth would have written about it. If the powers-that-be want us to have an education, this is the best way to do it. Please say you're with me?'

She laughed, ruefully. 'I'm here, aren't I?'

A smile transformed his face. 'You are, at that.' He leaned forward and kissed her full on the lips. 'When we get to Piers's flat I'm going to ravish you. Up, down, sideways and straight through the middle.'

'Don't be disgusting. I might not even be awake.'

'No. Seriously. He's got the most monstrous double bed you've ever seen. He and Jean probably get lost in it. And he's got a bath with golden taps. And gilded statues holding sconces. And tons and tons of that ormolu furniture you usually find in brothels. He's even got champagne in his fridge.'

'You can't steal your uncle's champagne, J.'

'In a revolution other people's property becomes the property of the people.'

'What? Even Piers's? That doesn't sound very revolutionary to me. Are you sure we're not simply over here for an adventure, J? You haven't just been spinning me a yarn?'

'Perish the thought.' He hesitated, unsure, suddenly, whether she was being serious or not. 'No, Fran. I really mean it about the riots.' He grinned down at her, the pre-adolescent smoothness of his features belying his years. 'And about the seduction too, of course.'

At ten past midnight they arrived at Paris's *Gare du Nord*. The harsh, artificial lights of the station made the dark patches under Frances's eyes seem even more intense. For the first time Jonathan realised the enormity of what he'd asked her to do and just how much she stood to lose by it. 'I'm sorry, Fran. You must be exhausted.' The empty noises of the station made him shiver, and he put an arm around Frances's shoulders as much to comfort himself as to comfort her.

She snuggled closely in to him, tucking her hands up either sleeve of the oversized polo-neck pullover they'd bought for her in a charity shop at Dover. 'I thought it was meant to be warm in Paris in May?'

'Not in the middle of the night.'

She looked up at him. 'J, you do realise that Piers's concierge is going to be asleep by now? One o'clock in the morning may not be the exact right moment to tap her for his key.'

'I was just thinking about that.'

'Have we got enough money for a hotel?'

'A cheap one.' He glanced around. 'Come on. That one over there's still got a light on.'

They crossed the road, dodging through the late-night traffic. Jonathan scanned the price-list nervously. 'Thirty francs for two. It could have been worse, I suppose. But we'll have to pass up a room with a bath. That's five francs extra.'

'I don't mind.'

They entered the lobby. Jonathan put on a brave face for the half-asleep night porter. '*Une chambre, s'il vous plaît. Sans bain. Mais avec un grand lit.*'

Frances tucked herself tightly in behind his arm.

'*Et vos bagages?*' The porter was watching them suspiciously, his eyes still hooded with sleep.

'*Ils sont à la gare. Notre train est en retard. On ne part qu'à dix heures demain matin.*'

'*Trente francs alors. En avance.*'

Jonathan counted the money into the man's outstretched palm. 'I don't think he trusts us somehow,' he whispered.

'I *am* still wearing my school uniform. Perhaps he thinks you've kidnapped me?'

Jonathan glanced down at her. 'White slavery, you mean? I can see the headlines now. "Schoolgirl Valedictorian Snatched From Benenden Sunday Matins. Worst Feared." '

'The headlines? I thought you said...'

'A joke, Fran. It was a joke.'

They squeezed inside the antediluvian lift. Inadvertently Frances's hip brushed against his. He was shocked anew at the womanly weight of her, for some part of him obstinately persisted in clinging to the old image he had of her as a child. She rested her head sleepily against the cubicle. 'Are we really in Paris, J? Twelve hours ago I was coming out of chapel and getting ready to oversee junior break. Now here we are in France. It's verging on the surreal.'

He took her face in his hands. 'You do realise this will be our first whole night together, don't you?' The elevator yo-yoed drunkenly to a stop. Frances lurched towards him. He encircled her smoothly in his arms. 'In fact I haven't been able to think of anything else for the past twenty minutes. Have you ever done it in a lift?'

'J. You know very well I haven't.' She could sense the weight of him pressing against her. The assertive force. Her throat felt momentarily dry. 'But couldn't we wait just five minutes until we get to the bed? I'm desperate for a wee. And I've got a funny feeling I'll fall fast asleep on your shoulder otherwise.'

Twenty-two

Monday, 6 May

From early that morning a little meagre sunshine fought valiantly against the obstinate grey skies over the *Gare du Nord*. Like an elderly Napoleonic veteran rejuvenated by the thought of a new campaign, Paris was awakening to yet another possible future.

Jonathan closed his eyes and pulled quickly back from the brink. Frances was hunched on her knees in front of him, the swell of her hips miraculously curving in towards the slender diameter of her waist.

'Did you pull out in time? You didn't come inside me?'

'Wait. Wait.'

Steadying himself against her buttocks, he took himself the last few steps of the way. At the final moment he fell forwards and she collapsed underneath him. 'God, J. It's all wet. I'm sticking to the bed. It's all over my stomach.'

He flopped over onto his back. 'Jesus, that was close.' He put out a tired hand and caressed her bottom languidly. 'But oh so good.'

She pulled the sheet across her and snuggled towards him. 'Good, huh?'

'Really, really, good.'

She hitched up on one elbow, watching him. 'So good you didn't notice something?'

He glanced towards her. 'What?'

'In feminine parlance, I'd call it *orgasmus interruptus*.'

'Oh.'

She hitched herself a little higher. 'Otherwise known as "master gets his oats, but his trusty mare gets none." '

He groaned and moved towards her, lifting the sheet. 'Hmm. What have we here?' He dropped the sheet back over himself and burrowed down the bed. 'Are you there, Miss Cherry?'

'J, what are you doing!'

'It's all right. I saw it in one of papa's books.'

Frances closed her eyes. She drew in a quick breath. As he began to arouse her she delicately began to touch the tips of her nipples with her thumbs.

An hour later, Jonathan took a deep, demonstrative breath and squinted into the sunlight. 'Ah, Paris! A mixture of diesel fumes, rotting vegetables and strong cologne.'

Frances dug him in the ribs. 'Well, *I* like it.'

Overnight, a market had sprung up outside their hotel. Street vendors were calling out their prices. Newspaper parcels full of fruit and vegetables were passing from stand to shopping basket – the aroma of freshly baked bread wafted enticingly from the *boulangerie* across the road. 'Come on, Fran, what shall we do? Go to the rue de Florence and freshen ourselves up, or make Paris our own?'

'Hmm. I've always wanted to own a city.' She took his hand and kissed it. 'Do we reek of sex, do you think?'

He sniffed his forearm. 'I don't know about you, but every time I move I exude the odour of three rutting steers.'

Frances squinted up at him. 'Steers have had their goolies cut off, J.'

He cracked a grin. 'Bulls, then. Three rutting bulls.'

'That's better.' She reached up and shielded her eyes from the slowly intensifying sun. 'Rue de Florence and a bath, I think. Then Paris. Don't you?'

'Sold.'

'But just one thing. And you mustn't make a fuss. I'm going to phone my stepmother and tell her I'm all right.' Jonathan opened his mouth as if to speak, but she shushed him. 'I won't tell her where we are, I promise. But I want her to know I'm with you and that I'm safe. It's not fair on them otherwise. Then she can tell Daddy and he won't call the police, or Pinkerton's, or something equally silly. Please J. You must understand.'

He let out his pent-up breath. 'You promise you won't let yourself be talked around – won't tell them we're in France?'

She shook her head, swallowing. 'I promised that yesterday, didn't I?'

He hesitated for a moment, his spirits clouding. 'Okay, then.'

They had less trouble than they'd expected in securing the key to Piers's flat from the concierge. The old woman had known Jonathan ever since he was a child.

'*Monsieur Jonathan?*' She'd thrown her hands up in the air. '*Mais quel horreur! Monsieur Piers et Monsieur Jean ne m'ont pas prevenu de votre arrivée. Je n'ai même pas eu le temps de nettoyer. Et les draps!*'

Jonathan crossed his fingers behind his back and wagged them at Frances. '*Ne vous gênez pas, Marise. On ne vient que pour se baigner. Nous rentrerons tard ce soir.*'

Marise smiled at them, revealing a pristine set of new dentures. Her thin, grey hair was held back by a bewildering variety of clips, culminating in a fake brown bun that jutted from the back of her head like a bagel. She exuded a rank country smell even in the heart of Paris. She had comprehensively adopted Piers, Jean and Charles following their removal into her building after the war, and now she prided herself above all on her partial, albeit extensive knowledge of their convoluted genealogies.

'*Vous êtes la cousine de Monsieur Jonathan, n'est-ce pas? La fille de Madame Hélène? Comme vous êtes jolie, Mademoiselle.*'

'*Merci Marise.*'

'Marise has always had good taste,' said Jonathan, as they climbed the stairs to Piers's flat. 'She thinks you're beautiful.'

'She also thinks I'm your aunt Helen's real life daughter. Which makes what we're doing incest. So no canoodling when she's around, mister, or she might not understand. *Capisco*?'

'*Capisco.*'

'And she said "pretty", by the way, not beautiful. My French isn't as bad as all that.'

'You *are* beautiful, Fran, do you know that?' He leaned forward and blew warm air into her ear. 'And very, very sexy.'

'J! I thought you said we were here for a revolution?'

'To hell with the revolution.'

* * *

They emerged, squinting, into the late-afternoon sunlight. Frances pinched Jonathan playfully on the arm. 'You're a beastly pre-vert, keeping me locked inside all day to minister to your pleasures.'

'A pervert, please.'

'No, a pre-vert. Haven't you seen *Dr Strangelove*? When that American sergeant won't let Peter Sellers raid the Coca Cola machine?'

'And you're the Coca Cola machine, I suppose? Is that why you're walking so funnily? I don't remember that bit in the film.'

'You bastard. I'm walking like this because I'm sore. If the riot police chase us, I shall lie down and pretend I'm dead. Perhaps they'll think I've been run over or something.'

Jonathan sniffed the air. 'Can you smell anything?'

'Now come on. I've had two showers and a bath already today.'

'No. Not you. Something else.' He shook his head incredulously. 'I bet it's tear-gas.'

Frances turned around, flaring her nostrils. 'Yes. I've got it. It's a sort of smoky smell. Not that unpleasant, really.'

'Wait until you get close to it.'

'Come on, J! When did you ever get close to tear-gas before?'

They turned instinctively south, passing from the rue de Florence, down the rue d'Amsterdam and towards the Place de la Concorde. Small groups of students were gathering at every corner, discussing, falling back, then moving forward again into larger groups. There were remarkably few police on the streets. The *groupuscules*, as they had begun to call themselves, in mockery of being written off by patronising politicians, were moving inexorably towards the Left Bank.

'Come on, Fran, I think we ought to cross the river. There's something building over there.'

They followed the flow of young people across the Pont de la Concorde and up the boulevard St Germain. Now dozens of police officers, in long black mackintoshes and carrying their square shields and long wooden truncheons at the ready, were lounging inside their vans, inspecting the phalanxes of passing students like predators before a kill.

'J, I'm scared. Are they suddenly going to run out at us?'

'Not yet. My guess is that they'll wait a while, get us all together, then try to cut us off.'

'Where are we going?'

Jonathan looked up at the street sign, then checked the map in his *Leconte*. 'We're on Raspail. If we keep on like this we'll eventually reach Place Denfert-Rochereau. That's the square with the lion statue in it. When I was a child papa let me climb up on top of it. A policeman helped him steady me. Sounds unlikely, now, doesn't it? I've a funny feeling the flics won't be helping many children today.'

The closer they got to Denfert-Rochereau, the more damage they began to see. Cobblestones and pavés had been torn up and heaped in piles across the side roads. Shop windows were shattered and boarded, and across from the Montparnasse Cemetery was a burnt-out Renault Berline. Someone had daubed 'Here, Imagination Rules' over the main wall of the École d'Architecture.

'J. This is terrible. Whatever happened?'

'There was a major riot here three days ago. All over the Latin Quarter. Six hundred people were arrested.'

'I didn't imagine it would be like this.'

As she spoke, a wave of black-clad students burst from the cemetery and ran up the street, shouting and waving banners.

'Come on, let's follow them. They seem to know where they're going.'

'J, are you sure?'

'I'll look after you. Just remember, if we ever get separated, we'll meet back at the apartment. Okay?'

They were running behind the students now, holding hands, part of an ever-burgeoning, ever-increasing street army.

'*A bas les réacs! A bas les réacs!*'

The massive wave of humanity began to take on a life force of its own. The blunt vanguard of the students fractured instinctively into lines, spanning the entire width of the road. Cars were stopping, bumping onto kerbs, reversing wildly down the street in front of them.

'*Vive les anars! Vive les anars!*'

The students had hold of each other's shoulders, their arms interlocked. The police simply moved apart and let them through. Everywhere people were smiling at each other, heady with short-term triumph.

'CRS-SS! CRS-SS!'

'What are they shouting?' Frances was running beside Jonathan, her face excited.

'The CRS are the guys on motorbikes who stand up in the saddle before the *Tour de France*. Papa says they're known as the grandmother-kickers because they have to kick their grandmothers around the parade square before they can be inducted.'

'You can't be serious. Which ones are they?'

'It's all right. They're not here yet. They only call in the CRS when things get *really* tough!'

The wave of students flooded into Place Denfert-Rochereau, seething either side of the stone lion. Half-a-dozen students climbed up onto the lion's back. One of them began haranguing the crowd through a megaphone.

Each minute brought new police reinforcements. The police officers were out of their vans now, standing in unbroken lines against the façades of the buildings. Some of them were even smiling.

'Come on, Fran. I don't like the look of the flics. They're mustering. Getting ready for a charge. They've got us all hedged in here now. Let's go over by the *Ossuaire* gates. That way, if things get bad, we can slip through and down into the catacombs. They're not likely to follow us in there.'

Some of the student demonstrators were starting to pull up the pavé stones, lobbing them wildly towards the police lines. The police responded with a barrage of tear-gas grenades, fired from the hip.

'Quick. Tie this handkerchief over your mouth.'

He helped Frances secure the knot behind her neck. The tear-gas was already making their eyes smart. There was a volley of blast-effect grenades, then some shouting.

'Shit. They're charging. They've got their batons out.' Jonathan pulled his shirt up to cover his face.

The crowd of students wound back in front of them like an elastic band, then surged forward again. They found themselves being pushed inexorably towards the police lines from behind.

'J, I'm scared.'

Ten feet in front of them two burly policemen swung a student around by his shirt, then began beating him with their wooden batons. The student curled up in a foetal position on the ground. A third policeman ran over and kicked him viciously in the kidneys.

'Come on. This is no good. We'd better take shelter.'

Grabbing Frances's hand, he made a sudden break for the black-grilled gates of the *Ossuaire*. An attendant was standing just inside, a handkerchief held tightly to his face. Jonathan pushed roughly past him, followed by four or five more students, their eyes and noses streaming from the tear-gas.

'Jonathan, I think I'm going to be sick.'

The attendant held up a hand and tried to stop the rush. No one took any notice of him. Police were forcing their way through the student lines towards them. More and more students had noticed the open catacomb doors and were sprinting for cover.

'Quick. Down the stairs. There's an exit in the rue Cassini. We'd better hope the bastards haven't locked it.'

A slim young man was running alongside them. 'Did you say there is a way out of here?' His English was heavily accented.

Jonathan nodded. 'We have to go all the way through the catacombs. About a kilometre. Then you go up some stairs and come out in a side-street.'

'Can I come with you?'

'Of course.'

'How do you know this place?'

'My father. He used to bring me down here whenever we visited Paris. I think he felt at home here, among all the fossils.'

'Ha. Very funny. You must be English.'

'Half French. My girlfriend is English.'

The slim young man smiled. 'Well I am Italian. My name is Giancarlo Brancardi.'

Twenty-three

The corridors got narrower the deeper inside the bowels of Paris they went – now, when they spoke, their voices boomed mysteriously against the damp stone walls, then echoed flatly back at them in a dying whisper. Sparse amber lighting illuminated a few small patches of disintegrating plaster.

'J, what is this? Where are we going? Are you sure there's a way out of here?'

They stopped near a cement plaque, set over a low door. Two white triangles were inset against the coal-black background of the walls: *Arrête! C'est ici l'empire de la mort.*

Jonathan put on a lurid Vincent Price voice. 'This is it, then. The Empire of the Dead. There's no turning back now.' He twisted his face into a grotesque leer. 'Surely you remember "The Cask of Amontillado"?'

'Shut up, J! You're scaring me.'

Five students racketed past them and on into the catacombs. '*Vite! Les flics.*'

'We better go.' Giancarlo was still with them, it seemed.

Jonathan felt a brief surge of male-on-male resistance. What was the bastard thinking of, ordering them around? They'd only met two minutes ago.

Despite his misgivings he ushered Frances through the passageway and on into the catacombs proper. 'This way. We've got to follow these arrows.'

Piles of skulls were stacked ten feet high along the corridors, supported by row upon row of gnarled, bleached shin-bones. Morbid verses by Legouvé were set at intervals into the concrete, between the bays. Someone had fixed two of the shin-bones into one of the skeletal structures as a sort of macabre joke, and varnished them to mimic a skull and crossbones. Frances made a disgusted face as they passed by.

'Come on.' Jonathan fervently hoped he wasn't sending them around in a circle. Each of the bays was wired off with a heavy grille – impossible to pass between them except via the corridors. He hesitated at the next underground crossroads.

'Listen!' Giancarlo held up his hand. The rattle of heavily booted feet was echoing up the passageway behind them. 'It's the flics! Let's sprint. It can't be far now.'

Jonathan couldn't believe his luck. They were actually being chased by the police. He felt instantly and passionately alive amidst the crazed reminders of death surrounding them. He grabbed hold of a skull and attempted to prise it loose from the grotesque pyramid of bones encasing it. In the sudden silence that followed he could hear the ever-fainter sound of Frances's and Giancarlo's footsteps disappearing ahead of him. Without any warning he trembled, his body convulsing as if someone had just stepped over his grave. He let the skull drop to the floor with an abrupt, almost instinctive abhorrence. It landed with a dull crack and rolled around in a circle, coming to rest against the toe of his shoe.

There was a shout five yards behind him. '*Eh vous. Restez là!*'

Jonathan turned. The three policemen had stopped, like a trio of vultures uncertain whether their prey was alive or dead. They stood in a line across the corridor, their black-leather jackets, trousers and boots bizarrely illuminated from behind.

'*Allez. Viens mon gars. C'est fini la comédie, non?*'

The voice was almost comforting, as if the owner was trying to coax a potential suicide back from the edge of a building. Jonathan found himself remembering the mysterious black-clad motorcyclists in Jean Cocteau's film *Orphée*, which he'd recently seen at school. These men, too, looked like the guardians of hell. He took a step towards them, as if about to give himself up. His heart felt as though it were trying to force its way up his windpipe, through his throat, and out of his mouth.

At the last possible moment he kicked the skull at them, flicked them a two-handed V-sign, swivelled, then sprinted up the corridor, easily outpacing the police in their bulky riot gear.

'*Petit con. On t'aura. Et ta gonzesse.*'

As their footsteps fell further behind, and despite the furtive glory of his narrow escape, Jonathan followed Frances and Giancarlo's trail back up to the surface with a strange and unwanted foreboding.

An attendant was waiting for them at the top of the stairs. 'Wait. I have to check your bags.'

'We're escaping from the riot. The flics are after us.'

'I still have to check everybody's bags. It's my job. We have many thefts here. People are always trying to steal the skulls.'

'But we don't have any bags. Where do you think we're hiding your bloody skulls? In our trousers?'

Giancarlo was staring wildly down the stairs as if he expected the police to appear at any moment behind them. It pleased Jonathan to think that their unwanted companion might have weak nerves. 'It's all right. You can relax. I lost them. I don't think they realised that the white arrows actually point towards the exit.' The words came out more flippantly than he intended. He hunched his shoulders questioningly at the attendant, in an effort to divert attention from his tone. '*Eh bien alors*?'

The attendant shrugged and waved them irritably through. Jonathan conceived a sudden, vivid picture of himself pelting the pursuing flics with eighteenth-century skulls as they tried to force their way towards Frances up the spiral staircase. It was one of his better heroic visions. As the final *coup de grâce*, he imagined kicking Giancarlo down on top of the flailing bodies – purely as a diversionary tactic, of course. He turned around, smiling. The sooner he got rid of the slimy Italian, the better. 'Well, it was great meeting with you, as our American cousins say. Remember us to your next riot.'

Giancarlo flashed him a smile. 'Look. Why don't I invite you both for a coffee?'

'A coffee?' Jonathan tried to instil five hundred years of supercilious de Montigny disdain into the words.

'Yes. Not all the streets are sealed off. And life goes on, you know.'

'We'd love to.' Frances was speaking for both of them. 'I've got to sit down. My legs feel like jelly.' She gave Jonathan a pointed look.

Jonathan felt a surge of anger. What was the bastard trying to do? Muscle in on Frances? He gave Giancarlo his best Burt Lancaster smile. 'Do you know of a café around here, then?'

'There's one behind my father's gallery. The coffee is good. Nearly as good as Italian coffee.'

Frances was peeling off her polo-neck pullover. 'I don't need coffee. I need an ice-cold coke.' Her breasts were plainly visible beneath her thin school blouse. Giancarlo was noticing them too. Jonathan felt like thumping him one on the ear. He stepped up and put a possessive arm around Frances but immediately got caught up in what she was doing with her pullover.

'Follow me.' Giancarlo moved off with estimable style, brushing his glistening, floppy mop of black hair lightly over his ears.

Oh you smooth, smooth bastard, Jonathan thought to himself. He flicked another unobtrusive V-sign behind Giancarlo's back.

They took the avenue de l'Observatoire route down towards the river. As they walked, Jonathan couldn't help noticing Giancarlo's mirror-polished Dexter loafers and immaculately creased white trousers – even the chase through the catacombs hadn't succeeded in dirtying them. The silhouette of his black bikini underpants showed through the thin material of his trousers, which were themselves set off by a near-fluorescent orange shirt, with thin white stripes and a wide collar. A small gold crucifix nestled at Giancarlo's neck, beneath a loosely knotted red silk bandanna.

Jonathan glanced morosely at his own get-up – a grubby pair of Levi's and a cotton shirt with a seaman's half collar. It had never really seemed to matter before. Now he felt humiliated.

'What sort of gallery does your father have?'

They were walking through the Jardin du Luxembourg. Birds were singing, mothers were wheeling their children past the lake, nannies were taking their charges for a late-afternoon airing – it seemed senseless, even obscene, to Frances to think that there was still a riot going on two or three blocks away. She wondered idly whether Giancarlo was homosexual. Those absurd clothes...

'A picture gallery. My father specialises in post-impressionist and late nineteenth-century French painting. It's on the quai de Conti. It's called Brancardi's. That is my name. Giancarlo Brancardi.'

'So you told us,' said Jonathan. 'And isn't that rather far?' Jonathan felt the urge to show that he, too, knew Paris intimately. And he was damned if he would introduce Frances formally to Giancarlo.

'Not if you take the short cut through the rue de Condé.'

Jonathan was about to suggest an even quicker route, when Frances cut in on him. 'I'm Frances, by the way. Frances Champion. And this is Jonathan Audley.'

They shook hands. Giancarlo's handshake struck Jonathan as rather limp.

'I'm studying history of art when I go up to Cambridge.' Frances had on her interested look. '*If* I go up to Cambridge, that is.' She crossed the fingers of both hands in front of her. Had she flashed him a brief, accusing look from under her eyelashes? 'So I'd love to see your father's gallery. Does he have a Cézanne?'

Jonathan could hardly believe what he was hearing. The guy was a total stranger for God's sake, and here was Frances, panting like a mare on heat to see his etchings. So it was true. Women really were fickle.

'Only a drawing, I'm afraid. There is an early Gauguin aquarelle, however. From his time at Pont Aven. And then we have a Vuillard.'

'A Vuillard!'

Jonathan made an 'A Vuillard! Wow!!' face behind their backs. If this was what alienation felt like, he wasn't interested.

Some way to the rear of them, as if to echo the tenor of his thoughts, a series of blast-grenades went off. From that distance they sounded like fireworks at a far-away Guy Fawkes celebration. 'Perhaps we ought to go back and see what's happening?' he interjected into their conversation. 'People may be getting killed back there.'

Jonathan's revolutionary fervour was waning rapidly, however. For the first time in his life he felt totally at the mercy of another person's actions. What if Frances changed her mind? What if she decided she preferred another man to him? Giancarlo, for instance? What would he do then?

'Please, J. I've had enough rioting for one day. Let's all have a drink and go and see Giancarlo's gallery.'

'His father's gallery, surely.' It sounded petty the minute he said it.

Frances gave him an unbelieving look, which Giancarlo immediately picked up on. Jonathan flushed to the roots of his hair. 'Yes, okay. Let's do it. It's a great idea.' His burst of belated enthusiasm sounded lame even to his own ears.

* * *

'How could you?' It was after midnight. Frances was confronting Jonathan outside the entrance to Piers's apartment. She'd been holding herself in for the last twenty minutes. Now she began to cry. 'How could you, J?'

Jonathan flopped wearily against the door. His head was spinning. His ears felt as if someone had stuffed them full of cotton wool and then plugged the gaps with wax. What in God's name had made him bolt those last two whiskies like that? Squinting heroically, he watched the tail-lights of Giancarlo's car all the way up the road until they disappeared in a sudden flash down the rue de Turin. Yes. The bastard even had a car.

He fumbled in his pockets. The key was still there, thank God. His barked knuckles stung abominably where they rubbed against the hard denim of his jeans. He cleared his throat. 'I didn't...'

'Shhh. Lower your voice. It would be the final straw if we woke Marise.'

They mounted the stairs in silence. A fearful headache was building behind Jonathan's eyes. Wordlessly, he unlocked the apartment door. Even the motion of bending down to find the keyhole gave him a pain in his temples.

'Thanks for nothing.' Frances's cheeks were shiny with tears.

Jonathan straightened up, then ducked his head against the throbbing in his skull. This wasn't how he'd imagined their return at all. Their first night alone in Piers's flat, and he'd already blown it. He tapped fatalistically at the light switch.

Marise had obviously been in to clean. There was a bowl of freshly cut flowers on the coffee-table. Romantic. Now all they needed was a bottle of champagne and a rolling-pin.

'I'm going to wash my face,' he said.

'Good idea. You do that.'

He hesitated, hunting for something to say. Frances scowled through her tears. She flung her pullover angrily onto the sofa.

'Right. I won't be a minute.'

Jonathan lurched into the bathroom. He stepped up to the mirror and prodded himself. Not too bad, considering. He had a livid red mark down the side of one eye, and his cheek was scratched. But that was all. No blood to speak of. No loose teeth. He filled the basin with cold water and dunked his head. The red mark stung like the blazes.

He padded back into the drawing-room. Frances was sitting on the sofa, next to her discarded pullover. He patted himself dry and draped the towel self-consciously around his neck. 'Do you want a drink?'

'Haven't you had enough already?' Frances's legs were primly tucked beneath her, and she was clutching her knees. She'd managed to stop crying.

'I meant you, not me. Something soft. Piers keeps crates of the stuff in his store cupboard.'

She raised her chin. 'A coke then.'

Jonathan slid the towel from around his neck and flicked idly at the back of a chair.

'I suppose you'll be wanting to hit me next?' She was crying again.

He cursed silently. How did girls manage to turn it on and off like that? He was badly irritated, but didn't dare show it. 'Look, Fran. I'm really sorry. It was a stupid thing to do.' His mind refused to settle on one response – one moment he was replaying, in heroic slow motion, everything that had happened at the club, the next he was feeling excruciatingly guilty.

'But you promised, J. You promised me you'd never get angry. Never get like Daddy.'

His heart lurched in his chest. 'I didn't mean to, Fran. Really I didn't. But when that sod started to paw you, it got too much for me.'

'He wasn't pawing me. And I can look after myself.' Each sentence came out as a gulp of air between sobs.

'I know you can, Fran. I know that. But I want to look after you.' Tears of frustration were building behind his eyes.

'And what about Giancarlo? It was his club. They all knew him there.'

'It was him I wanted to thump, not that drunken sot who asked you to dance.'

'Giancarlo? Why would you want to hit him? He's sweet.'

'Sweet!' He threw the towel onto the floor. His head began to throb abominably. He held up a placatory hand, as much to still his pulsing temples as to calm a tense situation. 'Look, Fran. Okay. Maybe I did behave badly. But what did you expect me to do? Just stand by while that bastard slobbered all over your neck?'

Frances opened her mouth to speak.

'No! Don't say it.' He closed his eyes. God, his head hurt. Perhaps when that guy had hit him it had perforated an eardrum or something? He took a ragged breath. 'Do you want to know the real reason I lost my rag?'

Frances nodded. She dabbed at her eyes with a tissue.

'Because you'd been ignoring me all evening, that's why.' He held up his hand again to still her. 'No. Listen to me. Because you made it perfectly obvious that you'd rather be with Giancarlo than with me, chatting about exhibitions, and auction houses and picture dealers and all that stuff. I don't blame you, of course. I can perfectly well see why you'd prefer him to me, with all his money, and his swish clothes, and his oozy, greasy charm.' His voice broke unexpectedly. 'You know something, Fran? You made me feel like a lump tonight. A mindless, sexless lump of bog-Cornish peat.'

'Oh, J. I didn't mean to.'

He was finding it increasingly hard to keep the tears of self-pity at bay. It was dawning on him, as he spoke, that if he didn't have Frances, he didn't have anything.

'Come over here,' she said at last.

'Why?'

'Just come over here. Then I'll tell you.'

He bent down and picked up the towel. He could tell she was getting ready to forgive him. If only he were still bleeding. Down the side of one cheek, perhaps?

'Let me see.' She took hold of his head, turning it towards the light.

'Ouch!'

She leaned forward and kissed the sore spot near his eye. 'So you were jealous, huh?'

'I'd liked to have cut his fucking balls off.'

She pulled back, disturbed once again by his tone. 'Do you often get into fights like that? With total strangers?'

He'd blown it again. Why, oh why, couldn't he keep a lid on his temper? 'Oh, all the time.' He could detect the rancour in his own voice.

Frances caught it too. She pulled back a little more. 'Is it going to happen again, J? Every time I notice another man? Every time I'm nice to someone?'

He felt the bitter gall of adulthood hammering to be let in. 'Of course it's not.'

'Aren't you sure of me? Is that it?' She was looking at him now as if he were some sort of wild animal, temporarily muzzled in its cage. 'You never have to worry, you know. As long as you're kind to me, and treat me gently, you'll never need to doubt me.'

He gave an ironical laugh. The night had given him a sudden flash insight into his own nature, and he wasn't happy about it. He wet his lips. 'It isn't you I'm not sure of, Fran. Don't you see that? It's me.'

Twenty-four

'Wake up. Wake up.' The hiss of the voice seemed to come from somewhere inside her own head.

Lisa realised that she had been dreaming. Clara had been drowning. In some sort of bog or quicksand. She'd been holding up her hands and sliding slowly under the water which was thick with weed and scum. But Clara's face had been strangely calm. Her hair had bloomed out like Ophelia's as her shoulders sank below the surface. Terrified, Lisa had run towards her, but her feet had become snagged in the mud. She'd tried to pull them out, but each time she managed to release one foot, the other dug deeper in. Now the mud was covering Clara's nose. Only her eyes and hair were visible. No!

'Come on. Lisa. Wake up!' The voice was more urgent now.

Lisa opened her eyes. Clara was crouched by the side of her bed. Clara? She sat up, her chest aching.

'Shhh. Don't make a sound.'

Lisa couldn't make out whether she was awake or still dreaming. She looked distractedly around the dorm. The other girls were all asleep. It was dark outside. She glanced at her bedside clock. Quarter past two. 'What are you doing? What is it?'

'Come with me. But don't make any noise.' Clara tiptoed quietly out of the dormitory.

Lisa sat up in her bed. What was happening? She was still half in the dream. She'd had it many times. Or variations of it. Each time Clara was drowning. Sinking somewhere. And Lisa would try to save her. But she never succeeded.

Sometimes she'd get as far as touching Clara's hand, feel the fingers closing over hers, but that was it. She'd never yet managed to pull Clara free.

Had she been dreaming this time? Had Clara really come into the dorm and woken her up? She pushed back the sheets and slipped her feet into her slippers. She felt quickly around for her dressing-gown. It was cold, all of a sudden. Bitterly cold for May. And she hadn't been sleeping well for weeks. It was beginning to tell on her. Sometimes she would have hallucinations – see things creeping up the walls.

She shuffled to the door and eased her way through into the corridor. No sign of Clara. She hurried down the passageway towards the study block. Perhaps she was going mad? Sometimes it felt like it. Her fixation on Clara was beginning to get her noticed. Mrs Renton had spoken to her about it on more than one occasion. Told her that her form-work was suffering. That she shouldn't take friendship so seriously. *Friendship*? She opened the door to her study and looked in. No one. She was wide-awake now. It *had* been Clara. Of course it had. But where had she gone?

'Lisa. Come on. In here.'

Clara was beckoning to her from the prefects' common-room. Lisa ran up the corridor, holding her dressing-gown tightly about her. Clara! Wanting to see *her*? Clara had cut her dead ever since their last summer holiday together in France. Ignored her. Nine months. Nine months of sheer agony. And now here she was. Calling to her.

Clara bundled her through the door. It was warmer in there, with the electric fire on. Clara fastened the door behind her and jammed a chair against the lock. Lisa turned to her. She wanted to hug Clara. Enfold her in her arms. But she could only stand there. Waiting. Hoping. 'Why did you bring me here?' she said. 'You know I'm not allowed. It's for prefects only.'

Clara snorted. 'It's the middle of the night, Lisa. Nobody's allowed.' She shook her head as if to clear it of some invisible irritation. 'Why do you think I brought you here?'

'I don't know.'

'Come on, Lisa. Tell me where Frances is. I'm her sister. And I know you know.'

So that was it. Lisa closed her eyes. 'I was just having a dream about you. That you were sinking. I tried to save you. But I was too late. I'm always too late.'

Clara made a face. She bounced down onto the sofa. 'Oh, God. Don't tell me you've still got a crush on me?'

'It's more than a crush. I'm in love with you.' Lisa stood there shivering. Outside, a solitary nightingale began to sing. It was the same one she'd been hearing for two weeks now, all through her sleepless nights.

'You'd better come over here then.' Clara patted the sofa cushion beside her.

Lisa hesitated. She was not so far gone that she didn't realise that Clara had something devious up her sleeve.

'Come on. Don't be shy. I won't eat you.'

Lisa took a deep breath. Despite her good intentions, she found herself walking across to the sofa. She sat down beside Clara.

'I suppose you want to kiss me.'

'Not if you're going to imagine I'm Jonathan again.'

Clara made a quizzical face. 'What?'

'Last summer. When you let me do those things to you. You told me you were pretending I was Jonathan.'

Clara groaned. 'And you wonder why I won't have anything to do with you?'

Lisa sprang up from the sofa.

'Oh, come on. I didn't mean anything. Come here and snuggle down beside me again. I'm freezing cold.'

Lisa hated herself bitterly. She hated herself for loving Clara, and she hated Clara for causing her to love her. She sat down again, her shoulders stiff with outraged pride. 'Why are you doing this? It can't just be because you want me to tell you where Frances is. Even you couldn't be that cruel.'

'Of course it isn't. But I always thought we were friends. We used even to be best friends. Or so you told me. You once said I was your best friend.'

'That was seven years ago. You've changed a lot since then.'

'Then why do you still say you love me?'

'Because I do! I can't explain it. If I could explain it, I wouldn't be putting myself through all this hell, would I?'

'Shhh. Did you hear anything?'

'No.'

'Are you sure it wasn't one of the teachers?'

'Of course not. They're all asleep.'

'Do you want to give me a cuddle then?'

Lisa closed her eyes. Why? Why was she always so stupid? Why did she let herself be manipulated so easily? In every other way she could cope. Be strong. She was good at games. Even better at lessons. There was talk of an English scholarship. A possible exhibition to Oxford, even, if things kept up.

Loathing herself, she reached out for Clara. Clara snuggled up against her. Lisa began to weep, her shoulders rocking.

They'd slept a little. A faint hint of dawn underlay the blackness outside. Clara pushed her hair back and stretched luxuriously. 'Do you want to kiss me?'

'No.'

'Why not?'

'Because I don't trust you. Or myself. After that last time. I'm scared. I'm scared I won't be able to pull back.'

'Why pull back?'

'Oh Clara. Do I have to tell you?'

'I suppose not.'

Lisa sat up. Clara hunched forward and lay with her head on Lisa's lap, looking up at her. Lisa began to stroke her hair. 'You're so beautiful. I stare at you sometimes, in the showers. Or in the changing rooms. I wish I had a body like yours.'

'What's wrong with your body?'

'It's like a man's. I'm skinny all over.'

Clara reached up and touched one of Lisa's breasts through her nightgown. 'That doesn't feel very male to me.'

'You know what I mean.'

Clara tilted her head back so she could see Lisa's eyes. 'Don't you like boys?'

Lisa looked away. 'Of course I do. What do you think? But I like you, too. There'll be tons and tons of time for boys later.' Her voice didn't carry much conviction.

'Why won't you talk about it?'

'Why should I? You'd probably tell all your friends about me. Then they'll make even more fun of me than they do already. Call me a lesbo.'

'Did Jonathan used to do things to you? When you shared a bed with him? Is that why you don't like boys?'

'Of course not! Don't be disgusting. Jonathan's got nothing whatsoever to do with it.'

'He saw us, you know. That day at the pool.'

'He didn't!'

'Yes, he did. He told me about it afterwards. Tried to get me to do the same thing with him. More than that, even.'

'I don't believe you. Jonathan would never do such a thing. He loves Frances.'

'How loyal you are, Lisa.'

'Did he really see us?'

'Yes.'

'He never told me.'

'Are you surprised?'

Lisa shook her head. 'Whatever you think about Jonathan, he'd never let me down. Never betray me.'

'So where has he gone, then? Where has he taken Frances? I spoke to daddy today on the telephone. Jonathan's run away from school. So Frances is obviously with him.'

'You'd just tell your father if I told you.'

'No I wouldn't. I promise. But I'm worried for Frances. They'll expel her if she stays away too long.'

Lisa stopped caressing Clara's hair. 'Clara, I may have a crush on you, but that doesn't mean I'm stupid. You couldn't care less if they expelled Frances. You've always hated her. Ever since you were little. I've never understood that about you. Frances is sweet. I'm really happy that she's going to be my sister-in-law some day.'

'Sweet!' Clara sat up. 'She's sweet like arsenic. Sweet like prussic acid. And believe me, she'll never be your sister-in-law. Jonathan will blow it. Somehow. Somewhere. But he'll blow it. And Frances doesn't forgive. She's got an ice-cold streak in her. She sits there, holding a grudge like that Malbecco character in *The Faerie Queene*, and she never lets go.'

'You sound as though you're talking about yourself.'

'Maybe I am.'

Lisa was standing by the window, looking out over the playing fields. The early morning sun was turning the grass a cold, brilliant orange. 'It's beautiful.' She pulled her dressing-gown closer around her. 'Even the nightingale's stopped singing. We'll have to go back to our dorms before everyone wakes up.'

Clara came up behind her. 'Did you like our kiss?'

'Of course I did.'

'You've wanted to, haven't you? For a long time. I see you looking at me sometimes. As if you could eat me.'

'Then why do you turn away? Why do you cut me dead like that?'

'God, Lisa, you can be dumb sometimes. You're so obvious, that's why. The teachers all know you've got a crush on me. If I were to chum up with you, an older girl with a younger, everyone would become suspicious. We'd be lucky not to get kicked out. It's better like this, believe me. This way they'll just think you've grown out of it.'

'I'm only seven months younger than you. And I won't grow out of it.'

'I know that.'

Lisa turned towards her. 'Do you? Do you really?'

'Do you want to see me sometimes? Secretly. Like this?' Clara was standing in front of her. She was fiddling with the neck of her nightgown.

'Of course I do.' Lisa could feel her desire for Clara burning in the pit of her stomach. She put a hand up to her chest.

'Then tell me where Frances is. Show me you trust me. Prove how much you love me.'

Lisa closed her eyes. Clara was leaning towards her. She could smell Clara's body. Her hair.

'Then I'll let you touch me again. Just like I did at the swimming pool last summer. I promise. Not pretending you're Jonathan.'

Lisa opened her eyes. Her head had fallen forward and she was looking at the floor. At Clara's bare feet. They were dirty. Grubby from the dust. She wanted to wash them. Dry them with her hair. Kiss them all over.

She sighed in tortured resignation, her voice shuddering. 'They're in Paris. Probably staying at Uncle Piers's flat in the rue de Florence.'

She looked up, meeting Clara's triumphant gaze. The passion of her physical desire melted like spring ice in the face of the dull, mundane reality of her betrayal.

Twenty-five

Tuesday, 7 May

This was to be the innocent day of the revolution. The day when ideas, not politics, would reign. Throughout that crisp spring morning, students from all over Paris congregated on both sides of the river. By midday, already in heavy sunlight, the crowd was beginning to converge on the Place de la Concorde. The good weather and the universal sense of expectation ensured an almost holiday mood.

By one o'clock more than twenty-thousand young people had gathered near the site of Robespierre's guillotine. Schoolboys, even the *Grandes Écoles* themselves, had abandoned their work to join the students. They assembled under red and black flags – the ancient colours of blood and death; of communism and anarchy. It was to be a joyous occasion. A ramble around Paris. A romp. The students wanted to own the city, not lease it from their elders.

'You see? I told you. Didn't I? Something is happening here. It would be foolish to miss it.' Giancarlo waved his hand airily to encompass the crowd in front of them.

They were standing near the eastern corner of the Pont de la Concorde. A phalanx of students had just charged the thinly guarded bridge. Now they were hurling defiance at the editorial offices of the right-wing *Le Figaro* newspaper.

Giancarlo had come by earlier that morning and sweet-talked Marise into letting him upstairs. Frances had still been in bed. Jonathan had been standing naked by the window, looking out into the street, the curtain held across his midriff.

'I'm sorry. I didn't realise...' Giancarlo started politely backing out of the door.

'It's all right.' Jonathan stepped back into the middle of the room. 'Just give me a moment and I'll get some clothes on. I want to talk to you.'

He was very aware of Giancarlo watching him as he walked towards the bedroom. Perhaps he was a queer, after all? That would be a joke, given his ludicrous behaviour the night before over Frances. To be jealous of a homosexual. Perhaps he'd introduce Giancarlo to Jean and Piers's circle? Get rid of him that way?

'You're very fit, aren't you?' Giancarlo was leaning against the door frame, admiring him. 'There's hardly an ounce of spare flesh anywhere on your body.'

Jonathan turned to him, quizzically. He was tempted to burst out laughing. 'Only here.' He hefted his cock and balls, giving Giancarlo a withering smile. 'Do you like it? Does it turn you on to look at men? Is that it?'

'Sometimes I like it. I like women more, though.' Giancarlo seemed curiously unfazed.

'Don't we all.' Jonathan turned mournfully back towards the bedroom. 'See if you can find yourself something to drink. I'll go in and rouse Frances. How about putting on some coffee? You're particularly fond of coffee, as I remember?'

Giancarlo ignored the jibe. 'Do you have any?'

'Only one way to find out.'

The sound of their voices from the drawing-room had woken Frances. She squinted up from the bed. Jonathan walked over and sat beside her. He bent down and gave her a kiss. 'Good morning, sleepyhead. Guess who's here? Your favourite Italian.'

'Oh no.'

'Oh yes. I think he's forgiven me for last night, though. He says I haven't got an ounce of spare flesh anywhere on my body.'

'He didn't! You didn't walk around in front of him like that?'

'It was a test. To see his response. I'm a dyed-in-the-wool naturist, remember? Impervious to bodily shame.' He shook his head ruefully. 'I think he fancies both of us if you ask me. He's one of those.'

'You're kidding.'

'No, I'm not. He's got that same way of looking that some of Piers's friends have. As though they're measuring you for a particularly tight-fitting suit.'

'How ghastly.'

'What say we get rid of him? Lose him somewhere on the streets?'

'J! We couldn't.'

'We'll let him buy us lunch first, of course. It would be unfair not to, in the circumstances. And then we'll dump him.'

'You're disgusting. You've no morals at all.'

Jonathan bent forward and began nuzzling one of her nipples.

'J!'

'I've found the coffee.' Giancarlo was calling from the other room. 'Do you want me to go down and buy some croissants? And you don't seem to have any milk.'

'Great. That would be great.' Jonathan made a face at Frances. He lowered his voice so that Giancarlo wouldn't hear what he was saying. 'It'll give us just enough time for a quickie.' He hung out his tongue and panted like a dog. Frances punched him on the arm.

'What's that you say?' shouted Giancarlo.

'Yes. You do that.'

'Okay. I'll be back in a few minutes.' The outside door slammed shut.

'J, I think you're starting to enjoy this.'

'Well, you've got to admit it, the possibilities are startling.'

'They'll never let us get away with it.' Giancarlo was shaking his head sagely. 'Never.'

The body of students, now some thirty thousand strong, was moving off towards the Champs Élysées. Jacques Sauvageot and Alain Geismar, two of the student leaders, had just spoken. The Arc de Triomphe was to be their goal. They would sing the *Internationale* on the Tomb of the Unknown Soldier.

'They'll massacre us. I can just see it now. There will be a line of them waiting...'

'Like in *Doctor Zhivago*? A line of Cossacks with drawn sabres? Or maybe you're thinking of *Battleship Potemkin*? The massacre on the Odessa Steps?'

'You know what I mean, Jonni.'

The crowd was in extravagant mood. Jonathan and Frances found themselves caught up in the heady carnival atmosphere. Only Giancarlo was holding back. Jonathan spun in a circle and threw his arms into the air. 'This is crazy. There are so many of us now, the police wouldn't dare to interfere. Don't you see that?'

And it was true. The police presence was little more than token. Shopkeepers and café-owners were emerging from their premises to watch the procession, which had begun to take on the appearance of a medieval revel. Even commuters and passers-by were joining in the fun. There was music and dancing – lines of students were linking arms and swinging around and around in the centre of the boulevard. Scooter cyclists were weaving in and out of the throng on their Vespas and Lambrettas, beeping their klaxons and waving.

'Can you ever see this happening in England?'

'Or in Italy.' Giancarlo was all in black today – black leather trousers, black silk shirt, narrow leather tie. Even his mood seemed black. 'Of course the politics are stupid. It will end badly. But it will be fun while it lasts.'

'What do you mean?'

Giancarlo gave a cynical sniff. 'Do you really think that de Gaulle is going to hand this country over to the students? He'll give them enough rope, then let them hang themselves with it.'

'But what about the workers? What if they go on strike?'

'The workers? Oh yes. They will go on strike. For a few days. For a few weeks maybe. Who knows? But after that they will go back to feeding their families. Just as they've always done. And nothing will change. Nothing will be different. Except us, of course. We'll become nostalgic. Waste the rest of our lives looking back on a non-existent past. A non-existent ideal.'

'Oh for God's sake, Giancarlo. Which side of the bloody bed did you get out of this morning? I don't know about you, but I'm looking to a better future.'

'Really? You told me last night that you left your school to come here. That you will no longer go to university. So? You are lucky. Your family is rich. They can accommodate you. You won't starve. How convenient. But what about these kids? If they don't graduate, they will have nothing. Not even self-respect.'

'What makes you such an expert?'

'Because I am like them. I come from there.' He threw out his arm. 'When I was young, my father didn't own a gallery. He swept the gallery floors.'

'Then how the hell…'

'I will tell you. Listen!' His face had taken on a darker, more dangerous expression. 'Because slowly, over many years, he dragged himself up. Went to night school. Studied art. Kept his eyes open. Watched what people were buying. How much they were paying. Who they were. He wanted to improve himself. His condition. The condition of his family. In the only way he knew how.'

Giancarlo and Jonathan stood facing each other in the centre of the street. The crowd parted around them like waves around the Red Sea, then merged again on the far side. Frances moved in behind Jonathan.

'How do you think I have the money to buy these clothes?' Giancarlo threw up his hands, pinching at his shirt and tie. 'To live and work here in Paris? Eh? Because he risked us. He risked his family. Risked our health and our future to save money to buy a painting. One painting. From an old lady he used to clean for.' He smoothed himself down, his fingers fluttering nervously. 'He knew how valuable it was, of course. And so did she. How very valuable.' He held up his hand, palm open. 'It took him five years to save up enough for even a down payment. Five years. Then he stopped a man at the shop. One of the collectors. A well-chosen man. And he spoke to him. Told him of the painting. The collector was fascinated. He came to our house. He could not believe that a family that lived as we did could hold something of such value.' He shrugged his shoulders. 'So he bought the painting from my father. For fifty million lira. My father gave half to the old woman to pay off the debt. With the other half he bought his own gallery. Now he has three. In Venice, Milan and Paris.'

'Christ, Giancarlo. I didn't know. You seem…well, the way you dress. I assumed…'

'It's all a lie. I didn't even own a pair of shoes until I was eight. If my father hadn't done what he did – if he hadn't pulled us up by sheer force of will – we would still be living in a tenement in Rome. And my mother would probably be dead.' He crossed himself superstitiously. 'She had leukaemia. After he sold the painting, my father was able to pay for the best treatment. They gave her a bone-marrow transplant. Now she has her own house in Venice. With a kitchen. And a bathroom she doesn't have to walk up four floors to reach.'

'I'm sorry. I wasn't trying to be flippant.'

'I know you weren't. But education matters. You're crazy to throw it away.'

'I'm going to enrol at the Slade. To study painting.'

'Good. But you owe it to Frances to make sure that she isn't harmed by all this, too. You must take the responsibility. Tell them you persuaded her to come with you. You mustn't spoil her chances. She has a natural dealer's eye. It is rare. She must be allowed to train it.'

Jonathan turned to her. They were walking with the crowd again. Everyone was smiling. Clapping each other on the shoulder. Calling to onlookers to join in. 'He's right you know,' he said. 'I've been thinking about it. That I should call your school. Tell them you're here with me. That it's all my fault.' He cleared his throat. 'You've got your A levels in a month. I don't know what I was thinking about.'

'J, I wouldn't have missed this for the world.' She smiled contentedly, and put her arms around both of them. 'Look. I want to spend today with you and Giancarlo. Understand? I want us to be happy. I want to eat the day. Gorge myself on it. I want the sun and the day and Paris and all these people to sink into me, right down to my bones. I want to come back home tonight exhausted with joy.' She looked up. 'Then you can call my school, barrack my teachers, and ride to my rescue like Sir Lancelot and the Lady of Shalott. Okay?'

Jonathan glanced across at Giancarlo, then back at Frances. He was tempted for a moment to tell her that Sir Lancelot had never succeeded in rescuing the Lady of Shalott; that loving him had killed her. But he took in the unconstrained joy on her face – the orgasmic way she threw back her head to breathe in the essence of the day – and said nothing.

For some reason that he couldn't entirely fathom, his feelings of jealousy seemed, temporarily at least, to have fallen into abeyance.

Twenty-six

By six o'clock that evening they had all but circumnavigated the city of Paris. Twenty-five kilometres of crazy, rebellious, joyous, anarchy. They were exhausted but happy. People were dropping out of the crowd and collapsing into cafés, bistros, restaurants, on the pavements – talking to each other, shouting, calling excitedly, going over the day and the march and the unfamiliar freedoms they had enjoyed.

'A beer. A cold beer. A Peroni would be best, but it is too much to expect. I shall settle for a Kronenbourg.'

'That's big of you.'

'We Romans are a modest people. We have always believed in encouraging the rest of Europe to make their best efforts for our delectation. That's why we conquered you. You would still be barbarians otherwise.'

'Happy barbarians.' Jonathan cocked his head to one side. 'Hey! That would be a good name for a pop group. The Happy Barbarians. You could play the electric mandolin, Giancarlo. And Frances could sing.'

'But I can't sing.'

'That hardly matters.'

They bantered and joked and ragged each other for the rest of the evening. On a whim Giancarlo took them to the Carosse d'Or, and they sat amongst the bourgeoisie feeling bohemian. The waiters seemed to smile at them benevolently for once, whilst their fellow diners watched them wistfully – the beautiful girl and her two handsome chaperones, unwittingly making their elders a present of their youth. Giancarlo paid for everything. As far as

Frances and Jonathan were concerned, it was only their due. They had youth, beauty and the future on their side. For that night only, they were convinced that life was good, that the world was a benevolent place, and that it would fulfil all their dreams.

After the restaurant they hung out around the Sorbonne. There were fire-eaters in the streets, and clowns and would-be magicians. Barriers were down. People spoke to each other, moving from table to table, from bench to bench, from wall to wall, small groups turning into larger ones and back again, couples going off together on assignations, having met only ten minutes before.

At midnight they went to a showing of Godard's *A Bout de Souffle* at the Action Christine. Watching Belmondo and Seberg on the screen perfectly encapsulated the way they felt about themselves. They emerged into the soft night air at two in the morning, still heady from the accumulated pleasures of the day.

'Come on. We'll take a taxi.'

'Can we afford it?'

'I can.' Giancarlo smiled. 'You can repay me when you are both rich.'

They sat in the taxi with all the windows open. The driver watched them in the mirror, a smile crinkling the corners of his eyes. 'You've been on the march?'

'Yes.'

'How can you kids expect me to make a living if you walk everywhere? Why don't you do a march with taxis?'

'With the clock on or off?'

'On, of course. That way you would get the best of both worlds. You make your point, and you feed the workers at the same time. That's what I call a revolution.'

They drove through the backstreets of Paris, empty now after the massed demonstrations of the day. The driver dropped them off at the rue de Florence.

Jonathan peered up at the apartment while Giancarlo paid the fare. 'Hey. We left the lights on.'

Frances pushed sleepily against him. 'No we didn't. It was morning, remember? Maybe Marise has been in?'

'Oh shit.' Jonathan made a face. 'We forgot to muss up the spare bed. Come on, Gianni, you can have the spare room tonight. Marise has got the convenient idea that Frances and I are first cousins. Now you can do the job for us. I hope you toss and turn a lot?'

'That all depends.'

'Sorry. No dice. Frances and I may be incestuous, but we're monogamous too.'

'Ha, ha, ha.'

They clattered up the stairs, forgetting the time and the fact that anyone else might be so mad as to actually be asleep.

'Piers has oodles of champagne stashed away. Let's plunder it.'

'Brilliant idea.'

They burst into the apartment, laughing. Frances, who was marginally ahead of the two boys, stopped dead in her tracks. 'Daddy!'

Jonathan stumbled to a halt behind her. Giancarlo came pushing up beside them. At the last possible moment he noticed the strange tweed-covered man standing in front of Piers's Second Empire sofa. 'Heh! We've caught a thief. *Vous êtes coincé, mon vieux*! *Haut les mains*!'

Henry Champion took a step towards them. 'I am not a thief. I'm Mr Champion, Frances's father. And who the bloody hell are you?'

Jonathan turned around, white-faced. 'Giancarlo. You must go. Please.'

'Is this who I think it is?'

'Yes,' said Jonathan through gritted teeth, making urgent shooing motions with his hands.

'All right, then. I go. But remember what I said to you this morning.'

'I will. I promise. And thanks. Thanks for the day.'

'No problem.' With a quick glance at Frances, Giancarlo backed out of the door. At the last possible moment Frances tore her eyes away from her father and raised her hand. Giancarlo made a chin-up sign with his head.

Jonathan turned back to the room. 'I can explain, sir.'

'There's no need to explain. I've seen the state of the bedroom. I think it's absolutely disgusting what you've done to my daughter. If you weren't Helen's nephew, I'd consider laying criminal charges against you. And if you were a little older, I'd give you a bloody sound thrashing. As it is I'll trouble you not to bother Frances ever again.' He turned his back on Jonathan. 'Frances, as you appear to have no luggage to speak of, I will expect to see you down at my car, ready to go, in five minutes. You have exactly that long to explain to…' He couldn't bring himself to utter Jonathan's name. '…to explain that I will not have this person either in my house, or around you, or around Clara ever again. You are neither to see him, speak to him, write to him, telephone him, nor to communicate with him in any way whatsoever. Do you understand me?'

Frances hesitated. For a moment Jonathan thought that she was going to defy her father. Argue with him. Then she dropped her head and turned her face away from his. 'Yes, Daddy.'

'Good. Five minutes, then. It's a great deal more than either of you deserve.'

Jonathan moved grudgingly aside to let his step-uncle through the door. Henry Champion stopped, as if he were about to say something, then shook his head disgustedly. He strode into the corridor and down the stairs. 'I shall be speaking to your father about this. You mark my words.' His voice echoed eerily off the stairwell.

Jonathan stood rooted to the spot, his face deathly pale. 'Oh God, Frances. I'm sorry.'

She ran towards him and buried herself in his arms. 'It had to happen. It just had to. It was too good to go on.'

'Whatever he says, I'm going to see you.' He closed his eyes, nuzzling her hair. 'Look! What if I write to Stacey? He's always liked Dad and me. And he hates your father. Well, not hates but…'

'It's all right. I know what you mean.'

'If I write to him, enclosing a letter to you, he'll make sure you get it. Then we can arrange how to meet.'

A car horn honked angrily in the road below.

'That's Daddy. I've got to go.'

'I really hope you're not going to get into trouble at school. I'll speak up for you. Write a letter to your headmistress. How about that?'

She rolled one of his shirt buttons between her fingers. 'What are you going to do, J?'

'I'm going to stay here. See the riots through. I can't go back to school now.'

'Will you apologise to Giancarlo for me. And thank him?'

'Of course.'

The horn beeped again.

'J, I've got to go.' She kissed him. He responded, hugging her tightly to him. 'I love you, J. It's a real passion with me. I'd die if anything happened to you.'

'Me too.'

She broke away from him and ran down the stairs. He listened to her footsteps all the way to the bottom. Then he ran through the apartment to the window overlooking the street. He unlocked it and threw it wide open, craning his body down. Frances was just stepping into her father's car. Instinctively, she looked up.

'I love you, Fran.' He raised a hand. 'I love you!'

She blew him a kiss, then ducked inside the car. The headlights came on before she'd even closed the door.

Jonathan watched the car all the way up the street until it rounded the corner of the rue de Stalingrad. He waited until the sound of its exhaust had long died away in the distance.

Twenty-seven

Penhallow, Cornwall. 1999

Frances moved closer to the window. She eased her head around the curtains and peered down. What was Jonathan doing, standing there like a zombie in the garden? What was he looking at? Was he in a bate because she'd run off? And what exactly had he told Cosima? She ducked back inside.

When she glanced out again he had his hands in his pockets and he was staring towards the woods. She wished she'd thought to bring her specs with her when she bolted. She could see perfectly well close to, but she had a problem with distances – Jonathan looked fuzzy. It was the story of her life.

She had an idea. She went into her father's dressing room and rummaged through his drawers. Yes. Here they were – Daddy's old pair of Ross binoculars. At least Clara hadn't pawned them. She hurried back into her bedroom and made straight for the window. Jonathan was still there, in exactly the same position, as though the gorgons had turned him to stone. She put the binoculars to her eyes and focused them. If only he'd turn this way; she could only really see the back of his head. Well he still had all his hair, at least. And he certainly hadn't run to fat – in fact he erred a little on the thin side, if anything. She supposed it was the result of his illness.

As she watched, he seemed to make up his mind about something, for he took his hands out of his pockets and struck out determinedly for the woods. Frances followed his progress with the binoculars until he disappeared into the shadow of the trees.

'Mummy!'

Frances jerked around. She dropped the binoculars guiltily to her side. 'I was just looking at the sea. It's so beautiful.' She pointed airily westwards. 'This was my old room, you know. My bed used to be over there. Mr C used to lie under that rug, hiding from Cruikshank.'

Cosima moved towards her. 'You were spying on Jonathan, weren't you?'

'Then where's he gone? Do you see him out there? I can't spy on someone who's not there, can I?' She raised her chin angrily. 'I wish you wouldn't be so impetuous, Cosima. You have a way of steamrollering over people's emotions. I hope you don't do the same with your boyfriends. Men don't like it, you know.'

Some instinct made Cosima bite back her cutting retort. 'Look, Mummy, I am sorry for what I said down there in the hall. It was out of order, I know it was. It's just that Jonathan seemed so sweet and vulnerable in the car. By the end of the journey I felt as if I'd known him all my life. Not just for five or six hours.'

'Well I knew him for eleven years, and he can charm the petals off a daisy.' She scowled at her daughter. 'He obviously charmed your petals off.'

Cosima blushed. 'He's a bit old for me.'

'That's the understatement of the year!'

'Oh, come on. He's only forty-nine. And he looks younger. I pretended I thought he was fifty-one in the car. You should have seen his face.'

'You shouldn't play games with people, Cosima. One day they'll ricochet back and hurt you.'

'It's all right. I don't fancy him if that's what you mean. It would be almost like incest, wouldn't it? Knowing he's been your lover too?'

Frances squared her shoulders and made for the door. 'Take these binoculars back, please, and put them in your grandfather's dressing room. I'm going for a walk. I don't like the way this conversation's turning.'

'To the woods? Are you going to the woods?'

'Cosima, you can stop all this right away! You're making it impossible for Jonathan and I to meet in a remotely normal way. Just belt up about whatever he told you. Please? For me? Otherwise I shall go to an hotel. And that would make your Aunt Clara deliriously happy.'

'So where is my delirious Aunt Clara, then?'

'God knows! I certainly don't.'

Frances flounced off knowing she hadn't played the scene very well, but what could she do about it? Every word that Cosima uttered seemed to strike a raw nerve. She hurried down the front stairs. Should she leave? Things were only going to get worse when Clara came back from wherever she was. And then the rest of the family were going to turn up tomorrow. The whole thing was a nightmare. She felt like running outside, jumping into a taxi and heading straight for the nearest airport.

She stopped briefly by the hall mirror. She was wearing a cream silk blouse, a French linen sheath skirt in grey, transparent tights, and a pair of flat-soled loafers which she'd had made for herself by Lobb one year in a rare fit of extravagance. When Giancarlo had seen the bill he'd thrown one of his rare tantrums.

'One thousand pounds for a pair of shoes? It's impossible!'

'They're hand-made. And it's my money. And they'll last a lifetime. Unlike me,' she'd added, as an afterthought.

And it was true. The shoes had worn well. She patted the crow's feet at the corners of her eyes – nothing much she could do about them. But the spat with Cosima had given her face a heightened colour, which suited her – such a shame the health gurus had taken all the pleasure out of lying in the sun. She remembered the long naked days on Levant. Up at eleven and down to the rocks for the first swim. Then back for a leisurely lunch followed by a siesta – with or without sex. With, mostly. Hot, sweaty, afternoon sex. The sort she liked best. Then back for another session on the rocks, rolling through the water, cleansing herself like a seal. She'd been as brown as a berry by the end, and felt marvellous with it. Until Jonathan went and spoiled everything with... God, she could hardly bring herself to think about it, even after all these years.

Well, it was now or never. If she bolted again she'd never come back. She knew it. She felt flustered but determined. Might as well get it over with. She stepped out through the front door.

The light rain of thirty minutes ago had given way to strong September sunshine. She could feel the warmth of it through her blouse. Smoothing her skirt down over her hips, she set off towards the woods. She knew exactly where Jonathan would be – the tree house. It was obvious.

And the tree house, as she had to admit, was as good a place as any to begin the long delayed process of confronting her past.

Jonathan arched his head backwards. Had the tree house really been this close to the ground? He could very nearly reach up and touch the hatch. The rope ladder had long since rotted away, of course – he scuffed some fresh leaves with his foot to reveal a decomposing rung. And it had always seemed so large. Now he saw it for what it really was. A five-foot by six-foot rectangular box with two rough windows cut into the sides. Even if he could climb up there, the thing probably wouldn't take his weight. Some of the planks had rotted, and he could see daylight leaching through the roof. Another year or two and it would be gone.

He turned unwillingly back towards the house. Something was missing. Some element of the equation. He felt dissatisfied with his experience. Standing in the garden he'd been tempted not to come out here – and perhaps that would have been best. It didn't do to dwell on the past.

'Jonathan?'

He glanced up.

Frances was standing at the far edge of the clearing, watching him. The fresh sunlight was filtering through the trees behind her, creating an artificial halo around her head. He grinned with an unholy sort of joy. The picture she made seemed so apt. It had been the stuff of his wilder, less rational fantasies for years.

How long had she been there? Why hadn't she come down to greet him? He started up the slope towards her.

'It doesn't look like much, does it?' he said.

'The past never does.'

'Oh I don't know.'

He kissed her on both cheeks, his skin clenching with her remembered fragrance. He stepped back and gazed at her, just as she was gazing at him. They were both smiling.

'Well? How do I look?' All her good intentions had fallen by the wayside. She stood there, as she had stood all those years before on the hillside, a scant quarter of a mile away in distance, a great deal more than that in understanding, and let him admire her.

'You look bloody marvellous. Better than ever.'

'I seem to have heard this conversation before. Only you were knee high to a grasshopper at the time, and I was nursing a swollen foot.'

'I've run out of handkerchiefs, though, since then. It's never been the same since that maid of ours left.'

She turned and slipped her arm through his. 'Come on. Shall we go and take a look?'

'Yes. I'd like that.'

They walked back through the trees together. Jonathan felt curiously at peace, as if some holy man had laid a healing hand on his forehead, blessing him and bringing him succour.

'Are you really all right?'

'You mean the cancer?'

'Yes.'

'So it seems. I spoke to Mézières last week. He's the doctor in Toulouse who treated me. He appears to think I might last out the millennium. With maybe a decade or two tacked on the other side, if I'm especially lucky.'

'Was the treatment horrible?'

'Indescribable. Just like they say.'

'I'm so sorry, J.'

He stopped and turned to her. 'I'm not. Really. It sort of made me grow up.' He allowed his eyes to graze across her face. 'You know what I was like before. Well I carried on being like it after you left. Only worse. And Uncle Piers leaving me his money didn't help. You were well rid of me.' She opened her mouth to speak, but he hushed her by shaking his head. They walked on tacitly, not looking at each other.

'My only sadness is that I can't have children any more. I know I left it too late. Selfishness. Ego. What have you. But I would have liked a child.' He laughed ironically. 'Mind you, I suppose that's only vanity, too. The unregenerate male's desire for a spurious immortality – to see yourself reflected back in the eyes of someone who'll outlive you.' Frances remained silent, and Jonathan was grateful for her intuitive tact.

They reached the bottom of the bluff.

'This is it, isn't it?' She turned to him, expectantly. 'This is the place.'

He nodded. 'You were up there. And I came blundering in from over that direction. Come on. I want the full effect.'

'Aren't we being terribly silly?'

'Of course not. We're just *being*. Do you mind?'

'No.'

They approached the crest. 'You were in this hollow. Lying just there. Mr C was beside you.' He let go of her arm and backed up the hill. 'I came running down here.'

'You had yellow shorts on. And a white shirt. And a crew-cut. And those sandals with holes in them.'

'What happened then?'

'I screamed.' She smiled wryly. 'Well. Not exactly screamed. Gasped is more like it. I thought you might be a bull or something, come to get me. I only saw your shadow at first.' She hesitated. 'Do you know something? I always wondered why Mr C didn't bark.'

'Perhaps he knew something we didn't?'

'Perhaps. I thought you were terribly dashing, you know.'

'Really?'

'Really. When you brought out that handkerchief and started binding my foot, I nearly swooned.'

'*Swooned*?'

'Yes. Just like the ladies in all those bodice-rippers. I felt quite faint. All fizzy. I can't explain it.'

'Is that why you let me kiss you?'

'Probably. I must have had my guard down.'

He laughed. 'Was that your first ever kiss?'

'Yes. Of course it was. We were only ten. You must have known.'

'I suspected.'

'How about you?'

'It was mine too.'

She glanced down. He'd taken off his jacket and had slung it over one shoulder. He had his shirt rolled up to just below his elbows. The hair on his forearms was still very blond. He was wearing faded black jeans with no socks – just bare feet in well-polished loafers. She could see his ankles. She'd always liked the look of them. They were so brown and slim and masculine.

'Could I kiss you now?' he said.

'That might not be a good idea.'

'Then again it might.'

She looked up at him, considering. 'Will you close your eyes? Just like you did back then?'

'If you want me to.' He was smiling.

'I do. And just once. Agreed?'

'For old time's sake?'

'If you like.'

Twenty-eight

Clara swerved her Volvo through the Penhallow gates. A thick cloud of gravel pattered off the retaining walls. A hovering kestrel soared up fifty feet in front of her and began dancing on the eddies. Lucky buggar.

Seeing that man at the cottage had given her the absolute willies. Had he really noted down her number? Maybe he'd already told the plods? She'd heard all about these new-fangled police computers. Would they turn up at her door and try to take her away? Or would they phone up, all polite, and ask her to come down to the station to answer a few questions?

Well, either way, it would be her word against his. There wouldn't be any 'it's a fair cop, lads,' as far as she was concerned. She'd bloody well fight.

She brushed nervously at her face. Her hand came away covered in perspiration. Must have another drink. Maybe she was getting the DT's? Maybe it was all just a case of hallucinations? She *had* been hitting the juice a little harder than usual in the past few weeks – furtively, while Helen was still alive, and a good deal less furtively since. Perhaps she had alcohol poisoning? That would explain a lot of things.

She allowed the Volvo to drift around the final bend of the drive, then hunched forward across the wheel, her shoulders tensing. Damn! There was a car parked in front of the house. She squinted through the greasy windscreen. No. It was a convertible Aston Martin. Thank God for that. Must be Jonathan's. Just the sort of stupid, flamboyant car he would have – an overgrown schoolboy's sort of car.

She pulled up and switched off the engine. Pity she'd been forced to miss the first pregnant meeting between the lovebirds. That would have been a sight for sore eyes. Perhaps Frances had hauled off and given him a whack? No. That would have been too much to hope for.

'Aunt Clara?'

Clara stopped halfway through the act of getting out of the car. She looked up myopically. Christ. The model. She'd forgotten all about her. She fixed what passed for a welcoming smile on her face.

'It is you, isn't it? Can I give you a kiss?' Cosima ran up to her. 'I've been dying to meet you. It's crazy, isn't it? All these years and we've never even spoken to one another.'

Clara made a sour face and offered her a cheek. 'We might as well have. I've seen all your pictures. Helen used to cut them out of the magazines.' She steadied herself against the roof of the car. 'Couldn't miss them, really. She insisted on leaving them around the house for people to trip over.' She stumbled backwards as if subconsciously echoing her words, then caught herself. 'You're even more beautiful than I expected. The photos don't do you justice.'

'Thanks. But don't tell that to the photographers.' Cosima sighed, and hunched her shoulders dramatically. 'Actually I'm over the hill. I've retired. Strutted down my final catwalk. I never was that hot, if the truth be known. Only second league, really.' Her self-deprecating smile turned into a quizzical frown when she realised that Clara wasn't listening to her. 'Are you sure you're all right, Aunt Clara?'

'Just a little unstable on my pegs, that's all. Nothing to worry about.' Clara squinted at her niece. Over the hill? Well at least the girl had a lively sense of humour. Perhaps she was okay after all? Maybe she'd try the truth on her. Make a welcome change. 'Actually, I'm blasted.' Clara made an extravagant gesture towards her hair. 'Stopped off on my way back from town and had a few at the Gurnard's Head. Your mother always has that effect on me.'

Cosima sniggered, then abruptly caught herself before it turned into a fit of the giggles. 'Come on. I'll help you carry in your shopping.'

'Sorry. Forgot the shopping.'

Cosima gave a snort, then doubled up, clutching at her stomach. 'Oh, God. I'm sorry! Wait. Wait.' She flapped a hand and gulped in some air. Her nose was turning numb with the strain of trying to control herself. Clara stared at her, her head cocked to one side like a pointer's.

Cosima forced herself upright. She mopped fruitlessly at her eyes with a crumpled tissue. 'Christ, how embarrassing. I haven't corpsed like that in years.' She could feel the giggles still hovering at the back of her throat. 'Not since school, actually. But I had a sudden vision of you and Mummy housekeeping together, and it just murdered me. I think I'm finally beginning to understand.'

'Understand what?'

'Your relationship.'

'Well that's great. Because I certainly don't. Where are our ageing lovers, by the way?'

'Couldn't tell you.' Cosima had things more or less under control again. 'I've been in the doghouse once already today for interfering. She went off in a huff.'

'In a huff? Fancy that. She threw a plate at me this morning. During breakfast.'

'You're kidding!'

'No. I promise. Ask her if you don't believe me. It missed of course. She bust the dining-room window instead.'

'I can't believe it. Mummy? Throwing dishes? Breaking the dining-room window?'

'That's not the half of it. Come on in and I'll tell you all about it.' Clara hesitated on the threshold, weighing Cosima up. 'You haven't brought any booze with you, by any chance? No? Then we'll have to raid what's left of your grandfather's cellar.' She made a face. 'Although, to be perfectly honest, vintage plonk has never really punched my ticket.'

'Clara's back. That's her car.'

Frances wished she had pockets in her skirt because she suddenly didn't know where to put her hands. She ended up folding them awkwardly across her chest. What she really wanted to do was to slip her arm through Jonathan's again, as she had done coming out of the woods, but she felt constrained. Their kiss had got a little out of hand, and she'd panicked, pulling away from him. It would seem perverse to cosy up to him again so soon.

'Look. I'm sorry. About taking advantage like that. But you wouldn't believe how long I've been dreaming of that moment.' He shook his head disconsolately. 'I haven't felt lost like that – completely lost – for years. Nearly thirty, actually.' He dared a look at her.

'Well if it's any consolation, I felt exactly the same way. But it just won't do, Jonathan. It's not thirty years ago. It's now. And things have changed. I can't revert to being a schoolgirl again.'

'You'd just finished at Cambridge, actually.'

'Well a young graduate then. It's too late for all that.'

'Why?'

She dropped her hands to her sides, and sighed. 'Well for one thing, I haven't forgiven you for what you did on Levant. It completely rocked my life. It changed everything. It was like one of those cataclysmic events that...well...that killed off the dinosaurs or something.'

'I was drunk, Fran. Stupidly, sickeningly drunk. So drunk I passed out.' He thrust his hands deep inside his pockets and shook his head. 'When I woke up I was in Clara's bedroom, stretched out on her bed. Believe me, to this day I haven't the faintest idea how I got there, or what I did when I was there. It's a blank. It's always been a blank. I can only assume I did what I think I did. I certainly have no recollection of it. I imagine that Clara thoroughly enjoyed filling you in on all the salient details later.'

'She said you'd been taking drugs.'

'Taking drugs?'

'Yes. She crowed about it yesterday, in the car. Then later she told me she'd baked a hash cake and you ate it. Then you were drinking something with a... Slivovitz. That was it.'

'I remember the Slivovitz. It was long-dong Ludo's – you know, that ghoul-faced Frenchman two terraces down who had the hots for Clara. I only had a couple of shots, though. He'd left a bottle of it iced-up in her and Lisa's fridge.'

'Iced-up? Clara told me that something else got iced-up, too.'

'Did she? Well, good old Clara. She probably meant the Slivovitz.' He squinted, trying to remember. 'Look, I know it was stupid. And God, yes, I did eat some of that cake, I admit it. I didn't know it was a hash cake, though. Crafty little bitch!'

Frances stopped and turned towards him. 'Look, Jonathan. What are you trying to tell me? That you didn't sleep with Clara? Is that it? Because I don't believe you. I saw you in there. And Clara exhibiting herself out on the terrace like the cat that finally got the cream. You were stark naked – flat out on top of her rumpled bed. The whole place stank like a brothel.'

Jonathan winced. 'Seriously, Fran. I don't know what I did. I'm not trying to make excuses for my behaviour. I was perfectly capable of it, I'll admit that. But I had a head on me before I even started drinking. It was stupid, I know. I'd probably taken too much sun the day before.' He briefly closed his eyes, concentrating. 'The rot set in after our row, when I went down and had a couple of gins at the *Pomme d'Adam*.'

'Gins? You never drink gin.'

'Hair of the dog – you know the sort of thing. I thought something stiff like a gin would do the trick better. It didn't do any good, of course. It never does.' He shook his head, still bewildered by his own gullibility. 'Then I saw Clara saying her fond goodbyes to Ludo – she and Lisa had just had a blistering spat over him. Needless to say she wanted a drink too. So I had another with her. Or two. I don't remember now.'

'You don't have to go on, you know.' They were standing at the edge of the clearing, looking down towards the house.

'Yes I do.' The expression on his face belied his words. 'I know I should have gone after you. Chased you all the way back to Venice. But I was in shock. Or muzzy. Or... I don't know what. Instead I just hung around papa's house like a rabbit blinded silly by a set of oncoming headlights – as though I deserved to lose you, or something.' He glanced across at her, his eyes blurring with remembered pain. 'But I realise now I should have stopped you. Should have tried to explain.'

'All right. You can explain now.'

He held out his hand. 'Look, will you sit down? Please. It's dry. You can use my jacket.'

Frances hesitated, then stepped back to let him clear a space for her. He spread his jacket across the still damp ground. She sat down and drew her legs beneath her, then looked up at him. He hovered above her, his eyes strangely distant. She had a sudden unwelcome vision of what the past few years must have been like for him. Alone. Sick. With no one to love and look after him.

She forced her misgivings to the back of her mind. She would remember all her own empty years instead. The rottenness of her marriage to Giancarlo. The lies. The infidelities. That was the reality. Not this. Not some vaguely remembered dream that a mere half-dozen casually taken drinks had contrived to shatter.

Jonathan's throat was dry. What a fool he was not to have thought this moment through – all those years wasted in speculation, and now it had finally come to it, he was totally unprepared.

Frances glanced up at him with cold eyes. 'Well?'

Twenty-nine

Ile du Levant, France. 1971

The old man bent over to reveal a pair of pancake-coloured buttocks the texture and consistency of tanned leather. He rummaged around in his holdall and withdrew a leopard-skin G-string. Lisa lit a cigarette and watched him, her grey eyes narrowed against the smoke. He hopped precariously from one foot to the other while he struggled to slip the flimsy material over his hips; then he straightened up, checked to see if anyone was watching, flexed his knees, and arranged the G-string more comfortably around his crotch.

Lisa turned to her brother. 'What do you think he can possibly get out of it?'

'God knows.' Jonathan took a sip of his beer. He watched moodily as yet more tourists descended in their shaky droves from Lulu Le Corsaire's yellow-striped fishing boat. 'Doesn't look like they're on this boat either, Liss.'

Lisa shook her head in exasperation. 'I must be mad. When I was twelve, I vowed I'd never come back to this beastly island again. Now look at me. Panting with anticipation every time the ferry comes in.'

'You know what I think about all that.'

Lisa stubbed her cigarette out on the metal table top. 'Yes, I know. I know. Clara's bad for me. She doesn't love me. She's going to waltz off with the first man who eyes her up. How do you think that makes me feel?'

'Sorry, Liss.'

'Yes. Sorry. You've chosen the perfect word.' Lisa thrust the straw from her coke bottle between her teeth and started chewing on it. 'Sorry for myself.'

Jonathan hunched forward in his seat. 'Look, I know this is going to sound stupid, but what is it about Clara? You're nineteen, gorgeous, intelligent – come on, Liss, you can take your pick. Why has it got to be Clara?' He felt the words slipping out despite his best intentions. 'And why not give the male sex a chance for a change?'

'Why not indeed?' Lisa stood up. 'But thanks for the endorsement, anyway.' She gave him a fractional smile and slipped her feet neatly back inside her flip-flops. 'I'm going down to the ferry in case we've missed them. Coming?'

Jonathan sighed and drained the last of his beer. 'Look. I didn't mean that last thing I said. Of course it's up to you who you fall in love with.' He put a placatory hand on her arm. 'I'll tell you one thing, though. This is going to be a miserable bloody holiday if they don't turn up.' He bent down and picked up their beach bags. 'Perhaps we can improve on our scrabble scores?'

Lisa shook her head vehemently. 'They will turn up.'

'How can you be so sure? They hate each other.'

'Frances loves you and Clara wants you. How's that for an equation?'

He winced. 'Yes, Liss, but I don't want Clara.'

She turned to him, rolling her eyes. 'Why the fuck do you think I'm here?'

Frances glanced furtively at her sister. Clara had outdone herself today. She was wearing a huge pair of dark glasses *à la* Sophia Loren, a pink chiffon headscarf, a black Playboy-style top, and a matching velvet miniskirt. One of the young sailors was busily inspecting the engine simply to afford himself a waist-high view of Clara's crotch.

'Clara, can't you see he's looking at you?'

'So what?' Clara spread her legs a little wider. The sailor dropped his spanner, tried to catch it, and slammed his head teeth-gratingly hard against the top of the cowling. 'Serve you bloody well right,' she murmured under her breath.

Frances was staring at her own distorted face in the mirror-like surface of Clara's lenses. She waved two-handed at her reflection. 'Anybody in there? What have you done with my sister?'

'Go to hell, Frances.'

Frances leaned back against the wooden bench. 'You know, I can't for the life of me understand why you ever insisted on coming on this trip. You're just playing with Lisa. You know you are. And Jonathan doesn't want anything more to do with you. I'd have thought that would have sufficed for most people?'

Clara flashed her a fake smile. 'Haven't you forgotten that I'm Lisa's guest, not Jonathan's? And that she's paying for my ticket, my accommodation, my food, and, presumably, my time. So you don't have any say in the matter, it seems to me.'

'You're disgusting. Why don't you just set her free? Tell her what the score is?'

'Because I don't want to. And I'm poor. And I find her amusing.'

Frances snorted. 'I only hope that she and Jonathan haven't taken cabanon next door to one another. I don't want to have to be the one to sweep up the pieces.'

'No one's asking you to. Anyway, what's eating you all of a sudden? Scared Jonathan will get a hard-on every time he sees me naked?'

Frances sprang angrily to her feet. 'I wish I had a tape recorder sometimes!' She pushed her way through the main passenger cabin towards the front of the boat. Still fuming, she wedged her hips against the prow and stood watching the gradual approach of the island.

The main hill was dominated by an ancient, flat-roofed fort, surrounded by pines and reached by a stone staircase that bisected the slope like a sacrificial Aztec walkway. Mimosa, dwarf oak and eucalyptus trees dotted the surrounding hillside, with occasional houses breaking up the thick green blanket – some were painted a brilliant white, some were mud-coloured, and some were of stone construction to match the textures of the encircling coast. A thin scattering of people lay sunbathing, like naked seals, down by the rocks.

As she watched, a slender young man stood up, stepped languidly onto an outcrop and executed a neat scissors dive into the sea. Frances could almost feel the cool slap of the water on his skin.

'God. Just look at them all.' Clara had followed her outside. 'Pretending not to eye each other up. No wonder Jonathan and his pervy old father have been coming here for years.' She sniffed. '*Coming* being the operative word, of course.'

Frances pretended not to hear. It was easier that way. If only she could manage the trick all the time. 'Can you see them anywhere?'

Clara gave her a knowing look. 'Are you absolutely sure we're on the right island? It's not the next one, by any chance? Or the one after that?'

'No. It's this one.'

'Well they're not here then. What a laugh if they decided to stand us both up. The screwees screwed!' Clara took off her sunglasses and began to massage her neck. 'How much money have we got left, by the way?'

'About three hundred francs.'

'Christ. We could always go on the game, I suppose. Pick ourselves some rich lovers. Fuck our way back to England.'

'Clara, you're absolutely disgusting.'

Clara winked at her young sailor who had tentatively come forward to throw out the bowline. He turned away, shaking his head disconsolately. 'I just say what other people think. What's the harm in that?'

'If you don't know, I can't tell you. Let's get our things and go before you cause a riot.'

Their fellow passengers, apart from a few conventional souls who were travelling on to the neighbouring islands of Port Cros and Porquerolles, were already seething off the boat and out onto the dockside.

Clara shaded her eyes. 'Look. There's a van. Let's get a move on or it'll fill up. Broke or not, I'm not lugging my bag all the way up to the village – that much I promise you.'

'Clara!' The shout had come from somewhere above them.

'Who's that?' Clara squinted around in the bright sunshine. 'Is it Lisa?'

Lisa stepped to the edge of the track, raised her hands and waved. Jonathan gave her a nudge. 'She can't see you, Liss. The sun's in her face. Why don't you run on down and welcome her? I'll bring our bags along.'

Lisa darted along the road, still waving. She picked up pace going down the incline, dodged past the beaten-up van and sprinted nimbly out towards the wharf. At the very last moment one of her flip-flops broke. She hopped the last few yards, tugging vainly at her sandal, her chest heaving, her forehead beaded with perspiration. 'Oh my God, Clara. You're really here!'

Clara stepped languidly off the gangplank. 'Sexy. I like the sarong. I'm surprised it stayed on with all that exercise.'

Lisa blushed crimson beneath her tan. 'It's a pareo, actually. They sell them in the village.' She swallowed awkwardly. 'They're from Tahiti. I'll buy you one if you want.' She limped forward, unable to control herself any longer. 'Can I kiss you?'

'Might as well.'

She pecked Clara chastely on the corner of the mouth.

'Doesn't the porter get a kiss too?' Frances stepped onto dry land and gave Lisa a one-armed hug. 'Last off the boat. As always.' She grimaced hopefully up the track. 'Is Jonathan here?'

'Don't worry. He's just coming. I left him carrying our beach things.'

Frances's belly tightened in anticipation. She put on her most matter-of-fact voice. 'The van's about to leave. Why don't you two hitch a ride up to the village with the bags? I'll wait here for Jonathan. I'm dying for a swim, anyway.'

'Don't you want a swim, Clara?'

'You must be joking.'

'Okay, then.' Lisa gesticulated at the van driver. 'I can't wait to show you our cabanon. It's got a really big sun terrace and the best possible view of the sea and the other islands. And the sunsets are gorgeous.' She grabbed the bags and hobbled forward, Clara following more sedately behind. 'There's no generator, unfortunately, so we have to use oil lamps and candles instead. But that's romantic, don't you think? We've got a gas cooker, and a gas refrigerator, and there's even a shower which you have to heat up with hot water from old Evian bottles they leave out all day on the terrace…'

'There are two beds, I hope?'

Frances couldn't bear to watch. It was like animal baiting at a circus. 'See you both later.' Her voice came out unnaturally high.

She hurried up the hill without waiting for Lisa's reply. Jonathan was just breasting the corner. She had to stop him from going down there and poisoning the situation even further. She broke into a nervous run. 'Jonathan!'

Jonathan dropped his bags and held out his hands, smiling. Frances rushed up and buried herself deep inside his arms. He smelled wonderful, as if the sun had concentrated all its essence on his skin. Animal-like, she abandoned herself to him, while he kissed her passionately over her forehead and eyes and hair.

He rested his chin on top of her head. 'God, I'm glad you're here – glad both of you are here, actually. Lisa's been climbing the walls for the past three days.'

'That's nothing to what she'll be doing over the next two weeks.'

Jonathan stepped back, holding her at arm's length. 'What do you mean?'

Frances made a face.

'Oh Christ. You're not serious?' Jonathan's eyes wandered down the hill to where Clara and Lisa were entering the van.

'You know what our darling Clara's capable of. Well she's in one of her drop-dead sarcastic moods. And she's been making eyes at any man remotely over five-foot tall since we left London.'

'Shall we just leave and go somewhere else? Tasmania, maybe?'

'J, we can't. We owe it to Lisa to look after her.'

'Fran, believe me, Lisa can look after herself.'

'I'm not so sure.'

He gave a grudging wave as the van went past. Clara doffed her sunglasses and blew him a flamboyant raspberry. Lisa averted her face and pretended she hadn't seen him.

'See? I told you. It's started already.'

Jonathan planted a firm kiss on Frances's forehead. 'Well how about your father, then? Any trouble in that direction?'

'He thinks I'm on holiday with Giancarlo. In Sicily. Separate rooms, of course.'

Jonathan straightened up, scowling. 'Giancarlo?'

'Oh, come on, J. He's only a convenience. And what's more, he's promised to get his mother to post all the fake cards I wrote before I left Venice – they're mostly of the Leaning Tower of Pisa, but Daddy won't know the difference.' She grabbed him by the chin. 'So don't be jealous!'

Jonathan forced the smile back onto his face. 'Of course I'm not jealous. In fact I'm rather grateful to him.'

Frances let out her pent-up breath. 'That's better.' But still she didn't quite believe him.

'How about going up and seeing our cabin? We could test out the bed.'

'It's not next to Clara and Lisa's, is it?'

'You must be joking! It's in an entirely different place altogether.'

'Thank God.' She reached up and gave him a wet kiss. 'Come on, J. Cheer up. You're still scowling. Can we go for a swim first? Please? Then you can rape me.'

'I hope you've brought your swimming costume?'

'No, I…it's in my bag.'

He chucked her under the chin. 'It was a joke, silly. This is a naturist island.' He tipped her a wink. 'And you know what that means, don't you? It means we can stop off in the bushes whenever we want to for a quick one. Everybody does it. In fact, we'll probably have to force our way through half a hundred wildly thrashing bodies to even get down to the rocks.'

Frances faltered – then her face cleared and she punched him playfully on the arm. 'Ha, ha, ha!' Then, still not sure if he was joking or not, 'Do they? Do they really, J?'

'Oh, God give me strength.'

'Well? Do you like it?'

Clara sat down on the bed and took off her sunglasses. 'I could do without the communal shower bit. And the communal bed bit, too, for that matter. And does everyone really have to walk around starkers all the time?'

Lisa took off her pareo and spread it over her chair. 'People here don't like it if you walk around dressed. It makes everyone else feel uncomfortable.' She stepped out onto the terrace. 'I used to hate it too. But it actually feels pretty good after a while. Once you get used to men ogling you.'

'Oh, I don't mind that bit of it.' Clara followed Lisa outside. She walked to the edge of the terrace and looked around. 'Well the view's nice, at any rate. But it's a bit public, isn't it?'

Two levels down a man was doing limbering exercises. He straightened up and waved.

Clara waved back. 'God. Look at the dong on him. Do you think only men with big dongs come to naturist islands? Sort of showing themselves off?'

'I've never thought about it that way.'

'No, I don't suppose you have. Oh well. *Tant pis*. Here goes.' Clara slipped off her top. The man was still watching them. 'Just look at him. The bastard can't believe his luck. I really ought to charge.' She turned to Lisa. 'Have you at least got some sun-cream?'

'No. We all use coconut oil here. But I'll get you some from Le Bazaar this afternoon.'

Clara shrugged off her miniskirt and draped it over the back of one of the chairs. She made a face. 'Well that's that then. As nature intended.'

'Don't you ever wear underwear?'

'Not if I can help it.'

Lisa swallowed. She couldn't tear her eyes away from Clara.

Clara sighed. 'Oh God. Come on then. Let's get it over with.' She turned on her heel and walked back inside the cabanon.

Lisa hesitated, watching her. She put out a tentative hand and caressed the velvety material of Clara's discarded miniskirt. Then she furtively lifted it up and buried her face in it. Some instinct caused her to glance backwards over her shoulder. The man was still watching them.

She straightened up and walked inside out of the sun.

Thirty

Lisa stood in front of the mirror and circled her breasts with her hands. She turned around. 'Do you mind that they're so small?'

'Why should I mind?'

'No reason.'

Clara rolled over onto her tummy and buried her face in the pillow. 'That wasn't your first time, was it?'

Lisa hesitated. 'No.'

'I knew it.' Clara squinted at Lisa from under her arm.

Lisa moved over and sat down beside her on the bed. She ran her finger up and down Clara's back. 'It's not enough for you, is it? That I can please you every bit as well as any man can?'

'Maybe for your other friends. Not for me.'

'What if I…'

'That wouldn't be enough either.'

Lisa threw back her head. 'What would be enough, then?'

Clara turned over onto her back. 'Now that's a question.'

'Would Jonathan be enough for you?'

Clara pushed herself up into a sitting position. 'Give me a cigarette.'

Lisa reached across, slid a cigarette out of her pack, lit it, and handed it to Clara. She lit another for herself. 'It's more than sex with me. You know that. You've always known it. That's why you keep me dangling, isn't it?'

'I didn't keep you dangling just now, did I?'

'I was scratching an itch. I'm not blind.'

'Then why did you ask me here?'

'Because I'm a fool.' Lisa stood up and walked over to the basin. She took one of the plastic jugs of water and poured it into the bowl. She placed her cigarette on the tiles, lowered her head until it was just below the surface of the water, let it rest there for ten seconds, then straightened up. She patted herself dry with a towel. 'Just promise me one thing. Please.'

Clara blew a distorted smoke ring. 'What?'

'That for these two weeks you'll be faithful to me.'

'Oh God.'

'Please, Clara.'

'*Please, Clara.*'

Lisa took a step towards the bed. 'I'll do anything you want. Anything. But can't you just pretend?'

'Until I slowly fall in love with you? Is that it? Won over by your devotion and constancy?' She shook her head. 'It won't wash, Lisa.'

'I can look after you, if that's what you're worrying about. Papa gave me ten thousand pounds as an eighteenth-birthday present. And I've hardly spent any of it.'

'Ten thousand pounds?'

'Yes. And to Jonathan, too. But Jonathan doesn't need it. Uncle Piers just left him his house on the Cap and all his money.'

'You're kidding!'

'No, I'm not. He's rich. Almost richer than Daddy now.'

'Jonathan? God. That cow Frances never told me.'

'She doesn't know yet. Jonathan's going to tell her today. Then he's going to ask her to marry him. I know he is.'

'The jammy little bitch!'

'Clara!'

'Well she is.' She crushed her cigarette out in the candle tray. 'All she does is moon around with her bloody frescoes, then some old poof dies and leaves her childhood sweetheart a fucking fortune. I call that being a jammy bitch, don't you?'

Lisa could feel her throat tightening with anxiety. It was never any good when Clara got onto the subject of Frances. It brought out all her perversity and contrariness. And something always went wrong. She walked over to the fridge and poured herself some water, then took a long time drinking it.

'You're not so bad, you know.'

Lisa turned around, astonished at the change in Clara's tone. 'What do you mean?'

'You may be a bit skinny, but you've got a good bum.'

'Thanks.'

'And you come easily. You'll find that a blessing later.'

'Clara, I don't understand you sometimes. Is sex all you care about?'

Clara's expression darkened. 'Of course it isn't. But it's a means to an end.' She inspected a smudge of something on her stomach, then looked up. 'If you've got it, flaunt it, I say.'

'But what about when you lose it?'

'That's a long way off. Why bother to think about it when you don't have to?'

Lisa put down her glass. 'Can you think about the next two weeks then? About what I said?'

Clara narrowed her eyes. 'You'll buy me whatever I want? Do whatever I want?'

Lisa swallowed. She felt almost physically sick. She could feel the hand that was holding her cigarette begin to shake. She clamped it tightly against her thigh. The next fortnight loomed like a bottomless chasm in front of her. She nodded slowly, humiliated.

'Well it's a deal, then.'

'How much!?' Frances was propped up with her back against a rock.

Jonathan was lying with his head across her lap, playing with her fingers. 'Oh, a lot. I don't know how much yet exactly, because he was a member of Lloyds and they take three years or something to sort things out. But it's in the millions.'

'In the millions? J, you're joking?'

'No. Really. This time I'm not.'

'But why did he leave it to you?'

Jonathan raised his hands and let them fall onto his thighs. 'Because I was kind to him, I think. In Paris. After you left. And then again later, when Jean was dying. And I think he sort of always loved papa. More than just as his nephew, anyway. More like a son. And when papa married and had us, he transferred a lot of that love onto me.' He swallowed.

'But that's rather a nice story, J.'

'It still needs a happy ending.'

'How do you mean?'

He squinted up at her. 'What happens in fairy tales, Fran? At the end? With the prince and princess?'

'They live happily ever after.'

He grunted impatiently. 'But what do they do before that?'

'The princess kisses him and he stops being a frog.'

Jonathan clambered to his feet. 'You're doing that on purpose.'

Frances cocked her head to one side. 'What's sauce for the goose is sauce for the gander, wouldn't you say?'

'You little minx.'

She sprang up, ready to run. 'So what are you going to do about it?'

He glanced around. They were already the subject of considerable discreet interest from the other bathers on the rocks. Changing his mind on the spur of the moment, he bowed formally to her, making an extended reverence with his fingers. 'Mademoiselle Champion.' He fell gracefully to one knee and took her right hand in his. 'Despite my lack of a suitable covering, may I have the honour – *l'honneur* – to request your chaste hand in marriage.'

Frances looked around in embarrassment. 'J. Get up. You can't be serious.'

'Far from it. I'm deadly serious. In fact, if you don't give me an answer I shall remain here, my arse to the setting sun, until you do.' He cleared his throat. 'Think of our audience, if of nothing else.'

Every face was turned their way. A gentle buzz of amused conversation was beginning to compete with the waves. Scattered words of encouragement issued from the rock niches surrounding them. '*Mais allez-y, jeune homme!*' '*Ne le laissez pas comme ça, mademoiselle!*'

'Well?'

'J, we're naked!'

'So were Adam and Eve.' He eased himself onto his other knee. 'Fran, these rocks are killing me.' He leaned forward and kissed her on the palm of her hand. 'Well? Miss Champion?'

'J, do you really mean it? Do you really want to get married?'

'I really mean it. And I really do.'

She glanced around again, taking comfort from the kindly aura surrounding them. She took a quick breath. 'Yes, then.'

'In French, please. And louder. Remember our audience.'

'*Alors oui!*'

He stood up and hugged her. Spontaneous cheers broke out from the niches around them. Jonathan turned and bowed once again.

'If you think I'm going to curtsey looking like this, you've got another think coming,' she hissed. She put on her most regal smile and bobbed her head. Under her breath she said, 'J, you can be a real bastard sometimes.'

'And don't you just love it. Come on then. Let's go for a swim. Get ourselves a little privacy. They'll forget all about us in two minutes.' He helped her down onto the diving rock. 'Both together now. Okay?'

'Okay.'

They parted hands at the last moment and plunged deep into the cooling water. Jonathan broke the surface, turned over onto his back and kicked himself seawards. Frances side-stroked beside him. 'Where are we going?'

'If we get far enough out, no one will be able to see us and we can make love. That's the full extent of my fiendish plan. I can't hold out much longer, you see. I've been fighting nature for the past two hours and it's finally won.'

'But I haven't got any protection.'

'That doesn't matter now, does it? We're getting married. And the sea water will dilute it anyway.'

'J, you're crazy.'

'Crazy with love for you.' He turned over onto his front. 'I want to spend my life with you, Fran. I want to make you happy.' He pushed back his wet hair. 'And thanks to Uncle Piers, I can. I can buy you anything you want. Paintings. Books. A gallery of your own. We've got everything anybody can ever need.'

She turned to him, floating on her side. 'Don't say that, J. It makes me shiver. I'm superstitious. Mummy used to say you mustn't paint the devil on the wall.'

'Then I take it all back. The wedding's off.'

'I didn't mean that, and you know it!' She splashed some water at him with the heel of her hand. 'Do you know, in a few days it's going to be the eleventh anniversary of our first meeting?'

'Why not choose that day to get married, then? We could get the mayor of Heliopolis to do it. There's a church at the top of the island.'

'I'm not getting married naked.'

He snorted. 'God. Just imagine. It would give the whole concept of a line of raised swords a radically new meaning.' He caught her dismayed expression and smiled. 'No. Scout's honour. Everyone will be clothed. But we might have trouble finding enough morning suits. Birthday suits no problem, of course.' He began to tread water. 'It looks like we're far enough out now, anyway.'

'Far enough out for what?'

'Turn away from me and you'll see.'

'Well, congratulations.' Clara sat back in her wicker chair and took a sip of Pastis. 'Double congratulations, in fact. Lisa tells me you've won the lottery. How did you do it? Was it a contract killing, or did you simply rely on old age to do the job for you?'

'Ha, ha. Very droll.'

'So where's the celebratory slaughter taking place?'

'I've booked a table for four, tonight, at *La Réserve*. I presume I can expect the pleasure of your company?'

'You presume right.'

Jonathan put down his glass of wine. 'Look. Clara. All joking apart. And before the girls get here. What's the score between you and Lisa?'

'One nil. And twenty more minutes to go until half-time.'

He sighed. 'I suppose that means you're not going to tell me?'

'Give the man a kewpie doll!'

'Will you promise me something then?'

'Probably not.'

He bit back his words. 'Will you promise me that you won't go out of your way to hurt her? Just for these two weeks?'

'It seems to me I've heard this somewhere before.'

'I don't know what you mean.'

'Lisa. She's asked me to be faithful to her for a fortnight.'

'Oh God.'

Clara sat up straighter. 'What do you mean, "Oh God"?'

Jonathan shook his head. 'Don't you realise how much asking you that will have cost her? How much humiliation?'

'Frankly, I've no idea. I rarely, if ever, feel humiliation myself.'

Jonathan closed his eyes. 'So how did you answer?'

'Bollocks to you, Jonathan. You can ask Lisa if you're so fascinated about her sex life.'

'You know I wouldn't do that.'

'Well you'll be forced to speculate then.'

Frances appeared from across the square and plumped herself down beside Jonathan. She'd bought herself a diaphanous pale-blue Indian pareo from Le Bazaar, and her hair was pinned back with a coral brooch. 'I'm utterly exhausted. What is it about sea and sun and rocks that just drains you of the will to do anything more active than sipping a Campari and watching people?'

'Sex, probably.' Clara held up her hand before anyone could answer. 'Lisa, darling!'

Lisa looked at the others uncertainly, then took Clara's proffered hand. Jonathan rolled his eyes heavenwards. Frances gave him a kick underneath the table.

'Clara.' Lisa sat down, looking anxious. 'Did you go swimming in the end?'

'No. I fell into conversation with our well-hung Frenchman and he invited me for a drink out on his terrace.'

Lisa whitened perceptibly. 'Did you go?'

'Of course not, darling. He would probably have made a pass at me and then what would I have done?'

Jonathan leaned forward in his chair. 'Lay off, Clara. I warned you.'

'Oh yes. I forgot to tell you. Your big brother has been warning me to be nice to you. "You be nice to Lisa," he said, "or it'll be smacked botty time." Are you going to smack my botty, Jonathan? Shall we do it here? Or over in the bushes. It's your call.'

'Just forget it. Just forget I ever said it.' He stood up. 'I'm sorry, Lisa. I shouldn't have interfered. You'd think I'd have learned my lesson by now.' Lisa took his hand and gave it a quick kiss.

He glanced across at Clara. 'Are you sure you all want to go to *La Réserve* tonight? I'd quite understand it if you both wanted to do your own thing.'

Clara inclined her head and smiled brilliantly up at him. 'Jonathan, darling. I wouldn't miss it for the world. Such a celebration.' She held out her glass. 'And while you're up I'll have another one of these, if it's not too much bother.'

Thirty-one

'I don't know how much more of this I can take.' Jonathan was standing on the terrace of their cabanon, looking out towards Port Cros. 'Four bloody days. And each one worse than the last. One minute butter wouldn't melt in her mouth; the next she's acting like a harpy. Do you think she's mad, by any chance?'

'All too sane, I'm afraid.' Frances finished oiling herself and collapsed backwards onto her towel. 'It's simply second nature for Clara to manipulate everyone. She's done it all her life. Daddy trained her too well.'

'But what does she get out of it? One day even Lisa will turn on her. Then where will she be?'

'In bed with somebody else.'

Jonathan snorted. 'Do you think she's really having it off with that Frenchman?'

'Probably.'

'Jesus. Isn't she scared of VD?'

'I should think she's immune by now. The NHS could probably use her as an antibody bank.'

Jonathan let out a bark of laughter, then threw himself onto the towel next to Frances. 'Do you know, I've never heard you talk about her this way before.'

'I've never felt about her this way before. Last night marked a new low point in our relationship.' She sighed. 'In fact I think we've finally reached the parting of the ways, Clara and I.'

'It's about bloody time.'

Frances raised her sunglasses a fraction of an inch and gazed at him. 'J. Be honest. I won't be angry, but did you ever fancy her?'

Jonathan inhaled sharply, then let the air whistle out through his nose. He was tempted not to answer, but that would have been even worse than telling the truth. 'Briefly, I suppose. In a sort of masochistic way. You'd have to be a masochist to want anything to do with Clara. But it never occurred to me to do anything about it. You do believe that, don't you, Fran?'

'Of course I do.'

'And you. What about Giancarlo? You've been living pretty close to him for the past year. Don't tell me he hasn't got a crush on you, because I know he has.'

'He asked me to marry him.'

Jonathan sat up. 'He what?'

Frances turned over onto her side and looked at him. 'I told him "no", of course. Just as he knew I would.'

'Then why did he ask you?'

Frances closed her eyes. *Because he was putting in his bid in case you ever let me down. Telling me he was there. Placing all his cards on the table. Trusting me.* She stretched out onto her back again. 'I don't know. Perhaps he's a masochist too.'

'Did you encourage him in any way?'

'Of course not.'

'What? Don't tell me! He simply came out of the blue and asked you, "Frances. Please will you marry me." Just like that. You had no idea at all that it was coming?'

Frances began unconsciously chewing on her lower lip. God! Why had she ever started this conversation? You'd have thought she'd have learned by now never to mention Giancarlo to Jonathan when he was feeling fragile. 'I'm parched. Have we got any water in the fridge?' The moment she'd uttered the words she knew she'd taken the wrong tack.

'Fran. I want an answer. Now.'

'You don't have to be so aggressive about it.'

'Aggressive about what? Has he had you? Is that what you're telling me?'

'Jonathan!'

He was standing up now, his face congested. 'I've been wondering, you know. You haven't been yourself these last couple of days. And when I came to visit in March he was acting a bit bloody possessive for a "friend"!'

She raised herself on her elbows. 'I don't want to carry on this conversation. Are you drunk or something?'

'That's a good one. Change the subject.'

'I'm not changing the subject.' She was sitting up all the way now, her heart beating frantically. 'All right then. No. Of course I haven't slept with him. I've only ever slept with you. But you've lost my respect by asking.'

'I've lost your respect? Just like that? Wham! Ask a silly question, bang goes the respect? That's fair is it?'

'Jonathan, look...'

'I tell you, there's more to this than meets the eye.'

'No, there isn't.'

'You would say that wouldn't you?'

'God, now you're sounding like...who was it? Christine Keeler.'

'Did he kiss you then?'

Silence.

'Well?'

Frances put her face in her hands.

'Has he ever kissed you? Is that such a difficult question?'

Frances hesitated fractionally, then nodded her head. She was crying.

'Now we're getting somewhere. How far did he go? Did he touch you?'

She shook her head.

'What? Not even on the tits? I don't believe you.'

'Well don't believe me then!'

'I won't. Take it from me, I won't.' He was standing close to her, hating himself. Hating the outrage that was feeding like a cancer on his heart. He felt like hitting her. 'I can't believe this. You let that little rat kiss you. Did he stick his tongue in your mouth?'

'Jonathan! Stop it! He'd just asked me to marry him. I felt sorry for him.'

'So you let him kiss you?'

'Yes.'

'Did you think about me? What I might feel?'

'Do you want an honest answer,' she wailed, 'or a lie?'

'Right. That's it! I've got a splitting headache and I've just found out my fiancée's been unfaithful with the man I mistrust most in the world. Brilliant! When did you say our eleventh anniversary was? In two days? Well we didn't make it, did we?'

'We did. We have.' She was crying badly now.

Their neighbour appeared on his terrace, took a quick look around, frowned, then slipped back inside his hut again. They could hear him giving the low-down to his wife.

'At least we're entertaining the neighbours.'

'Then stop!'

'Stop what? There is nothing to stop. I've had it. I'm off.'

'You can't go just like that!'

'Try me.'

He marched into their cabanon, hunted wildly amongst the scattered bedcovers, and came up with his wallet and sarong.

Frances ran through the door behind him. 'Where are you going?' She backed up against the window.

'To the village. I need some fresh air. And a drink.'

'You won't go and see Clara?'

'Why should I go and see Clara? She's all I need. The pair of you can go to hell as far as I'm concerned.'

'I shouldn't have told you. I knew you wouldn't understand.'

'Understand? Understand what? That you fancy Giancarlo? That you'd like to marry him, but oh dear, unfortunately boring old J came along first? That's taking loyalty to ridiculous extremes, don't you think?'

'I love you, J. I always have. And I don't love him.' She pushed herself a foot further into the room. 'I was stupid to let him kiss me. I know I was. But he was crying.'

'Oh, well, that's all right then. Remind me to burst into tears when I next want something from you.'

She took two more tentative steps towards him. 'J, why don't you stay? Please.'

'What? And make love, maybe?'

'If you want.'

He stood by the door, watching her, watching himself, his heart beating, his face clammy with righteous anger. 'Fran, at this minute, I wouldn't touch you with a ten-foot shovel.'

The moment he found himself alone on the track, he realised what a bastard he'd been. He hesitated, wondering about going back, but then changed his mind. She'd probably be having a good cry. Best leave her to it. They could always make up again later. It would be that much nicer then.

Still not sure of himself, he set off towards the village. He'd have one drink, just to pass the time, then come back. He'd bring a pizza or something with him. As a peace offering. And a bottle of champagne, maybe. No, not champagne. He didn't feel in a champagney mood. Wine.

The stones were hot under his bare feet. People were coming back from the beach thinking about showers and a siesta. He tightened his sarong and riffled through the contents of his purse. If there were more than a hundred francs in there, he'd stay out; if less, he'd go back to Frances.

Dead on a hundred francs: a fifty, a twenty and three tens. Frances must have used up all his change that morning. So it was up to him then. Perhaps he should let her suffer a bit after all? Teach her a lesson.

He allowed his mind to dwell on her kissing Giancarlo. He'd never thought of Frances in relation to another man before. Not really. Now the thought was strangely exciting. He fantasised about breaking in on them, beating Giancarlo to death, then making love to Frances beside his body. God. He was getting freaky.

He shivered convulsively. His head was throbbing badly now. Probably the beers he'd had at lunch. It was never any good drinking in the sun. He hurried across the square and bagged the best seat on the *Pomme d'Adam* terrace. He could see everyone from here. A bit of girl-watching wouldn't do him any harm. The best bottom. That's it. He'd give them marks out of ten. Even as he allowed the thought to cross his mind, he felt the shabbiness of it.

'*Un gin-tonique*.'

Why had he ordered that? He didn't even like gin. He leaned forward and rubbed his eyes with the palms of his hands. His neck felt as if someone had rabbit-punched it. Perhaps the waiter would have an aspirin? He glanced up. Uh-oh. There was Clara with long-dong Ludo. They were sitting on the terrace of the *Escalet*, drinking coffee. She had her back to him. She obviously hadn't seen him yet. Well thank heavens for that!

He swallowed his gin in one. Oh, that tasted good. He could feel it dulling his head – arrowing its way straight to his brain. He signalled for another. He felt better already.

Now what was Clara doing? She was leaning across the table. Ludo was lighting her cigarette, but he was making a bit of a meal of it. Jonathan craned over to his right for a better look. God! The little tart. She was feeling him up. He felt instantly aroused. Perhaps he *had* missed something in not going with Clara all those years ago in St Tropez. She must have been a virgin then – or a semi-one at least. Like Frances. He knew, deep in his heart of hearts, that he'd probably have succumbed to her blandishments if she hadn't been so bloody untrustworthy. But just one word from her would have scuppered him with Frances forever. Mind you, Frances had just proved beyond a shadow of a doubt that she wasn't such a saint herself. He still found it hard to believe of her, though. He'd always looked up to her as sort of immaculate, somehow. *Better* than he was. A nicer person.

To keep his indignation going, he allowed his thoughts to focus on Giancarlo again. He'd known something had been going on in March. Sensed it. He just couldn't acknowledge it, that was all. The enormity of it. How could Frances prefer someone else to him?

When he looked up again, Ludo was kissing Clara goodbye. Ludo reached over and gave her bottom a final squeeze and she gave him a wiggle, a bit like Lauren Bacall in *To Have and Have Not*.

I bet that pareo's all she's wearing, Jonathan thought to himself, gulping some more gin. If she were to come towards you, with the sun behind her, you would probably see right through the thing. Right down to her manicured little...

'Jonathan! How nice. I didn't see you there.' She was walking towards him, her breasts bobbing beneath the flimsy material.

'Well I saw you all right.'

'Can I sit down?'

'If you're not too sore from all that squeezing.'

'Ha, ha. Is this your first or your second gin?'

'My third.'

'What a naughty boy. Have we been having a spat then?'

'I don't know what you mean.'

'It's five o'clock; you're drinking gin and tonics. Come on, dummy. It doesn't take an Einstein.'

'Maybe a little one.' His words were starting to slur.

'Then we're both in the same boat. We might as well get drunk together. Lisa walked out on me earlier.'

Jonathan looked up. 'I'm not surprised. Did she catch you humping old LD?'

Clara weighed him up. 'Sort of.'

'What does that mean?'

'I was sucking him off.'

'Oh Christ.'

She raised herself in her seat and cocked her eye over the lip of the table. 'Is that a carbuncle beneath your sarong, or are you just happy to see me?'

'You're so original, Clara.'

'The thought of me juicing old Ludo turns you on, doesn't it?'

Jonathan hesitated for a moment. 'A bit.' What did he have to lose?

'Hmmm. Honesty at last.' She weighed him up some more. 'Do you want to come back to the cabanon with me? I've baked a cake. We can polish off the last of Ludo's Slivovitz with it.'

'You baked a cake?'

'I was feeling domestic.'

'Why do I feel like vomiting?'

She concentrated her most calculating gaze on him. 'Well? Are you going to come or not? Last chance.'

'And no passes?'

'Perish the thought.'

Thirty-two

'So where did Lisa go to?' Jonathan stretched his legs out onto the bamboo table, noting with pleasure how satisfyingly brown they were. He smoothed a hand admiringly across the ridges of his stomach. He took a deep breath in an effort to clear the slight numbness from his nose.

'How the hell should I know? To Timbuctoo, probably.' Clara was inside the cabanon preparing the Slivovitz. 'Ludo says you've got to drink this stuff ice-cold. Straight from the freezer. Ideally in frozen glasses. And with a sprinkling of cumin seed.'

'I can't wait.' Jonathan craned around and peered at her through the bead curtain. 'Ludo's not the jealous type, by any chance? Not going to burst in on us brandishing a knife?' He cleared his throat ironically. 'Mind you, he could probably beat me to death with his cock if it ever came to it.'

'I thought you saw our fond farewells at the café?'

'Don't tell me he's gone for good?'

'On the last boat.'

'Must leave quite a gap in your life.'

Clara grimaced. 'Save your innuendoes for Frances. She's a much better target than me.' She walked out and handed him a glass. 'You won't mind if I take off my pareo? We're on a naturist island, after all. And I've got rather used to walking around in the nude.'

Jonathan swallowed. 'Of course I don't mind. In fact I'll join you. Wouldn't want you to feel embarrassed.' He untied his sarong and threw it self-consciously over the chair next to him. Why did Clara always have this effect on him? His limbs were beginning to feel curiously unco-ordinated, as if someone had stuffed them full of wire wool.

Clara stood at the edge of the terrace, sipping her drink and watching him with unconcealed interest. 'The last time I saw you naked was four years ago. On Pampelonne beach. You've put on a bit of muscle since then. In all the right places.'

'I'm afraid I don't compare very well with your friend Ludo.'

'Don't you believe it. With Ludo, what you saw was what you got. Damn thing didn't get any bigger. Just hardened up a little.' She smiled. 'I was rather disappointed, actually.'

Jonathan took a gulp of his Slivovitz. Clara had shaved the hair on her pudendum into the shape of a heart. He couldn't take his eyes off it. He watched her sit down, idly wishing he was underneath her.

'You, on the other hand…' she pointed at his groin with her glass. 'Doesn't take much to trigger you off, does it? Just a teensy little heart sculpted in the right place. I'm surprised you don't get lynched down on the rocks.' She crossed, then uncrossed her legs. 'You must be diving in and out of the sea most of the time. Or in and out of Frances.' She frowned. 'Offhand, I can't think which would be the wetter.'

Jonathan lay back, refusing either to cover himself or to answer. He was slowly learning about Clara. Once you let her take the initiative, you were done for.

'Fancy another drink?'

'Okay.'

'How about a piece of cake?'

'What is it with you and your cake?'

'I baked it for Lisa. By special order. Now she's obviously not going to eat it. It'll go off in no time in this weather.'

'Then stick it in the fridge.'

'Touchy, touchy.' Clara came over and took his glass. She bent across him, allowing her breasts to dangle six inches in front of his face. Jonathan could smell her; smell Ludo on her. He glanced involuntarily at her mouth. 'Back in a sec.' She swivelled abruptly and flounced back inside the hut.

He knew he should go. Now. Before it was too late. If only his mind didn't feel so woolly.

'I think I'd better go in a minute,' he said, when Clara re-emerged. 'Frances will be wondering where I've got to.'

'And we can't have that, can we?' Clara handed him his replenished glass and a piece of cake on a plate. 'You don't have to eat it, if you think it's forbidden fruit.' She walked to the edge of the terrace and stood looking out over the bay, allowing Jonathan a good long stare at her bottom. 'So when's the wedding?' She turned around and sat on the tiled wall. Beneath the heart, she was shaved bare. Nothing was left to the imagination.

Jonathan slurped some more Slivovitz. 'We thought about having it here. But then we decided it wouldn't be fair on Aunt Helen and my mother. So we'll decide when we get back.' He took a bite of the cake. 'It's good. What is it?'

'Just a little invention of my own.'

'Well it's good. I mean it.' He took another bite. 'It goes really well with the Slivovitz.' He knocked back the rest of his drink.

'There's a lot more where that came from.' Clara found something to squint at on one of her breasts. She flicked whatever it was off with her fingernail, then massaged the spot with the heel of her hand.

Jonathan was loath to admit it, given the circumstances, but his head was starting to spin again. He took a deep breath. Then another. The spinning didn't stop. The skin on his face felt tacky and dull to the touch. 'Look. I know this is rather wet – and it isn't a pass, I promise – but do you think I could lie down on your bed for a moment? I must have taken a bit too much sun this morning. I'll only need a minute.'

'Go right ahead. I'll be out here waiting for you.'

He stood up, faltered, then caught himself. 'God, I feel wuzzy. I shouldn't have drunk this bloody stuff of Ludo's.'

'You're not going to be sick, are you?'

'No. No. I don't think so.' He put down his glass, paused to drag in another deep breath, then stumbled through into the cabanon. He was dead to the world before his head hit the pillow.

'Frances? Are you there?'

'I'm inside.'

Lisa walked around the cabanon, hesitated, then ducked through the bead curtain. She looked nervous. 'Is Jonathan here?'

'No.'

Frances was huddled on the bed, covered by a single sheet.

'Oh. I'm sorry. You were having a siesta.'

'No I wasn't.' Frances drew her legs up beneath her and rested her head on her knees. 'Be a darling and get me a glass of cold water, will you? And help yourself to some juice.'

Lisa stepped across and rummaged in the fridge. She came back with the glasses and sat down beside Frances on the bed. 'Are you all right?'

'Bit of a headache. Dehydrated, probably. I'll feel better with some liquid slopping around inside me.' She attempted a smile, but it failed atrociously.

Lisa sipped her drink. 'Look, Fran. I wanted to ask you and Jonathan a favour.' Her eyes darted across Frances's face, taking in nothing. 'It'll be irritating, I know, but do you think I could sleep out on your terrace tonight? I'll try not to get in the way. But I've made the decision to go back home, you see, and I've just missed the last boat.'

'Whatever's happened?'

'Oh. Nothing surprising. You won't be surprised at all.'

'Tell me.'

Lisa swallowed. Her mouth moved spasmodically, fighting off tears. She stretched her legs out on the bed, and leaned back wearily against the headboard. 'Do you mind?'

'Of course I don't.'

She squeezed her eyes shut. 'I can hardly bring myself to say it, even now.'

'Say what, Lisa? What's the matter?'

'I caught Clara with that Frenchman.' Lisa rested her glass on her thigh and began constructing a sequence of wet rings, one on top of the other. Then she threw back her head and stared up at the ceiling. 'So, so predictable. I've been walking around the island ever since trying to get up the courage to face her again. Have it out. But I just can't do it.'

'Oh God, Lisa. I'm so sorry.'

'He was sitting in a chair on our terrace with a bovine smile on his face and she was down on all fours in front of him.' She glanced across at Frances, her eyes misting up. 'You know.'

'Lisa, you don't have to tell me this.'

'I do. It makes it easier to go…easier to cut off, if I acknowledge it.'

'What did she do when she saw you?'

'Stood up, licked her lips, and asked me if I wanted to join them.' Lisa's face seemed to freeze for a moment in suspended animation, then she burst into tears.

'Oh, Jesus.' Frances reached across and took Lisa in her arms. She began gently to stroke her hair.

'I love her, Fran. It's awful. And I hate her, too.' She looked up, sobbing. 'I simply don't know what to do. I'm scared to go down and get my things in case he's still there. He's so gross. He just looks at you as though you're an object – some sort of walking hole he can fit that obscene thing of his into.' She shuddered, and began wiping her eyes on her pareo. 'And I'm *not!* I wouldn't let him touch me. I don't know how Clara could ever have thought that. How she could have said that to me.'

'Shh. Don't worry. It doesn't matter.'

'But it does!'

'Not nearly as much as you think.' Frances kissed Lisa on the cheek, then raised her chin with her hand.

'It's easy for you to say that.'

'I know. I know.' She brushed Lisa's hair away from her forehead. 'Look. I'll tell you what we'll do. I'll go down with you. Then we'll collect your things and you can come back up here and stay with us.' She held Lisa at arm's length. 'Then Jonathan and I will travel back to Canteloube with you tomorrow. On the ferry. Back to St Tropez. How will that do?'

'Really?'

Frances smiled, happy that Lisa was at last responding. 'I think we've all had just about enough of this island, don't you?'

Clara spread her legs and inspected herself, then stood up, hefted her shoulders, and smoothed her fingers along the tops of her breasts. She checked over her shoulder in the window glass, running her hand along the line of her bottom.

She gave it another minute, then walked inside and sat down beside Jonathan's recumbent body. She fluttered her hands over his nipples, then down across his stomach and over his groin. 'Sleepy, sleepy,' she said, 'oh you sleepy, sleepy.' She began a rhythmical movement, glancing down occasionally, then back to his congested face. 'Jonathan. Are you awake?' she whispered. 'You are awake, aren't you?'

He groaned, but made no further response.

Clara speeded up her movements, touching herself at the same time, a smile playing across the corners of her lips. At one point she glanced out of the window, threw back her head and closed her eyes; then she hunched forward and carried on what she was doing with her mouth. Jonathan grunted, and made a disconnected movement with his hand.

'We've come for Lisa's things.' Frances stood on the terrace, watching Clara. Lisa was standing at her right shoulder, looking nervous.

'They're inside.'

'Your friend's not still in there, is he?'

'Which friend's that?'

'You know who I mean, Clara.'

'Oh him. No. He's gone back to Paris.'

'Okay, Lisa. You can go on in then. It's quite safe.'

Clara leaned back in her chair. 'You make a terribly impressive bodyguard, Frances. It must be all those muscles.'

'Clara, you're disgusting. And you haven't even washed yourself. How do you think Lisa feels?'

'I don't know. I'm not a lesbian.'

Lisa emerged, pale-faced, from the hut. 'Frances, I think we'd better go.'

'But you haven't got your things yet.'

'I'd rather just go. I can always come back later and get them.'

'Nonsense. It'll only take a minute.'

'Please, Frances. What I actually mean is, you go, and I'll stay here. I want to talk to Clara. I'm feeling better, now. I'll be up later, all right?'

Frances hesitated. 'All right then. If you're sure.'

'I'm sure.'

Clara crossed her legs and took off her sunglasses. 'Could you possibly take Jonathan away with you, then? Save yourself the journey later?'

Frances turned to her, her heart rigid with shock. 'Jonathan? What do you mean? Do you know where he is?'

Clara flicked her chin. 'The last sight I had of him, he was asleep on my bed.'

Lisa hurried across and parked herself in front of the cabanon door. 'Frances. Please. This is some trick of Clara's. Don't go in.'

'I don't understand?' Frances furrowed her brow. 'Why should Jonathan be asleep on your bed?' Her arms felt terribly light all of a sudden – as if her hands might take off by themselves without her knowing it.

'Exhausted, I should think.' Clara moistened her lips, then smiled. 'Shagged out.'

Frances hesitated. Her eyes were refusing to focus properly. 'Jonathan?' She took a leaden step towards the cabanon door. 'Are you in there?'

Lisa moved towards her. 'He's out cold, Fran. He's probably ill or something.'

Frances pushed past her and into the cabanon. The bamboo beads clattered back into place with an eerily conclusive sound. She couldn't get her bearings at first. The blinds were down against the sun and the room was gloomy, despite the intense heat outside.

Jonathan snorted and rolled over onto his back. Frances flinched. She stumbled three paces towards him and looked down. She instantly took in the rumpled covers and the dried semen stains on his stomach. Her head began to tremble spasmodically, as if she were trying to shake off a fly. She fell back against the cold, whitewashed wall. Then she pushed herself away from it, flung herself wildly at the bead curtain, and ran outside.

'See. I told you.' Clara was tilting back in her chair.

Frances rushed up to her, straightened her arm, and slapped her hard on the side of the head. Clara's sunglasses flew off into three separate pieces. Her chair tipped backwards and she fell heavily onto the tiles. Frances kicked her, then raised her hand for a second time. Lisa grabbed her from behind and pulled her away.

'Let go of me. It's all right. Let go of me.'

Lisa dropped Frances's hands as if they were scalding her.

Frances backed away. She pointed at Clara with all five fingers, as if she were uttering a curse. 'I never want to see you again. Ever. Or Jonathan either. You can both keep away from me. I never want to see any of you ever again. You're all sick.'

Lisa made a spasmodic movement towards her, then stopped.

'Suits me fine.' Clara was collecting up the shattered pieces of her sunglasses. She looked up. 'He's a lousy lover by the way. Passive's not the word. But then you probably know that already.'

Frances made as if to go for her again, then moaned, turned violently on her heel and ran with broken steps back in the direction of her cabanon. Lisa hesitated for a second as if she, too, wanted to speak, then she spun around and hurried after her.

Clara stood up. She swivelled her head tentatively back and forth, then reached up and felt her cheek. When the sound of Frances and Lisa's feet had finally diminished, she stepped back inside the cabanon. She walked across to the bed and looked down. 'Sleep on, sweet prince.'

She hesitated for a moment, still looking down, then tiptoed to the far side of the bed. She clambered carefully between the sheets. She froze once, watching the door, then slowly reached across and drew Jonathan onto her breast. He groaned, fluttered his eyelids, then fell back into a heavy sleep. Clara eased her head cautiously back onto the pillow. When she was finally settled, she lay, her eyes wide open, staring up at the ceiling, cradling him. After a little while she whimpered, almost imperceptibly, and in the gloomy light of the hut it was impossible to tell whether the silent tears which came tumbling down her cheeks were tears of sadness or of joy.

Thirty-three

Penhallow, Cornwall. 1999

Jonathan reached forwards and hugged his knees. 'So I woke at ten the next morning feeling like hell warmed up. Hung over. Dehydrated. Disorientated. The works.' He cleared his throat self-consciously. 'Far too late to catch you and Lisa at the first ferry.' He glanced across at Frances. When she didn't respond, he squinted in the direction of the sea. 'Even if I'd wanted to, that is.'

Frances had her back to him. She was lying very still. If it wasn't for the gentle movement of her shoulder and hip, she might almost have been asleep.

He shook his head, as if he were still attempting to clear it of a thirty-year hangover. 'Clara did try to get me to stay on with her. On account of Piers's money, I suppose. But I wasn't having any of it. I followed you back to the mainland that very afternoon.'

'Then why didn't you come after me? To Venice? While there was still time?'

He screwed up his face. 'That's the million-dollar question, isn't it?'

'You knew I'd go there.'

'I had a pretty fair idea.'

She kept her face averted from him, although she could tell by the sound of his voice that he was looking at her. 'Was Lisa still at Canteloube when you got back?'

'No. She'd gone too. After dropping you at the station she simply headed on up to the chateau. To lick her wounds, I shouldn't wonder. It took me nearly a year to get things straight again with her. To explain. By that time it was way too late for any of us.'

'Did she ever see Clara again?'

'That's the weirdest bit of all. They carried on seeing each other for years. Whenever Clara was between lovers or had somehow managed to land herself in the mire, she'd go to Lisa for a bit of comfort. A bit of R and R, I suppose.' He shrugged his shoulders. 'Lisa's love, absurdly enduring as it was, must have been a sort of security for her. A counterweight to the men she let use her. Or whom she used. I could never quite get that clear in my mind.'

'And you honestly mean to tell me that you didn't make love to her that day?'

'Does it make any difference now?'

Frances turned to him for the first time. 'To me it does.'

He shook his head ruefully. 'Well I didn't. Ever. Though God alone knows what she got up to while I was out cold. But I can't remember a thing of it, I promise.' He glanced at her, desperate for even the smallest sign that she might be believing him. 'I racked my brains about it for years. As to whether I could have done something like that without knowing it. But now you've told me about the hash cake, things finally make sense. I've never had any tolerance for drugs. I just go out like a light. Clara must have known that from Lisa.'

'Lisa?'

'Lisa's always liked to get it on. Have a spliff or two – although I don't suppose she calls them spliffs any longer.' He attempted a laugh, but it didn't come out right. 'That's why Clara made the cake. The pair of them were probably planning an orgy or something. Then Lisa caught Clara with long-dong, and that was the end of that.' He snorted. 'I'm willing to bet that when Clara saw her money-bags going out the side door with Lisa, it immediately occurred to her that I might be persuaded to take over.'

'Why didn't you then?'

'Oh come on, Frances. Clara was always what the French call an *allumeuse*. A prick-teaser. She got her kicks out of keeping people lit up. Look at poor Lisa. She was on the hook for years. God alone knows how many thousands of her money Clara got through before Lisa finally called a halt and chucked her out.' He caught himself just in time. 'What's more she was your sister. I wouldn't have gone with her for that reason alone.' He realised that he was starting to sound holier-than-thou, and quickly changed his tone. 'And that's not to say that she didn't succeed in tempting me, because she did,' he ended lamely.

Frances sat up. She looked him straight in the eye. 'Are you still angry with me?'

'What do you mean?'

'At the way I just left. Without letting you explain?'

He hesitated, wondering whether to admit the truth or not. He wasn't entirely sure, yet, how she would respond, and he was terrified of alienating her again. 'I was. Yes. I've got to admit that. For years and years. I thought it was some sort of plan you'd hatched with Giancarlo. Find a pretext to dump me, then you could move on to him.'

'You can't be serious.'

'I'm not. Now.' He smiled at her. 'When I heard you had a daughter, I started getting things clearer in my mind. It sort of put a line under everything. There's no comeback from that. From then on I began to accept that it had been my fault. That you were right to protect yourself from me. I'd probably have made you very miserable.'

Frances watched him. He'd turned slightly away from her, and was following the wake of a fishing boat with his gaze. She took in the grey hairs at the nape of his neck; the fine lines at the corners of his eyes; his familiar smell. She unconsciously lifted the sleeve of his jacket and toyed with the fabric. 'She's yours, you know.'

'Who is?' Jonathan half turned to her.

'Cosima. She's your child.'

Jonathan jerked the rest of the way around. 'That's not funny.'

'It's not a joke.' Her eyes were wide open with shock. She hadn't meant to tell him. In fact she was never going to tell him. She'd vowed that to herself all those years ago. Now she was at a loss to understand quite what had happened. She closed her eyes fatalistically, feeling numb. 'Do you remember that time in the sea? When you'd just asked me to marry you?'

'And we didn't use anything?'

'Yes. It was then.' She began to cry. 'I didn't know. I didn't know for another three weeks. And by then it was too late. I was married to Giancarlo. Stupid, dumb bitch that I was.'

Jonathan could hardly trust himself to speak. 'Did you tell him?'

'He couldn't have taken it. He was such a baby. He was touchy enough about you as it was. He was always expecting me to leave at the first sign of a spat and hurry back to you. When he found out I was pregnant he was over the moon. And I let him be. I owed him that much by then.'

Jonathan flopped full length on the ground. He stared up at the sky. He ran his hands shakily through his hair, then twisted around and looked at her. 'You can't be serious, Frances. Are you honestly telling me I have a twenty-seven-year-old grown-up daughter? And that I sat in the car with her all the way to Cornwall and I didn't know?'

'Why should you?' She was leaning towards him, urgent now. 'But Cosima suspected something. There was some connection between you that she didn't quite understand. She as good as told me.' She hesitated momentarily. 'She was attracted to you. But not like a lover, of course.' She shook her head in wonder. 'It was quite out of the ordinary. Not like her at all.' She dabbed impatiently at her eyes with her sleeve. 'Now's when I need that steadfast old hanky of yours.'

Jonathan stretched across and rummaged in his jacket pocket. He felt shell-shocked – as if the earth's tectonic plates had just shifted, very slightly, beneath his feet, skewing his horizon onto another level. 'It's only kitchen roll. Sign of the times, I'm afraid. It's clean, though.' He put out a hand and touched her hair.

She looked up at him, her gaze skirting the contours of his face. 'Now I'm going to ask you again. Do you hate me?'

He attempted to pull her towards him, but she resisted.

'Jonathan, I can't live a lie. I've got to know how you feel. About me. About what I've done.'

He took a deep breath. He chose his words carefully, knowing she would detect any confusion – any duplicity – and that their whole future might rest on it. 'You did what you had to do. I can't blame you for that.'

'But I deprived you of your daughter's childhood.' She was weeping badly now, her eyes fixed on his face, wearing an expression of frozen grief. 'She hasn't even got your name, for God's sake.'

He swallowed. He could feel the smarting of tears behind his own eyes. His hands were turning numb with the pressure of supporting himself for so long in a prone position. 'You didn't deprive me of anything, Fran. I deprived myself. It was my test, and I failed it.'

She raised a hesitant hand and touched his cheek.

'I should have come after you. Any normal man would have done. Sorted things out. There was ample time. But I didn't.' He shook his head. 'The joke is that I don't feel I'm any closer to explaining my actions now than I was then.'

'Yes, you are. You couldn't have said what you've just said otherwise.'

'Perhaps.' He was pleased to see that she was calmer now. More herself. 'No, Fran. The truth is, you've haven't deprived me of a daughter. You've given me one.'

She swayed towards him. He reached across and embraced her. They lay back onto the grass and she curled herself small in the crook of his arm, just as she'd done all those years ago.

They stayed like that for some time, witnessed only by the sea, and the gulls, and the gradually diminishing clouds.

Clara fluttered her hand and tipped some cigarette ash onto the floor. She was sprawled across the sofa like a senator at some Roman orgy. A vein was pulsing heavily at her left temple. Cosima found herself fascinated by it. The parchment-thin membrane of flesh that marked the difference between life and death. 'Do you really think you should have any more?'

'Yes, I do.' Clara noticed a smudge above her left knee, and rubbed at it, frowning. Her dress fell back to reveal a grubby-looking petticoat.

Cosima shook her head ruefully. 'God, I sound just like Mummy. Vaguely disapproving but still wanting to be liked.' She was out of her depth, she knew it. She'd never met anyone who could drink as much as Clara – or as fast. 'Where do you think they've got to?'

'What do you care?' Clara could barely string two words together. She'd already got through the bottles they'd liberated from her father's cellar – except for the glass that Cosima was cradling in her lap – and now she wanted more. 'Well? Are you going to drink that or not?'

'No. Here. You have it.' Cosima handed her the wine.

Clara knocked it back, shivering. 'That damned dragon's walking all over my grave again.'

'What do you mean? What dragon?'

'Ever since I killed that child.'

Cosima sat up straighter. 'Child? What child? What are you talking about?'

Clara squinted up at her. 'Did I say child?' She shook her head woollily. 'I meant dog. Ever since I killed that dog.'

'I still don't understand.'

Clara scowled. 'Who does? Do I?' She snorted disgustedly. 'Hardly. Do you?' She shook her head until her hair danced in rat's tails. 'Not a chance. Does God? Why? What's the point?' She punctuated each unco-ordinated statement with an intake of breath, as if she were reciting a breviary.

'Why did you kill the dog, then?'

Clara made an attempt to hoist herself upright. She fell backwards, brushing uselessly at her skirt. 'Oh, I didn't mean to, if that's what you're thinking. I like dogs. Stupid, tender animals, with no brain. Rather like men, when you come to think of it.' She chuckled. She grabbed a cushion and clutched it to her chest. 'No. I hit it. With my car. Then it lay in the road and died.'

Cosima stood up, listening. 'Speaking of cars...' She walked a few paces towards the window, her head cocked. '...did you hear something?'

'No.'

'Perhaps it's them?'

'Who's them?'

'The others. Uncle Charles and Aunt Geneviève. And Lisa.'

Clara sat bolt upright, giving the lie to her former languor. 'Impossible. They're coming tomorrow. It must be someone else.' She swallowed awkwardly. Her face had gone sheet white. 'It's the police.' She struggled, like an upended tick, to push herself to her feet. 'If it's the police, tell them I'm not here.'

'Why should it be the police?' Cosima gave her a quizzical stare. 'Haven't you been paying your parking fines, Aunt Clara? Tut-tut-tut.' She strode the final few feet to the window and peered through the glass. 'No. Look. It is them. I knew it. I'm going outside.'

'Well thank God for that.' Clara fell backwards again. She felt around for her cigarette, which had fallen underneath her on the sofa. She held it triumphantly up and took a puff. 'Go on then. Spear the fatted calf!' She let the smoke trickle through her nostrils. 'You can bring me another bottle when you come back.'

'I'm not sure that's a good idea.'

'Wait! Change of plan.' Clara shook her head in an exaggerated negative. 'No, no, no. On second thoughts, ask old Charley-boy if he's brought any drink with him from France. He's probably good for a litre or two of cognac.'

Cosima hesitated, wondering whether it was wise to leave Clara alone – then ruefully decided that she was probably used to it. She ran through the house and out onto the drive. The sunlight took her by surprise and she was forced to shade her eyes 'It *is* you! I knew it.' She ran up to Lisa. 'It's been so long. We were expecting you tomorrow.'

'Papa couldn't get a Friday flight.' They kissed affectionately. 'So we bumped everything forward by a day. It all fitted in rather well. I hired a car at the airport.' She glanced at the house, then back at Cosima. 'Where are the others?'

'Mummy and Jonathan you mean? They're up there.' She began to point, then let her arm drop limply to her side. 'I don't believe it. They're holding hands.'

Lisa swivelled sharply on the spot, following Cosima's incredulous gaze.

'Lisa!' It was Charles, from over by the car. 'Come here and help your mother. I can't manage these bloody bags of hers on my own. I think she's moving in for the winter.'

'Yes, papa.' She glanced at Cosima. 'Come on and give me a hand. I'm sure we'll find out what's been going on later.'

Cosima stopped her. 'Look. I'd better warn you. Clara's been on the bottle. I left her in the drawing-room, rather the worse for wear.'

'You're joking?'

'No. It's true.'

'Oh God.' Lisa's face seemed to change and become older. 'Look. You help my parents in with their luggage. Jonathan will give you a hand, too, if you can manage to attract his attention. I'd better go and sort Clara out.' She grimaced. '*Maman* doesn't really approve of her, you see. And she can be horrifyingly abrupt when she wants to be.' She hesitated. 'You do understand, don't you?' She squeezed Cosima's arm and hurried inside.

'Jonathan. And Frances.' Geneviève was walking towards them up the hill. 'I know we're a day early. And I was so stupid. I left Helen's number at home, so we couldn't telephone you.' She took Frances's hand in hers. 'And they no longer have telegrams, of course. It's such a shame. It was always so exciting receiving one.' She kissed Frances three times, her eyes taking in everything.

'Jonathan. *Ton père est fatigué.* Will you take him upstairs? I'll stay here with Frances. We have so much to talk about.'

Charles bellowed from down by the car. 'I'm not as tired as all that, Geneviève.'

'You never are, papa.' Jonathan gave Frances a quick smile, then started down the slope towards his father.

Geneviève focused all her attention back on Frances. 'My dear. It's been so long.' Her eyes moved sideways. 'And is this your beautiful Cosima? Come and give me a kiss, child.' She took Cosima's face in her hands. '*Ah, tu es magnifique, ma petite. Vraiment magnifique. Toute aussi belle que ta mère.*'

'*Merci, madame.*'

'*Appellez-moi Geneviève.*'

Frances caught Jonathan's eye over by the car, and shrugged guiltily. He made a wry face back at her.

'Come on, Dad.' He took his father's arm.

He glanced furtively back at Cosima when he knew the others weren't looking. He could feel himself flush. Was this really what it felt like to be a father? He could hardly believe that after all these sterile years he was looking at his own flesh and blood. She was so like Frances. He yearned to be able to go across and hug her. Tell her the truth. Watch her face. But Frances had forbidden it. And he'd promised to take his cue from her.

Charles pulled free of him. 'I'm not an old crock yet. And I will not have Geneviève telling me when or when not to take my afternoon rest. Antonia doesn't do that.'

Jonathan turned back to his father. 'But she's not your wife, Dad.'

Charles stopped in his tracks. 'Now don't you start. I've had it all the way from the airport and I'm fed up to the back teeth with it. They both ganged up on me in the car. Even Lisa. I thought at least she'd understand.'

'Understand what?'

'I'm sorry, Jonathan. There's no easy way to put this. But a man can't run his life according to a fifty-year-old piece of paper.'

'Shh. *Maman* will hear.' He took his father's arm again.

'I wish she would. Instead of sitting in that bloody castle of hers waiting for me to remember my marriage vows. She's got some ghastly Catholic notion that I'll repent my infidelities on my deathbed and sail up to heaven beside her. On a golden chariot, probably.'

Jonathan snorted. He looked at his father with grudging respect. What an absurd day. What did they say about family funerals? Skeletons toppling out of cupboards?

Charles cocked an eye at him. 'Where are we going?'

'What do you mean?'

'You're taking me to the stables. Your sense of direction must be even worse than I thought.'

'I'm sorry, Dad. I must have been dreaming.'

Charles looked sharply at his son. 'You were holding hands with that Champion girl. I saw you. Coming down the hill. Didn't you two have a fling some years back?'

'In Paris. Yes, Dad.'

'Oh, it was her.' He paused in his walking. He stood with his hands held by his sides, shaking his head. 'Of course it was. My memory isn't what it used to be.' He cleared his throat. 'Nothing else is either, I regret to say.' He straightened up, sighing. 'What do you think of your mother, then?'

'How do you mean?'

'Well? How do you think she looks?'

'Dad, I've been seeing her at least three times a year for the past twenty years. And I was living with her at the chateau all the time I was being treated.'

'Of course you were, of course you were.' Charles started back towards the house. 'Perhaps I am a little tired after all.' He glanced up, his eyes glistening foxily. 'I didn't like that bloody airplane, you know. Didn't like it at all.'

'Why ever not?'

'They had some blighter in a blazer to serve me my drinks.' He shook his head sombrely. 'In my day they used to have pretty young stewardesses. Much more fun. Made flying an event.'

Thirty-four

'Please.' Lisa took Clara's hand in hers. 'There'll only be a scene if *maman* comes in.'

'I'm quite happy here.'

'Just to your room.'

'Why? Do you want a shag for old time's sake?' Clara grimaced when she saw Lisa's tormented face. 'It's all right. You don't have to make excuses. I know how I look.' She poked at her hair. 'I can't even get a man to bed me any more, let alone a woman.' She focused on Lisa with some difficulty. 'Are you still having it off with all those undergraduates? Like that blonde piece you paraded in front of me last time I was in London? What was she? Nineteen? Probably illegal.'

Lisa cocked her head to one side, listening. Then she let go of Clara's hand and hurried to the door. She poked her head into the corridor, crooking her finger anxiously at Jonathan as he started up the stairs. 'Come here,' she whispered.

'What is it?'

Charles was moving slowly ahead of him up the staircase.

'You've got to keep *maman* out of the drawing-room.'

'Whatever for?'

'Because Clara's in there!' Clara's words erupted from inside the room in a hoarse schoolgirl screech. 'And she's drunk!'

Lisa made an 'I-told-you-so' face. Jonathan moved to her side and peered around the door. Clara waved at him. 'Oh, boy. The man himself! Old Johnny-Jack the wanker.'

Lisa gripped his arm. 'She can't even stand up, J. I don't suppose you could carry her upstairs, could you? *Maman*'s still gossiping with Frances and Cosima. We've got two minutes at the outside.'

Jonathan grunted. He squeezed past her and made for the sofa.

'Hi, lover. Come to get me?'

He hoisted Clara up by the arms, ducked underneath her and let her drop onto his shoulder.

'Oooh-wee. Caveman!'

He was surprised at how light she was. 'All clear?'

'Yes. Hurry!' Lisa held the door open for him.

He ducked through into the hall and started up the stairs. He felt all right at first, but the pressure of Clara's weight soon began to tell on his weak left leg. By the time he got to the landing, the pain was so intense that he was obliged to lean against the oak banisters and take a rest. 'Sorry, Liss. This bloody leg.'

Clara raised her head from his jacket. 'I think I'm going to be sick.'

Lisa called up to him from downstairs. 'Jonathan, hurry. They're coming in.'

Jonathan eased Clara into a more comfortable position. He took a shambling run at the last ten steps. 'Which way's her room?'

Lisa overtook him at the trot. 'I don't know. It's years since I've been here.'

Jonathan craned back his head. 'Clara. Can you hear me? Where's your room?'

'How the hell should I know? I'm fucking upside down.'

'Go on, Lisa. You'd better check them all. If we can't find the right one we'll just have to take pot luck.' He stood in the shadow of the first-floor landing, gasping for air – they'd told him at the hospital that the chemotherapy would temporarily affect his lung capacity, but this was ridiculous. He could already hear his mother's voice rapidly approaching from outside.

Clara began to fidget. 'I need to pee.'

'Well hold on, Clara, for God's sake.'

'Too late.'

'Oh Christ. Thanks a bundle.' He could feel the warm liquid cascading through the lining of his jacket. He took a few steps forward. 'Hurry it up, Lisa.'

'It's in here.' Lisa beckoned to him from down the corridor.

Jonathan stumbled across the landing and through into Lisa's room. 'Hurry. Close the door. She's bloody wet herself.' He dumped Clara unceremoniously on the bed. 'And me too.' He held out his arms. 'God it stinks.'

Lisa slipped the latch and moved swiftly across the room. She took in Clara's state, then looked up at Jonathan. 'We seem to have come full circle, haven't we? It used to be me that wet myself.'

Jonathan's face darkened. 'Oh, Liss.'

She smiled ruefully. 'Come on. You'd better get out of that jacket and wash up. I'll see to Clara. I'm used to this. She'll be out for hours now.'

He hesitated. 'Look, it's probably not the right moment, but I've got something to tell you.'

Lisa glanced up from undressing Clara. 'What? That you're going back to Frances?'

He snorted. 'Am I that transparent?'

'You shouldn't be seen holding hands if you don't want people to jump to conclusions.'

He grimaced and shook his head. 'No. It's more than that.'

'What then?' She straightened up. She'd already stripped off most of Clara's clothes.

Jonathan averted his eyes. 'Are you sure she's out cold?'

'As a raw chilli.'

He swallowed. 'All right then. Here it is.' He shuffled nervously. 'You couldn't possibly help me out of this jacket, could you? I smell like a nineteenth-century Parisian *pissoir*.'

'Come on then.' She walked ahead of him into the bathroom.

Once inside, she dropped Clara's wet clothes into the bathtub. He shrugged back his shoulders and she slipped off his jacket. She dumped that into the bathtub too. 'Now the shirt. I'll get you another one from your room.' He unbuttoned the shirt, watching her. Her eyes strayed across his stomach. 'God. What a mess.'

'Thanks.'

'They really had it in for you, didn't they?'

'They thought I didn't look interesting enough. There's more, if you'd care to see it.'

She ran her fingers down his biopsy scar. She swallowed, more shaken than she cared to acknowledge. 'So what is it, J? What do you want to tell me that can't wait until we've got this mess cleaned up?'

He threw his shirt into the bathtub. He went over to the basin, ran some hot water, soaped a flannel and washed himself thoroughly. When he was finished, Lisa handed him a towel. He patted himself dry. She was watching him with a quizzical expression on her face.

He took a deep breath and fixed his attention somewhere over her left shoulder. 'Cosima's my daughter.' He swallowed. He slid his gaze unwillingly down until he met her eyes.

'What?'

'Frances just told me.' He hesitated, his mouth beginning to work of its own accord. 'I suppose that makes her your niece.' His face creased up and he began to sob. He eased himself slowly down beside the bathtub, raised a hand to his face and curled up towards it. 'I'm sorry. I'm sorry. I didn't think this would happen. I thought...' He clutched the towel to his stomach, as if he wished to hide the testimony of his scars.

Lisa squatted beside him, resting her back against the bathtub. She put out a hesitant hand and touched his hair. 'It's all right, J.'

'God.' He shook his head, still turned away from her. 'I haven't cried like this since...' He couldn't get it out.

'Since then.'

'Yes.'

'But you're happy? Happy about Cosima?'

'I'm over the bloody moon.' He laughed through his tears. 'You wouldn't think it, though, would you, to look at me?' He dabbed at his face with the towel.

'So what's wrong?'

He swallowed, shaking his head. 'I'm scared at how she's going to take it, I suppose. I'll be stealing some of her history. Stealing some of her past life away from her. And only offering her me instead.' He looked up, his face still fragile. 'And I'm not much of a bargain, as you'll readily admit.'

'Oh come on, J. Creak, creak.'

He hesitated, weighing her up. 'You'll think this is silly, but there's a part of Frances that doesn't want to tell her. And there's a part of me, too.'

'You can't be serious!'

'Think about it, Liss. I can see Frances's point. Cosima's twenty-seven. She's lived nearly half a lifetime without me.'

'What's that got to do with it?' She glowered at him. 'If Frances won't tell her, I will.'

'You wouldn't!'

'J, you can't go around the world leading other people's lives for them. It's not fair. If you're really her father, it's her right to know. What if she ever has children? And what about Penhallow? And *La Giraudère*? You'd expect to leave them to her, now, wouldn't you? How are you going to explain that away?'

He let his head sink onto his chest. 'I suppose you're right.'

'Of course I'm right. And Daddy? And *maman*? They both have a right to know. She's their solitary grandchild, for heaven's sake. This doesn't just affect you and Frances. It affects everyone. You talk to Frances about it. Persuade her.'

'I'm going to ask her to marry me.'

Lisa cocked her head at him. 'That's pretty rapid, isn't it?'

'I asked her for the first time thirty-nine years ago. Does that sound rapid to you?'

'So what's changed?'

'I told her what really happened on the island. And she forgave me.'

'It always struck me there wasn't much to forgive.'

'How do you mean?'

'Well the problem was always elsewhere, wasn't it?' She squinted at him. 'With you, actually.'

'That's not very funny.'

'I'm not trying to be funny. But I always suspected you were secretly rather relieved that your marriage with Fran never took place.' She glanced sideways at him, measuring his capacity for the truth. 'I mean, look at you. You've spent the better part of the last twenty-five years neurotically fucking your way through vast swathes of Europe, Africa and the Far East. Not to mention North and South America.' She sighed wearily. 'I hate to disappoint you, J, but you never did strike me as the marrying kind.'

'That's a bit rich, coming from you.'

She cupped her hand to his cheek. 'Now don't get all upset and catty. I'm sure you've changed since then.' She hesitated, aware that perhaps she'd gone a little too far. 'The cancer's marked you, for one thing. And age has probably slowed you down a bit.' She ran her hand back through his hair. 'And maybe becoming a father, albeit a belated one, will have its effect on you too? But I'm going to give you a bit of sisterly advice nevertheless.'

'Oh boy.'

She took a solid grip on his topknot, using the pressure to reinforce her words. 'Take it easy with Frances, J. Rekindle your affair by all means. Build up your relationship with her and Cosima. But don't jump the gun. It would be criminally unfair to let her down again. You're pretty damn old to be marrying for the first time.'

She let go of his hair, and allowed her hand to fall gently down the contours of his cheek. She sighed, and eased herself up from the bathroom floor. 'And now, after that little bit of flannel, I'm going to take a real flannel and get to work on Goody Champion.' She smoothed down her blouse. 'And for that, I'll need you out of the room. Think you can corridor hop as far as your bedroom without getting caught? You must have had enough experience by now, so help me God.'

He stood up, grunting in mock contrition.

While Lisa was getting a flannel ready, Jonathan walked on ahead of her into the bedroom. He looked at the bed in disbelief. 'Oh shit!'

'What is it?'

'Clara's gone.'

'Gone? Gone where?' Lisa appeared beside him at the door. 'She hasn't got any clothes on, for God's sake.'

Jonathan darted out into the corridor. Charles was standing at the top of the stairs with a bemused expression on his face.

'Dad. Have you seen her?'

'Woman's gone completely mad. She just ran past me. Stark bollock naked.'

'Which way did she go?'

'Down the stairs and out into the garden. Was she streaking, do you think?'

Jonathan motioned to his sister. 'Come on, Liss.'

They clattered down the stairs. There was the sound of a motor car revving on the driveway. Jonathan sprinted through the front door, clutching his leg. 'Christ Almighty. She's taking my Aston.'

'Then stop her!'

Clara let out the clutch. The Aston Martin slewed around on the gravel.

Jonathan made a megaphone with his hands. 'Clara. Stop being so bloody stupid! Get out of the car. You're drunk.'

Clara's sheet-white face flashed briefly at him. He dived to one side as the Aston accelerated violently up the driveway. At the first corner the car wobbled, then corrected itself. It disappeared in a cloud of dust towards the main road.

'Come on, J. We can take my car. Are you all right?'

'Have you got a mobile phone?'

'We haven't time for any of this.'

'Lisa. Listen to me. It's already too late to stop her. So we've got to call the police. She could kill somebody in the state she's in. We can follow her later. Either way we'll have to take a punt on the road she took. She must have been going sixty-miles-an-hour up the drive.'

'You can't, J. You can't call the police. They'll take away her licence.'

He was already limping back inside the house. He stopped. 'It wouldn't be such a bad idea at that.'

'Oh, J.'

Grim-faced, he steadied himself against the door. 'It's better than risking Clara's life. Or somebody else's. Some innocent party. Isn't it? Isn't it, Liss?'

Thirty-five

Clara clutched the steering-wheel and craned her head forward myopically. She'd seen it again. In the bedroom. The white thing. It had come closer this time. Blood had been dripping from its mouth. The red had stained her stomach. She could still feel the viscous texture of it. She shivered, rubbing her belly violently with her hand. Without consciously deciding to, she began to retrace her journey of the night before.

The Aston Martin juddered around the right-angled bend near the Gurnard's Head Inn, then again on the corner before Gear Farm. Each time the tyres barely held their traction. Clara forced the car into third, the mesh protesting. She accelerated along the Try Valley in third gear, at a little over sixty-miles-an-hour, the engine screaming throatily beneath the bonnet.

She squinted vacantly at the road, massaging her face. A camper van was approaching fifty yards ahead of her. It was hard to judge the distance. Probably just enough room to get past it. At the final moment she closed her eyes.

There was the scream of tearing, rending metal, then a teeth-jarring crunch. The Aston surged off the ground, shook itself, then veered off to the left. It stuttered to an unwieldy halt, fetching up against a fence. The engine conked out.

Clara reached up and touched her split lip – blood began to drip onto her breasts and belly. She moaned.

'What the flaming hell do you think you're doing?'

A man was approaching from the camper. She could see him in the rear-view mirror. It was the man from the cottage. She was sure of it. His face flushed with anger, he was jogging the fifty yards that now separated their cars. He meant to kill her. Revenge himself on her. That must have been why he'd driven at her with the van. She felt for the door handle. For some reason it wasn't in the usual place. She looked around herself uncomprehendingly. What was she doing in a strange car? Ah. There it was. She opened the door and stepped out into the road.

'John. She's naked. Look.'

It was a woman. She'd emerged from the van and was following behind her husband. Probably the mother. Clara raised her voice. 'Keep away from me! You…you…keep away from me.' It came out as a croak.

'John. Stop. She might be mad.'

The couple stood watching her. Clara prodded at her stomach, unconsciously smearing more blood across her belly and breasts.

'Look. She's injured. Perhaps you'd better go and help her after all.'

'Keep away! Just keep away from me!'

'What shall we do?'

Clara spun round. A police car was approaching from the direction of Chysauster. That was it, then. A trap. And she'd fallen for it. They'd sent the van in first to stop her. Then the police car to take her away.

She lurched to the side of the road, bent down, and began to ease herself through the barbed-wire fence.

'Miss. Wait. We're here to help you.'

Two policemen had stepped out from either side of the police car. Clara glanced up a second time and lost her footing. She fell onto her back, snagging herself badly on the wire. She screamed in pain.

'Bloody hell.' The first policeman signalled to his companion. 'Get over the fence. Quickly. Stop her if she tries to get through.' He started slowly up the road, his hands held out calmly in front of him. 'Miss. It's all right. Just stay where you are. There's an ambulance on its way.' He raised his voice a little. 'You two get back inside the van. Please. The situation is under control.'

Clara fell clumsily through the wire. She curled up into a tight ball, keening to herself.

'Don't run, you fool. Walk!' The first policeman was talking to his companion.

Clara looked up. One of the policemen was climbing through the fence thirty yards from where she was lying. She unclenched her knees and got shakily to her feet. The wire cuts hurt abominably. She dabbed unthinkingly at her lip. 'Don't come near me. I know what you're here for. I didn't mean to do it.'

'Do what, miss?' The policemen were coming closer.

'Kill the child. I didn't mean to kill the child.'

'Which child is that, miss? We haven't heard about any child.'

'You know very well. His child.' She pointed shakily back towards the camper van. 'That's why you've come, isn't it? To take me away.'

'That's not why, miss. No. We're here to help you.'

The policeman in the field started running.

'No!' Clara turned away from him and sprinted up the hill.

'Cut her off from the marsh! Quickly.'

The marsh? Clara reached the top of the bluff and stopped for breath. The land spread around her on all four sides, falling away towards the sea and the coastline behind her and towards Treen Downs swamp to her right. Treen Downs? She recognised where she was for the first time. She uttered an eerie wail.

'Jesus. What was that?' Both policemen stopped in their tracks.

'I'm not going near that bloody bog,' said the one who'd come through the field. 'That's where the Sherman Tank went down during the war. Whole bloody tank and its crew.'

The older man blanched. 'You're joking? You're bloody joking?' He turned swiftly towards Clara. 'Miss! Miss! Stay where you are. We're not going to hurt you. You haven't done anything wrong. But you mustn't go any further. You must stay exactly where you are.'

Jonathan poked at the electric button below the dashboard of Lisa's car. He craned his neck out of the side window. He could only see the camper van at first, skewed across the middle of the lane. Then the lacerated wreck of his Aston Martin came into view, with the police car parked nearby. 'Damn. Just as I thought. She's caused a bloody accident.'

'Look.' Lisa pointed at the hillside.

Clara was standing on the bluff. Even at that distance the full extent of her uncontrollable, spasmodic trembling was visible to the naked eye. The two policemen were just below her, separated from each other by about thirty feet of common. All three were seemingly frozen to the spot. The brown smudge of Treen swamp loomed thirty yards from where Clara was standing.

Jonathan leapt out of the car. For a moment he lost his balance, but he instantly found his feet again and began running. 'Clara! It's Jonathan. Stay just where you are. The policemen don't mean you any harm. You'll be perfectly all right if you stand still.'

Lisa was clambering through the barbed-wire fence. 'Please!' she cried out. 'Please don't approach her anymore. You'll scare her. Please. She's hallucinating. She's got the DT's.'

'We've got to get her, miss. She told us something about killing a child.' He made a signal to his companion. They broke into a run.

Clara turned on her heel and stumbled down the far side of the hill.

'Clara. No!' Lisa ran as fast as she was able towards Clara's position, one hand clutched to her breast. Jonathan, desperately trying to ignore the agony in his leg, sprinted behind her.

Clara struck the edge of the swamp and came to an abrupt halt. She sank slowly in up to her calves, instinctively throwing out her arms to balance herself.

'Miss!' The older policeman froze ten feet away from her. 'Clara. That's your name, isn't it? Clara. Stay there. Stay exactly where you are. Don't go any further. It's all right. You're quite safe. But don't go any further in. I'm going to begin walking towards you.'

Panic-stricken, Clara tried to extract one leg from the bog. She twisted awkwardly and fell onto her back.

The policeman broke into a run. He made a flat dive and grabbed hold of Clara's calf. 'It's all right. I've got her.' He twisted his head and shouted over to his companion. 'You grab my leg and hold on.'

Clara shrieked and wriggled away from him. He lost his grip in the mud, but before he could regain his hold, she was away. She backed violently towards the centre of the bog, her legs and arms windmilling and throwing up great splashes of mud.

'Oh Jesus.' Jonathan reached the edge of the bog and began to wade in. He fell to his knees with the suction.

'Don't anyone else go in there!' The first policeman was holding up his hand.

Clara doubled up. The slimy water had already risen as far as her waist. She made as if to wade towards the edge, then found she couldn't move. She moaned. The whites of her eyes turned up into themselves.

'Clara. For God's sake put out your arms! Support yourself.'

Clara could no longer hear him. She began a primeval shrieking. The swamp water bubbled up above her bare breasts.

Jonathan surged forward. Lisa plunged in behind him and grabbed his shirt. 'J, don't! Please. It's too late. It's too late.'

The second policeman was already dragging his companion back onto firmer ground.

As they watched, Clara's disembodied head hovered for a moment above the swamp water, then disappeared beneath the surface.

Thirty-six

'But she said she'd killed a child?'

Jonathan shook his head. 'The police assured me that there have been no fatal road accidents involving children anywhere in the neighbourhood for more than a year.'

'What then? What did she kill?' Frances shook her head uncomprehendingly.

'They traced her last known route, the one she drove on the night you arrived. They checked every single house along the way. They finally found a place called Badger's Cross. It's just a mile or two outside Penzance.'

'I know it. She told me there were roadworks that way. That we should go the long way around.'

Jonathan grimaced. 'Well there weren't any roadworks. She simply didn't want you to use that route because she'd hit something there, just before she picked you up.'

'But what? What did she hit?'

'A badger.'

'A badger?'

'The man at the cottage remembered it. It happens all the time. They use the road as a crossing point, apparently. Hence the name. He's buried three this year already.'

'But she can't have thought...'

'She was hallucinating, Fran. Who knows what she thought?'

Frances dropped her face into her hands. 'It's ghastly…ghastly. I can't bear to think of her lying all alone in that bog.'

He hesitated, weighing his words, fearful that he might sound flippant. 'She's got the American boys, Fran. The crew of that Sherman Tank. The one that was lost during the war. Remember when Stacey told us the story?'

Frances looked up, frowning.

'They're down there with her. So she's not alone. Not really.' He bit off the remainder of his words, feeling that he'd already gone too far.

They never did find Clara's body. A double funeral was held four days later, with one of the coffins empty. At the last moment Lisa begged to be allowed to place something inside the casket, and was permitted to do so. No one had the nerve to ask her what it was. There was some talk of a plaque, too, up on Treen Downs, well away from the road, so as not to tempt people up to the bog out of sheer curiosity.

On the day of the funeral, Frances stood beside Jonathan in the pale September sunshine, watching the final committal. 'I feel like an absolute fraud. I'm standing here, watching an empty coffin, feeling empty.' She took Jonathan's arm, leaning tightly against him. 'Something happened, some awful thing, to make Clara the way she was. It must have done. You don't turn in on yourself like that, keeping the rest of the world at bay, for no reason whatsoever.'

'Don't torture yourself about it, Fran. It's too late.'

'I'm not. I promise. But I'd still like to know.'

She crouched down, when it was her turn, and threw a little dirt onto the coffin. Jonathan did the same. Then he took her arm and they walked away.

When they'd passed the line of mourners and reached the churchyard gates, he leaned across and whispered in her ear. '*Ashes to ashes, and dust to dust. If the men don't get you, the whisky must.*' He cleared his throat, hesitantly. 'I think Buddy Bolden must have had our Clara in mind when he wrote that.'

Frances glanced up at him, her face magically clearing.

Cosima came up beside them. 'A smile at last. God, Mummy. It's about time.' She squinted across at Jonathan. 'Are you both coming to the pub, then? With the rest of us? We're going to give Helen and Aunt Clara the sort of send-off they would have appreciated. Well, that Clara would have appreciated, anyway. I'm not so sure about Helen.'

'A minute. We'll be there in a minute. I've got something to say to your mother first.'

They watched Cosima as she moved forward and took Charles's arm. He turned to her, smiling, already half in love with a granddaughter of whose existence he was entirely unaware.

Jonathan turned Frances towards him. 'Don't you think it's about time?'

She shook her head uncertainly. 'I don't know. I'm scared. Scared for her.'

'We may not have too long.' He nodded towards Charles. 'We owe it to them. To both of them, don't you think?'

Her eyes misted. 'Oh God, J. I'm so bitterly ashamed of myself. I seem to have spent my entire life avoiding confrontations.'

'And I seem to have spent my entire life causing them.' He laughed ironically. 'So I may as well end my career with a bang.'

Frances brushed at her eyes. Her brow lost its furrows. 'You're right. It's absurd, isn't it? That a grotesque thought like that should be comforting. But it is.'

He reached for her hand. 'Shall we go now, then? And see our daughter?'

She froze for a moment. Then she slowly looked up into his eyes. 'Yes,' she said. 'Let's.'

Internet: **www.houseofstratus.com** including author interviews, reviews, features.

Email: **sales@houseofstratus.com** please quote author, title and credit card details.

Hotline: UK ONLY: **0800 169 1780**, please quote author, title and credit card details.

INTERNATIONAL: **+44 (0) 20 7494 6400**, please quote author, title and credit card details.

Send to: **House of Stratus Sales Department**
24c Old Burlington Street
London
W1X 1RL
UK

A Worthwhile Life

ISBN: 979-8-9867934-0-5 (paperback)
ISBN: 979-8-9867934-1-2 (ebook)

Ordering Information:
Special discounts are available on quantity purchases by corporations, associations, and others. For details, contact AWorthwhileLifeBook@gmail.com.

A Worthwhile Life

How to Find Meaning, Build Connection, and Cultivate Purpose

Michael Westover

Table of Contents

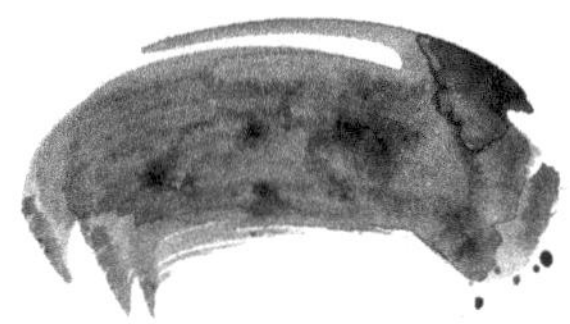

Meaninglessness in the Mirror

This book was born of a midlife crisis. I stared at my reflection in the bathroom mirror one afternoon and asked what my life meant. The blueness of my eyes seemed to be fading. The old hockey scar wrinkled the skin below my right eyebrow. Worry lines extended from the corners of my eyes, past graying temples and down my cheeks. My whole countenance sagged in the bright lights.

I had achieved many of my aspirations by then. I had a wonderful wife, and we had exceeded the financial goals set early in our marriage. I had a great education and a supportive extended family. I was healthy, and I was well-respected in my field. And yet a surprising hollowness was still seeping into my life.

I understood myself and the world better at that time than I had at any previous point in my life. I had opportunities to be involved with a staggering array of activities and causes… and yet, aimlessness was creeping in. I had tried to distract myself from the emptiness, but it had raged back louder and deeper than before. So I increased the dose of distraction and experimented with new entertainments. They dulled the pain and made me forget for a moment.

So, in that moment of introspection, I strained to look beyond my image in the mirror. Was I here on earth to sit in meetings all day and then watch television until I fell asleep? Why did I try so hard, and why should I try at all? I wondered if the world would be any different without me in it.

The popular answers to these questions seemed incomplete. So I studied what I could about how to squeeze more meaning from life. I gathered sources from the fields of philosophy, theology, business, evolutionary biology, and the social sciences. I reflected on the meaningful moments from my own history. These pages are the result.

This book is not about the nature of reality and the universe. It does not attempt to answer questions of where we came from or where we are going, but it does propose reasons for us being here. It is about what makes existence worthwhile. If you are looking for a book to tell you, "Nothing really matters, so do whatever you want," you might prefer the writings of Camus or Sartre. If you want to see your life as valuable, keep reading.

In these pages, we will explore why some people perceive their lives as worthwhile while others do not. We will ask hard questions about what it means to have a meaningful life, and we will face uncomfortable answers. Some activities are conducive to meaning while others are not. We will investigate the differences, and we will expose the counterfeits.

The concepts in this book are rooted in the literature, but I extend some of the research findings into new territory and add a few thoughts of my own. Who am I to write on this topic? There may be others with stronger credentials and sharper pens, but I can state with conviction that there was a time when my life felt empty, and now it is meaningful. I hope this book can help you in some small way.

At 6'8", Clayton Christensen was a wiry intellectual giant who knew something of the meaning of life. As a child, he could be found navigating a local river with his brothers and friends in home-built canoes. By age 12, Clay had read the entire *World Book Encyclopedia*.[1]

With more than a little understatement, his youngest brother said that Clay "was not a passive participant in life."[2] He was his high school's student body president and attended college with a full-ride academic scholarship. After graduating with high distinction, Clay won a Rhodes Scholarship and finished the rigorous graduate program in two years instead of three, all while playing on the school's national championship basketball team.

Clay graduated from Harvard's business school with high distinction. He founded and ran a successful company and then returned to Harvard to receive an advanced degree in business. Then he joined the Harvard faculty, teaching a popular business course. He was a best-selling author of 10 books. *Forbes* called him "one of the most influential business theorists of the last 50 years" and featured him in a cover story.[3]

But Clay's life was not universally charmed. In the space of only a few years, he had a heart attack, three cancerous tumors, and a major stroke—and he was only in his fifties. Of the three experiences, he described the stroke as the most trying.

Clay described his vocabulary as an organized file cabinet filled with words. When he had his stroke, it was as though the file cabinet tipped over and scattered the contents.[4] Clay retained his keen intellect but lost the words to share it with others.

So, Clay began the painstaking work of refilling his mental file cabinet—one word at a time. He made vocabulary lists and purchased English learning software. He challenged his six-year-old granddaughter to noun-naming competitions and lost badly each time.[5]

His progress was maddeningly slow. Clay began spending more and more time in his basement, and he fell into a profound sadness—something he had never experienced before. Years later, he spoke openly of how discouraging it was, as a supposedly brilliant academic, to lack the power of speech. He said, "Sometimes I just wanted to quit trying to learn and speak and write again and just go into my basement and build furniture. Then I [would not] have to talk to people.... The more I focused on myself, the unhappier I became."[6]

After Clay rose from the fog of depression, he said, "I screwed my head on straight" and "I learned that focusing on my own problems does not bring happiness. God didn't say, 'Okay. For those with problems it's okay to focus on [yourselves]. And for those who don't have problems, I want you to focus on helping others.'"[7]

So Clayton Christensen stepped out of his basement and into the world. He wrote and he taught. He mentored and he inspired. Sometimes it was more difficult for him to find the right words as quickly as he had been able to before the stroke, but he cared more about the people in front of him than about how they perceived him.

We are going to draw from the lessons of Clay's life in this book. We will investigate the effects of accomplishments and high status on our perception of self-worth. We will explore suffering and what it has to do with the value of our lives. And we will consider taking responsibility for others despite our pains. So let this be a modest start on our journey toward a worthwhile life.

Purpose versus Meaning

The stirring call to find purpose and meaning is part of the human condition. Most of us loathe the idea of accepting our lives as pointless—as only as meaningful as an insect's.[8]

The phrases "purpose of life" and "meaning of life" are used interchangeably, but the word "purpose" and the word "meaning" have different connotations. Purpose is a perceived direction—something to do and to achieve. On the other hand, the social psychologists Costin and Vignoles state that "those pursuing meaning need assurance that their lives have value."[9] They seek confidence that their existence is worth the suffering.

People need both purpose and meaning in their lives. One is not necessarily preferable to the other. We need to have direction and to know that we matter.

It is possible to have a purposeful life that is devoid of meaning. Imagine someone who dedicates his time to collecting artisanal cookie jars. He spends nearly all his disposable income on ceramic containers from around the world. But this man is embarrassed by his hobby. So he keeps his cookie jars in a vault and shares them with no one. Without more to his life than cookie jars, this man may wake up one day to find his life an empty vessel.

It is also possible to experience meaningful moments when you have no clear sense of purpose. These are the times when a friend drags you to sing at a nursing home and you come away wondering how such a trivial activity suddenly made life worthwhile, or when someone thanks you for a gift that seems insignificant to you.

The Meaning of Life Through the Ages

The universal desire for meaning is debated in Eastern and Western philosophies, addressed by every religion, and found in myths and stories throughout the records of human history. The quest for meaning belongs with other great questions: How can I be happy? Is there a God and does he care? Who am I?

The visual below summarizes the meaning of life according to different philosophers over the ages. It conveys the general confusion on the topic. Some philosophies advocate for pleasure-seeking and self-fulfillment while others promote hard work or self-sacrifice. Some say meaning is universal while others say we create our own. Each of us subscribes to one or more of these philosophies, and they are each enticing in their own way. A few choose their life philosophy

How to Have a Worthwhile Life

ACCORDING TO DIFFERENT PHILOSOPHIES

PLATONISM

Think more, understand beauty, contribute to society

ARISTOTLEIANISM

Build good character and intellectual virtues

CYNICISM

Reject custom and live in agreement with nature

EPICUREANISM

Avoid pain, live humbly, make friends

HEDONISM

Maximize total pleasure

STOICISM

Achieve wisdom, temperance, justice and courage

CONFUCIANISM

Live an ordinary life

MOHISM

Care for people impartially

THEISM

Do God's will

CLASSICAL LIBERALISM

Protect individual freedom

PRAGMATISM

Bring the most good to people

KANTIANISM

Do as you'd have others do

EXISTENTIALISM

Life has no meaning until you give it one

NIHILISM

Do anything because life has no inherent value

WILL TO POWER

Impose your will in your life and on others

EXPRESSIVE INDIVIDUALISM

Find and reveal your authentic inner self

deliberately, while the rest pick theirs up somewhere along the way. They manifest in how we spend our time, how we treat other people, and how we view religion.

Take the pickup artist, for example. His life revolves around the study and practice of wooing as many women as possible. The set of beliefs that undergird his behavior likely include hedonism, liberalism, and some nihilism. He may not have studied these philosophies in depth, but they are enmeshed in the cultural fabric and impossible to avoid. The Casanova will chase thrills in the short term and negative consequences over the long term if his behavior persists.

Each of us internalizes a system of values that directs our priorities, decisions, and behavior. What we believe about the source of a meaningful life is just such a motivator. We don't follow our beliefs all the time, but they are there in the background, nudging us. Although there is a dizzying array of conflicting perspectives on *how* to have a meaningful life, a growing consensus among academics is emerging around *what it means* to have one.

Attributes of a Meaningful Life

The author and researcher Emily Esfahani Smith wrote that people have meaning in their lives when three conditions have been satisfied:

1. They evaluate their lives as significant and worthwhile—as part of something bigger.
2. They believe their lives make sense.
3. They feel their lives are driven by a sense of purpose.[10]

These descriptions aptly capture the sensations that accompany a meaningful life, but they raise other questions: Can I just decide that my life is significant and find meaning? What is the "something bigger" I should be a part of? Why do some peoples' lives make sense? And where does the perception of purpose come from?

More important than understanding what it feels like to have a meaningful life is understanding how to create one. And without some understanding of the causal mechanism, you might search for meaning in all the wrong places. You may choose to follow a lonely path away from meaning instead of toward it because some actions give people a greater sense of meaning than others do. Gandhi's path of peaceful resistance delivered a nation. Charles Manson's path led his cult members to murder.

The clinical psychologist Jordan Peterson once said, "Our modern societies have criticized the idea of meaning so much that many do not even believe in it anymore."[11] Some people wonder if the meaning of life is unknowable or decide that the answer is not worth pursuing. A quick search on social media will surface thousands of posts declaring that nothing really matters. One that just popped up on my Twitter feed states, "Life is just made of meaningless moments."

If you are willing to entertain the possibility that your life could be valuable and that some pursuits are more meaningful and purposeful than others, then it is important to explore the sources of that variation. The questions then become "How can I maximize the meaning in my life?" and "What am I willing to sacrifice to obtain it?"

There is hope. If we look outside ourselves, we will find individuals and communities with a deep sense of meaning. Like the Russian novelist Dostoevsky, we will meet humble people who know why they are here and that they matter. Across all countries and belief systems, most people believe that their lives have purpose and are meaningful.[12]

A Reliable Source of Meaning

A nurse named Cindy once told me a story about a woman who went to the emergency room 12 times in only six months for various ailments. Cindy called this woman one of her "friendly faces," which is a euphemism for patients who go to the hospital or emergency room too often.

During her initial conversation with this friendly-faced patient who we'll call Jane, Cindy asked about Jane's health history, financial situation, eating habits, social support network, transportation access, and medications while motivating her to live a healthy lifestyle. Cindy discovered that Jane was lonely and not getting enough exercise. Instead of challenging Jane to lose weight or buy a gym pass, Cindy bought her a dog—a mutt named Mochi.

The results of this simple act were surprising. Jane began taking Mochi on morning and evening walks. Jane took her medication more regularly. And, importantly, Jane stopped having health crises and going to the emergency room. Cindy attributed the change in Jane's demeanor to the exercise, but I believe it is deeper than that. Jane recognized that the dog needed her and accepted responsibility for him. In fulfilling that responsibility, Jane found the meaning and motivation missing from her life. She found that her life was worthwhile.

Here is the heart of it. Meaning comes from *taking responsibility for another individual.* It is having a vested interest in a life and being willing to sacrifice. If you want your life to be a part of something bigger, connect it to other people. If you want your life to make sense, make it about the ways you can serve other people. If you desire a sense of meaning, decide to improve the lives of people with whom you come into contact.

How Responsibility Leads to Meaning

Responsibility is a commitment to the well-being of another. We commit to those who, in our judgment, have value. If we didn't believe them to have value, we would not commit. Taking responsibility for others is the acceptance of their worth and potential.

In this book, you will learn how the accepted worth of another can become a motivating principle in your life. If our charges have intrinsic value, then we are willing to support them, which requires sacrifice. Willingness to face discomfort and pain for the benefit of another is the mark of responsibility. If the person I help along the way has value, then my life is important. My life is valuable. I have meaning.

You will also discover the nuances and complexity of responsibility in this text, like how a belief in God or something higher is not required to find meaning in others. The only prerequisite is to recognize the spark of potential in the one before you. Everyone lacks something, and we can take responsibility for helping them along their way.

The source of meaning can be counterintuitive to those hoping that a meaningful life is an individual pursuit and not a communal one: *Are you seriously telling me that my life is only worthwhile if I am willing to sacrifice my time, energy, and resources for other people? I want to feel like my life is worthwhile—not that others' lives are. Is there another way?*

Likely no. The German philosopher Martin Heidegger described feeling like a stranger thrown into the world and alienated from it.[13] Many of us have also felt lonely, useless, and disconnected at some point. Responsibility is an antidote to those feelings. Of course, there are other ways to feel like life is worthwhile: status-seeking, achievement, pleasure, dominance, and wealth, to name a few. These activities may give you purpose, but, as we will discuss throughout this book, they do not create much meaning.

I recently attended a Halloween party with a 10-month-old baby named Chloe. Both she and her mother had painted green noses, sparkling silver onesies, and spikey blonde troll hair. Chloe had a probing interest in face paint and costume accessories and showed off her new clapping skills throughout the evening. Someone speculated that Chloe's curiosity and friendliness portended an amazing life.

I sat on the carpet and played blocks with her for a few minutes. I put them back in the Tupperware box while she removed them. I built up while she destroyed—always with a toothy smile. When I looked into Chloe's innocent face, I saw near-infinite potential. When I search the countenances of people from all walks of life, I perceive similar worth.

The desire to take care of those in our orbit, especially children, is ingrained in our DNA, our histories, and our culture.[14] Our species has been so successful in part because of our ability to protect and watch over each other. We should not resist the nurturing aspect of our natures; we should encourage it.

The Potential Range of Meaning

Meaning can be described as the value or worth that you perceive in your life. The potential range is not from no worth to infinite worth. The spectrum is broader. It is from infinitely positive to infinitely negative. If people believe they are doing more harm than good, they may perceive their lives as having less than no meaning.

Those who perceive their lives as meaningful improve their world through the lives they touch, while those who see their lives as meaningless refuse to take responsibility or do not act on it when friends need them. People who see their lives as having less than no value use other people instead of caring for them. They are willing to trade on and benefit from human suffering.

Augustine of Hippo was 31 when he dedicated his life to Christianity and became Saint Augustine—a theologian, philosopher, and bishop. Before then, he had been a brilliant student with a devout Christian mother and a pagan father.

Augustine relates a not-so-saintly story from his childhood for which he tortured himself later in life. He and some friends secretly raided a neighbor's yard and ate all the ripening pears on a tree. Augustine writes that he was not even hungry and that more delicious pears were waiting for him at home. Augustine considered this an act of pure wickedness and thought that it would not have been so grievous if he had been hungry or had had no other means of securing a pear.[15]

The boy Augustine clearly felt some responsibility to protect his neighbor and understood that he had violated that commitment. Sticky regrets from this experience fill seven chapters of his book *Confessions*. Augustine went on to do great things. After his conversion, Augustine restored the confidence of the Christian world, which had been shaken after the sack of Rome by Visigoths in 410. His words carried down through the centuries, influencing untold masses, but he never forgot the pear tree.

Augustine is like many of us: we sometimes take what we want instead of giving what is needed, producing meaning at times and destroying it at others. We do our best to come through for those we care about, knowing that we may fail. We should still try. Assuming Augustine was able to deliver on his commitments to help others more often than he let them down, he would have seen his life as meaningful.

Like meaning, purpose in life can be benevolent, malevolent, or something in between. As an employee of General Motors in 1921, Thomas Midgley Jr. discovered that adding tetraethyllead to gasoline prevented car engines from making irritating knocking sounds. General Motors named the substance "Ethyl" to avoid any mention of lead in its advertising, and Midgley received several prominent awards.[16]

Even after witnessing hallucinations, insanity, and multiple deaths in the production factory, Midgley advocated for his creation. During a press conference in 1924, he poured the substance on his hands, inhaled the chemical's vapor, and declared that he could repeat those actions every day without any issue.[17] He was soon diagnosed with lead poisoning and had to take a leave of absence.[18] Choose a worthy purpose.

The Potential Depths of Meaning

You take on responsibility for others when you believe you can help them and you desire to do so. You would not make the commitment without thinking you could deliver on your promise. As your responsibilities grow and you fulfill them, you will see yourself as more useful to others. So, the meaning you experience in life is proportionate to the responsibility that you take on. The deeper the responsibility, the greater the sense of meaning. And each of us has an endless potential supply.

Is it possible to take responsibility for only one person and have a meaningful life? Absolutely, and you will see your life as more meaningful as your commitment to that individual deepens. You may have the time, energy, and capacity to look out for others too. If you can barely take care of yourself, take a small measure of responsibility for others. Take some, though, and remember that the commitment is to do what you can to help when your charges cannot help themselves.

Profound meaning is achievable but generally found through the accumulation of small commitments or the deepening of existing responsibilities. Outside of comic books, no one makes the leap from no responsibility to heroic levels without setting themselves up for failure. We progress incrementally and through trial and error.

We are each like glass soda bottles that can be recycled endlessly. In the recycling process, metal lids and any contaminants are removed.

The glass is crushed and then mixed with sand and other raw materials. All these are melted in a furnace with temperatures exceeding 1000 degrees Fahrenheit. The glass is finally molded into new shapes for new purposes.

As we take on seemingly overwhelming responsibilities, we remove as many of the contaminants keeping us from being as successful as we can. We are crushed under the weight of new commitments, but we gain new resources and skills through the effort. We are then melted and slowly molded into new shapes, larger than before and capable of carrying more liquid for more people.

Drew Harmon required total care for his entire life. He was born prematurely and barely survived pneumonia when he was seven weeks old. He had open-heart surgery at four months old, and he had a stroke during his recovery. He visited almost every department in the local children's hospital before the age of five.

Through his numerous surgeries and constant medical issues, his mother Jill and other family members stood by him. Jill took care of Drew full time. She took him on walks, listened to music with him, brought him to amusement parks, and took him to the beach.

When Drew passed away at the age of 17, Jill crumpled for months. She expressed her anguish online with comments like "Goodbye angel baby. I will miss you every day!!!" and "Really need one of his hugs right now. Miss him too much!!!" Despite Drew's physical limitations and the constant worry, work, and cost associated with caring for him, Jill missed the love and fulfillment that came with total responsibility.

Families with disabled members suffer physical and emotional trials that many find overwhelming. I have a close friend whose child has severe autism and other physical limitations. My experience with his family and others who endure caring for disabled loved ones is that they gain a closeness that most other families simply do not enjoy. One man with a disabled child said, “This is a challenge that only a family unit can handle, [and it] has strengthened our family.”

The research supports this. Families with disabled members report increased sensitivity and caring on the part of siblings and other relatives. Siblings in particular report having developed greater maturity and a greater sense of responsibility.[19]

Meaning in life lasts for the duration of our commitment to the well-being of another. And that commitment is not bound by the end of an official relationship or the beginning of another. A teacher, for example, can connect with a student years after the school year is over. Neighbors can check in on one another decades after one moves to the other side of the world.

You might be thinking, “Wait! If I refuse to take care of the puppy, someone else will do it for me. If the puppy would have been cared for regardless of my behavior, did I really create value?” The answer is of course yes. The puppy required care. You provided it. The value accrues to you. To shirk your responsibility, hoping that someone will pick up the slack, is a missed opportunity for meaning.

The Substance of Meaning

Adding a new source of meaning is typically accompanied by a period of rapture. Think of a mother holding a newborn or the acceptance of a new job. The more meaning you extract from life, the more you want. In this way, meaning is like an addiction. In fact, destructive addictions can be inadequate replacements for the meaning we all need.

How can we say our lives are worthwhile? We perceive positive meaning through feedback from those to whom we are committed. The feedback comes in the form of gratitude or the recognition that our behavior is helping in some way.

With gratitude, you see your value reflected in the eyes of those you serve. Strive to recognize the imperfect expressions of appreciation that you receive as proof of your value, and remember to find an appropriate "thank you" for those who take responsibility for you.

Of course, you do not always receive gratitude for valued service. I do not believe any of my children thanked my wife for spending hours teaching them how to read. They seemed much more pleased with their own progress than with their good teacher's contribution. With every new sound and successful word, though, my wife could sense that her efforts were successful. And that evidence of valuable service is another small proof that my wife leads a valuable life.

Interestingly, we receive gratitude not just from those we serve but from others who feel responsible for those we serve. I am grateful my wife spent so much time teaching my children to read. I did not benefit directly from her work, but those I care for did.

So what is the substance of meaning? It is a growing certainty that one's life is valuable. It is the accumulation of valuable contributions made to the lives of others. And we receive that certainty through gratitude and evidence of effective service.

If meaning is just a perception of life value, can I trick myself into thinking my life is meaningful? Could meaning-affirmation exercises alone do the trick? Sadly, meaningless activities do not generate worthwhile feedback. They are like companies that create products no one wants.

How Purpose and Meaning Interact

My mother, Susan, enters St. Peter's Basilica in Vatican City with her husband and turns, slowly taking in the pillars, arches, paintings, and sculptures. As she crosses through the vestibule, Susan bumps into stunned tourists gazing upward. And, turning to the right, she sees Michelangelo's Pietà: a sculpture of Mary cradling her just-crucified son, Jesus Christ.

Michelangelo portrays Mary not as careworn and furrowed, but as an elegant young mother—almost as though she is back in Bethlehem and holding a newborn in swaddling clothes. Lifelike folds of milk-white marble drape Mary from head to foot. She looks down on her son with graceful acceptance in place of mourning or devastation.[20] Christ appears not broken but peaceful—almost like an injured youth who drifted to sleep listening to his mother's comforting song. Mary's left hand is extended, inviting the onlooker to come and consider.

Susan is speechless as she stands before Michelangelo's masterwork. Her tears mingle with those of countless others on the marble underfoot. As a young mother of three small children, she sees a little of herself in Mary's idealized features. She comprehends Mary's love, loss, and willingness to sacrifice for her son—not just in that burnished moment, but in every moment from the manger to the tomb. The tenderness and beauty chiseled from Carrara marble imprint on Susan's character, and her voice is still filled with emotion when she relates this experience 35 years later.

Michelangelo was not always known as *Il Divino*, or "The Divine One."[21] He honed his skills over a decade of focused painting and sculpture. He used the output of that effort to generate masterpieces that have moved unnumbered masses over 500 years. As a premier artist of the High Renaissance, he even benefited from the work of classical Greek artists and philosophers who lived millennia before his time.

Through a singular focus and natural gifts, Michelangelo discovered both purpose and meaning. He found a profession in which to lose himself and converted his talent into art that will inspire through the ages. Michelangelo took responsibility for those who commissioned his work and the apprentices he trained. Most of us are not so gifted or focused, but we should still build talents and seek opportunities to employ them for the benefit of others.

Purpose and meaning are intertwined in a virtuous cycle. Those with purpose strive to grow, produce, and achieve. When others see the lives touched by that service, they are inspired to work harder and grow further. The result is someone with a purpose-filled and meaningful life who now desires to stretch for more.

The opposite case is also true. Those with a decreased responsibility for others feel like their lives are lacking the meaning they once had. They begin to ask themselves what the point of trying is. So they have trouble working as hard as they used to. They spend more time coping and trying to have fun. And this decrease in purpose leads to less meaning, and the downward spiral continues.

CHAPTER 3

Meaning's Hard Questions

The search for meaning requires that we grapple with challenging questions:

- If those to whom I am responsible fall short, am I at fault?
- For whom should I take responsibility?
- Are there limits to the responsibility I can take on?
- What is the brain's mechanism for taking responsibility?
- Can I take responsibility for inanimate objects?

- Does taking responsibility for people require that I take over their lives?
- Do I really know what's best for someone else?
- What happens when someone else takes responsibility for me?

Let's take a closer look at each question in turn.

Are Their Failings Your Fault?

When my oldest daughter was six months old, she loved stairs. Over and over, she would crawl up the carpeted staircase and slide on her belly back down, feet first. During one of these trips, I was following her absentmindedly… and she slipped. It happened so fast that I did not have time to react. She rolled backward between my legs and snowballed until she met the rough stone floor. She screamed in my arms until her mother arrived and calmed us both down. My daughter's tears and cries still sting a little 16 years later.

My responsibilities for my daughter included protecting her and helping her learn to crawl and walk. It is fair to say that I failed in my desire to protect her that evening. We all see those we want to thrive tumble down the stairs sometimes: a baseball coach whose player strikes out, a counselor whose patient relapses, a teacher whose student never grasps the material. When you are devoted to people, you cannot help but share in their pain. And if you don't share that pain, then you really were not taking responsibility for them in the first place.

It is helpful in these situations to look into the void and ask if you could have done anything differently. You can learn from your mistakes how to better care for the people you are responsible for in the future. I learned from my daughter that I needed to remain a few steps behind her while she climbed so that I had time to react. Now, I'm proud to say that I've caught more children falling down the stairs than I've allowed to barrel past me. And, now that my daughter is a teenager, it is even more important that I stand a few steps back.

It is inevitable that we will share in the pain and triumph of those we are responsible for, but we should avoid taking and assigning blame for their failures. Blame takes energy away from overcoming and directs it toward punishment. When I blame someone for a misdeed—especially when I blame myself—I feel anger, shame, and a desire for vengeance. None of these impulses is productive. So unless you are a judge, a Human Resources professional, or an insurance claim examiner, you should refrain from determining who is at fault. It will make you a happier and more effective caregiver.

The social commentator JP Sears once spoke about the blunder he made when he "took responsibility for his parents' marriage" while they were going through a divorce.[22] I believe JP was saying that he took it upon himself to keep the marriage alive and accepted blame for his parents' behavior. As JP recognized during the interview, this is not a healthy brand of responsibility. Their behavior leading up to the divorce and their decision to part ways was not JP's fault. No one could spare his parents from the consequences of a dissolving marriage.

Healthy responsibility is the commitment to help others through difficult circumstances like divorce, particularly in situations where those involved cannot help themselves. It is not accountability for others' choices, actions, or feelings. And healthy responsibility does not require that you punish yourself for someone else's bad decisions. Healthy responsibility is being there for them and with them.

So whose fault was my daughter's slipup? I'm not going to decide. I don't blame my daughter for the misstep, and I try not to blame myself for her fall. I'm still working on that.

The Limits of Responsibility

Every baby is born at a certain time and place in history and interacts with a limited subset of the human family. Our time and community strongly influence the challenges we face and our opportunities to take responsibility for others. In other words, a newly pregnant mother does not know if she will be raising a golden child or a troublemaker.

We each have some capacity to take responsibility for each other, but that capacity is limited by our environment, our natural gifts, and our choices. We all have weaknesses and blind spots.

I imagine what the world would be like if we each had an infinite capacity to serve. We could build or fix anything instantly to resolve or protect anyone from the problems endemic to our earthly experience. We could reach across time and space to do good. In short, it would be wonderful.

But that power to aid would have to also come with the ability to destroy all people and obstacles blocking the path of those we love. The impulse to control or manipulate those under your care would be great indeed. It would also be tempting to use that power to enrich yourself and sate your lusts at the expense of those under your power.

I take it back. It wouldn't be wonderful at all.

For Whom Should We Take Responsibility?

A pastor once told me that one thing he came to appreciate after interviewing thousands of people was that everyone suffers. This means that everyone could use another person to look out for them and ease those burdens. Each of us has distinct skills, knowledge, and experience that can help an individual or group of individuals address certain problems. Think about what your small offering might be and how to match that offering with the needs of the people around you.

Excluding the widespread desire many people have to care for small children,[23] the needier people are, the less likely it seems that others are willing to help them. Many draw back from the truly needy—those with deep emotional, physical, or intellectual deficits. They avoid the sour spouse, the grumpy coworker, or the clingy youth. And they gravitate to those who suffer least—those with something to give instead of something missing.

This means people with the least need of service are the most likely to receive it: talented, friendly, and articulate people who embrace everyone who walks into their lives. When deciding who to invite to dinner, these are the first people to come to mind—popular people who are surrounded by adopted friends and admirers. And these are the people most likely to invite you in return.

The most insufferable attributes of human behavior are often the loudest cries for help: frustration, selfishness, incompetence, anger, stupidity, and sadness. The last-place finisher in a race likely needs a kind word more than the champion, but which of the two is more likely to receive it? Many even have a natural tendency to pile on suffering when they recognize weakness. Bullies are most likely to pick on children who are insecure, have mental health issues, have few friends, or are recognizably different in some way.[24]

If you want to maximize the sense of meaning in your life, seek out not just those who are easy to care for but those who would benefit most from care. Find the difficult people, the outcasts. Work to understand them. You know you are beginning to understand someone when you know how to help. Everyone struggles with something and could benefit from a friend. There is deeper responsibility and meaning in lifting the outcast than in passing time with impressive people.

Taking responsibility is more than showing disinterested politeness or shallow kindness. It is a commitment. Be reasonable, though. If the idea of taking some responsibility for a difficult person fills you with dread, consider starting with an easier relationship—someone relatively safe. You can then work your way up to the advanced levels.

As we take on responsibility for more people, our capacity to serve will increase. Meaning in life, like other worthy pursuits, compounds over time. As you get to know people deeply and they open up to you with their secret fears and pain, your ability to accept responsibility for them expands. Your capacity to fulfill your responsibilities also expands through trial, error, and practice. Others then see your ability to commit and deliver. So they seek you out, and you want to help. And the positive feedback loop of meaning continues.

The Brain's Responsibility Mechanism

To take responsibility for people, you need to know their names or their faces—preferably both. The human mind is not built to take responsibility for faceless statistics. The name might be a nickname or a placeholder, such as "The bearded guy who wears jean shorts." The face could be a memory from long ago or a photo on the nightstand.

You know when you have taken responsibility for people when you desire good for them and are willing to sacrifice for their benefit—and you can picture their faces or know their names. When you meet someone for the first time and talk face-to-face, you may feel a sense of responsibility that only lasts for the duration of the conversation. When the new acquaintance is no longer in your line of sight, your commitment might just go with them.

As you forget an old friend's name and face, your sense of responsibility fades. And when that individual comes back into your life and you remember, you may feel a resurgence of meaning and responsibility, but only if you are committed to that individual. Perhaps you have the experience of looking at a long-lost friend in an old photo and feeling the connection anew.

If you do not know the names and you cannot picture the faces of those under your stewardship, then you have not taken responsibility for them. You should go out into the world and spend enough time with people that you can clearly picture their faces and know their full names and stories. Study their face shapes, worry lines, and eye colors. If you care or want to care, you will find a way to remember.

The psychologists Douglas Kenrick and Vladas Griskevicius proposed that our minds are composed of multiple competing "subselves," or modules. Each of these subselves evolved to perform a specific function, including self-protection, mate attraction, making and keeping friends, kin care, social status maintenance, and disease avoidance. There is no clean separation between the modules, and the same portions of the brain contribute to more than one module.[25] The "making and keeping friends" and the "kin care" subselves may be particularly relevant to whether people perceive their lives as worthwhile.

At times, one subself will war with another in our minds, and each subself can grow or shrink in comparison to others over time. If someone were trying to break into your home, you might feel the self-protection module telling you to run while the kin care one urged you to defend your family. Kenrick and Griskevicius theorized that the type of entertainment you watch can influence which subself is in control. A scary movie puts your "self-protection" module in charge while the show *Friends* might favor mate attraction or making and keeping friends.

The moment you take responsibility for people, I believe you add them to one of these modules—the making and keeping of friends or the kin care subself. When you decide that someone is a friend, a member of your team, a family member, or someone worth looking out for, you are adding them to a module.

When someone belongs to a module, your subconscious mind begins to serve the individual up to your conscious one for service opportunities. The greater your commitment, the more frequently your subconscious brings your friends to mind. When you are trying to decide who to invite over for a game night, it is the people you are most committed to who come to mind. They are also the people who pop into your head unexpectedly when your mind wanders.

Taking Responsibility for Objects

If anything for which you take responsibility has value, why can't you take responsibility for a rock or for your apartment where you live alone without visitors? Wouldn't that give your life just as much value? In the act of taking responsibility for the rock, wouldn't you be imbuing it with meaning?

The gem has no value without someone to see it sparkle. A dollar is only paper if it cannot be employed to purchase the solution you need. Building a beautiful home will not generate lasting meaning until that home is filled with family and guests—people to admire its beauty, bask in its comforts, and feel protected under its supports.

Value accrues to living things—not to inanimate objects. Those objects may be means to helping others, but an object's value is proportional to its ability to create short-term well-being or long-term growth in an individual. If an object cannot make you better as a person or make life better for someone else, then it has no value and can create no meaning.

Take responsibility for beings that grow and progress: pets and local wildlife, gardens and front yards, your friends, and other people's children. If it can benefit from service, then it is potentially a source of meaning.

Taking Responsibility and Taking Over

Jacqueline, a friend from my time in Connecticut, was cursed and blessed with a demanding mother. Other children had friends and free time, but Jacqueline practiced violin and studied music theory for hours every day. Her mother sharply criticized her for perceived laziness and careless mistakes during practice and in recitals.

She had to enroll in Rice University because of its strong string program. There, Jacqueline studied under the renowned violinist Sergiu Luca. Her mother visited regularly to poke at her violin play and her weight.

After graduation, Jacqueline was finally out of her mother's control. She pushed her violin to the side. Jacqueline despised that instrument. It represented a loss of freedom and everything she had missed in life.

After two years, she felt the draw of music and picked up her instrument again. Jacqueline still played beautifully, but this time it was her choice. She shared her work over the internet and with her church congregation. She joined an orchestra.

Jacqueline's mother still visits and still comments on her daughter's inadequacies.

So the question arises: Did Jacqueline's mother gain a sense of meaning from pushing her daughter to musical greatness? The answer would be yes, if she was taking responsibility for her daughter, or no, if she was trying to live vicariously through her. Is the mother's ambition for her child or for herself?

If you asked Jacqueline's mom why she drove her daughter mercilessly, the response would likely be that she saw potential in her daughter and was willing to do anything to draw it out. Jacqueline might only have achieved mediocrity in music without a firm hand. Jacqueline's mother would probably cite the thousands of dollars and hours sacrificed for her daughter's education as evidence of her commitment to that goal. And the results speak for themselves: Jacqueline is an accomplished musician, wife, and mother who is active in the community—a person who is a pleasure to be around.

When you take responsibility for others, you may have to decide whether a strong hand is needed to guide them in the direction you deem best. It is possible that a light touch will be more productive, depending on the person and the situation. Our modern world prefers gentle persuasion over tyranny (I strongly prefer kindness for reasons outside of the scope of this book), but both approaches can create meaning for the caretaker if done for the benefit of someone else.

Some have asked if it is too forceful or presumptuous to *take* responsibility for another person. Why not *accept* responsibility only when asked? The reply is that there are people in need who are hesitant to reach out for assistance. Some cannot see their struggles clearly or have no idea how to solve them. They may not know that you are willing to help and that you are capable of doing so. When you see someone fall through the ice, you do not wait for a formal invitation to help. You continue to offer a lifeline and call for help until the person disappears. It is good to accept responsibility when asked, but there is more meaning out there for those who take it.

Do You Really Know What's Best for Someone?

To trust that you can help someone, you must believe that people and situations can improve and that all circumstances are not equally desirable. Without a belief in "good" and "better," you would not waste your energy helping someone move from one pointless circumstance to another equally useless one. As Aristotle pointed out, all of your goals, dreams, and actions depend on your concept of the good.[26]

So what is good then? We do not have space for a thorough evaluation of ethics, personal taste, or the concept of moral good here. When it comes to meaning and purpose in life, though, it is good for a seed to become a tree. It is good for a fawn to grow into a 10-point buck. The good is progress. The good is to build up stores of excellence that can be used in service of others.

Individuals are constantly growing or declining in capacity along every conceivable front. They can understand their world more fully, develop in health and strength, and produce output more skillfully. Most believe it is better to play Scriabin's Sonata no. 5 expertly than it is to tap out "Mary Had a Little Lamb" with one finger on the piano. And with greater mastery on the piano, they can soothe and inspire listeners or train the next generation of pianists. The more their skills progress, the more we consider their output beneficial.

Most of us have heroes who embody the traits and talents we wish to cultivate. We seek exemplars who can show us exactly how to improve. If purpose in life means having something to achieve, then a proper hero can increase our sense of purpose by showing us how to accomplish more and how to do it more skillfully.

So how do you know what is good for people? Part of the answer lies in what they need to progress. Do they need knowledge? Help them find answers. Do they need support and inspiration? If so, be there for them. Do they need help dealing with a painful situation? Face it with them. If your actions are helping them improve in some way, then you are providing meaningful assistance.

When my daughter was three years old, she once shouted so that everyone could hear, "I'll do it myself!" She then whispered to her mom, "Can you help me do it myself?" There is a lesson in my daughter's humble boasting. Instead of solving problems for people, give them what they need to overcome similar situations in the future. They are not progressing if they need you to push past their obstacles for them. If physical limitations or other circumstances prevent someone from moving past a roadblock, you can step in.

Because there are so many skills to improve and characteristics to more fully develop, look to your charges for direction on how to help them progress individually. The better you understand someone's needs, the better you will be able to make choices that actually help. And, when all else fails, do something in place of hanging back. It will help more often than it will hurt. If you miss, you will learn, correct your aim, and get closer to the bullseye on the next attempt.

The thought that "anything I do for others could backfire" is paralyzing, and therefore, unhelpful. Humans are social creatures and flourish when we look out for each other. Although individual attempts to help will sometimes fail, the cumulative impact of an engaged community is generally positive. People with strong social lives live longer and have stronger mental and physical health than those who do not.[27] Wildebeests kick dust into each other's eyes, but they are still better off in a herd.

When Someone Takes Responsibility for You

A friend recently told me that her son is going through a rough time. She can no longer see the cheerful boy who loves cars and working with his hands. He is steeped in drug addiction and despair. Far from home, the young man cannot envision a way past the suffering. He recently wrote to his parents, "Your prayers are the only thing getting me through."

When you believe that someone has accepted responsibility for you, you feel a sense of belonging. When a parent or sibling looks out for you, you belong to a family. When you realize that a supervisor or mentor has your interests at heart, you belong to a company. When a neighbor goes out of his way to brighten your day, you belong to a community.

It is difficult to see your life as worthless when someone cares enough to take responsibility for you. The young addict carries on because his parents continue to see the value and potential in him. Despite his troubles, someone is willing to accept him and invite him into their home. This is the power of responsibility and belonging. This is the power that comes from the realization that "Someone noticed me. Someone knew I was there. Someone cared."

Emily Esfahani Smith wrote that "When people feel like they belong… it's because two conditions have been satisfied. First, they are in relationships with others based on mutual care: each person feels valued by the other…. Second, they have frequent pleasant interactions with other people."[28] Good traditions reinforce a sense of belonging because they occur on a consistent basis and communicate that each participant is a valued member of the group.

Your traditions can be as simple as having frequent family dinners and asking each participant to talk about the highlights of his or her day. They can be as complicated as setting up an annual service project to support a community to which you all feel connected. Carefully consider your traditions and how to make them more meaningful. Create new traditions and include new faces.

Belonging is a pleasing yet tenuous source of meaning. You cannot force people to accept responsibility for you or demand that they deepen what you consider shallow commitments. And the source of your belonging can be severed at any time. Your caretaker could pass on, move away, or lose the means to take responsibility for you.

During the moments you have it, belonging should be treasured and should fill you with gratitude. And once you recognize and appreciate the majesty of belonging, you may be more willing to offer it to others. Belonging is among the greatest of gifts, and you give it each time you commit to a friend. Taking responsibility for others, though, is a more certain path to meaning because it does not depend on others' choices. You decide who to watch over, and the meaning begins to flow.

In truth, those with great responsibility generally have a deep sense of belonging. They take responsibility for others and deliver on their commitments. Then those who benefit reciprocate by taking responsibility for their supporters. Just as the best way to get a hug is to give one, the path to belonging is through responsibility.

The reciprocal nature of responsibility is clear when we look at the 40.4 million unpaid caregivers of adults ages 65 and older. These are the people who do errands and housework, help with finances, and assist with personal care, such as bathing and getting dressed. A vast majority of those who receive unpaid personal care in America are the caregivers' parents, friends, grandparents, spouses, and other relatives. These caregivers are generally assisting people who cared for them in the past.

It's also important to note that 88% of people found providing care to an aging parent rewarding while only 5% found it not rewarding.[29] I imagine that part of that reward was a sense of meaning. Take responsibility for people, and there is a very good chance they will take care of you.

CHAPTER 4

Independence and Meaning

T*his chapter asks how and if* we can find meaning in the darkness of isolation. Let's explore how independence interacts with purpose and meaning.

The Meaning House Analogy

Each of us owns a meaning house. The house is small and simple when we are young, but over time, it is filled with family members and neighborhood friends. It has the kind of cottage feel that makes people want to stay. We don't remember letting people in, and it seems like they have always been there. We don't always get along with these people, but we all belong to each other. And life is happy.

Then one of our guests does the unthinkable and betrays us. And it hurts. Drastic action is required. We tell our guests that they are no longer welcome. As they leave, we slam the door and bar it shut. We also close the windows—just to be safe.

We feel calm and safe in our isolation for a while. Luckily, the house is filled with entertainments and food. It is fun for a while, but it becomes progressively more difficult to have fun. One day, we wake up and realize that our house feels more like a tomb than the cottage we once loved. The pain is not as sharp as it was during the betrayal, but the dull emptiness intensifies. So we crack open the door and peek outside. Someone outside notices the door ajar, stops, and waves. Hesitantly, we wave back, then quickly close the door. Nothing terrible happens.

Soon thereafter, we hear an urgent knock at the door. Someone is sitting on the porch, injured, and needs help. We hope that a parent or a neighbor will notice the situation and deal with it, but no one comes. The stranger seems safe enough, so we eventually relent, open the door, and escort him in. We patch him up and send him on his way, but before he leaves, he gives us a quick hug.

The next time we see the now-healed guest, we invite him in. Soon, he brings a friend. We remember the joy of having a full house as a child. So we begin calling out to the neighbors and letting them in.

We may not let everyone into the house, though. The one who betrayed us so long ago appears on the doorstep. We are polite and even generous, but we resolve to keep him outside.

Eventually, we gain the confidence to leave the safety of the home. We seek out those who could use a little friendship, food, comfort, and advice. We bring them home and let them stay as long as they wish. We treat them like family. Most leave, but some return year after year. A few stay.

The Meaning of Pleasure

I open my eyes in the darkness and reach for my buzzing phone. I lie there in my sweaty sleeping bag on my minivan floor while wondering why I do this. I pull the powder-blue hoodie over my head, climb into the driver's seat, and travel the short distance to the beach. I remember why when I spy the brightening pre-dawn sky and smell the salty air rolling in on lines of waves.

I wriggle into my hooded wetsuit and booties, attach three fins to my board, and hide my car keys under a nearby shrub. I place my board on the grass near my van and find a thumb-sized stick of sweet-scented wax. I rub the wax onto the board using gentle circular motions until small sticky bumps appear.

In the cold shallows, I attach one end of the leash to my board and the other to my right ankle. I ease onto my board and paddle over, under, and through the overhead swells.

As soon as I reach beyond the breaking waves, a large swell approaches. I sit on the back of my board, swing it toward the beach, and then kick and paddle. As I slide down the face of the wave, I push up and draw my legs up underneath me. I reach the bottom of the wave and turn to my right to see a glorious wall of water extending over a hundred yards. The wave urges me forward, and I carve along its face. As the wave reaches shallow water, it pitches over my head, and I crouch in a cascading tunnel of water. When the barrel collapses in front of me, I fall backward off the board and let the whitewash take me.

Near the horizon, Haystack Rock juts out of the water like a lopsided arrowhead in the fog. Cape Kiwanda extends into the ocean to my right, a great dune capped by a tuft of Oregon forest. Waves crash against the rocks of the cape and spray water into the air.

When I'm surfing, the world and the voices in my head are silenced. I'm in the zone and in the flow of the ocean. I have never been talented, but the ocean and my friends never seem to mind. I enjoy surfing so much that I am willing to work for it. I study the great ones like Kelly Slater and skateboard for practice in my driveway. There was a time when I might have called surfing the most important part of my life.

Any activity can become your purpose in life with rewards that can feel meaningful for a time. Each pleasurable activity comes with a staircase of accomplishments. Surfers can work on new tricks and feel the rush of landing an air for the first time. They can enter surfing competitions and receive profitable sponsorships. And one person will outcompete everyone and become the World Surf League champion. That person's competitors will shower him with champagne and crowns and trophies. At that time, he will be at the pinnacle of success. But does he have a meaningful life? Not necessarily.

Many confuse pleasurable purpose and meaning, and it's no wonder. Activities like surfing are so enjoyable that they can feel like the reason we are on this earth. And with increased skill and experience, the pleasurable moments can become even more intense, but those moments are fleeting. For every perfect day in the water, there are 10 choppy ones. Even the best surfers in the world lose more competitions than they win. It simply isn't possible to string together enough pleasurable surf sessions to create a meaningful life.

A popular young surfer named Nathan Monchet heard that the Indonesian government was going to close the airports because of COVID-19. He assumed that the lockdown would only last a few days. So he and his best friend's family booked flights. They arrived in the Mentawai Islands—a surfing paradise with coral reefs, yellow sands, and green rainforests—two days later.

It was supposed to be a 10-day trip, and it ended up being three months. Nathan described his days as follows: "You'd forget what your life was and think that [surfing] was your life. I'd have a breakfast surf between 8 and 10. Lunch surf at exactly 12 and I'd have dinner surf at 8 exactly for three months straight. And all I had to think about was surfing.

"[One day] I went surfing out there, and in the first 20 minutes, I probably got 10 waves and got 10 barrels.... And there was nobody to share it with.... Then my mate came and was like 'Dude, I'm going fishing.' And I was like 'I'm going fishing with you.' Just because I needed to do something. And I was bored.

"Two months in—that's when I went really cuckoo. One night, I drank a little bit, and I was just gone. I woke up in the morning and my head was shaved on top.... And it's like, you don't care because nobody's there [to see you].... I've got a full... reverse [friar] thing [going].... You're just sitting out there, you're going like, 'Dude.

What is going on? Is this real life?'"[30]

Nathan was filled with more pleasure and purpose than any surfer could wish for. And it took only two months for him to realize that a lonely life of surfing can feel meaningless. He even had trouble coping with the boredom and pain of eternal paradise.

You are unlikely to find lasting self-worth in isolation and meaning derived from individual pursuits. If there is no one to share your happiness with, then eventually it is exposed as hollow pleasure. Often, the pursuit of pleasure is not a search for meaning but a temporary escape from meaninglessness.

Am I saying that professional surfers or football players or Olympians cannot have meaningful lives? Absolutely not. They can experience awe and grow in skill and knowledge. They can have rich and meaningful lives, but not if they live only for themselves.

They can be the ones in the water hooting for an insecure surfer who could use encouragement. They can give a welcoming smile to a stranger coming into the lineup—even if that stranger might take the wave of the day. They can teach others how to surf and share why the cold water is worth it. The way to make surfing or any other fun activity truly worthwhile is to make it about others. And the more lives you influence, the more worthwhile the activity becomes. If it also gives you a sense of accomplishment and purpose, so much the better.

Can I Find Meaning in Individual Pursuits?

Perhaps I could make my own life more valuable by fulfilling my every want. And why can't I just decide to take responsibility for myself and recognize the value in my own life? Can't I just serve myself? Is there something wrong with the person of whom it is said, "Of all her mother's children, she loved herself the most"?

You can focus on yourself if you choose to. Many do. You can grow in knowledge and skill. You can achieve. This is the essence of having a purpose in life, but purpose without sacrifice for others may not create meaning. If you do not share your knowledge and skills with someone else, you will find yourself in a life of limited contribution.

There is a good kind of selfishness where you have the courage and awareness to know what you need to sustain serving others over the long term. Bad selfishness has no great end in mind. It is not marshaling your resources to provide a greater gift down the line. You just can't be bothered.[31]

Before the *Pirates of the Caribbean* movies was the Disneyland ride where passengers sat in damp boats gliding past animatronic scenes of adventuring pirates. One scene etched in memory from my childhood is that of a skeleton sitting on a mound of treasure. The captain's hollow skull smiles, still covered by a black hat trimmed with gold. His treasure cave is filled with paintings, stacks of gold bars, goblets, jewels, tapestries, and other finery. The captain clearly fought hard for his vast wealth. Bony fingers still clutch a sword. No other skeleton decomposes in the glittering tomb. The captain's bones are alone with his wealth.

If that synthetic captain had sailed the Caribbean, he would have led a purpose-filled life of blood and booty. He would have hoarded his treasure deep in a cave where it could do no good for others. During his life, the pirate may have considered his existence to be meaningful, but he would have begun to question that value near the end. It is clear to every child and parent passing by the plastic skeleton that if he had been real, his life would have been empty.

Modern Western society is obsessed with selfhood and individual identity.[32] Our proclivity for self-worship is apparent from the words we use. We talk about self-love, self-improvement, self-reliance, self-discipline, self-care, self-actualization, and being self-made. Our language reflects our society's belief that personal growth comes from within—that we can fix ourselves without help and without helping others.

The problem with the expanding importance of selfhood is that it diminishes the roles of community and mutual responsibility. The cult of the self prioritizes the needs of the individual while disregarding the needs of others. This is the definition of selfishness and is a pathway to meaninglessness. Adherents of the self-cult feel increasingly isolated and disconnected from the world. Studies show an association between self-centeredness and feelings of loneliness.[33]

Emphasis on the self magnifies all parts of you, including your weaknesses. As you focus on yourself, your problems appear larger and more desperate. Your deficiencies seem more pronounced and difficult to overcome. You do not notice those around you in need and can only perceive your own deficiencies. You may one day write

"I made myself so large and impressive that I eclipsed the sun and everyone else, but my problems and loneliness grew with me until I collapsed into a self-absorbed speck."

De-emphasizing the importance of self, on the other hand, contracts your problems. Your personal trials seem more manageable, and your weaknesses cease to obscure opportunities to serve. With increased selflessness comes the recognition that others can help you in areas where you cannot help yourself.

If you are only a source of value in your own life, then the rest of the world would be the same with or without you in it. If you are willing to help yourself but no one else, it's as though you are not there. This is meaninglessness. It is a realization that many self-focused people eventually face, too late at times. To find lasting meaning, you need a connection to the world and to individuals within it. You need the tethers of responsibility.

Alone in the Wilderness

My preference is to exercise alone. I often go jogging through an untamed grassy valley near my home. There is something soothing in how the long grass sways in waves on the breeze. Occasionally, I see a great blue heron standing alone in the field, unmoving and peaceful on spindly legs. The long-necked bird appears to have dark eyebrows that extend past its head like a feathered horn.

Scenes like this one can leave me with a sense of wonder that I am witness to something greater than myself. Part of me lives for those runs. The workouts clear my mind and make room for flashes of understanding. My problems seem insignificant next to the grandeur of the outdoors, and nature speaks to the caveman within me, whispering that I'm in the right place.

Can we find meaning alone in the wilderness, though? The way we define our terms is important here. If meaning in life is the perception that you matter, your actions should create value for someone other than yourself. Meaningful activities produce immediate benefits for others or the promise to help them in the future. If we adopt this perspective, then awe-inspiring experiences in nature can only produce a sense of meaning if they are shared or could potentially help someone else.

If we change our definition of meaning to "anything that diminishes your sense of self," then natural splendor would qualify as meaningful whether or not it helps someone else. So would high art, music, and anything else truly beautiful or moving. As when listening to a stirring song with an uplifting message, some shared activities can be meaningful as well as awe-inspiring.

Instead of combining "awe" and "perceived self-worth" into a single concept of meaning, though, it is easier to understand them as distinct ideas. Both awe and meaning can inspire you to change for the better, but the two concepts have different connotations. Awe recognizes and appreciates what is inspiring but outside of you. Meaning is a growing certainty that your life is worthwhile. We should seek and appreciate both awe and meaning.

Nature provides ample opportunity to experience awe and produce meaning. When you go out into the unforgiving wilderness and help a friend overcome its obstacles, you are doing something meaningful. When you move a tree branch off the path or pick up a plastic and aluminum granola bar wrapper on the trail, you generate meaning by taking care of those who follow.

Caring for nature is also a worthwhile pursuit. When you plant a seed and watch over it as it sprouts, you realize that the young life depends on you. As you water it and remove competing weeds and unnecessary branches, you are helping it grow. Your life is valuable to that tree, that garden, or that field of crops.

Two-Faced Meanings

Some roads just end without an apparent destination. This chapter covers popular pathways that may or may not lead to a meaningful life. Some are clever distortions and half-truths. Others generate meaning in certain circumstances but destroy it in others. We will attempt to take a nuanced view on existentialism, the promise of everlasting meaning, hierarchies and status, medals and honors, and ideology.

The Modern Conception of Meaning

First, we will briefly explore the roots of existentialism and the modern conception of the meaning of life. We can then evaluate its effectiveness as a worldview.

In 1517, Martin Luther penned the 95 Theses denouncing, among other things, the conspicuous wealth of church leadership and the sale of indulgences to absolve sin. Because of the recent invention of the printing press, Luther's ideas spread across Europe. They were debated in every city and argued across thousands of dinner tables.

New Protestant churches sprang up throughout Europe, each one with a new understanding of the Bible and Christian doctrine. Lutheran and Anabaptist churches appeared in Germany, Anglican churches in England, Reformed churches in Switzerland and France, and Presbyterian churches in Scotland. They warred among themselves, and some churches split again into smaller sects.

Philosophers witnessed the spiritual revolutions and imagined where the divisions would end. Some foresaw a world in which all people would have their own interpretations of the truth. They asked whether our species has any hardwired purpose. They wondered how God could be the author of such confusion, and some even questioned the need for a supreme being.

More and more people began to wonder if there was a single path to a worthwhile life. The gradual shift from a belief in a religious-centered purpose to a free-for-all increased in popularity during the nineteenth and twentieth centuries. Some people no longer found purpose in the same rituals and community events. They searched for meaning through a broader range of activities, many of which were discouraged by church leaders.

About 75% of Americans now believe that there is an ultimate purpose and plan for every person's life.[34] College-educated people and those younger than 30 are less likely to believe in a universal purpose, but most still think that a seed of meaning exists somewhere within each of us and that if we could just discover and nurture it, we could have a meaningful life.

One philosophy that has been growing in popularity during the last century is existentialism. The foundation of existentialism is that life is, at its core, meaningless.[35] Humans have an innate desire to seek meaning in a world where it does not exist. The experience of searching for answers in an answerless world is referred to as "the absurd." For existentialism's adherents, there are at least three approaches to life:

1. We all need to create our own path and meaning.
2. We distract ourselves from pointlessness with whatever we can. Albert Camus taught that the meaning of life is whatever you are doing that prevents you from killing yourself.[36]
3. We accept the seeming fact that life is meaningless and that nothing really matters. This is called existential nihilism.[37] Brent Weeks took this line of thinking to the extreme in one of his novels when he wrote, "Life is meaningless. When we take a life, we take nothing of value."[38]

Existentialism is seductive in a way, and many find it liberating. If life is inherently pointless, then you can do whatever you feel like—that is, if you are willing to live with the consequences. Jean-Paul Sartre called this "radical freedom."[39] The downside, of course, is that nothing really matters. Underneath your personalized path to meaning is the acceptance that you are a non-entity equally worthy of affection and destruction.

Either we came to this world prewired with a path to meaning, or each of us has to make up our own. Regardless of which worldview we adopt, taking responsibility can lead to a growing certainty that life is worthwhile. Looking at it one way, we each need to discover the God-given—or evolutionarily dictated—reality that taking responsibility for others leads to a meaningful life. From the existentialist's point of view, on the other hand, we can choose whatever road to meaning we want, but only those that involve responsibility will actually lead to meaning.

With the benefits of taking responsibility for others in mind, I believe existentialism is a half-truth. It captures the notion that meaning is one's perception of self-worth, but it misses that life at its core is worthwhile, or at least potentially so. We do have the capacity to lighten the load of those around us. Anyone who cares for a goldfish, a child, or a houseplant can demonstrate their self-worth.

Meaning Does Not Have to Be Everlasting

Yuval Noah Harari wrote "If planet Earth were to blow up tomorrow morning, the universe would probably keep going about its business as usual.... Hence, any meaning that people ascribe to their lives is just a delusion.... The scientist who says her life is meaningful because she increases the store of human knowledge, the soldier who declares that his life is meaningful because he fights to defend his homeland, and the entrepreneur who finds meaning in building a new company are no less delusional than their medieval counterparts who found meaning in reading scriptures, going on a crusade or building a new cathedral."[40]

Apparently, life can only be considered meaningful if it accomplishes something that persists beyond the destruction of the earth! That is a high bar. Too high. Harari's comments hint at the desire for infinite meaning. A meaning so great that it fills the cosmos. A meaning that persists in one's absence. We do not want just a glimmer of meaning. We want the stars—cascading supernovas of meaning.

So is life only valuable if it endures? If death erases any meaning, then there is reason to despair. Everyone fades and is soon forgotten. Most people are remembered for about 70 years after their final breaths.[41] Relatives born during your lifetime remember you. Those born after generally have no concept of your life's work, story, or even your name. And only a handful of people are remembered for centuries. It is unclear whether any memories will survive the earth's eventual destruction.

Fortunately, it is unnecessary to accept never-ending responsibility for finding meaning. And short-term responsibility for someone can generate high levels of meaning until the commitment is cut short. A genuine smile directed toward a stranger can create meaning even though it does not echo through time and even if it is soon forgotten. For that moment, you took responsibility for a stranger and lifted her on her way.

The only way we can connect with life and its meaning is in the present moment. The past and the future can only be experienced in stories.[42] Time beyond this instant is filled with fading memories and hopes for uncertain futures. Meaning is in the moment. Even though it is impossible to help all your loved ones simultaneously all the time, you can still be willing to help any one of them any time you can. You can spend your moments in needful service.

Hospice workers know something of the meaning available in the end. They work with the dying and their loved ones to help them say goodbye and let go. Most of their patients have fewer than 100 days left to live. An instance of hospice care workers knowing the importance of a short life is exemplified in the story of a young mother named Kelly.

While pregnant with her third child, Kelly learned that her unborn son, Riley, had a congenital defect affecting his brain. Her newborn would likely be stillborn or die soon after childbirth. When Riley was born, the doctors wanted to take him away for procedures and tests, but Kelly refused. "I didn't want to do anything unnecessary to him. I just wanted to enjoy every minute I had."

One of the nurses overheard Kelly and referred the family to a pediatric hospice. Surprisingly, Riley lived more than a year, and Kelly is forever grateful she made the call that she did. "Other people told me not to get too attached to Riley because he'll be leaving soon, but the pediatric hospice nurse told me 'Riley is worth loving.'" Kelly said that "the hospice team members were the first ones to acknowledge my son was a human being."

The team helped prepare Kelly, her husband, and their two other children for Riley's death. They made three-dimensional handprint molds with the kids, hired a professional photographer to take pictures of the family, and talked to the kids about their experiences. When Riley died, the hospice workers helped with funeral planning, brought coloring books for the kids, and even attended the funeral. They sent birthday, Mother's Day, and Father's Day cards after Riley's passing.[43]

These hospice workers understood that meaning does not require a long-term relationship. The death of one source of meaning can be the beginning of another or the deepening of existing sources. Moving to a new area, for example, severs existing ties but can draw families together and expose them to new neighbors and opportunities to serve.

Life is a sort of glorious hospice. All of us are taking care of other patients, slowly dying, and watching our loved ones approach death's veil. We need someone to help us when we cannot help ourselves, and we need someone to watch over in return. And time is short.

Hierarchies of Meaning

People organized into hierarchies get big, hairy, audacious projects done.[44] Good luck bringing a large group together to collaborate on tasks without one. Hierarchies also give people a soothing sense of structure and stability in a disorderly world.

Hierarchies seem to appear wherever there are large groups. We find them in wolf packs, chimpanzee communities, elephant herds, and even in beehives and termite colonies. Hens actually do have pecking orders, where the stronger and more aggressive birds use their sharp beaks to establish the priority order for eating, drinking, and dust bathing.[45]

Organizational pyramids are prominent in academics, religion, sports, politics, social groups, and families. Underlings report to superiors who themselves are subordinate to their own superiors. Those who successfully claw their way up through the ranks are rewarded with prestige, wealth, and influence. As you rise in the ranks of the corporate world, for example, your pay and number of people reporting up through you can increase exponentially. You also begin to enjoy the perks of the office: travel, company-subsidized events, and corporate swag.

Hierarchical structures allow large groups to deliver complex products and services. They give people within the structure something to do and to achieve together, which is the essence of purpose. They can also allow workers to master a small part of a larger task and thus better serve their customers or constituents. Although many complex organizations fail, the successful ones benefit their customers, congregations, voters, communities, or family members.

Those who sit near the top of a pyramid may feel responsible for more people in the organization than those who are lower in the pyramid do. This heightened sense of responsibility is a potential source of meaning for leaders. Sadly, some leaders seem to avoid taking responsibility for underlings and become careless toward those they could serve.

The healthcare system I work for was founded by hardy nuns on horseback over a century ago. Their dedication to the poor and vulnerable is captured in the motto "Know me, care for me, ease my way."[46] Most of my coworkers find inspiration in the company's orientation toward underserved populations. Some healthcare employees are even willing to accept lower salaries because of the meaning, purpose, and pleasure they derive from helping patients.

The Status Mirage

Status-seeking is a motivating principle in many peoples' lives. We jump up out of bed a little earlier and toil a little later, hoping that someday we will be recognized as special and elevated above our peers. We hope that with status will come the love and respect we so deeply desire. And when we miss out on a promotion, are rejected for a job, or are passed over for that award, we feel crushed and worthless.

Hierarchies are necessary, but they have potentially sinister aspects. It appears that the bigger the pyramid and the higher someone sits in it, the more valuable that person's life is. The leader of a large and fast-growing company is often perceived as the most valuable person in her empire because all her aggregate numbers are bigger than those of the people beneath her. The young unpaid intern, on the other hand, is sometimes seen as having hardly any value at all.

Many CEOs even place their corner offices on the top floor of luxurious corporate headquarters as a physical reminder of their ascendance. I imagine some of them gazing longingly at taller and more impressive buildings nearby. And the desire to climb to the top of a social ladder is not limited to the business world. Politicians, athletes, religious leaders, academics, social media influencers, and those in every other sphere of life compete to reach the summit and remain there as long as possible.

David Brooks wrote about our society's tendency to favor "résumé virtues" over moral character. Résumé virtues are those skills and advantages that you bring to the social marketplace: privileged upbringing, education, job training, physical ability and appearance, technical know-how, and so on. These virtues are easy to identify in others and make memorable first impressions.[47] The skills apparent in résumé virtues are vital to a functioning society. We need gifted and educated people with technical acumen to get certain work done. We also need people of strong moral character.

Particularly in work and academic environments, I hear people make sweeping judgmental statements about others. "That person is really good" or "This employee is terrible" are whispered in the hallways of every building where social hierarchies are present. It's as though everyone's value falls on a continuum from "nothing" to "the best" based on the number and quality of her résumé virtues.

Instead of assigning each person his relative worth, consider the combination of attributes that each group member has to offer. You should ask yourself if someone is well-suited to a role instead of how "good" the person is. In other words, stratify the group horizontally based on skill instead of vertically based on status. An individual's value depends on his ability to help others, not on where the person sits in the hierarchy. Meaning abhors class distinctions.

Kristen Bell is an A-list actor with talent, beauty, humor, wit, and wealth. Disney even chose her to play Princess Anna in the *Frozen* movies. Kristen is the kind of person who admirers stop and listen to during light-hearted interviews with late-night talk show hosts. Throngs hope to discover in the petty details of her life the secret of how to rise to the top of the social hierarchy and find that missing something. They reason that, if anyone has it, she must.

When asked about what makes her life worthwhile, though, Kristen said something unexpected: "I think if you walk into situations with an open heart and someone says, 'I'm stressed' or 'I have to move,' you say, 'I'm not doing anything on Saturday. Do you need any help?' You're not saying it because you're trying to get points in the afterlife or make your life better. You're doing it because you [think], 'Oh. I can spend the day with this person and make their life a little bit easier.' And out of that I get self-esteem, which makes me feel great."[48]

Even though Kristen is draped in the markings of status, these things appear to be secondary to the perceived self-worth she receives from service. She is known for dedicating her time to causes, both the people and animal varieties. She donates her time and money to good causes like the organization "charity: water" and advocates that others do the same.

Josh Radnor is a successful actor who starred in the show *How I Met Your Mother*. He talks about the experience of running into a woman who asked, "Are you just, like, so happy all the time?" Josh remembered thinking, "Does she really think that when [the television station] picked up the show it left me with an inability to feel anything other than unbridled joy? But the joke was on me because I kind of thought it would. I had bought into the not uncommon notion that when I taste success… then I will be happy. But the strangest thing happened. As the show got more successful, I got more depressed."[49]

You may be thinking, "Status may not be enough for Kristen Bell and Josh Radnor, but it would be more than adequate for me." And who could blame you? Those at the top appear to have it all. However, here are a few reasons why the road to status can be simultaneously crowded with strivers and empty of meaning.

Self-Worth Derived from Status Is Fleeting

Status is alluring to those who do not have it and a letdown to those who do. The instant status arrives, you stop caring about it.[50] You immediately turn your attention to the next rung on the status ladder and begin to climb again. And you hope the next rung will bring the feelings of self-worth you have sacrificed so much for. The feelings do not come, though, regardless of how many sit below you and how far above them you have risen. The psychiatrist Lance Dodes captured the impact of the status-seeking trap when he wrote, "When someone is forced to achieve just to have any value, then they can't stop. Stop achieving, and they stop being lovable. It's a terrible burden."[51]

Those looking for fulfillment or a sense of self-worth through advancement will encounter disappointment and disillusionment. After reaching the coveted level of success, they will continue to face the same petty problems and aggravations as before.[52] Just as most people feel no different the day after a birthday than they did the day before, those with elevated status recognize that they are no more capable or productive with status than without.

You may not find lasting meaning while rising through the ranks, but those witnessing your ascent will likely burn with envy. To others, it can appear that your advancement came with the self-worth and happiness that they so desperately crave. So they redouble their efforts and begin lobbying behind the scenes for their next big break—continuing down a path that may never lead to meaning.

Status Relies on Relative Superiority

The perceived value of enhanced status comes only with comparison and dominance. You may feel worthwhile because you are smarter, more successful, wealthier, more beautiful, younger, or better educated than your neighbors or coworkers. The problem is that, even if you are gifted in some way, there is always someone more so.

And if, through hard work and the luck of nature and nurture, you become the best in the world at something, your records will eventually be eclipsed, and your strengths will fade. Your trophies will gather dust on a shelf and your accolades will be fading memories—and with them, any sense of meaning will fade too.

Maybe though, you are thinking, "If I can just find a pond small enough, maybe I can be the biggest fish in it—the most impressive person around. Maybe then I will feel like my life is worthwhile. Everyone will recognize my greatness." It is true that this strategy may give you a temporary sense of meaning, but it would be devoid of purpose. And you need both. Purpose requires that you stretch the limits of your capabilities.[53] The process of purposeful progress inevitably brings you into contact with other people who are at least as talented as you are.

Smart and driven teenagers, for example, attend good colleges and join good companies where other smart and driven people work. They move into manicured neighborhoods with similar-looking houses. Selecting remedial courses or a dead-end job would be pointless and boring for these talented people. They might feel special when surrounded by mediocrity, but they would also feel aimless.

Few Achieve High Status

In most pyramidal hierarchies, there can only be a few at the top. Generally, there are significantly fewer people in each higher tier than the one below it, with most employees working somewhere near the bottom of the pyramid. Yet masses press upward, hoping to arrive as high up on the ladder as possible and remain there for as long as possible.

In most status games, the number of failures for every individual who reaches the top is staggering. An estimated 0.0086% of people on planet earth are considered notable or famous.[54] This number pretty much rounds to zero. The road to status is steep, and almost all who cherish it must face disappointment.[55] For every LeBron James or Elon Musk, there are uncounted failures who can only watch and dream. It is a pity that so many include "become famous" as a life goal when there is so little room on the precarious summit of life's hierarchy.

Status Is Slippery

A reported 78% of former NFL players go bankrupt or are under financial stress just two years after retirement.[56] And the average NFL career only lasts 2.5 years.[57] Status is sought over a lifetime but can be lost in a moment. A poorly worded email, an injury, or an unguarded comment to a coworker can end a career built over decades.

My young daughter Margo summarized my life with the following: "I don't want to be a dad. You have to work all the time. Then you're a grandpa. Then you die." Life from about the age of 35 onwards is characterized by watching things pass away. Your looks fade. Your energy and athleticism slowly ebb. You are fired from your job or retire. And finally, you lose the ability to perform even basic tasks and your mind drifts away. Holding on to status as a strategy to find self-worth is doomed to fail. You may end up like the stereotypical high school football star who spends his time reminiscing about the good old days when life had value.

In the end, status-seeking is not the secret to a meaningful life. It may be its antithesis. Status asks you to wait to take responsibility until you have ascended to a certain rank. It is inherently self-seeking instead of self-sacrificing. Status-seekers miss opportunities to find genuine meaning. Pursuit of status drives them to compete and win when they should be looking out for others. Status is a mirage on the sweltering horizon and the siren song of the competent.

Happiness versus Meaning

Meaning does not stand in opposition to happiness. Meaning is one of happiness's attributes and overlaps with it. Studies show that people who consider their lives meaningful are more likely than not to describe their lives as happy.[58]

So many have elevated the word "happiness" to an exalted state. We all seem to be chasing happiness, sharing it over social media when we have it, and then mourning its loss. If happiness is the whole aim and end of human existence, then we should understand exactly what it is, how it relates to the meaning in life, and where to find it.[59]

Happiness is not one but many interrelated concepts. The word is overburdened with meaning. Let's unpack some of the attributes of happiness and see if we can make any use of it. Here is a working list.

Happiness Term	Definition
Pleasure	A pleasant state of emotional, physical, and/or intellectual stimulation
Cheerfulness	The quality of being noticeably happy and optimistic
Absence of Pain	The state of being largely free from unpleasant events
Flow	The state of being in the zone while performing a "Goldilocks Task" — a task not too easy and not too hard
Contentment	The absence of feeling that something is missing from life - a deep feeling of satisfaction and gratitude
Novelty	To experience something new, including knowledge, people, cultures, and sensations
Eudaimonia	Human flourishing and prosperity; human excellence
Affect Balance	An evaluative assessment based on the relative frequency of pleasant and unpleasant emotional states across time
Life Satisfaction	An evaluative assessment of one's life as a whole from "worst possible life" to "best possible life"
Joy or Fulfillment	The positive sensation accompanying achievement of something desired, promised, or predicted; the greater the accomplishment, the greater the joy
Peace	A state of tranquility, quiet and harmony
Meaningfulness	The perception that one's life is worthwhile and valuable
Purpose	Having something to do and to achieve
Eternal Bliss	A state of perfect ecstasy that persists regardless of circumstances
Reconciliation with God	State of alignment with instead of opposition to God's will; the presence, comfort, and approval of God

Attempts to synthesize all these definitions into a single concept make it bland and unhelpful. Perhaps you could say that happiness is a general sense of well-being. Or maybe you could say that it is rooted in biology and comes from having your needs and desires satisfied, including being largely free from unpleasant events and sensations.[60] These efforts miss the richness of a multifaceted perspective though.

More helpful is to hold each of the 15 definitions in your hand and turn them about individually. Evaluate each one fully and determine how important it is to you. This is how you create a Happiness Hierarchy—a rank-ordered list of the different attributes of happiness and why they are listed in that order. Ties are acceptable. Here is my Happiness Hierarchy for the day.

Happiness Concept	Rank
Meaningfulness	1 (Best)
Reconciliation with God	2
Contentment	3
Joy or Fulfillment	4
Purpose	5
Peace	6
Flow	7
Novelty	8
Eudaimonia	9
Life Satisfaction	10
Affect Balance	11
Pleasure	12
Cheerfulness	13
Absence of Pain	14
Eternal Bliss	15 (Worst)

Looking through my responses, it is clear that I want my life to matter. The good life, to me, is one where I feel deep gratitude and that nothing is missing. I want a strong connection with God but do not seek eternal bliss. It also strikes me that most of my top five happiness definitions can coexist with pain and self-sacrifice.

Take the time to establish a Happiness Hierarchy that reflects your innermost desires. For me, this exercise clarifies what I want out of life and inspires me to prioritize the happiest activities. Perhaps this exercise will also influence your decisions and how you spend your time. You might just find happiness under all those meanings.

Medals and Honors

Shirin Ebadi probably never said, "Lawyers have a dangerous job in Iran," but it would have been true if she had. She made a name for herself as a lawyer defending political dissidents, women, and children. She even represented the family of a political dissident and his wife who were murdered by employees of the Iranian Ministry of Intelligence.

Shirin defended many child abuse cases, including that of a nine-year-old girl named Arian. Iran's religious code of justice had automatically conveyed Arian's custody to her father, even though her mother had told the court that the father was abusive. Arian's father, stepmother, and stepbrother physically abused the waifish child for years and eventually killed her.

The murder so unnerved Iranians that about 10,000 people turned out for a memorial service—an unusual public display in a country where speaking out against the government can lead to jail time.

Shirin spoke during that service, reminding the mourners of the law's preference for fathers and of the failure of the system to act when Arian was torn from her mother's arms. She implored them, "Anyone who is against the law of Iran take all the white flowers and throw their petals on the street."

"After a few minutes," Shirin said, "we saw the street all white. People were crying and protesting. Angry women raised their fists and [shouted] the law must be changed." This case led to a change in the Iranian law, allowing a court to remove a child from a home if the custodial parent was unqualified to care for the child.[61] There is still a black-and-white photo of Arian on the shelf behind Shirin's desk.

Shirin once found a message thumbtacked to her front door that read "If you go on as you now are, we will be forced to end your life. If you value it, stop slandering the Islamic Republic. Stop all this noise you are making outside the country. Killing you is the easiest thing we could do."[62]

Shirin Ebadi did not stop, though. She became the first female judge in Iran in 1979. After all female judges were dismissed during the Islamic Revolution, she wrote books and articles, performed pro bono and other legal work, wrote legislation, and established human rights groups. In 2003, she deservedly won the Nobel Peace Prize.[63]

As a recipient of this prestigious award, Shirin received:

- A gold medal stamped with Alfred Nobel's profile
- A diploma graced with original art
- A large monetary award—$1,300,000[64]

- The privilege of being referred to as a "laureate"
- Let's look at each of these markings of status in turn.

Symbols of Honor

The medal and diploma are not necessarily symbols of social triumph that will fade into the background. They were reminders that Shirin helped people in the past and that she could take responsibility for others in the future. Objects do not make life meaningful in themselves, but they can remind us of our responsibilities and inspire us to take them seriously.

More meaningful than the medal and diploma is the picture of Arian in Shirin's office. The image represents the children and women who Shirin Ebadi lives to defend. Arian is one example of the Iranian people who Shirin serves with such dedication. After stopping to look at that picture of the waifish girl, I wonder if Shirin is a little more focused and hard-working.

Consider surrounding yourself with representations of those for whom you bear responsibility. Hang pictures of extended family members around your home. Proudly display pictures of friends and trinkets from coworkers around your office. If you feel affinity toward members of a certain community, place the symbols representing that group somewhere to remind you whom you are willing to sacrifice for. And share with those who come into your life why you are so committed to the people behind these symbols.

Wealth and Resources

Shirin said she was glad to receive the $1.3 million cash prize, and she committed to using the funds to benefit the people of Iran.[65] This generosity likely gave her an increased sense of meaning. If she reconsidered and spent the money on her own comforts, her reward would be comfort instead of meaning. And in the unlikely event that she used the money on vengeance, the money could only drain Shirin's reserves of meaning.

Honorifics

Since 1901, only 107 individuals have earned the designation "laureate" for receiving the Nobel Peace Prize. The word hearkens back to ancient Greece, where laurel sprigs were fashioned into wreaths of honor and presented to heroes.[66] Shirin has also received at least 26 honorary degrees from prestigious academic institutions.[67] These honorifics mark her as a person who is set apart and special. Did they give her a sense of relative superiority and self-worth? Most likely yes. Did that feeling last very long? Likely no.

Shirin has even written about others questioning her worthiness. When a reporter asked the Iranian president why he had not congratulated Shirin, he said, "This isn't such an important prize. It's only the Nobel in literature that really matters."[68] I wonder if Shirin has doubts about whether she deserves to be among the chosen few when so many are deserving. I wonder if she is hard on herself when she acts in a way unbecoming of a peacemaker.

All of these symbols represent new responsibilities that Shirin received with her illustrious prize. She is not just responsible for Iranian women, children, and dissidents anymore. She is now responsible for educating and inspiring the whole world about issues facing her region of the world. And although Iran is her home, she is involved with human rights organizations with global scope.

Meaning for the Powerless

Through a blend of loving support, self-discovery, and obstacles overcome, the archetypal youth grows beyond all expectations and transforms her world. Coming-of-age stories touch on a primal yearning for us. We identify with the awkward youth who is coming into her full power because, regardless of age, we are still works in progress. We hope that, just maybe, we carry a kernel of magic, a superpower, or greatness within us.

Power has a kind of gravitational force. It attracts wealth, attention, criticism, sycophants, and everything else. Power draws people in and changes them into something more like the one who wields it.

Many understandably feel hamstrung because of a perceived lack of power. They grieve for the control and influence they deserve but never acquire. In this they are misguided. Power itself is not a worthy goal but a means to fulfill the worthy needs of others. And all have some capacity to improve their neighbors' lives.

Although the concepts are related, power differs from responsibility, and you can have one without the other. Take a father, for example. A father has the power to influence his children—for good or evil—throughout their lives. The father may choose to take on responsibility for the children or abandon them to pursue his own dreams. If he wants meaning, though, the father will embrace his charges and employ his power to prepare them for the world.

You can employ power to help those under your influence or you can use the influence on others to satisfy your selfish whims. Power can even be used to spread misery or mete out vengeance. Misuse of power will waste your potential and destroy the sense that your life is meaningful.

Those with responsibility may find that they require less power and not more. Talented managers and military leaders do not exercise the full extent of their power. They allow subordinates some leeway to find creative solutions to high-level objectives and then implement them. When a seasoned parent finds out that someone at school is bullying her son, she does not threaten him in the school hallway, yell at the bully's parents, or call the principal. She helps her son devise his own solution and then supports him through it.[69] Restraint is an unheralded form of service and a potential source of meaning.

Instead of seeking power, use the power you have to help those around you. Flexing your service muscles will expand your capacity to serve and prepare you to take on greater responsibility in the future. This is genuine power—the power displayed by Clayton Christensen at the opening of this book. In taking care of others, you find the strength to take care of yourself.

Ideology and Meaning

Each one of us is a lead character in an internal narrative. We have to place ourselves in a plot that has some purpose and meaning, or we can't get our bearings in life.[70] We can write our own narratives or adopt them from thinkers of the past. Ideologies, paradigms, creeds, philosophies, identities, values, theories, heuristics, knowledge, dreams, cultures, languages—they all contribute colored fragments to the stained-glass lens through which we each interpret the world. And those with similar worldviews possess fragments of a similar shape and color.

Through the feedback received while engaging with life, narratives are constantly built upon, broken, and then formed anew. They provide context for individuals to decide whether their sacrifices are worthwhile. The purpose of this book is in essence to help us craft the internal narrative that "My life is meaningful, and I know how to make it more so!"

Some ideologies build meaning. For example:

- Adherents of John Locke generally believe that all individuals are equal in the sense that they are born with certain inalienable rights that should be protected (i.e. life, liberty, and property).
- An evolutionary biologist might say that all life on earth shares a common ancestry.
- The religion Jainism states that life, meaning the soul, is sacred regardless of faith, caste, race, or even species.[71]

These perspectives each contain the notion that all people belong to a broader whole and that they are connected to each other. Those embracing one of these ideologies are likely to accept at least a sliver of responsibility for those with whom they come into contact. And with that responsibility will come meaning.

There is danger in ideology, however. People gazing at the world through an ideology tend to look at the world in terms of "us" and "them"—the lovable in-group of those who accepted the set of beliefs and the despicable out-group. They naturally prefer and trust members of the in-group and are wary of and more likely to discriminate against the out-group.[72] Refusal to take responsibility for outsiders will limit the amount of meaning available to ideologues.

Some believe that the one and only meaning in life is to embrace a certain ideology, be it political, religious, or practical. Adherents of the one true set of beliefs are likely to see those who reject it as wasting their lives. Worse, they may identify the non-adherents as threats and treat them as enemies. Those who have never heard of or understood the ideology are also seen as missing the entire point of life.

There must be more to a meaningful life than to accept an ideology and then continue learning more about it so that you can accept it even more fully. If the set of beliefs does not lead to action and responsibility, then it will not lead to a more valuable life. Even if your ideology is correct, it cannot lead to purpose and meaning unless you act on it.

Let's explore the effects of ideology on meaning and purpose through the story of the siege of Jerusalem in 1099.

In 1095, Pope Urban II gave a stirring sermon calling Europeans to liberate the Holy Land. He said that "Whoever for devotion alone... sets out to liberate the church of God in Jerusalem, this [act] will be counted for all his penance."[73] The Pope's address instigated the first of many Crusades over the next 400 years.

The Crusaders arrived before the defenses of Jerusalem on June 17, 1099. The walls surrounding the city were 50 feet high and 10 feet thick with five gates, each flanked by a pair of towers. Six days later, the Europeans assailed the fortifications, but the defenders thwarted the first assault because of the lack of wood for siege equipment. Jerusalem's inhabitants had cut down all the trees outside of the city as the Europeans approached.

On June 17, Italian sailors arrived with the equipment to build siege towers, and troops secured lumber from nearby forests. In only three weeks, the Christians used these materials to construct the most advanced siege weapons known at the time, including an iron-headed battering ram, scaling ladders, and a number of protective screens fashioned from woven lattices of thin branches.

The Crusaders launched their attack on the morning of July 14, 1099. The knights were repulsed in fierce fighting on the southern side but broke through the outer defenses along the northern wall. The Crusaders recommenced their assault the next day and quickly gained a foothold. Knights in chain mail with red crosses stitched onto their white mantles flooded the city, and waves of panic rippled through the populace.[74]

A contemporary wrote of the carnage, "In this temple almost ten thousand were killed. Indeed, if you had been there you would have seen our feet colored to our ankles with the blood of the slain. But what more shall I relate? None of [the Muslims] were left alive; neither women nor children were spared."[75] The Jews, who fought side by side with the Muslims, retreated to their synagogue, where the

Crusaders were said to have "burned it over their heads."[76] After the victory, all the clergy and laymen went to the sepulcher of the Lord and his glorious temple, singing.[77]

Jesus Christ had taught his followers to love their enemies and turn the other cheek instead of retaliating. He forgave all—even the Roman soldiers who crucified him. By the Middle Ages, the Christianity of the Crusaders had been debased and twisted into an ideology of Holy War. How did those who professed to believe in such gentle doctrines commit such crimes? Let's look more closely at these events with an eye toward meaning and ideology.

Before his fateful speech, Pope Urban II received a plea for help from an ambassador of the Byzantine Empire. Calling the European nations to the aid of his Christian allies was likely a factor in his speech. Muslim incursions into Europe instilled fear in the people, as well as a desire to establish a bulwark against the threat. Urban II and the crusading horde may have ventured out in part to protect their families and their way of life. In safeguarding neighbors with similar religious beliefs and their own nations, Urban II and those who responded to him likely found some meaning.

Ideologies are too easily co-opted for selfish motives by those in power. From the day of his ordination, Urban II faced the challenges to his papal authority with diplomatic finesse. He may have desired to reunify the disparate shards of the Catholic Church behind a common enemy. And as the head of the Christian faith in Western Europe, Urban II had the means and the incentives to centralize his power through this Crusade.[78]

Urban II and many of those who heeded his call apparently saw the call to arms as the will of God. Christian theologians had declared that a "just war" could be rationalized if proclaimed by someone in authority.[79] Many so strongly desired to serve their God that they were willing to leave their homes and trudge across Palestine's burning sands to lay down their lives for their Lord. A perceived desire to serve God is a deep well of potential meaning that many of these zealots clearly felt.

Not all who responded to Urban II's call did so out of religious devotion, though. Many European nobles were tempted by the prospect of increasing their land holdings and riches during the venture. These nobles were responsible for the death of a great many innocents, both on the way to and in the Holy Land. They happily absorbed the riches and estates of those they conveniently deemed opponents to their cause.[80] This was self-serving masked in piety and ideology.

In marching through the gore with songs on their lips, the Crusaders and clergy showed no apparent remorse. Refusal to take any responsibility for others is akin to dehumanizing them. At best, those toward whom you feel no responsibility are invisible. At worst, they are obstacles to be swept aside or trodden underfoot. The withdrawal of responsibility is a prelude to monstrous behavior.

Many of the Christians clearly felt no responsibility for the Muslim soldiers or for the cowering innocents. They saw the non-Christians as adversaries and threats to their faith. Without any sense of responsibility for the outsiders, the Crusaders could kill them without feeling a loss of meaning. There was no commitment to the Muslims that the Christians could betray.

Most of the Crusaders likely felt a surge of meaning during their journey and after the siege. They sacrificed years of their lives fulfilling their responsibilities to their countrymen and to their God. They stood shoulder to shoulder with and bled for the knights around them. And when they had retaken the sacred city and their enemies lay scattered and dead before them, most of the Christians likely saw their contributions as valuable and perceived their lives as worthwhile.

Likewise, the Muslim defenders felt an increased sense of meaning when they agreed to protect the city's inhabitants, even if it meant giving up their lives. I imagine that, as many of them died, they thought of their loved ones and hoped that their sacrifice was enough to save their people. With complete sacrifice comes supreme meaning.

There were likely others who could see the hopelessness of the situation and that they would not be able to protect their sacred city or their people. Those who realized that they could not defend their loved ones would have felt some loss of meaning. They would have shared the pain of knowing that friends would suffer and that they were powerless to prevent it. Some probably felt some solace in knowing that they had sacrificed everything, even if they had failed in their responsibilities.

The crusading narrative, like ideologies through history, gave its adherents an inspiring purpose and a deep sense of meaning. It produced a shared means to sacrifice for country, family, fellow knights, and God. Unfortunately, it also provided cover for ambitious men to rise in status and wealth, and the ideology created an enemy who could be abused and slaughtered without any sense of responsibility for the victims.

CHAPTER 6

Institutes of Meaning

Certain institutions promote a sense of meaning and purpose in their participants: marriage, family, work, and faith. There may be others too. These are bedrock institutions that citizens are more or less expected to participate in, even if they do not fully comprehend them. Participation is not always easy or pleasant, but these institutions tend to generate meaning over time.

Involvement in the institutions of meaning does not guarantee anyone a worthwhile life. The institutions invite participants to take and fulfill responsibility for others, but some refuse. Those who attempt to extract sacrifices from others without being willing to sacrifice themselves will find some pleasure and much emptiness.

We do not need to participate in all the institutions of meaning to find worthwhile lives. We can deeply engage in one or two and still have meaning. Research shows that childless elderly couples, for example, become invested in other social relationships and activities and do not suffer from loneliness, unhappiness, or emptiness.[81]

This chapter talks about these institutions, how they are eroding, and how that erosion impacts our societies.

Marriage and Meaning

When you think of marriage, you imagine the moments: an infatuated young man's realization that this is the woman with whom he wants to spend the rest of his life, the fairy-tale proposal on one knee when the ring is unveiled, or the white-clad bride's slow walk down the aisle toward an eager groom. Romantic movies often end with the wedding ceremonies, implying that a couple's life is a "happily ever after" from there, but in real life, too many couples do not consider the ongoing rules and requirements of the marriage contract.

Marriage comes with a series of rights that singles do not have. It entitles a couple to share all marital property. If one spouse passes away, the other inherits the assets. Married couples can open bank accounts, buy health insurance, and file tax returns together. Typically, spouses are the only ones allowed to visit their partners during medical emergencies.

The marital rights come with responsibilities too. According to the law, spouses cannot lie to each other about finances, criminal behavior, or secret second marriages. Without consent, they cannot hide money from one another, waste assets, or share money with secret lovers. Like in a patient–psychiatrist relationship, spouses do not have to disclose information from private communications to the courts.

Husbands and wives are also legally bound to treat one another with respect. If one spouse commits adultery or abuses or abandons the other, he or she is engaging in marital misconduct. This behavior can be grounds for a fault-based divorce and could impact alimony and property division.

Some marital rights and responsibilities persist even after a marriage ends. The only way out is death. One spouse may be required to provide maintenance payments to the other after divorce, either in installments or in a lump sum. And no prenuptial agreement can excuse a spouse from supporting his or her children financially until their maturity.[82]

Popular culture emphasizes passionate attraction in romantic relationships and marriage. Without the continued sparks of desire, many believe that their marriage is unsuccessful. Some choose to cheat on their spouses, believing that they will find the missing sensual excitement or emotional intimacy. When these affairs turn into passionate love, popular culture whispers that adulterers should be committed to their love and not to their spouses—so they divorce and select new lifetime mates based on temporary attraction, and the cycle begins again.[83]

In marriages that endure, passion is secondary to deepening commitment to the well-being of a spouse. Meaningful marriages arise when spouses "are truly one—united, bound, linked, tied, welded, sealed, married.... [Spouses] work together, they cry together, they enjoy Brahms and Beethoven and breakfast together, they sacrifice and save and live together for all the abundance that such a totally intimate life provides such a couple."[84] They say, "I'll be there for you even when you are not there for me."

Studies have found that suicide rates are generally higher for unmarried people than married ones and among people without children compared to those with them.[85] It is harder to step away when loved ones depend on you. Some have also commented that marriage creates meaning but not necessarily happiness.[86] Married couples share one another's pain and expose themselves to the possibility of betrayal. Such is the price of meaning.

Lasting marriages are not carved in stone and then jealously protected. They are formed from wet clay. The shapes and contours of the marriage are ever-changing as the partners develop and the memories fade. The relationship sags and splits in places from neglect and ill-advised behavior. The commitment of the sculptors is the only constant. And the marriage grows in beauty and strength each time it is formed anew.

There is a deep part of me that desires the kind of marriage that comes with increasing responsibility for my wife, Rachael. I want one of those marriages that last 50 years—one that improves as I understand myself and her better so that I may better care for her and our relationship. I want a marriage commitment that is so strong that it breaks the bonds of mortality and lasts forever.

The scientist and religious leader Richard G. Scott and his wife, Jeanene, were married for over 41 years. After Jeanene died, Richard spoke tearfully of his devotion to her. "When she passed away, I found in her private things how much she appreciated the simple messages that we shared with each other. She not only kept my notes to her, but she protected them with plastic coverings as if they were a valuable treasure. There is only one that she didn't put with the others. It is still behind the glass in our kitchen clock. It reads, 'Jeanene, it is time to tell you I love you.' Please pardon me for speaking of my precious wife, Jeanene, but we are an eternal family."[87]

Children and Meaning

Before their expulsion from the Garden of Eden, I imagine Adam and Eve living a peaceful life—one without pain or death. One of beauty and harmony. Food. Comforts. Companionship. Fairness. They had everything an individual could desire. Then Adam and Eve ate the forbidden fruit and came down to a world of thorns and nettles. The rest of us followed them here, some cursing God because we long for a Garden and not a land of sorrows.

Having children is akin to eating the forbidden fruit and being cast out of Eden. A life of relative tranquility is replaced with stretches of agony and moments of the sublime. Instead of peace and comfort, life seesaws between pleasure and pain, triumph and failure, progress and setbacks.

It may not even be possible to fully appreciate the good without knowing an evil with which to compare it. I remember being so sick one day that I had to crawl on my hands and knees to my toddler's room after she threw up. I did my best to clean up her crib while she bawled. That was a day of great responsibility and pain.

I also recall the day that same daughter took her first steps through the grass and fell into my wife's outstretched arms. Her blonde whale spout of hair waved with each step, and she laughed and jabbered as she toddled from her mother to me. That was also a day of great responsibility, but one of joy as well.

Because child-rearing generally demands extreme levels of commitment and sacrifice, it produces a strong sense of meaning. Parenting gives people an opportunity to put aside their own interests for the sake of another.[88] If parents feel as though they have mastered one stage of parenting, they enter the next one feeling just as unprepared. And each new sibling comes with his own set of needs and challenges.

Parents are not the only ones committed to their children. Many kids take care of their own siblings. We have a 15-year-old family friend named Talmage. He has an easy smile and freckles splashed across his cheeks and nose. He loves video games and wakeboarding and makes friends easily. My wife once overheard Talmage saying that he would let his younger sister take the spare bedroom for herself while he would share with his eight-year-old brother.

"Why don't you take the spare room for yourself?" my wife asked.

Talmage responded without any hint of annoyance, "My brother has trouble sleeping when he is alone. When I am gone, he puts a light under the covers of my bed to make it look like I am there. He needs me to share a room with him."

This teenager understands what taking responsibility for someone is. Does Talmage feel like his brother needs him and that life has something to offer? Of course he does. Talmage has found lasting self-worth through self-sacrifice, and his brother rightly sees Talmage as a hero. We should strive to instill in our children the capacity and desire to take such responsibility for others.

One study of women with breast cancer shows the meaning-inducing power of familial bonds. These women often do a thorough reappraisal of their priorities. A large number conclude that the most important and meaningful aspect of their lives is their family.[89] After interviewing several dozens of these cancer patients, one researcher was even persuaded to change her own life plans and have children herself.

Given the helplessness of babies and the self-destructive nature of many adolescents, no wonder so many find children a powerful source of responsibility, connection, and meaning in their lives. Studies overwhelmingly reveal that relationships, particularly relationships with family, are the most important source of meaning in people's lives in all cultures and age groups. When asked an open-ended question about what provides them with a sense of meaning, the percentage of Americans who mention family is 69%. Career is the next most common response at only 34%.[90]

Family meaning can accumulate with each new generation. This compounding of family meaning can only occur, though, if every new generation is firmly bound to the ones preceding it. Children should forge relationships with aunts and uncles. Grandparents should be there for each grandchild. The greater the size of the family and the strength of the relationships, the greater the shared responsibility and meaning. Divorce and the neglect of these familial ties can have a devastating impact on each family member's allotment of meaning.

Simple math can demonstrate the point. If each child in a family with five kids has five children of their own, then each of the grandchildren will have at least 24 cousins to look out for. Compare that with a family that has two children who each have their own set of twins. Each of the four grandkids will only have three cousins unless their parents marry into larger families. Cousins in the larger family may also feel a greater sense of responsibility for a larger number of cousins and would therefore have a great sense of meaning.

Of course, children with one or two cousins can find high levels of meaning, but only if they are truly committed to each other. In aggregate, nations with more children per capita tend to have higher self-reported levels of meaning than those that do not.[91]

Should we worry that the expected number of children born during the average woman's life has been cut in half since 1950—from over 5 down to 2.4?[92] There are reasonable arguments for and against limiting population growth around the world, but we should consider how the reduction in family size could impact the meaning available to each of the world's families.

The influential social psychologist and researcher Roy Baumeister wrote that we have so easily cast aside our marriage commitments because we do not find them sufficiently fulfilling. He warned that if we apply the same logic to our parental relationships, our social systems could have severe problems.[93] Children benefit from the sense of belonging and training that comes from attentive parents and committed families. If you have the opportunity and desire, raise children. If you do not, help the little ones that come across your path.

Invest Selfishly in Youth

Individual progress is not just an end to itself but the fostering of service potential. It is building future capacity for service. The motto of my undergraduate university states, "Enter to learn. Go forth to serve." The implication is that the purpose of gaining knowledge and expertise is to bless people with it in the future. Secret skills accumulated through great effort are treasures buried deep in the earth. They benefit no one until unearthed and shared.

People naturally feel the conflict between furthering the self and sacrificing it for others.[94] It is reasonable to spend significant resources as a youth honing service potential. The time spent honing service potential may decrease with age and as one employs progressively more time in service, but we should never stop learning or testing new concepts.

Community and Meaning

A Marine friend once asked me why I thought troops go into battle and why they are willing to face death. "Love of country," I responded. "Maybe soldiers are fighting for their nation?"

"No," he corrected. "Some may join the military for a love of country or because they have a military tradition in their families or whatever. By the time they go to combat, though, they are fighting for the guys in their squad."

Can we take responsibility for a nation? I find the notion of taking responsibility for abstract concepts unlikely. You cannot serve the flag, justice, or Limited Liability Companies (LLCs). They are only ideas. You serve individual countrymen, those suffering from injustice, or your customers and employees. A community—or group of people who feel fellowship with each other and have something in common—is a rich source of meaning. Because we each share something with everyone on earth, you could potentially form a community with anyone you meet. Community and friendship are strongly related concepts. Time spent together is a requirement for both.

Studies show that people have a higher sense of life meaning and purpose when they are part of a community and have strong social bonds.[95] 47% of people say that spending time with friends provides them with a "great sense of meaning." Interestingly, 45% of people say the same thing about spending time with animals.[96]

The question "Who is us and who is them?" is central to how we view our communities and how we interact with those around us. If it is you versus the world, or you and your family (the extensions of you) versus the universe, consider community as a potential untapped source of meaning in your life. Take a moment to consider who belongs to your communities or to your tribes. Do you feel a sense of community with those living in your neighborhood? Do you know their names? Maybe you have a community in your alma mater or with anyone involved in your child's school—or maybe with a group of like-minded people on the internet.

Many find themselves without strong communities, enduring the pain of social exile. Their neighbors are standoffish hermits. Their coworkers are competitive instead of collaborative. They don't have time to join volunteer organizations and are not quite sure how to make friends in the modern world. Like teenagers eating school lunch in a bathroom stall, they live separate and alone.

Luckily, the world is filled with outcasts. If we do not feel accepted or enjoy the culture of certain communities, then we can create our own subcommunities within them. When the pain of isolation and the lack of meaning is greater than the fear of rejection, it is time to find a stable community. Perhaps now is the time to reach out and see if an existing community is willing to have you as a member. Or maybe you should reach out and invite someone into a community of your own making. If that feels like too much of a commitment, just invite someone over for dinner.

A few years ago, my wife announced that she had signed me up to coach my son's T-ball team… without talking to me about it first. I was upset. I had never coached in my life. I hadn't played baseball since I was 12. We had a vacation planned for a week in the middle of the season. My job wouldn't allow enough time for the commitment. I don't even like baseball. I wanted to call the league office and tell them that I was out, but my son was excited to have me as his coach, and I wanted him to play. So, after considering my son's needs, I gave in.

Despite a bad start—I was a few minutes late to the first practice—I ended up having a great experience that season. There is nothing more entertaining than watching an over-eager five-year-old run in the wrong direction after getting his first hit. I enjoyed coaching so much that last year I coached two of my girls in volleyball, and I would have done so again this year if COVID-19 had not canceled everything.

An old maxim states that people in successful societies have "their hearts knit together."[97] In some ancient cultures, the heart was the source of all desire—not just romantic affection. So having your heart knit together with another's means that your thoughts, desires, and affections are directed toward that person. And the stronger and more numerous the arteries of connection become, the more meaningful the life. Healthy relationships and societies are based on mutual caretaking.

When all the members of a group are serving, teaching, and looking out for each other, the individuals in the community will progress and achieve more than they could otherwise. In isolation, we are too often unable to overcome our own weaknesses. This is a strength of the communal nature of humanity.

Meaning Across Nations

In a fascinating 2014 study, over 141,000 respondents from 132 nations were asked, "Do you feel your life has an important purpose or meaning?"[98] Respondents were also asked whether religion is an important part of their daily lives, and they assessed their level of life satisfaction on a scale from 0 (worst possible life) to 10 (best possible life). The responses were correlated with national suicide and childbirth rates. The results are so insightful that they are worth exploring in detail.

Amazingly, the study showed that residents of poor nations generally have a greater sense of meaning in life than those who live in wealthy nations. Over 98% of citizens in Togo, Sierra Leone, Laos, and Senegal, for example, reported having meaningful lives. On the other hand, less than 73% of people in France, Spain, Japan, and Hong Kong indicated that their lives have an important purpose or meaning. This is disappointing news for those debating the meaning of life outside cafes in Paris.

Perhaps unsurprisingly, the study found that a nation's suicide rate is strongly correlated with its residents' perceived meaning in life. People who have deeply meaningful lives are unlikely to end them. Nations with high levels of self-reported meaning are also more religious than nations with low levels.

I believe that citizens of these poor nations have meaningful lives because they feel needed. Citizens in poor countries can see the results of their sacrifices for the well-being of others. They can clearly envision what would happen to those nearby if they withheld service. They feel responsible for more children, and they have stronger connections to their gods. Contrast this with wealthy nations, where many are loath to ask for help or can't be bothered because of all the distractions in their lives.

Life satisfaction is substantially higher in wealthy nations than in poorer ones. Wealthy nations with high levels of life satisfaction are filled with modern conveniences, such as electricity, telephones, TVs, and computers.[99] Even though the study shows that meaning in life predicts a nation's suicide rate, there is no discernible relationship between life satisfaction and suicide rates. Wealth may bring some happiness, but shared suffering is a pathway to meaning.

Leaders of wealthy nations should remember that their nations may have a surplus of luxury and a dearth of meaning. If a government desires to increase its residents' sense of meaning and reduce the number of suicides, then creating wealth and contentment may not solve the problem. Instead, policymakers should ask themselves how a proposed law or program will impact their constituents' sense of meaning. Will the policy make it easier for citizens to delay taking responsibility or avoid it altogether? Will the program disincentivize marriage, childbirth, religious observance, hard work, community involvement, or other selfless activities? If so, reconsider.

Jobs and Meaning

In a time where many resist help and hide their suffering from others, business markets remain an acceptable venue for providing others with goods and services. My father likes to say that "Work is all about service. People enjoy it because they are making a product or performing a service that someone needs." Behind family and religion, work is the most often cited source of meaning.[100] Even boring dead-end jobs give people a chance to lift coworkers and clients.

I once had entrepreneurial ambitions. I came up with what I thought was an innovative idea and started building a company around it. I had a history of building successful teams and technology products and was lucky enough to get a strong business education. So I began designing the product and talking with investors and potential business partners. I created presentations and spreadsheets and schmoozed with everyone who would listen about my fledgling business.

Then I called Jay Desai, a friend from business school. He had started a successful healthcare company that was expanding across the country. After the pleasantries and hearing my story, Jay gave me the best business advice I have ever received. He said that I was spending too much time creating presentations for investors, searching for employees, and building the technology. "None of that matters," he stressed. "You need to be laser-focused on your customers. Don't worry about finding employees or investors or even building your product. If you have a group of clients who you understand and who trust you in return, the investment, technology, employees, and sales will follow. Go get your first client."

This was difficult to hear. I had fallen into the trap of doing what was comfortable instead of what was needed. And I learned my lesson too late. The investors were annoyed that I had not signed any clients, and my business partner ran out of money and needed to start looking for a job. So we shelved what I still think is a good business idea.

One of the keys to success in business is also the source of a meaningful life. The management guru Peter Drucker once wrote that "the aim of [business] is to know and understand the customer so well the product or service fits him and sells itself." The meaning of life is to know those around you well enough that you can provide meaningful services. The better you know someone, the better you can serve.

Toby Weston walked away from the world of investment banking to pursue his calling in music education. Now Toby is a middle school music teacher who has been helping young people learn how to play string instruments for more than 10 years. He is the kind of thoughtful instructor who is always perfecting his teaching skills and experimenting with tactics to connect with disinterested teenagers.

To help new violin, viola, cello, and bass students, teachers generally put bands of tape underneath the strings on the fingerboard. The tape, often in tan, blue, or red, helps students know where to place their fingers until they learn it themselves.

In 2017, Toby began teaching a group of 30 fifth grade students to play string instruments. After four weeks of slow progress, most students were still trying to figure out how to play the D string. Toby realized that colored tape is an ineffective teaching tool. He searched online and spoke with other teachers but could not find a viable solution. So Toby decided to solve the problem himself.

Toby spent three years developing "finger guides" for string instruments. These guides are essentially stickers that show beginners where to place their fingers for each note. They are made of thin, highly durable material that leaves no residue upon removal.

Toby now sells thousands of his finger guides to teachers and new students of all ages across the world. His patents and extra income are welcome, but they are not Toby's primary motivation. He describes his motivation this way: "In less than 10 minutes, nearly every student can play the song *Hot Cross Buns* and can tell you with confidence [his] first notes. Students come back to the next rehearsal beaming with confidence. And it's meaningful when I get notes from people saying that they always wanted to play a certain string instrument, and now they can."[101]

Toby Weston has a good job—one that makes a positive contribution to the world. A solid job can give you one or more of the following sources of meaning:

- Clients to serve—either through direct interaction or indirect activities
- Coworkers and subordinates to take care of

- Bosses and investors to help succeed
- Means to take care of your family's financial needs and to help the community
- Purpose—something to do and to achieve
- A sense of belonging if someone at work takes responsibility for you

Many jobs do not have all these attributes, but they should at least provide a couple of them to be worth your time. An eight-hour-a-day job occupies a third of your life, so make it meaningful or find one that is. If you must settle for pointless work, do what you can to make it meaningful by caring for your coworkers and customers, and use your paycheck to improve your communities.

When people pay you for a product or service, then you have some responsibility for them. Perhaps you are not responsible for every facet of their lives, but with every business transaction, you are committing to help them in some way. You should strive to understand your customers deeply, including what job you are helping them solve with your product or service. If you do so, you are more likely to have satisfied customers.[102]

Your job does not need to impress new acquaintances at cocktail parties to be valuable. Low-paying jobs can be high in meaning. I just returned from a whitewater rafting trip in West Virginia. Our river guide was an easygoing surfer-type in his midthirties with white hair down to his chest. The other guides called him Mustang. He knew every story, rock, and hazard of the river and organized our group of inexperienced rafters into a united force. Mustang receives below-average pay for his work, but he can see the good it does for families and friends in his raft. If your job lifts people up and gives you a sense of meaning, then the judgment of others should not amount to anything.

Erosion of the Institutes over Time

Have you ever cupped your hands and tried to keep water in the reservoir of your palms? You inevitably lose a drip here or a clumsy splash there. The more rights, wealth, and pleasures we discover, the more our community's sense of meaning seems to escape through our fingers—not because these innovations are bad, but because they do not generate new meaning. The water ebbs when we so desperately need our collective sense of meaning replenished.

Meaning wanes as we distance ourselves from each other and avoid taking responsibility. We may have excellent motives for doing so, and cultural norms can lead us down irresponsible paths. Regardless of the reasons for not taking responsibility, though, we are unlikely to find lasting meaning without it. We may find purpose, status, and fun, but meaning requires commitment to someone else's well-being.

Although many individuals are devoted to others, the aggregate levels of responsibility are diminishing over time in America and other Western nations. We are slowly drifting apart in both obvious and imperceptible ways. And with every loss of responsibility, another drop of meaning slips through society's fingers. Let's discuss how.

Our friendships circles are shrinking. Humans have the brainpower to maintain about five close confidants, those with whom we can discuss important matters. Most fall short of that number. Adults in the

US had three confidants in 1985, compared to just two in 2021. And in 2004, approximately one in four Americans reported having no close confidants—an almost threefold increase from 1985. A recent survey also found that 71% of millennials (those born 1981–1994) and almost 79% of Gen Z respondents report feeling lonely—a significantly greater proportion than other generations.[103]

How can we effectively take responsibility for people if we do not know them intimately?

We are physically isolating ourselves. New US homes today are 1,000 square feet larger than they were in 1973, and living space per person has nearly doubled since that time.[104] The percentage of US residents living alone has also increased dramatically in the last 100 years. In 1920, for example, only 4.9% of 60-year-olds lived alone. Now, 17.7% have no one to wake up to.[105] Today only 26% of Americans know most of their neighbors.[106]

How do we recognize opportunities to help others if we do not interact with them?

We are taking on responsibility later in life. Most young adults between the ages of 18 and 29 still live with their parents (52%) for the first time since the Great Depression. In 1960, only about 29% of young adults lived with parents, and that number has been steadily climbing since. There are economic and cultural reasons for this shift, but the result is fewer young people out in the world and taking responsibility for themselves and others.[107] Even the proportion of high school seniors with driver's licenses has been falling since 2006.[108]

The average age of first-time mothers is up from 21 in 1972 to 26 in 2020.[109] The median marital age for women rose as well, from 21.2 in 1920 to 28.1 in 2020. For men, it rose from 24.6 to 30.5.

How much meaning do we miss if we are unable to take on responsibilities until later in life?

Marriages are rarer and families are smaller. The median household size has decreased steadily since the 1960s (3.33 to 2.53 in 2020). The percentage of married adults in the US is at a record low of 48.5%. This is a long way away from the peak of 72% in 1960.[110]

If family is one of life's greatest sources of meaning, then why are we allowing ours to dwindle?

Working hours are declining. The typical American employee has decreased his or her working hours 12% since 1950, 24% since 1929, and 43% since 1870.[111] Fewer working hours could open up more time for volunteering and other meaningful service, but Americans dedicate most of that time to entertainment. The typical American spends over five hours a day engaged in leisure activities, with three of those on television alone.[112]

If we are not in the workforce or our work does no one any good, are we finding other ways to care for people?

Of course, there are good reasons to have a small group of friends, avoid neighbors, work less often, put off having children, or stay single. Just keep in mind that limited responsibility in one arena frees up time and energy to take responsibility in another. And rejecting all responsibility will likely lead to feelings of meaninglessness.

Religion and Meaning

N*ext to family, religious faith is* the most common response to the question "What is the most important source of meaning in your life?"[113] In the study cited earlier about wealthy countries with high suicide rates and poor but fulfilled ones, religion played a mitigating role. The study found that in wealthy countries with high levels of suicide and low levels of meaning, individuals were much more likely to have personally meaningful lives if they had a strong religious faith.[114] Religion can be a bulwark against the excesses and despair that are increasingly pervasive in Western society.

Religion offers purpose and meaning through the following means:

1. Religion allows adherents to participate in the work of God.

They **take responsibility for God's work** and serve him through active participation in the religion. Many religious people report feeling a strong connection with God.[115]

2. It provides adherents opportunities to take **responsibility for others who share their beliefs**. Most religions recommend that participants teach classes, take care of facilities, visit other members, or provide other acts of service to members of their congregations.

3. Religion allows adherents to take **responsibility for others in the community** through service and missionary work. Religious organizations commonly share resources with needy individuals in the community and across the globe.

4. Religion often provides adherents with the belief that their relationships, service, work, and legacy may **continue beyond the grave**, even into a heaven and the presence of God.

5. Religions often have **rites and ordinances** (e.g. Communion, weddings, bar mitzvahs) that symbolically bind adherents to serve each other and God.

6. Most religions have a **set of teachings, laws, or scriptures** that outline how to find both purpose and meaning.

7. Religions generally **advocate for behaviors that create meaning**: marriage, family, service, and other meaningful behaviors and beliefs. They also tend to discourage selfishness, addiction, and other activities that stifle one's ability to take responsibility for others.

8. Religion often gives adherents a **sense of belonging** to a com-

munity of like-minded individuals and a connection to God.

Religion gives us people to suffer for and reasons to pass through that suffering. It leads to connections that generate purpose and meaning for people from all walks of life. Some religious people would say that God instilled in people a desire to search for meaning. When found, meaning can be a marker that you are going in the right direction. Religion as a source of meaning should not be easily dismissed.

An increasing number of believers say that they are spiritual but not religious, meaning that they believe in God but do not participate in organized religion.[116] Holding all other factors constant, the spiritual but irreligious soul will likely have a less meaningful life than her religious counterpart. Organized religion allows each adherent to benefit not just from a commitment to God but also a connection to others in the religious community.

I can speak to this personally. I lived as a Christian missionary among the people of Rio de Janeiro for two years, trying to do good. This time in the hilly rainforests of Brazil was one of the most meaningful of my life. As missionaries, we helped people in extreme poverty establish new lives. While some struggled with drug addiction and joblessness, we struggled with them. Through hunger, blisters, diseases, and so many sunburns, we lived for others and our God.

Whether or not you believe in God, investigating the beliefs and practices of religious communities can help explain why so many derive meaning from faith. We will look at Islam, Buddhism, and Christianity (my faith), understanding that there are diverse views and activities within each of these broad belief systems.

Meaning and Islam

In the days of the prophet Muhammad, Arab communities were centered on tribal affiliations and blood relations.[117] Muhammad sought to establish a community that was not only for Arabs but universal. He said, "Arab has no merit over non-Arab other than godfearingness."[118]

Service to mankind is the essence of Islam.[119] Muhammad said, "You are the best people ever raised for the good of mankind because you have been raised to serve others"[120] and "It is righteousness... to spend of your substance, out of love for Him, for your kin, for orphans, for the needy, for the wayfarer, for those who ask, and for the ransom of slaves."[121]

One of the five pillars of Islam is Zakat, or almsgiving. The word "Zakat" means "purification," implying that through giving the believer is purified.[122] For those who qualify, Muslims annually contribute a minimum amount of 2.5%, or 1/40, of their total savings and wealth.[123] Islamic financial analysts estimated in 2012 that somewhere between $200 billion and $1 trillion are spent in alms and charity across the Muslim world each year.[124] Giving to those who cannot care for themselves can be a source of meaning if you can put a face to your donation.

The religion of Islam extends its adherents' sense of responsibility beyond kin to the entire Muslim community or "ummah."[125] As Muslims face Mecca and pray together five times each day, they are connected to each other and to Allah. Many make the pilgrimage to

Mecca wearing the same two white sheets so that there is no class distinction among them.[126] The believers indeed are brothers. And with this acceptance and willingness to sacrifice as a community comes an increased measure of meaning.

Islam encourages Muslims to show kindness to non-Muslims who are not fighting against them.[127] If Muslims take responsibility for caring for those who belong to all sects of Islam, including those who are half-hearted in their religious observance, they will perceive their lives as increasingly valuable. They will feel heightened levels of meaning if they look out for their neighbors of other faiths—or of no faith at all.

Meaning and Buddhism

Buddhists follow the teachings of the Gautama Buddha, who they revere as an enlightened being. One of my favorite stories of Buddha features an ailing monk with severe diarrhea. No one else would look after him because he was selfish and would not care for others. There was also the smell. Buddha rushed to the monk, bathed him, changed his clothes, and made him lie on a cot. Then he admonished the other monks: "Consider service to a sick one as a service to me. If one has fallen ill, you should not consider whether he is senior to you or junior."[128]

Buddha exemplified "metta," the Buddhist concept of unconditional loving kindness for all sentient beings. Rejecting the rigid class system in India during the fifth century BC, Buddha boldly taught that "It is not by mere birth that one becomes lowly or a noble but by one's own actions."[129] He dedicated his life to uplifting all of humanity and showed that generosity is giving more than is required compared with one's resources and circumstances.

Although Indian society at that time believed in the inferior status of women, he gave women a place of honor by allowing them to enter the Buddhist community.[130] Buddha taught that men and women could progress and be liberated from the endless cycle of death and rebirth and allowed women to enjoy equal privileges. He even directed his loving kindness toward animals and called people to abandon practices of animal sacrifice.

The goal of Buddhism is to overcome suffering that arises from craving objects and sensory pleasures, craving to dominate others, and craving to evade the pains of the world.[131] Buddhists overcome the un-satisfactoriness of the world by renouncing and then letting go of these wants, desires, and attachments. Buddha also wisely taught that attachment to the self is fruitless because no permanent self can be found anywhere. People change.

Embedded in Buddhist thought is the inherent value of sentient life—not only human life, but the value of all creatures that have subjective experience. This includes all who are capable of pain and pleasure or of suffering and not suffering.[132]

A central question for Buddhists is what to detach from and what to adhere to. Is life merely a stepping-stone on the escape path from suffering? Are the meaning and purpose derived from attachments to others worth the suffering?

The author and Buddhist practitioner Robert Wright said that the philosophy could potentially lessen one's attachment to family members and neighbors.[133] In reality, though, he says that Buddhism removes attachments to anger, jealousy, selfishness, and character attributes that get in the way of healthy relationships. Buddhists all over the world take responsibility for family members and neighbors.

Religious people should consider viewing responsibility not as a damnable attachment but as the means to escape selfish cravings. As Buddha let go of his personal desires so that he could heal others, so should we let go of the pleasures, fears, and ambitions that keep us from fulfilling our responsibilities to friends. And though the people around us are in a constant state of change—growing and backsliding and growing again—we should commit in each moment to do what we can for them.

Meaning and Christianity

A scriptural verse summarizing God's purpose states, "For God so loved the world, that he gave his only Son, that whoever believes in him should not perish but have eternal life."[134] The message in this scripture is that God takes responsibility for each of us from before the cradle to beyond the grave. His purpose is to help billions overcome and progress during their earthly sojourn. This work likely gives him a strong sense of meaning, and it demonstrates the potential value that he recognizes within each of us.

The passage stresses the extent of God's responsibility for us in the statement "he gave his only Son." God was willing to send Jesus Christ as a sacrifice for our benefit. Willingness to sacrifice is the sign of accepted responsibility. All Christian traditions believe that Christ outlined the path to follow and showed us how to navigate it through his example. Many also believe that Christ's sacrifice on the cross opens the door to life and progression beyond the grave.

So God's purpose is to help us grow, but how do Christians find meaning? And is there a way for them to serve God?

Christ addresses these questions directly when he states, "For I was hungry and you gave me something to eat, I was thirsty and you gave me something to drink, I was a stranger and you invited me in… Whatever you did for one of the least of these brothers and sisters of mine, you did for me."[135] Christ says that we serve God by taking responsibility for those around us, particularly the lowly and downtrodden. We participate in God's work by taking on a small measure of the responsibility he has for each of us. We find meaning in the same way that he does, through caring for others..

The Bible is replete with language of interconnectedness and mutual responsibility. It refers to Christians as parts of one body, each possessing different skills and abilities for blessing the whole.[136] It talks about heaven as a marriage feast where all are invited but few choose to attend.[137] The Bible describes God's people as the kingdom.[138] A primary attribute of heaven is the people to whom we are connected.

Daniel Becerra discusses how Jesus Christ equates himself with the hungry, thirsty, sick, and imprisoned. It is significant that Jesus sees himself not just in anyone but in the marginalized and disadvantaged of society. Christ's identification with the marginalized should also cause us to reflect on who he really was. He didn't just care for the poor; he *was* poor. He didn't just minister to ethnic minorities in the Roman Empire; he *was* one. He was also a refugee, was convicted of a crime, and was a victim of government-sanctioned oppression. In other words, Christ's ministry to the marginalized was not a charitable condescension to their level. Forgetting this risks inhibiting our ability to understand, love, serve, and see as equals those who are similarly marginalized in modern society.[139]

Christ showed that our circle of responsibility should not just include our loved ones and friends. Christ also asked us to love our enemies.[140] Christian believers cast a wide net of responsibility and are thus able to capture an expansive sense of meaning.

Some Christians are so eager for the meaning available in heaven that they miss opportunities to take responsibility for others today. Other believers look down on those who interpret the Bible differently than they do. The result is Christian tribalism. Christians should maximize the meaning in life today by treating everyone as equals and taking responsibility for them right now.

Meaning and an Afterlife

The statement "taking responsibility for another generates meaning" depends on the assumption that people can contribute to others. The arguments in favor of taking responsibility for others strengthen if there is an afterlife because a person's ability to grow and to give expands with the duration of that individual's existence. A child's life is worthwhile even if he spends only a moment in his mother's arms before passing, but a long life would likely provide more opportunities for growth and service.

In order for the additional benefits of an afterlife to accrue, the following requirements must be met:

1. Part of the person must continue after death.
2. Something gained during life must persist into the afterlife.
3. The "something gained" that persists into the afterlife can be enhanced by the contribution of others.
4. (Bonus requirement) A person can continue to grow and lift others at some point after death.

All four of these statements require religious faith. If the first three of these statements are true, then at least some of the good we do on earth follows us when we leave. If all four are true, then each of us has limitless potential for growth and for doing good.

If you believe in the eternal nature of people and the possibility of eons of progress, then you will likely treat those under your purview differently. Are you working with an elderly individual who has only a few weeks of existence left or are you working with an immortal being who you can help along the way and who will continue to develop long after death? There is some meaning to derive from either point of view, but the eternal view is a greater source of meaning than the finite one.

The presence of an afterlife is not required to find meaning and purpose in life, but it would extend the limits of meaning and purpose. Through resurrection, reincarnation, or a disembodied state, life after death would give the human family more to accomplish together and for one another. Imagine the depths of meaning in an eternal relationship.

Meaning and Atheism

A friend of mine was speaking with a wealthy venture capitalist, someone who works long and hectic hours making truckloads of money for other people and for his family. The venture capitalist asked my friend if he believes in God.

"Yes," my friend responded. "I do."

The venture capitalist acted surprised. My friend then asked, "If you do not believe in God, why do you do all this? Why do you work so hard? Why do you even come in to work at all? You have enough money to relax."

The venture capitalist responded, "I do it to make the world a better place for my daughter."

A belief in an almighty is not required to find purpose in life through accepting responsibility. This powerful businessman finds meaning in taking care of his daughter and making the world a better place for others. He understands that he can increase the frequency of happy moments for her and help her grow in knowledge and goodness. With a little luck, the venture capitalist's daughter will pass that knowledge down to her own children, and they will carry on the nurturing tradition.

So it is for agnostics and atheists around the world. They still donate their resources and time to good causes. They marry and raise good families. They treat others with love and compassion. Many atheists certainly have more meaning than the deeply religious who avoid committing to others.

Meaning and Trials

T*aking responsibility for someone leads to* heartbreak; the shock of a severed relationship, grief after death, or shared disappointment are just some ways responsibility hurts. Sometimes, the weight of responsibility seems greater than we can bear. This chapter discusses why it is still worthwhile.

The Impact of Responsibility Shocks

Mutual responsibility is a welding link between two or more individuals. This binding is not easily dissolved. What happens when committed individuals are torn apart?

I have a friend who worked as a registrar in a small emergency department near the California–Arizona border. Her role was to meet with injured people and their harried families when they entered the hospital. She would take down personal and insurance information before they received care.

Not too far away from her facility, a policeman responded to a serious car accident. As he blocked off the area surrounding the wreck and redirected traffic, a car struck him at high speed. He was rushed by ambulance to the hospital, where a team of clinicians attempted to save his life. My friend said the team worked on the policeman longer than they needed to, hoping for a miracle and demonstrating to family that they had done what they could. All the technology, expertise, and grit in that facility could not resuscitate him.

While the caregivers worked, the policeman's wife entered the hospital. My registrar friend was the first person to speak with the widow. She was sobbing, pacing, and ranting to no one in particular, "What am I going to do?! What am I going to do without my husband? What are the kids going to do without a father? Oh no, oh no, oh no…"

My registrar friend did her best to console the heartbroken woman. She could not be comforted, though. The experience so upset my friend that she cried into the night and eventually changed to an administrative role with a different healthcare system.

We recognize the sting that comes from losing a friend and companion, a dream job, or a meaningful activity. We ask ourselves what the loss means for our lives and for those around us.

When the ties of responsibility are cut, you feel a sense of loss.

What exactly are you losing, though? Of course, you are losing a person who you cared about, and you will no longer be able to laugh with them, talk with them, or enjoy their presence again.

But at the same time, you are losing the benefits of responsibility. Your sense of loss will be immediate and proportional to your level of commitment. You also lose any feelings of belonging that come from the individual's commitment to you. Involuntary losses of responsibility are particularly painful because they can come with rejection and feelings of worthlessness.[141]

The removal of responsibility tends to produce feelings of emptiness. In a study of role exits, researchers found that over 75% of those exiting roles went through a period described as feeling anxious, scared, at loose ends, or that they didn't belong. These emotions were accompanied by a pervasive sense of being suspended "between the past which no longer existed and the unknown future."[142]

One reliable predictor of the degree of distress at a romantic breakup is the duration of the relationship.[143] Because marriages destined for divorce are unpleasant, the transition to singlehood should be an improvement. Even so, the dissolution of most marriages comes with pain and sadness.[144] I believe that much of this pain comes from the loss of responsibility.

Let's look closely at the widow's grief-stricken words in the hospital waiting area. She seemed to be saying, "With my husband's death, I lose one of my purposes in life—to take care of my husband. I lose the meaning I derive from that responsibility. I lose a major source of belonging and the comfort that comes when he takes responsibility for me. The children lose a responsible parent and the sense of belonging that comes with that care. What matters most is lost."

This is an extreme example of a responsibility shock, but we face lesser instances frequently. We experience responsibility shocks when a work colleague moves to another department, when a neighbor leaves the area, or when a coaching job ends because the season is over. Some shocks are sudden and severe. Others are drawn out or preplanned.

The least difficult transitions are those in which a person can anticipate the transition and restructure life in advance.[145] When you feel responsible for someone, though, it is painful to say goodbye. "Congrats on selling your business," a longtime mentor said the day after Jeff Giesea signed the paperwork. "Now get ready for a depression."[146]

When someone severs responsibility, you can feel abandoned and betrayed. And a responsibility shock does not require that you remove yourself from someone's life. A father, for example, can cease to take interest in the welfare of his family while remaining in the home. One wonders if a detached zombie parent is preferable to an absent one.

Individual people and relationships cannot be replaced, but sources of meaning can.[147] When one person or group withdraws from your life, a space is created for another to enter. Feelings of pain and loss are not-so-subtle signs that you require a new supply of meaning. You may create deeper meaning in your remaining relationships.

Death—The End of Meaning?

Does the meaning of a life end with the firing of the last synapse or the final breath or heartbeat? Maybe yes, and absolutely not.

Let's cover the "maybe yes" part first. Because meaning is the perception that life is valuable, it can only continue beyond the grave if consciousness does. There is no perceived meaning without the capacity to perceive. So congratulations are in order for the believer. Meaning is eternal for you and has the capacity to expand forever. If, on the other hand, you are bound for dust and eternal sleep, then enjoy the meaning of this and every remaining moment.

The mystery of whether there is a great beyond will be solved as you step through death's door. Will you meet silence or immortality? If you are still a version of yourself at that point, you can shout for joy with me because we have endless potential to generate and recognize meaning. That would be a stirring moment.

Now on to why death is "absolutely not" the end of meaning. As stated earlier, you have the capacity to create value by making life better for others. And some of that value will endure beyond your life, even if you are not around to recognize it. Those you lift may continue lifting others. The ideas, products, and monuments of your life will continue to serve—maybe not forever, but for a time. Your charges can even multiply your value after your departure by preparing the next generation.

Loved ones feel responsibility for the deceased until they say a final goodbye. They show their continued responsibility as they escort dear friends through life's final moments. They organize the funeral and finances and notify others who are wound up in the deceased one's network of responsibility. They craft eulogies and share stories that establish a legacy.

Even though he died when I was 28 and lived an hour away from my childhood home, I never knew my grandfather, Gordon Westover, well. He was the type of person who would not intrude on the lives of others but was always willing to help. The truth is that most of what I believe about him comes from the eulogy my father gave at Gordon's funeral. Even the line about him not "[intruding] on the lives of others" came from the eulogy written by my father. Here are a few words from that document that give me a sense of connection to him and to others connected to him.

"[Gordon] had an irrational confidence in his ability to repair anything. He used to say, 'If a man can build it, I can fix it.' Invariably he could. [Gordon was] an aerospace engineer. He helped build and test the first surface-to-air and air-to-air missiles at White Sands missile testing range in New Mexico. He spent most of his career working with the Minuteman and Peacekeeper missile systems.

"When I was eight, I remember him taking me up on a hill to watch one of the test launches of a missile. We were miles away, but we had an unobstructed view. When the missile ignited, the roar was deafening and the ground shook. These devices were as ominous as the wrath of Almighty God. The Minuteman was 60 feet tall, weighed 78,000 pounds, and flew 15,000 miles per hour. In my mind, my father built the missile by himself. I was eight years old, and he was 10 feet tall.

"People say that Ronald Reagan won the Cold War. In fact, the

Minuteman missile system was the only bulwark that protected us from Soviet annihilation. When [Gordon] went to work every day, he was protecting us all. I understand that not everyone will agree with me that [Gordon] won the Cold War, or that he ended the Cuban Missile Crisis, or that he gave his life to defend America and all that we hold dear against powerful enemies. But in my mind, I'm still eight years old, and he will always be 10 feet tall."

My children love listening to heroic stories of their ancestors. These stories help the children understand what their ancestors sacrificed to make the world a better place and that some of that capacity was passed down to them. The stories give my children a sense of belonging and connect them to their great-grandfather and everyone related to him.

Many find meaning in serving and honoring their dead long after the funeral. Loved ones jealously guard their reputations and preserve inspiring memories. They feel a sense of belonging as they imagine a deceased loved one looking in on them from time to time. They place flowers at the gravesite or an urn in a prominent place above the mantel. This continued sense of responsibility comes with hope for an afterlife or refusal to acknowledge death in the first place.

It is difficult to draw a precise boundary between life and death. Doctors and coroners usually turn to the moment where electrical activity in the brain ceases, but I propose a new definition. A kind of death occurs when you are no longer responsible for anyone—when you are alone in a crowded world. Without someone to watch out for, the loneliness will precipitate a slide into emptiness, sickness, and death.

Meaning and Suffering

Lack of meaning is a kind of pain. It is an intolerable unease—a feeling that something vital is missing and that you are overlooking the moral of your own story. A shortage of meaning urges the ancient parts of you to seek out something greater than you now have.

A friend from my community named Kristie recently told me that she had been devastated to learn her unborn son had Down syndrome. Later, she had felt emotionally dissected when at five months old that same son, Josh, had open-heart surgery. She blamed herself for every milestone that he did not achieve. Now Josh is in his twenties, and Kristie still must take him to three to five doctor's appointments a week. Her total commitment gives Kristie a high degree of meaning, but at times the work seems overwhelming.

Through it all, Kristie's mother was her anchor and always there for her. Then, one day, Kristie heard that her mother was in the hospital. The diagnosis was encephalitis (or swelling of the brain) brought on by a virus. Now Kristie's mother has severe memory problems and seems to be a different person. She is no longer the go-getter she used to be.

When Kristie realized how serious her mother's condition was, she was angry at God for the first time. She thought that God would not give her more than she could bear, and this was far more than she could handle. She could take care of her son, but who would take care of her? Suffering like this cries out for a reason to carry on. All experience intense pain during the ups and downs of life. Almost all of us sense background levels of agony that swell and subside with each day and moment. Those who take risks fail and face rejection and injury. Those who play it safe wrestle with loneliness and boredom, which are forms of pain. No one escapes.

Most people consider the words "pain" and "suffering" to be synonymous or view suffering as more extreme or enduring forms of pain. Some psychologists, including Steve Stosny, look at pain and suffering differently, though. For the purposes of this section, we will follow his lead.

Pain is a physical or emotional sensation ranging from a minor itch to burning alive—or from a minor offense to being abandoned by a close loved one. It is an unpleasant activation of pain receptors or the trigger of painful feelings. Pain brings with it motivation to heal, repair, replace, or improve.

Suffering, according to Stosny, comes from attempts to numb or avoid the pain. It is intensely focused on the self—the greater the pain, the greater the temptation to block out the world, turn inward, and escape. Suffering manifests as blame, anger, resentment, or addiction. It blunts pain signals that could otherwise motivate healing, repairing, and improving.[148]

Pain is writing an essay on the yogurt production process for a science class. Suffering is wandering around the house complaining that the assignment is pointless, proclaiming that your teacher is an idiot, and then spending three hours on social media. Pain comes with purpose and the drive to seek meaningful connections to help. Suffering distracts from what matters.

Our modern world is built around coping with and escaping from pain. For many, days are filled with numbing pills, distracting toys, and monsters to blame. The modern world fills our lives with coping mechanisms and then tries to convince us that our suffering is happiness.

Kristie endured the pain of watching her newborn son go through surgery. It pained her to watch Josh—her responsibility—fail to progress. Kristie also felt a kind of agony watching her mother fade. The pain motivated her to sacrifice time, money, and energy for her son and for her mother. And in pain-motivated service, she found meaning.

It appears that Kristie also added some suffering onto her pain. She blamed herself when Josh failed to meet impossible progress milestones. She compared her situation with the seemingly charmed circumstances of those around her, and she resented God for taking away her mother. Much of this suffering is understandable given her circumstances, but unnecessary.

All meaningful pursuits come with exposure to pain. In truth, nothing worthwhile comes without some danger. Deepening responsibility increases pain's likelihood, duration, and acuity. You cannot apply for your dream job without the possibility of rejection. After your weaknesses are uncovered, you could face disgrace and dismissal.

Responsibility may not alleviate the pain, but it is an antidote to suffering. Those with a deep sense of responsibility accept the reality of pain and serve anyway. They do not waste much energy on anger, blame, escape, or resentment. Those with responsibility fight through the pain because they know the worth of the people around them.

Every generation asks why we endure pain and weakness. I do not know the complete answer, but part of it rests in others' difficulties. My life is valuable because I try to help out my elderly neighbor. His life is worthwhile because he comforts me during my trials. If suffering did not exist in the world, there would be no way to make yourself of use to others. You cannot fulfill your responsibility to help people if they have no burdens for you to lighten—no pain for you to ease.

Hiding your struggles limits the sense of worth those around you can feel. A close relative recently told me that he is getting divorced. I had no idea he and his wife were struggling until he tearfully announced his marriage was over. I wish he had let me in earlier. I could have been there for him and offered what strength I have. At least I can try now.

Mental Health, Trauma, and Human Touch

Rates of depression and anxiety have increased dramatically over recent decades. Martin Seligman concluded that the cause is our increased emphasis on the self.[149] The self is poorly suited to provide a source of meaning and value to human life.

Everyone has off days, but those with severe depression experience low moods or a feeling of numbness for extended periods of time, even for weeks, months, or years. According to one model of depression, the condition can be activated by stressful life events.[150] Depression is a disease that has a "tidal pull toward seclusion."[151] Many who suffer from untreated depression lack friends because it saps the energy that friendship requires and makes it hard for them to speak or hear words of comfort.[152] Research also shows that people suffering from depression are much more likely than others to find their lives empty and meaningless.[153]

Because of its recent wars and human rights violations, Cambodia is a good place to study whether people can rise above traumatic events to find meaning in their lives. Surprisingly, only 0.02% of the Cambodian healthcare budget is spent on improving mental health. A mere 35 trained psychiatrists labor to care for a population of over 15 million.[154] This is for a country still suffering from the aftershocks of Pol Pot's killing fields and the murderous regime of the Khmer Rouge.

In April 1975, a black-clad boy with a rifle came to Nuon Phaly's lovely home in Phnom Penh and demanded she leave. "I can't," she protested. "You can see I am nine months pregnant. My baby is due any day." The wiry boy explained that those who would not leave would be killed. Phaly said that when she looked into his eyes, they were "black, like a cavern, like a hole plunging deep into the earth." She understood that she did not exist for this boy, and it made no difference to him whether she lived or died.

So Phaly took her two sisters and two children into the pitiless Cambodian sun and walked with three million others who were ordered out of the cities and into the countryside. Stone-faced boys with rope-like muscles stood along the road and used their rifles to club anyone who fell behind. With the help of a few kind passersby, Phaly had her baby by the side of the road and named him Therac. Almost as soon as the baby was born, soldiers forced her to continue trudging down the road. They passed by children, women, and men lying lifeless on both sides of the road.

Phaly somehow found her husband in the migrating mob. His wealthy upbringing made him unaccustomed to hardship, though, and he died within a couple of weeks. A ferryman took Phaly's wedding ring to pay for a crossing and then stole her remaining rice. Soon after, Phaly's 12-year-old sister lost the will to carry on. While Phaly and her other sister scrabbled for roots and leaves to eat, the 12-year-old sat down under a tree and quietly passed away.

Deprivation dried up Phaly's breast milk, and she had nothing left to give her newborn. So, six months after entering the world, Therac slumped in her arms, and she washed and buried him. Phaly said that she had no words for such sadness. She continued moving, working, and fighting for survival over the next four years. She said that there was never a good day. The threat of starvation loomed on one side and summary execution for minor offenses on the other. Phaly wrote about this time, saying that she had no emotions left.

The Vietnamese armies eventually came in force and gained control of most of Cambodia. The Cambodian people in those days were treated like enemies and animals by the Khmer Rouge, the Vietnamese, and the Thai people. Many died. So, with hundreds of thousands of other refugees, Phaly eventually made her way to a refugee camp near Cambodia's border with Thailand.

In 1985, the United Nations built a new camp for people who had been driven from Cambodia into Thailand. Because of her education and usefulness as a translator, Phaly lived in a wooden hut that passed for luxury there. Phaly noticed that many women in the camp were seemingly paralyzed—not moving, not talking, not feeding, and not caring for their own children. One of those women said that she felt like "a frog living in a well." Phaly saw that the other women had survived the war but thought they were now going to die from depression.

Several foreign organizations in the United Nations camp and others nearby began offering mental health services. Phaly received training from Harvard University and other organizations from around the world. In the camp, though, she developed her own way of treating traumatized women. At first, she went around the camp, visiting people in their homes, and then they began seeking out her hut. Only five women at first, then 10, then 15.[155]

Phaly used traditional Khmer medicine, made with varied proportions of more than 100 herbs and leaves as a first step. Phaly would take her patients to meditate before a Buddhist shrine in her hut. If that did not adequately address the problem, Phaly would use antidepressants brought in by the foreign aid workers. She only had enough for the most severe cases.

After steadying each of the women, Phaly would teach them how to forget, how to work, and how to love and be loved. She would draw each woman out through daily exercises to help her forget horrific memories. She distracted them with purposeful activities like weaving or music and taught work skills such as cleaning houses or raising pigs. These became sources of income and pride.

And, when she felt the time was right, Phaly took them to a steamy lean-to where they could wash and give each other manicures and pedicures. Phaly described "little bottles of colored enamel, the steam room, the sticks for pushing back cuticles, the emery boards, the towels."[156]

After the prolonged crisis, Phaly returned to Phnom Penh and started an orphanage, where she cared for over 90 children. Many of the women she treated continue to work in the orphanage after Phaly's death in 2012.[157]

It is clear from Phaly's story that she suffered incomprehensible levels of trauma. She had every reason to curl up on a dirt floor and wither away. Walking through that camp, though, she could not help but notice others suffering and that she had the means to try to help. And, through her actions, Phaly apparently found a measure of solace.

Some sacrifice is so subtle that it is almost imperceptible: an accepting touch, removing the lint from a shoulder, taking the time to listen after a painful day, or accepting someone so completely that she feels comfortable showing her true self. Phaly did not serve through one monumental sacrifice, but through thousands of small and simple ones. She tapped into the primal human need for human contact and the need to be seen and heard.

Her grooming activities were effective because they put the women "in contact with the bodies of other people and [made] them give up their bodies to the care of others. It [rescued] them from physical isolation, which [was] a usual affliction for them. And that [led] to the breakdown of the emotional isolation. While they [were] together washing and putting on nail polish, they [began] to talk together. And bit by bit they [began] to trust one another. And by the end of it all, they [learned] to make friends so that they [would] never have to be so lonely and so alone again."[158]

When people feel the affectionate touch or embrace of those they are close to, they often interpret it as a sign they are safe, loved, and supported. Affectionate touch is so potent that one set of studies found that one second of contact on the shoulder led people with low self-esteem to be less self-anxious about death and more connected with others.[159] Grooming, such as manicures, pedicures, and massage, not only helps people bond, but it also reduces anxiety and improves mental health.

According to multiple studies, most people who received a course of massage therapy had less anxiety or depression than those who did not.[160] For those who have no desire to engage in grooming rituals, I wonder if watching a game with a group of friends, playing a contact sport like rugby, or having a game night ritual would have similar effects. These activities may provide opportunities to hear stories, have contact, and build trust. Small communities of trust and mutual responsibility can become bulwarks against the terrors of the world.

Research also shows that volunteering leads to lower rates of depression, especially for individuals 65 and older. Volunteering increases social interaction and helps build a support system based on common interests—both factors that have been shown to decrease depression.[161]

I am not saying that taking responsibility is a cure-all for depression or trauma. It is not. I am saying that it is a reason to persist despite the pain. So if you are on medication and receiving psychotherapy or other treatments, keep going. Facing your shortcomings each day is a valiant purpose in life. Also, take as much responsibility for others as you can muster—even if it is just a little. The added sense of self-worth may give you the energy needed to progress and overcome.

Meaning for Gang Members

Rio de Janeiro is beauty and chaos. It is a tangle of brick, concrete, wire, and sandals mixed in with hilly rainforest. Unlike in the United States, the wealthy tend to live in high-rises in the basin while poorer settlements climb haphazardly into the hills. Most of the people I met while living there were warm and generous—people who invite strangers in for a piece of cake.

Água Santa, like many of the towns in Rio, backs onto steep green slopes. No roads climb into these areas, so people can only reach their homes via winding staircases crowded by other dwellings. The higher I climbed up the uneven steps, the humbler the houses became. The staircase ended, I wiped sweat from my eyes, and I took in the splendid jumble below me.

It was on this hill in 2001 that I met a man I will call Eduardo. He wore a ball cap pulled almost over his eyes and was barefoot. I extended my hand and introduced myself. Seeing my tie and scriptures, he smiled and began referring to me as "brother" in Portuguese. After some small talk, Eduardo motioned over to a pair of shoes and said that I should look inside. I picked up one of the tan work boots, and inside, the handle of a small handgun glinted in the hot sun.

"Look in the other one," Eduardo suggested. I picked up the second worn boot and tilted it toward me so that I could see inside. Small bags, some filled with white powder and others with white irregular pebbles, slid into view. I realized what they were, put the boot down, and swallowed hard.

If you are going to sell drugs, the highest point in a Brazilian favela is as good a place as any. You have a dense population of potential clients around you, a good view of police or rivals approaching from below, a limited number of access points to defend, and time to prepare in case of trouble. I had interrupted Eduardo at his place of business.

I assume that because of my religious attire, Eduardo confided in me that he had done great wrongs. He needed two hands to count out the six people he had killed in wars with rival gangs on nearby hills. Eduardo detailed how he had done each of them. One of his victims was a young woman. He described waiting for her while pressed against a wall with a knife. The barrel of her rifle came into view around the corner…

I should have walked away, but his experiences captivated me. How often do you meet a murderer? Near the end of our conversation, Eduardo removed a laminated picture of his young son from a pocket. He let me hold the warped and peeling image while he told me of his love for his son. He said that everything he did was for that boy. We parted with a final handshake, and I scampered down the stairs toward safer ground.

So did my acquaintance have a life of purpose and meaning? He certainly had something to do every day. He probably had sales quotas to achieve and personal records to best. I imagine that he felt some responsibility for his loyal customers and a thrill when he made a new one. Many people likely depended on the drugs he provided to get through the day. And Eduardo was surrounded by a tight-knit group of fellow gang members who were willing to fight and die for each other.

Eduardo's actions may have seemed destructive, but his sense of meaning was not determined by how others perceived him. It was based on whether he felt a sense of responsibility for others. And from what he said about his son and his customers, Eduardo found some meaning in his life.

When we take responsibility for others, we assist them on their way. We help them to grow and to nurture others. When Eduardo sold crack cocaine to his delighted clients and witnessed them using it, perhaps he felt like he was making their lives better for a time. He offered escape, and this could have given him a sense of meaning.

Over the long run, though, I believe he will see a clearer picture of the harm his actions cause those he is supposed to help. I expect he will see fallen friends, ruined clients, and disappointed family members as the result of his behavior. And I imagine that this feedback will lead him to question whether his life is worthwhile or destructive.

The conversation on that hilltop felt like a confession, and Eduardo seemed to regret many of his actions. Someday, he might see that the illegal drugs he sells wither the human mind and both the capacity and desire to serve. In a way, every illicit transaction extinguishes someone's capacity to find meaning. Perhaps someday he will realize this and try to change course.

Nothing removes more potential meaning from the world than murder. Instead of helping people reach their full height, the murderer cuts them down. Concluding that an innocent's life has no value says much about how the murderer perceives his own worth. If an innocent is worth the knife, then the guilty is likely to see his own life as worthless.

When Responsibility Is Too Much

Reluctance to take on responsibility for someone is natural. All things being equal, who wants more work and sacrifice? Many of us have had the following thoughts:

- I can't manage another friend.
- I don't have enough energy for a needy family member.
- I don't want to be trapped by a new commitment to someone.
- Life is a little crazy right now, and I just need a break.

When Beth discovered that she was pregnant, she went to Graham, the man who had bedded her, in tears. He said that he didn't want anything to do with her or the baby. Graham just wanted to know if it was a boy or a girl and what she was going to do with it.

Beth fled the state to live with her brother and her sister-in-law. She kept her pregnancy a secret from close friends and even her parents. My mother, Susan, was born on December 8, 1955, in Salt Lake City with dark hair and rosy cheeks.

Beth was crestfallen after deciding to give her child up. Her brother had convinced her that it would be best for the newborn to be put up for adoption. My mother was then adopted by an elementary school teacher and his young wife. After Beth married and raised her own family, her other children did not know they had a half-sister.

Every year on December 8 for over 60 years, Beth would look up at the sky and pray that her daughter was okay. And she was. My mom is a great student, teacher, volunteer, and homemaker. She married a good man and raised five children.

By the time my mom tracked down her birth mother, Beth was slowing down and dragging oxygen tanks from room to room. The time had passed for mother and child to form a deep connection, but Beth was relieved to hear that her daughter had lived a good life. They now talk regularly.

All the circumstances of Beth's affair with Graham point to cruelty and misjudgment. I can understand how the physical toll of childbirth, the expense, the lost time, the regret, and the conflicting commitments to others would make abortion a tempting solution. I am grateful, though, that my grandmother took a measure of responsibility for her daughter and gave her a chance.

Unexpected responsibilities can overwhelm, and existing ones can grow too heavy to carry. Life tends to saddle us with obligations that are too great to carry alone. A natural response to pain and suffering is to detach from commitments, especially those that are causing anguish. Sometimes it is best to excuse yourself from responsibility because your care is doing more harm than good. At other times, deep responsibility for one requires that we limit it for another. In situations where you need to scale back your commitment to someone else, there is a right way and a wrong way to do so.

The wrong way is to express your frustrations with the situation publicly, sever all ties, and then just disappear. I had a coworker who was struggling in her job and falling behind. She was also sensitive to smells—a condition called hyperosmia—and requested that her coworkers not use perfume or strong deodorants in the office. One day, this coworker barged into her supervisor's office, slammed her

ID card on the desk, said something about how one of the administrative assistants was trying to kill her with the fragrances of essential oils, and then left.

Cut-and-run behavior may seem satisfying in the moment, but it leaves those remaining with a sense of rejection and betrayal. Worse, it means that the people who need help are left to fend for themselves. When my coworker left suddenly, we did not know where she had saved her work. We lost months scrambling to recreate it and hire a replacement.

When your cumulative responsibilities are negatively impacting your health or your other relationships over an extended period, carefully consider your commitments. You may decide that you should persist in them and that the burdens will lighten over time. It may be possible to reduce your commitment to a more reasonable level. Or maybe you will need to phase out a responsibility entirely.

When possible, stick with responsibility through dark times. Eight out of 10 couples who narrowly avoid divorce are relatively happy five years later.[162] Work, relationships, and other forms of responsibility carry in them the motivation to make it through trials.

Few responsibilities are "all or nothing." Many can cut down hours at work or take longer lunch breaks. Students can often change classes or take fewer classes instead of dropping out. Even in marriage, one partner can outsource certain chores so that he can focus on more important aspects of the relationship. The courage to ask for help from others can also lighten these burdens.

The right way to step away from responsibility is to prepare a path for it to continue despite your absence. A soon-to-be ex-employee can provide two weeks' notice, document her work, or even help to recruit and train a replacement. She can do everything in her power to ease the transition for her clients, coworkers, and supervisors. She can check in on them after she is gone.

Beth took on as much as she could for her unborn daughter. She cared for her own body during the pregnancy and faithfully visited her doctor. She and her brother worked closely with the adoption agency to find a good family who wanted a child.

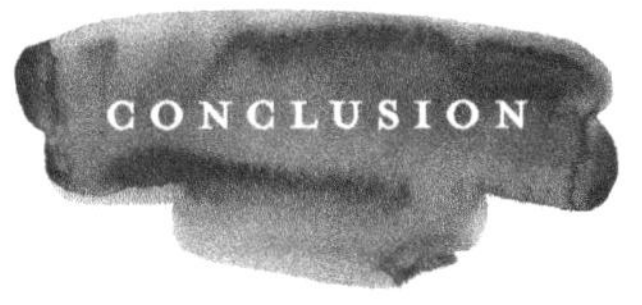

Take Responsibility

In *the movie The Princess Bride,* Billy Crystal asks his mostly dead patient, "Hey! Hello in there. Hey! What's so important? What you got here that's worth living for?" In moments of emptiness, I ask myself the same question. And what comes back to me are names—names of family, friends, coworkers, clients, pets, neighbors, and readers I am ready to help. And reflected in their eyes, I see my own value.

Our modern world is replete with messages warning people away from responsibility. Here are a few I've heard recently:

- Pull yourself together before taking responsibility for someone else.

- If you do not love yourself, then you cannot love others.
- You are only responsible for your own actions.
- Sort out your education and career before getting married and having children.

These messages may be helpful to those pursuing a dream or a purpose, but they are detrimental to meaning. Those who shun responsibility, even for good reason, lose the meaning in their lives. And every momentary delay of responsibility is a moment spent without a feeling of self-worth.

Our collective sense of meaning is shrinking as our communities splinter into smaller and smaller tribes. We view those outside our contracting rings of responsibility as enemies. We need a renaissance of meaning. To recapture it, we must reach out and invite people into our lives.

I was planning to stay the night in Neskowin last weekend and wake up for an early surf session. The surf report was predicting five out of five for the surfing conditions—with waves over 10 feet high, the perfect tide and swell direction, and a slight offshore breeze. Then my dishwasher broke.

With a large family, it is challenging to keep the forks clean even with a functioning dishwasher. The replacement parts arrived the afternoon I was planning to leave for the coast. I looked at the dishes piled around the kitchen and the food smeared on the counter. I told myself that I could quickly fix the dishwasher and still have enough time to drive the two hours to the coast. I was wrong.

By the time I finished, it was too late to risk the drive but not too late to start a load of dishes. I was disappointed that I could not go surfing, but I felt a small sense of accomplishment for successfully fixing a large appliance (I am by no means handy). I also felt a deeper satisfaction knowing that I could help a few people who needed me in that moment. And if I can do just a little good in the life of someone else, then my life has meaning.

A meaningful existence is highly personalized in that there are many people to take care of and a near-infinite number of ways to do so. Outside of making and keeping commitments to others, though, you may not be able to find a lasting sense of meaning. I would love to learn about other pathways to a valuable life, but I have not found any outside of responsibility.

If you are still uncertain about the benefits of committing to another person, go out into the world and give it a try. Agree to become a coach in a local league or commit to learning everyone's name in your neighborhood and saying "Hi, [name]" whenever you walk by them on the street. Experiment with volunteering somewhere. Agree to participate in a mentoring program at work. Make someone a part of your life. And don't just try it for one evening. Really experiment with different kinds of service for weeks and then months and years and for the rest of your life. This adjustment may send rippling waves of fulfillment into your life and the lives you touch.

As a toddler, my daughter Finley could smile with her whole face—blue eyes, Grandma's rosy cheeks, and a joyous mouth. I would come home from graduate school sometimes feeling overwhelmed or low. Finley would just fix me with that radiant smile, and I couldn't help but see the world as a brighter place. I would think, "She's shining her happiness beam right at me. Turn it away!"

We all have a kind of happiness beam—even those of us with sour dispositions. Some have art, a business, a technical skill, creativity, something to teach, money, stories, compassion, a calming demeanor, time, or networks of relationships. Perhaps you are just good company. Take your happiness beam and shine it at those with whom you come into contact. Or point it at one person with such intensity that it fills her life with joy.

THE END

Bibliography

Abbink, Klaus, and Donna Harris. "In-Group Favouritism and Out-Group Discrimination in Naturally Occurring Groups." *PLOS ONE* 14, no. 9 (September 4, 2019). https://doi.org/10.1371/journal.pone.0221616.

Al-Jahiz. "The Adab of Islam." Translated by Nuh Ha Mim Keller. Masud, 2001. http://www.masud.co.uk/ISLAM/nuh/adab_of_islam.htm.

Ali, Abdullah Yusuf, trans. *The Holy Qur'an*. London: Wordsworth, 2014.

Allen, S.J. *An Introduction to the Crusades*. New York: University of Toronto Press, 2017.

Arbesman, Samuel. "The Fraction of Famous People in the World." *Wired*, January 22, 2013. https://www.wired.com/2013/01/the-fraction-of-famous-people-in-the-world/.

Aristotle. *Nicomachean Ethics*. Edited by Lesley Brown. Translated by David Ross. Oxford: Oxford University Press, 2009.

Asbridge, Thomas. *The First Crusade: A New History*. Oxford: Oxford University Press, 2004.

Augustine of Hippo. *The Confessions of Saint Augustine*. Translated by E.B. Pusey. Mount Vernon: Peter Pauper Press, 1947.

Azzam, Amy M. "Motivated to Learn: A Conversation with Daniel Pink." *Educational Leadership* 72, no. 1 (September 2014): 12–17.

Barth, Brian. "The Secrets of Chicken Flocks' Pecking Order." Modern Farmer, March 16, 2016. https://modernfarmer.com/2016/03/pecking-order/.

Baumeister, Roy F. *Meanings of Life*. New York: The Guilford Press, 1991.

Baumeister, Roy F., Kathleen D. Vohs, Jennifer L. Aaker, and Emily N. Garbinsky. "Some Key Differences between a Happy Life and a Meaningful Life." *The Journal of Positive Psychology* 8, no. 6 (November 1, 2013): 505–16. https://doi.org/10.1080/17439760.2013.830764.

BBC. "Ahimsa," September 11, 2009. https://www.bbc.co.uk/religion/religions/jainism/living/ahimsa_1.shtml.

"Nobel Winner's Plea to Iran," October 10, 2003. http://news.bbc.co.uk/1/hi/world/middle_east/3181428.stm.

Becerra, Daniel. *3rd, 4th Nephi: A Brief Theological Introduction.* The Book of Mormon: Brief Theological Introductions 9. Provo, Utah: The Neal A Maxwell Institute, 2020.

Beilock, Sian Leah. "Why Young Americans Are Lonely." *Scientific American*, July 27, 2020. https://www.scientificamerican.com/article/why-young-americans-are-lonely/.

Bell, Kristen. "Kristen Bell." Interview by Dax Shepard. *The Armchair Expert*, February 14, 2018. https://armchairexpertpod.com/pods/kristen-bell.

Benda-Beckmann, Franz von, and Keebet von Benda-Beckmann. *Social Security Between Past and Future: Ambonese Networks of Care and Support.* Piscataway, NJ: Transaction Publishers, 2007.

Bloom, Leslie. "How Long Is the Average Career of an NFL Player?" Chron, March 5, 2019. https://work.chron.com/long-average-career-nfl-player-12643.html.

Brooks, David. "The Moral Bucket List." *The New York Times*, April 11, 2015, sec. Opinion. https://www.nytimes.com/2015/04/12/opinion/sunday/david-brooks-the-moral-bucket-list.html.

Bui, Quoctrung, and Claire Cain Miller. "The Age That Women Have Babies: How a Gap Divides America." *The New York Times*, August 4, 2018, sec. The Upshot. https://www.nytimes.com/interactive/2018/08/04/upshot/up-birth-age-gap.html.

Cacioppo, John T., Hsi Yuan Chen, and Stephanie Cacioppo. "Reciprocal Influences Between Loneliness and Self-Centeredness: A Cross-Lagged Panel Analysis in a Population-Based Sample of African American, Hispanic, and Caucasian Adults." *Personality and Social Psychology Bulletin* 43, no. 8 (August 1, 2017): 1125–35. https://doi.org/10.1177/0146167217705120.

Camus, Albert. *The Myth of Sisyphus: And Other Essays*. London: Hamish Hamilton, 1965.

Carroll, Robert, and Stephen Prickett, eds. *The Bible: Authorized King James Version*. Oxford: Oxford University Press, 2008.

Chaudhuri, Sukhomal. "The Ideal of Service in Buddhism." Vendanta Society of Southern California. Accessed June 24, 2022. https://vedanta.org/2001/monthly-readings/the-ideal-of-service-in-buddhism/.

Christensen, Clayton M. *Competing Against Luck: The Story of Innovation and Customer Choice*. New York: Harper Business, 2016.

Costin, Vlad, and Vivian L. Vignoles. "Meaning Is about Mattering: Evaluating Coherence, Purpose, and Existential Mattering as Precursors of Meaning in Life Judgments." *Journal of Personality and Social Psychology* 118, no. 4 (2020): 864–84.

Crotty, Robert, and Terence Lovat. "The Five Pillars of Islam." In *Islam: Its Beginnings and History, Its Theology, and Its Importance Today*. Hindmarsh, Australia: ATF Press, 2016.

Crowell, Steven. "Existentialism." Stanford Encyclopedia of Philosophy, June 9, 2020. https://stanford.library.sydney.edu.au/archives/sum2020/entries/existentialism/.

Curtin, Sally C., and Paul D. Sutton. "Marriage Rates in the United States, 1900–2018." Centers for Disease Control and Prevention, 2020. https://www.cdc.gov/nchs/data/hestat/marriage_rate_2018/marriage_rate_2018.htm.

Davis, Leslie, and Kim Parker. "A Half-Century after 'Mister Rogers' Debut, 5 Facts about Neighbors in U.S." Pew Research Center, August 15, 2019. https://www.pewresearch.org/fact-tank/2019/08/15/facts-about-neighbors-in-u-s/.

Dellasega, Cheryl, and Charisse Nixon. *Girl Wars: 12 Strategies That Will End Female Bullying*. New York: Simon & Schuster, 2003.

Diener, Ed, Daniel Kahneman, Raksha Arora, James Harter, and William Tov. "Income's Differential Influence on Judgments of Life Versus Affective Well-Being." In *Assessing Well-Being: The Collected Works of Ed Diener*, edited by Ed Diener, 233–46, 2009. https://doi.org/10.1007/978-90-481-2354-4_11.

Dodes, Lance. "Are You an Unhappy Achiever?" *Psychology Today*, August 31, 2017. https://www.psychologytoday.com/intl/blog/the-heart-addiction/201708/are-you-unhappy-achiever.

Doughty Street Chambers. "Dr Shirin Ebadi (Academic Expert)." Accessed June 28, 2022. https://www.doughtystreet.co.uk/

barristers/dr-shirin-ebadi-academic-expert.

Dudley, Chris. "Money Lessons Learned from Pro Athletes' Financial Fouls." CNBC, May 15, 2018. https://www.cnbc.com/2018/05/14/money-lessons-learned-from-pro-athletes-financial-fouls.html.

Ebadi, Shirin. *Until We Are Free: My Fight for Human Rights in Iran.* New York: Random House, 2016.

Ebaugh, Helen Rose Fuchs. *Becoming an Ex: The Process of Role Exit.* Chicago: University of Chicago Press, 1998.

Emison, Patricia A. *Creating the "Divine" Artist: From Dante to Michelangelo.* Leiden, the Netherlands: Brill, 2004.

Emmanuel, Steven, ed. *A Companion to Buddhist Philosophy.* Malden, MA: John Wiley & Sons, 2013.

Erikson, Erik H. *Childhood and Society.* New York: Norton, 1950.

Fantastic Finger Guides. "Meet Mr. Weston." Accessed June 27, 2022. https://www.fantasticfingerguides.com/pages/about.

Fernandes, Joynel. "Picturing the Passion: 'Pieta' by Michelangelo." Aletaia, March 26, 2018. https://aleteia.org/2018/03/26/picturing-the-passion-pieta-by-michelangelo/.

Fry, Richard, Jeffrey S. Passel, and D'vera Cohn. "A Majority of Young Adults in the U.S. Live with Their Parents for the First Time since the Great Depression." Pew Research Center, September 4, 2020. https://www.pewresearch.org/fact-tank/2020/09/04/a-majority-of-young-adults-in-the-u-s-live-with-their-parents-for-the-first-time-since-the-great-depression/.

Fulk of Chartres. "The Deeds of the Franks Who Attacked Jerusalem." In *Parallel Source Problems in Medieval History*, edited by Frederic Duncalf and August C. Krey, 109–15. New York: Harper & Brothers, 1912.

Gardner, Peter B. "The Disruptor." *Y Magazine*, Spring 2013. https://magazine.byu.edu/article/the-disruptor/.

Giattino, Charlie, Esteban Ortiz-Ospina, and Max Roser. "Working Hours." Our World in Data, December 2020. https://ourworldindata.org/working-hours.

Gibb, H.A.R. *The Damascus Chronicle of the Crusades: Extracted and Translated from the Chronicle of Ibn Al-Qalanisi*. Mineola, NY: Dover Publications, 2003.

Giesea, Jeff. "Dealing with the Emotional Fallout of Selling Your Business." *Harvard Business Review*, September 1, 2015. https://hbr.org/2015/09/dealing-with-the-emotional-fallout-of-selling-your-business.

Givens, Fiona, and Terryl Givens. *All Things New: Rethinking Sin, Salvation, and Everything in Between*. Meridian, ID: Faith Matters Publishing, 2020.

———. "MIPodcast #125—'All Things New' with Fiona and Terryl Givens and Spencer Fluhman." Maxwell Institute. YouTube, February 26, 2021. https://www.youtube.com/watch?v=-wHfeNkAa8g.

Goleman, Daniel. *Social Intelligence: The New Science of Human Relationships*. New York: Bantam, 2006.

Gordon, Sherri. "What You Need to Know About Victims of Bullying." Verywell Family, April 25, 2022. https://www.verywellfamily.com/characteristics-of-a-typical-victim-of-bullying-3288501.

Harari, Yuval N. *Sapiens: A Brief History of Humankind*. London: Vintage, 2019.

Heidegger, Martin. *Being and Time*. London: SCM Press, 1962.

History. "Pope Urban II Orders First Crusade," November 22, 2021. https://www.history.com/this-day-in-history/pope-urban-ii-orders-first-crusade.

Holland, Jeffrey R. "Of Souls, Symbols, and Sacraments," January 12, 1988. https://speeches.byu.edu/talks/jeffrey-r-holland/souls-symbols-sacraments/.

Jones, Robert A. *Emile Durkheim: An Introduction to Four Major Works*. Beverly Hills: Sage Publications, 1986.

Jorgenson, Eric. *The Almanack of Naval Ravikant: A Guide to Wealth and Happiness*. Magrathea Publishing, 2020.

Kearl, Michael C. *Endings: A Sociology of Death and Dying*. New York: Oxford University Press, 1989.

Kenrick, Douglas, and Vladas Griskevicius. *The Rational Animal: How Evolution Made Us Smarter Than We Think*. New York: Basic Books, 2013.

Kitman, Jamie Lincoln. "The Secret History of Lead." *The Nation*, March 2, 2000. https://www.thenation.com/article/archive/secret-history-lead/.

Klinger, Eric. *Meaning and Void: Inner Experience and the Incentives in People's Lives*. Minneapolis: University of Minnesota Press, 1977.

Kross, Ethan. *Chatter: The Voice in Our Head, Why It Matters, and How to Harness It*. New York: Crown, 2021.

Langan, John. "The Elements of St. Augustine's Just War Theory." *The Journal of Religious Ethics* 12, no. 1 (Spring 1984): 19–38.

Laurin, Kristin, Karina Schumann, and John G. Holmes. "A Relationship With God? Connecting with the Divine to Assuage Fears of Interpersonal Rejection." *Social Psychological and Personality Science* 5, no. 7 (September 1, 2014): 777–85. https://doi.org/10.1177/1948550614531800.

Lawson, Anette. *Adultery: An Analysis of Love and Betrayal*. New York: Basic Books, 1988.

Leavitt. "Why Hierarchies Thrive." *Harvard Business Review*, March 2003. https://hbr.org/2003/03/why-hierarchies-thrive.

Levinson, Daniel J. *The Seasons of a Man's Life*. New York: Ballantine Books, 1978.

Lifeway Research. "Ultimate Purpose and Meaning: Some Say They Pursue It, Others Do Not," December 27, 2011. https://research.lifeway.com/2011/12/27/ultimate-purpose-and-meaning-some-say-they-pursue-it-others-do-not/.

Lipka, Michael, and Claire Gecewicz. "More Americans Now Say They're Spiritual but Not Religious." Pew Research Center, September 6, 2017. https://www.pewresearch.org/fact-tank/2017/09/06/more-americans-now-say-theyre-spiritual-but-not-religious/.

LoLordo, Ann. "Girl's Murder Shames Iran Torture: She Was as Much a Victim of Iran's Child Custody Laws as of Relatives Who Killed Her." *Baltimore Sun*, January 28, 1998. https://www.baltimoresun.com/news/bs-xpm-1998-01-28-1998028066-story.html.

McLaughlin, Daniel, and Elisabeth Wickeri. "Special Report-Mental Health and Human Rights in Cambodia." *Fordham International Law Journal* 35, no. 4 (2017). https://ir.lawnet.fordham.edu/cgi/viewcontent.cgi?article=2590&context=ilj.

Merriam-Webster. "A Reading Break on 'Laurel.'" Accessed June 27, 2022. https://www.merriam-webster.com/words-at-play/word-history-of-laurel.

Miller, Adam. "Stories and Sin: A Conversation with Adam Miller." Faith Matters Foundation. YouTube, January 10, 2020. https://www.youtube.com/watch?v=KHvQaSaU12Y.

Monchet, Nathan. "He Surfed Lance's Right Alone For 3 MONTHS | Nathan Monchet in 'I Lost My Sanity In The Tube.'" Stab: We like to surf. YouTube, September 21, 2020. https://www.youtube.com/watch?v=gKWhzy1gG50.

Moyer, Christopher A., Jim Rounds, and James W. Hannum. "A Meta-Analysis of Massage Therapy Research." *Psychological Bulletin* 130, no. 1 (2004): 3–18.

Musick, Marc A., and John Wilson. "Volunteering and Depression: The Role of Psychological and Social Resources in Different Age Groups." *Social Science & Medicine* 56, no. 2 (January 1, 2003): 259–69. https://doi.org/10.1016/S0277-9536(02)00025-4.

The New Humanitarian. "A Faith-Based Aid Revolution in the Muslim World?," June 1, 2012. https://www.thenewhumanitarian.org/report/95564/analysis-faith-based-aid-revolution-muslim-world.

The New York Times. "Bar Ethyl Gasoline as 5th Victim Dies," October 31, 1924. https://www.nytimes.com/1924/10/31/archives/bar-ethyl-gasoline-as-5th-victim-dies-city-health-authorities.html.

The Nobel Prize. "Shirin Ebadi – Biographical." Accessed June 24, 2022. https://www.nobelprize.org/prizes/peace/2003/ebadi/biographical/.

Oishi, Shigehiro, and Ed Diener. "Residents of Poor Nations Have a Greater Sense of Meaning in Life Than Residents of Wealthy Nations." *Psychological Science* 25, no. 2 (February 1, 2014): 422–30. https://doi.org/10.1177/0956797613507286.

Otterstrom, Kristina. "Rights and Responsibilities of a Married Person." Lawyers.com, April 9, 2015. https://www.lawyers.

com/legal-info/family-law/matrimonial-law/rights-and-responsibilities-of-a-married-person.html.

Our World in Data. "Percentage of Americans Living Alone, by Age." Accessed June 27, 2022. https://ourworldindata.org/grapher/percentage-of-americans-living-alone-by-age.

Palliative Doctors. "Hospice for Baby Riley Leads to Memory-Making Activities for the Family." Accessed June 24, 2022. https://palliativedoctors.org/stories/riley.

Perry, Mark J. "New US Homes Today Are 1,000 Square Feet Larger Than in 1973 and Living Space per Person Has Nearly Doubled." AEI, June 5, 2016. https://www.aei.org/carpe-diem/new-us-homes-today-are-1000-square-feet-larger-than-in-1973-and-living-space-per-person-has-nearly-doubled/.

Peterson, Jordan. *Beyond Order: 12 More Rules for Life.* Toronto: Random House Canada, 2021.

Pew Research Center. "Where Americans Find Meaning in Life," November 20, 2018. https://www.pewresearch.org/religion/2018/11/20/where-americans-find-meaning-in-life/.

Phaly, Nuon. "Phaly's Story." eGlobal Family. Accessed June 24, 2022. http://www.eglobalfamily.org/phaly-story.html.

Price, Sharon J., and Patrick C. McKenry. *Divorce.* Beverly Hills: Sage, 1988.

Providence. "Our Mission." Accessed June 24, 2022. https://www.providence.org/about/our-mission.

Public Library of Science. "Why Do We Love Babies? Parental Instinct Region Found In The Brain," ScienceDaily. February 27, 2008. https://www.sciencedaily.com/releases/2008/02/080226213448.htm.

Radnor, Josh. "Josh Radnor: Fame's Lesson Plan." INKtalks. YouTube, October 23, 2015. https://www.youtube.com/watch?v=Jr7MkrHDGt0.

Rapley, Rob. *The Poisoner's Handbook*. PBS, 2014.

Rehmatullah, Nasim. "Service to Mankind Is the Essence of Islam." *Ahmadiyya Gazette USA*, 1999. https://www.alislam.org/library/articles/new/service-to-humanity.html.

Rempel, Judith. "Childless Elderly: What Are They Missing?" *Journal of Marriage and Family* 47, no. 2 (1985): 343–48. https://doi.org/10.2307/352134.

Roser, Max. "Fertility Rate." Our World in Data, December 2, 2017. https://ourworldindata.org/fertility-rate.

The School of Life. "How To Be Selfish." YouTube, April 5, 2017. https://www.youtube.com/watch?v=-kArjCybqpc.

Scott, Richard G. "The Eternal Blessings of Marriage." *Ensign*, May 2011.

Sears, JP. "How To Fight The Woke | JP Sears – MP Podcast #90." Interview by Mikhaila Peterson. YouTube, June 15, 2021. https://www.youtube.com/watch?v=mr1tjwWTkzI.

Seligman, Martin. "Boomer Blues." *Psychology Today*, October 1988.

Sententiae Antiquae. "Happiness Is Thinking… About Things Aristotle Didn't Say," June 10, 2019. https://sententiaeantiquae.com/2019/06/10/happiness-is-thinking-about-things-aristotle-didnt-say/.

Simpson, J.A. "The Dissolution of Romantic Relationships: Factors Involved in Relationship Stability and Emotional Distress." *Journal of Personality and Social Psychology* 53, no. 4 (1987): 683–92.

Slavich, George M. "Deconstructing Depression: A Diathesis-Stress Perspective" 17, no. 9 (2004).

Smith, Emily Esfahani. *The Power of Meaning: Finding Fulfillment in a World Obsessed with Happiness*. New York: Crown, 2017.

Solomon, Andrew. "Depression Is a Disease of Loneliness." *Andrew Solomon* (blog). Accessed June 28, 2022. https://andrewsolomon.com/articles/depression-is-a-disease-of-loneliness/.

———. *The Noonday Demon: An Atlas Of Depression*. New York: Scribner, 2001.

Solomon, Robert C., ed. *Existentialism*. New York: McGraw-Hill, 1974.

Stepler, Renee. "5 Facts about Family Caregivers." Pew Research Center, November 18, 2015. https://www.pewresearch.org/fact-tank/2015/11/18/5-facts-about-family-caregivers/.

Stosny, Steven. "Pain and Suffering." *Psychology Today*, April 15, 2011. https://www.psychologytoday.com/us/blog/anger-in-the-age-entitlement/201104/pain-and-suffering.

Taunt, Helen M., and Richard P. Hastings. "Positive Impact of Children with Developmental Disabilities on Their Families: A Preliminary Study." *Education and Training in Mental Retardation and Developmental Disabilities* 37, no. 4 (2002): 410–20.

Taylor, Shelley E. *Positive Illusions: Creative Self-Deception and the Healthy Mind.* New York: Basic Books, 1983.

Troyer, Angela K. "The Health Benefits of Socializing." *Psychology Today*, June 30, 2016. https://www.psychologytoday.com/us/blog/living-mild-cognitive-impairment/201606/the-health-benefits-socializing.

U.S. Bureau of Labor Statistics. "Time Spent in Leisure and Sports Activities for the Civilian Population by Selected Characteristics, Averages per Day, 2021." Accessed June 24, 2022. https://www.bls.gov/news.release/atus.t11A.htm.

Vaughn, Diane. *Uncoupling: Turning Points in Intimate Relationships.* New York: Oxford University Press, 1986.

Veit, Walter. "Existential Nihilism: The Only Really Serious Problem in Philosophy." *Journal of Camus Studies*, 2018, 211–32.

Wade, Nicholas. "Some Biologists Find an Urge in Human Nature to Help." *The New York Times*, November 30,

2009. https://www.nytimes.com/2009/12/01/science/01human.html.

Waite, Linda J. *Does Divorce Make People Happy?: Findings from a Study of Unhappy Marriages*. New York: Institute for American Values, 2002.

Watt, W. Montgomery. *Muhammad at Medina*. Oxford: Clarendon Press, 1972.

Weeks, Brent. *The Way of Shadows*. New York: Orbit, 2008.

Whelan, David. "Clayton Christensen: The Survivor." *Forbes*, February 23, 2011. https://www.forbes.com/forbes/2011/0314/features-clayton-christensen-health-care-cancer-survivor.html.

Wright, Robert. *Why Buddhism Is True: The Science and Philosophy of Meditation and Enlightenment*. New York: Simon & Schuster, 2017.

Yale University. "As Teens Delay Driver Licensing, They Miss Key Safety Instruction," ScienceDaily. July 7, 2020. https://www.sciencedaily.com/releases/2020/07/200707113234.htm.

Endnotes

1 Peter B Gardner, "The Disruptor," *Y Magazine*, Spring 2013, https://magazine.byu.edu/article/the-disruptor/.

2 Gardner.

3 David Whelan, "Clayton Christensen: The Survivor," *Forbes*, February 23, 2011, https://www.forbes.com/forbes/2011/0314/features-clayton-christensen-health-care-cancer-survivor.html.

4 Whelan.

5 Gardner, "The Disruptor."

6 Gardner.

7 Gardner; Whelan, "Clayton Christensen."

8 Roy F. Baumeister, *Meanings of Life* (New York: The Guilford Press, 1991), 62.

9 Vlad Costin and Vivian L. Vignoles, "Meaning Is about Mattering: Evaluating Coherence, Purpose, and Existential Mattering as Precursors of Meaning in Life Judgments," *Journal of Personality and Social Psychology* 118, no. 4 (2020): 864–84.

10 Emily Esfahani Smith, *The Power of Meaning: Finding Fulfillment in a World Obsessed with Happiness* (New York: Crown, 2017), 14.

11 Jordan Peterson, *Beyond Order: 12 More Rules for Life* (Toronto: Random House Canada, 2021).

12 Shigehiro Oishi and Ed Diener, "Residents of Poor Nations Have a Greater Sense of Meaning in Life Than Residents of Wealthy Nations," *Psychological Science* 25, no. 2 (February 1, 2014): 422–30, https://doi.org/10.1177/0956797613507286.

13 Martin Heidegger, *Being and Time* (London: SCM Press, 1962).

14 Nicholas Wade, "Some Biologists Find an Urge in Human Nature to Help," *The New York Times*, November 30, 2009, https://www.nytimes.com/2009/12/01/science/01human.html.

15 Augustine of Hippo, *The Confessions of Saint Augustine*, trans. E.B. Pusey (Mount Vernon: Peter Pauper Press, 1947), 354–430.

16 Jamie Lincoln Kitman, "The Secret History of Lead," *The Nation*, March 2, 2000, https://www.thenation.com/article/archive/secret-history-lead/.

17 "Bar Ethyl Gasoline as 5th Victim Dies," *The New York Times*, October 31, 1924, https://www.nytimes.com/1924/10/31/archives/bar-ethyl-gasoline-as-5th-victim-dies-city-health-authorities.html.

18 Rob Rapley, *The Poisoner's Handbook* (PBS, 2014).

19 Helen M. Taunt and Richard P. Hastings, "Positive Impact of Children with Developmental Disabilities on Their Families: A Preliminary Study," *Education and Training in Mental Retardation and Developmental Disabilities* 37, no. 4 (2002): 410–20.

20 Joynel Fernandes, "Picturing the Passion: 'Pieta' by Michelangelo," Aletaia, March 26, 2018, https://aleteia.org/2018/03/26/picturing-the-passion-pieta-by-michelangelo/.

21 Patricia A. Emison, *Creating the "Divine" Artist: From Dante to Michelangelo* (Leiden, the Netherlands: Brill, 2004).

22 JP Sears, "How To Fight The Woke | JP Sears – MP Podcast #90," interview by Mikhaila Peterson, YouTube, June 15, 2021, https://www.youtube.com/watch?v=mr1tjwWTkzI.

23 Public Library of Science, "Why Do We Love Babies? Parental Instinct Region Found In The Brain," ScienceDaily, February 27, 2008, https://www.sciencedaily.com/releases/2008/02/080226213448.htm.

24 Sherri Gordon, "What You Need to Know About Victims of Bullying," Verywell Family, April 25, 2022, https://www.verywellfamily.com/characteristics-of-a-typical-victim-of-bullying-3288501.

25 Douglas Kenrick and Vladas Griskevicius, *The Rational Animal: How Evolution Made Us Smarter Than We Think* (New York: Basic Books, 2013).

26 Aristotle, *Nicomachean Ethics*, ed. Lesley Brown, trans. David Ross (Oxford: Oxford University Press, 2009).

27 Angela K. Troyer, "The Health Benefits of Socializing," *Psychology Today*, June 30, 2016, https://www.psychologytoday.com/us/blog/living-mild-cognitive-impairment/201606/the-health-benefits-socializing.

28 Smith, *The Power of Meaning: Finding Fulfillment in a World Obsessed with Happiness*, 50.

29 Renee Stepler, "5 Facts about Family Caregivers," Pew Research Center, November 18, 2015, https://www.pewresearch.org/fact-tank/2015/11/18/5-facts-about-family-caregivers/.

30 Nathan Monchet, "He Surfed Lance's Right Alone For 3 MONTHS | Nathan Monchet in 'I Lost My Sanity In The Tube,'" Stab: We like to surf, YouTube, September 21, 2020, https://www.youtube.com/watch?v=gKWhzy1gG50.

31 The School of Life, "How To Be Selfish," YouTube, April 5, 2017, https://www.youtube.com/watch?v=-kArjCybqpc.

32 Baumeister, *Meanings of Life*.

33 John T. Cacioppo, Hsi Yuan Chen, and Stephanie Cacioppo, "Reciprocal Influences Between Loneliness and Self-Centeredness: A Cross-Lagged Panel Analysis in a Population-Based Sample of African American, Hispanic, and Caucasian Adults," *Personality and Social Psychology Bulletin* 43, no. 8 (August 1, 2017): 1125–35, https://doi.org/10.1177/0146167217705120.

34 "Ultimate Purpose and Meaning: Some Say They Pursue It, Others Do Not," Lifeway Research, December 27, 2011, https://research.lifeway.com/2011/12/27/ultimate-purpose-and-meaning-some-say-they-pursue-it-others-do-not/.

35 Robert C. Solomon, ed., *Existentialism* (New York: McGraw-Hill, 1974).

36 Albert Camus, *The Myth of Sisyphus: And Other Essays* (London: Hamish Hamilton, 1965).

37 Walter Veit, "Existential Nihilism: The Only Really Serious Problem in Philosophy," *Journal of Camus Studies*, 2018, 211–32.

38 Brent Weeks, *The Way of Shadows* (New York: Orbit, 2008), 155.

39 Steven Crowell, "Existentialism," Stanford Encyclopedia of Philosophy, June 9, 2020, https://stanford.library.sydney.edu.au/archives/sum2020/entries/existentialism/.

40 Yuval N. Harari, *Sapiens: A Brief History of Humankind* (London: Vintage, 2019), 391–92.

41 Michael C. Kearl, *Endings: A Sociology of Death and Dying* (New York: Oxford University Press, 1989), 210.

42 Adam Miller, "Stories and Sin: A Conversation with Adam Miller," Faith Matters Foundation, YouTube, January 10, 2020, https://www.youtube.com/watch?v=KHvQaSaU12Y.

43 "Hospice for Baby Riley Leads to Memory-Making Activities for the Family," Palliative Doctors, accessed June 24, 2022, https://palliativedoctors.org/stories/riley.

44 Leavitt, "Why Hierarchies Thrive," *Harvard Business Review*, March 2003, https://hbr.org/2003/03/why-hierarchies-thrive.

45 Brian Barth, "The Secrets of Chicken Flocks' Pecking Order," Modern Farmer, March 16, 2016, https://modernfarmer.com/2016/03/pecking-order/.

46 "Our Mission," Providence, accessed June 24, 2022, https://www.providence.org/about/our-mission.

47 David Brooks, "The Moral Bucket List," *The New York Times*, April 11, 2015, sec. Opinion, https://www.nytimes.com/2015/04/12/opinion/sunday/david-brooks-the-moral-bucket-list.html.

48 Kristen Bell, "Kristen Bell," interview by Dax Shepard, *The Armchair Expert*, February 14, 2018, https://armchairexpertpod.com/pods/kristen-bell.

49 Josh Radnor, "Josh Radnor: Fame's Lesson Plan," INKtalks, YouTube, October 23, 2015, https://www.youtube.com/watch?v=Jr7MkrHDGt0.

50 Eric Jorgenson, *The Almanack of Naval Ravikant: A Guide to Wealth and Happiness* (Magrathea Publishing, 2020), 137.

51 Lance Dodes, "Are You an Unhappy Achiever?," *Psychology Today*, August 31, 2017, https://www.psychologytoday.com/intl/blog/the-heart-addiction/201708/are-you-unhappy-achiever.

52 Daniel J. Levinson, *The Seasons of a Man's Life* (New York: Ballantine Books, 1978).

53 Amy M. Azzam, "Motivated to Learn: A Conversation with Daniel Pink," *Educational Leadership* 72, no. 1 (September 2014): 12–17.

54 Samuel Arbesman, "The Fraction of Famous People in the World," *Wired*, January 22, 2013, https://www.wired.com/2013/01/the-fraction-of-famous-people-in-the-world/.

55 Baumeister, *Meanings of Life*, 110.

56 Chris Dudley, "Money Lessons Learned from Pro Athletes' Financial Fouls," CNBC, May 15, 2018, https://www.cnbc.com/2018/05/14/money-lessons-learned-from-pro-athletes-financial-fouls.html.

57 Leslie Bloom, "How Long Is the Average Career of an NFL Player?," Chron, March 5, 2019, https://work.chron.com/long-average-career-nfl-player-12643.html.

58 Roy F. Baumeister et al., "Some Key Differences between a Happy Life and a Meaningful Life," *The Journal of Positive Psychology* 8, no. 6 (November 1, 2013): 505–16, https://doi.org/10.1080/17439760.2013.830764.

59 "Happiness Is Thinking…About Things Aristotle Didn't Say," Sententiae Antiquae, June 10, 2019, https://sententiaeantiquae.com/2019/06/10/happiness-is-thinking-about-things-aristotle-didnt-say/.

60 Baumeister et al., "Some Key Differences between a Happy Life and a Meaningful Life."

61 Ann LoLordo, "Girl's Murder Shames Iran Torture: She Was as Much a Victim of Iran's Child Custody Laws as of Relatives Who Killed Her," *Baltimore Sun*, January 28, 1998, https://www.baltimoresun.com/news/bs-xpm-1998-01-28-1998028066-story.html.

62 Shirin Ebadi, *Until We Are Free: My Fight for Human Rights in Iran* (New York: Random House, 2016), xiii.

63 "Shirin Ebadi – Biographical," The Nobel Prize, accessed June 24, 2022, https://www.nobelprize.org/prizes/peace/2003/ebadi/biographical/.

64 "Nobel Winner's Plea to Iran," BBC, October 10, 2003, http://news.bbc.co.uk/1/hi/world/middle_east/3181428.stm.

65 "Nobel Winner's Plea to Iran."

66 "A Reading Break on 'Laurel,'" Merriam-Webster, accessed June 27, 2022, https://www.merriam-webster.com/words-at-play/word-history-of-laurel.

67 "Dr Shirin Ebadi (Academic Expert)," Doughty Street Chambers, accessed June 28, 2022, https://www.doughtystreet.co.uk/barristers/dr-shirin-ebadi-academic-expert.

68 Ebadi, *Until We Are Free: My Fight for Human Rights in Iran*, 10.

69 Cheryl Dellasega and Charisse Nixon, *Girl Wars: 12 Strategies That Will End Female Bullying* (New York: Simon & Schuster, 2003).

70 Fiona Givens and Terryl Givens, "MIPodcast #125—'All Things New' with Fiona and Terryl Givens and Spencer Fluhman," Maxwell Institute, YouTube, February 26, 2021, https://www.youtube.com/watch?v=-wHfeNkAa8g.

71 "Ahimsa," BBC, September 11, 2009, https://www.bbc.co.uk/religion/religions/jainism/living/ahimsa_1.shtml.

72 Klaus Abbink and Donna Harris, "In-Group Favouritism and Out-Group Discrimination in Naturally Occurring Groups," *PLOS ONE* 14, no. 9 (September 4, 2019), https://doi.org/10.1371/journal.pone.0221616.

73 S.J. Allen, *An Introduction to the Crusades* (New York: University of Toronto Press, 2017), 13.

74 Thomas Asbridge, *The First Crusade: A New History* (Oxford: Oxford University Press, 2004), 295–316.

75 Fulk of Chartres, "The Deeds of the Franks Who Attacked Jerusalem," in *Parallel Source Problems in Medieval History*, ed. Frederic Duncalf and August C. Krey (New York: Harper & Brothers, 1912), 114.

76 H.A.R. Gibb, *The Damascus Chronicle of the Crusades: Extracted and Translated from the Chronicle of Ibn Al-Qalanisi* (Mineola, NY: Dover Publications, 2003), 48.

77 Fiona Givens and Terryl Givens, *All Things New: Rethinking Sin, Salvation, and Everything in Between* (Meridian, ID: Faith Matters Publishing, 2020).

78 Asbridge, *The First Crusade: A New History*, 11–21.

79 John Langan, "The Elements of St. Augustine's Just War Theory," *The Journal of Religious Ethics* 12, no. 1 (Spring 1984): 19–38.

80 "Pope Urban II Orders First Crusade," History, November 22, 2021, https://www.history.com/this-day-in-history/pope-urban-ii-orders-first-crusade.

81 Judith Rempel, "Childless Elderly: What Are They Missing?," *Journal of Marriage and Family* 47, no. 2 (1985): 343–48, https://doi.org/10.2307/352134.

82 Kristina Otterstrom, "Rights and Responsibilities of a Married Person," Lawyers.com, April 9, 2015, https://www.lawyers.com/legal-info/family-law/matrimonial-law/rights-and-responsibilities-of-a-married-person.html.

83 Anette Lawson, *Adultery: An Analysis of Love and Betrayal* (New York: Basic Books, 1988).

84 Jeffrey R. Holland, "Of Souls, Symbols, and Sacraments," January 12, 1988, https://speeches.byu.edu/talks/jeffrey-r-holland/souls-symbols-sacraments/.

85 Robert A. Jones, *Emile Durkheim: An Introduction to Four Major Works* (Beverly Hills: Sage Publications, 1986).

86 Baumeister, *Meanings of Life*.

87 Richard G. Scott, "The Eternal Blessings of Marriage," *Ensign*, May 2011, 94.

88 Smith, *The Power of Meaning: Finding Fulfillment in a World Obsessed with Happiness.*

89 Shelley E. Taylor, *Positive Illusions: Creative Self-Deception and the Healthy Mind* (New York: Basic Books, 1983).

90 "Where Americans Find Meaning in Life," Pew Research Center, November 20, 2018, https://www.pewresearch.org/religion/2018/11/20/where-americans-find-meaning-in-life/.

91 Oishi and Diener, "Residents of Poor Nations Have a Greater Sense of Meaning in Life Than Residents of Wealthy Nations."

92 Max Roser, "Fertility Rate," Our World in Data, December 2, 2017, https://ourworldindata.org/fertility-rate.

93 Baumeister, *Meanings of Life.*

94 Erik H Erikson, *Childhood and Society* (New York: Norton, 1950).

95 Daniel Goleman, *Social Intelligence: The New Science of Human Relationships* (New York: Bantam, 2006).

96 "Where Americans Find Meaning in Life."

97 *The Bible: Authorized King James Version* (Oxford: Oxford University Press, 2008) Col. 2:2.

98 Oishi and Diener, "Residents of Poor Nations Have a Greater Sense of Meaning in Life Than Residents of Wealthy Nations."

99 Ed Diener et al., "Income's Differential Influence on Judgments of Life Versus Affective Well-Being," in *Assessing Well-Being: The Collected Works of Ed Diener*, ed. Ed Diener, 2009, 233–46, https://doi.org/10.1007/978-90-481-2354-4_11.

100 "Where Americans Find Meaning in Life."

101 "Meet Mr. Weston," Fantastic Finger Guides, accessed June 27, 2022, https://www.fantasticfingerguides.com/pages/about.

102 Clayton M. Christensen, *Competing Against Luck: The Story of Innovation and Customer Choice* (New York: Harper Business, 2016).

103 Sian Leah Beilock, "Why Young Americans Are Lonely," *Scientific American*, July 27, 2020, https://www.scientificamerican.com/article/why-young-americans-are-lonely/.

104 Mark J. Perry, "New US Homes Today Are 1,000 Square Feet Larger Than in 1973 and Living Space per Person Has Nearly Doubled," AEI, June 5, 2016, https://www.aei.org/carpe-diem/new-us-homes-today-are-1000-square-feet-larger-than-in-1973-and-living-space-per-person-has-nearly-doubled/.

105 "Percentage of Americans Living Alone, by Age," Our World in Data, accessed June 27, 2022, https://ourworldindata.org/grapher/percentage-of-americans-living-alone-by-age.

106 Leslie Davis and Kim Parker, "A Half-Century after 'Mister Rogers' Debut, 5 Facts about Neighbors in U.S.," Pew Research Center, August 15, 2019, https://www.pewresearch.org/fact-tank/2019/08/15/facts-about-neighbors-in-u-s/.

107 Richard Fry, Jeffrey S. Passel, and D'vera Cohn, "A Majority of Young Adults in the U.S. Live with Their Parents for the First Time since the Great Depression," Pew Research Center, September 4, 2020, https://www.pewresearch.org/fact-tank/2020/09/04/a-majority-of-young-adults-in-the-u-s-live-with-their-parents-for-the-first-time-since-the-great-depression/.

108 Yale University, "As Teens Delay Driver Licensing, They Miss Key Safety Instruction," ScienceDaily, July 7, 2020, https://www.sciencedaily.com/releases/2020/07/200707113234.htm.

109 Quoctrung Bui and Claire Cain Miller, "The Age That Women Have Babies: How a Gap Divides America," *The New York Times*, August 4, 2018, sec. The Upshot, https://www.nytimes.com/interactive/2018/08/04/upshot/up-birth-age-gap.html.

110 Sally C. Curtin and Paul D. Sutton, "Marriage Rates in the United States, 1900–2018," Centers for Disease Control and Prevention, 2020, https://www.cdc.gov/nchs/data/hestat/marriage_rate_2018/marriage_rate_2018.htm.

111 Charlie Giattino, Esteban Ortiz-Ospina, and Max Roser, "Working Hours," Our World in Data, December 2020, https://ourworldindata.org/working-hours.

112 "Time Spent in Leisure and Sports Activities for the Civilian Population by Selected Characteristics, Averages per Day, 2021," U.S. Bureau of Labor Statistics, accessed June 24, 2022, https://www.bls.gov/news.release/atus.t11A.htm.

113 "Where Americans Find Meaning in Life."

114 Oishi and Diener, "Residents of Poor Nations Have a Greater Sense of Meaning in Life Than Residents of Wealthy Nations."

115 Kristin Laurin, Karina Schumann, and John G. Holmes, "A Relationship With God? Connecting with the Divine to Assuage Fears of Interpersonal Rejection," *Social Psychological and Personality Science* 5, no. 7 (September 1, 2014): 777–85, https://doi.org/10.1177/1948550614531800.

116 Michael Lipka and Claire Gecewicz, "More Americans Now Say They're Spiritual but Not Religious," Pew Research Center, September 6, 2017,

https://www.pewresearch.org/fact-tank/2017/09/06/more-americans-now-say-theyre-spiritual-but-not-religious/.

117 W. Montgomery Watt, *Muhammad at Medina* (Oxford: Clarendon Press, 1972).

118 Al-Jahiz, "The Adab of Islam," trans. Nuh Ha Mim Keller, Masud, 2001, http://www.masud.co.uk/ISLAM/nuh/adab_of_islam.htm.

119 Nasim Rehmatullah, "Service to Mankind Is the Essence of Islam," *Ahmadiyya Gazette USA*, 1999, https://www.alislam.org/library/articles/new/service-to-humanity.html.

120 The Holy Qur'an, 3:111, quoted in Rehmatullah.

121 The Holy Qur'an (London: Wordsworth, 2014), 2:177.

122 Franz von Benda-Beckmann and Keebet von Benda-Beckmann, *Social Security Between Past and Future: Ambonese Networks of Care and Support* (Piscataway, NJ: Transaction Publishers, 2007), 167.

123 Robert Crotty and Terence Lovat, "The Five Pillars of Islam," in *Islam: Its Beginnings and History, Its Theology, and Its Importance Today* (Hindmarsh, Australia: ATF Press, 2016), 57.

124 "A Faith-Based Aid Revolution in the Muslim World?," The New Humanitarian, June 1, 2012, https://www.thenewhumanitarian.org/report/95564/analysis-faith-based-aid-revolution-muslim-world.

125 von Benda-Beckmann and von Benda-Beckmann, *Social Security Between Past and Future: Ambonese Networks of Care and Support*, 167.

126 Crotty and Lovat, "The Five Pillars of Islam," 59.

127 The Holy Qur'an, 60:8.

128 Vinaya Mahavagga, chapters 5 & 7, quoted in Sukhomal Chaudhuri, "The Ideal of Service in Buddhism," Vendanta Society of Southern California, accessed June 24, 2022, https://vedanta.org/2001/monthly-readings/the-ideal-of-service-in-buddhism/.

129 The Middle-length Discourses 98, quoted in Chaudhuri.

130 Chaudhuri.

131 Steven Emmanuel, ed., *A Companion to Buddhist Philosophy* (Malden, MA: John Wiley & Sons, 2013).

132 Robert Wright, *Why Buddhism Is True: The Science and Philosophy of Meditation and Enlightenment* (New York: Simon & Schuster, 2017).

133 Wright.

134 The Bible: Authorized King James Version, John 3:16.

135 Matt. 25:35–40.

136 1 Cor. 12:27.

137 Matt. 22:1–14.

138 Matt. 7:21.

139 Daniel Becerra, *3rd, 4th Nephi: A Brief Theological Introduction*, The Book of Mormon: Brief Theological Introductions 9 (Provo, Utah: The Neal A Maxwell Institute, 2020).

140 The Bible: Authorized King James Version, Matt. 5:44.

141 Diane Vaughn, *Uncoupling: Turning Points in Intimate Relationships* (New York: Oxford University Press, 1986).

142 Helen Rose Fuchs Ebaugh, *Becoming an Ex: The Process of Role Exit* (Chicago: University of Chicago Press, 1998), 144.

143 J.A. Simpson, "The Dissolution of Romantic Relationships: Factors Involved in Relationship Stability and Emotional Distress," *Journal of Personality and Social Psychology* 53, no. 4 (1987): 683–92.

144 Sharon J. Price and Patrick C. McKenry, *Divorce* (Beverly Hills: Sage, 1988).

145 Baumeister, *Meanings of Life*.

146 Jeff Giesea, "Dealing with the Emotional Fallout of Selling Your Business," *Harvard Business Review*, September 1, 2015, https://hbr.org/2015/09/dealing-with-the-emotional-fallout-of-selling-your-business.

147 Baumeister.

148 Steven Stosny, "Pain and Suffering," *Psychology Today*, April 15, 2011, https://www.psychologytoday.com/us/blog/anger-in-the-age-entitlement/201104/pain-and-suffering.

149 Martin Seligman, "Boomer Blues," *Psychology Today*, October 1988.

150 George M. Slavich, "Deconstructing Depression: A Diathesis-Stress Perspective" 17, no. 9 (2004).

151 Andrew Solomon, "Depression Is a Disease of Loneliness," *Andrew Solomon* (blog), accessed June 28, 2022, https://andrewsolomon.com/articles/depression-is-a-disease-of-loneliness/.

152 Andrew Solomon, *The Noonday Demon: An Atlas Of Depression* (New York: Scribner, 2001).

153 Eric Klinger, *Meaning and Void: Inner Experience and the Incentives in People's Lives* (Minneapolis: University of Minnesota Press, 1977).

154 Daniel McLaughlin and Elisabeth Wickeri, "Special Report-Mental Health and Human Rights in Cambodia," *Fordham International Law Journal* 35, no. 4 (2017): 898, 937, https://ir.lawnet.fordham.edu/cgi/viewcontent.cgi?article=2590&context=ilj.

155 Nuon Phaly, "Phaly's Story," eGlobal Family, accessed June 24, 2022, http://www.eglobalfamily.org/phaly-story.html.

156 Solomon, *The Noonday Demon: An Atlas Of Depression*, 37.

157 Phaly, "Phaly's Story."

158 Solomon, *The Noonday Demon: An Atlas Of Depression*, 36–37.

159 Ethan Kross, *Chatter: The Voice in Our Head, Why It Matters, and How to Harness It* (New York: Crown, 2021).

160 Christopher A. Moyer, Jim Rounds, and James W. Hannum, "A Meta-Analysis of Massage Therapy Research," *Psychological Bulletin* 130, no. 1 (2004): 3–18.

161 Marc A Musick and John Wilson, "Volunteering and Depression: The Role of Psychological and Social Resources in Different Age Groups," *Social Science & Medicine* 56, no. 2 (January 1, 2003): 259–69, https://doi.org/10.1016/S0277-9536(02)00025-4.

162 Linda J. Waite, *Does Divorce Make People Happy?: Findings from a Study of Unhappy Marriages* (New York: Institute for American Values, 2002).

Ingram Content Group UK Ltd.
Milton Keynes UK
UKHW012003100323
418413UK00008B/60

9 798986 793405